"One of the best...books I have read in awhile."
- *Readers Helping Authors* (5 Stars)

"Changeling by Karen Dales was an amazing read...(it)kept me on the edge of my seat. I cant' wait to read the next one to see where his path will lead." - *Sizzling Hot Books* (4 stars)

"...full of wonderful characters... I highly recommend this book, it is very unique..." - *Paranormal Romance Guild* (4 Stars)

"In a word: AWESOME! ...you will not be disappointed."
- *Kyle Hannah, Author of Time Assassins.*

In Praise of Angel of Death

"A dark and gripping tale by a true mistress of supernatural fiction. Karen Dales brings fresh blood to the vampire genre."
- *Michelle Rowen, National Best Selling Author*

"A fresh and intriguing new look at the vampire mythos..."
- *Violette Malan, Author of the Novels of Dhulyn and Parno*

"For readers who adore textured layers in their literary tapestries, rich in colorful emotions, Karen Dales is one writer of vampire fiction they'll want to read." - *Nancy Kilpatrick, Author and Editor*

"...is a must-read for any fans of Twilight or other books in the popular Vampire genre." - *Oakville Today.*

"...a poignant and epic tale... a brilliant example of good overcoming and prevailing against evil and prejudice... an emotional ride of literary genius, both heart-warming and heartbreaking at the same time."
- *Bitten By Books* (5 Tombstones)

"a grand tale of eternal life and its many challenges... I greatly enjoyed Angel of Death by Karen Dales and ... recommend it..."
- *Two Lips Reviews (5 Stars)*

"I would definitely recommend this book to vampire fans... a good solid read for ... I'm definitely looking forward to where Dales goes with this in the future." - *Once Upon A Bookshelf*

"OOOO!!!!! I need more. Ready for book two no doubt about it... OMG!!!!! Great plot, great characters. Just loved it. Glad I read it. She makes you fall for Angel. I did....." - *My Book Reviews*

"This was a amazing book and should not be missed. It has murder, romance, betrayal, lies, and some graphic violence. There is surprise after surprise. The characters are wonderful ...The author has done an amazing job...I can't wait for the next book."
- *Paranormal Romance Guild* (5 Stars)

"...dark, layered and intricate. The story was fast paced and gripping with an ending that will leave you breathless...I enjoyed the book and would recommend it to those who love vampires but crave something out of the ordinary." - *Open Book Society*

"...you never know which direction it will take...left me with my mouth hanging open and waiting impatiently for the next chapter in this exciting world. I highly recommend Angel of Death: Book One of the Chosen if you enjoy a fast paced adventure with all the twist and turns of a road map!" - *Sizzling Hot Books* (5 Stars)

"...one of the best stories by a new and upcoming writer that I have read...This tale was wonderfully written. Every character has a complete and utterly unique personality ...The Angel of Death will make you smile, and it will cause your heart to break. Very few stories are the equal to this tale. When you read this story, have a box of tissues handy. Ms. Dales I am trying to await the next installment patiently, and it is not working out so well." - *Siren Book Reviews* (5 Tombstone)

In Praise of Shadow of Death

"A dark, compelling thriller that will keep readers turning the pages well past bedtime."
- *Kelley Armstrong, #1 New York Times Best Selling Author*.

"Dales doesn't disappoint with 'Shadow of Death'...left me gasping in surprise... by far the best in the series so far and I will certainly be devouring any future additions." - *Open Book Society*

"Shadow of Death...takes you on a nail biting ride across the pond to her home town ... That never slows down and is as exciting on the first page as it is on the last...Ms. Dales I can only say one thing about Shadow of Death Book Two of the Chosen Chronicles and that is WOW! You have left me in suspense and teetering on the edge of a nervous breakdown!" - *Sizzling Hot Books* (5 Stars)

"... as impressive as the first...a fabulous story, well conceived and illustrated in such a way that the reader will not put it down until they've completed it...You cannot miss with Karen's book. You will love it... This is the kind of story that leaves you both begging for more..."
- *Siren Book Reviews* (Siren Books Best Stone Review)

"Oh wow, that is the only expression that can describe a great book. I can't wait for the next book in the Chosen Chronicles...I loved every minute of it...It leaves the reader anxious for more. "
- *Night Owl Reviews* (5 Stars Top Pick)

"A distinctive and addictive voice in the paranormal genre, Karen Dales has once again delivered a must-read piece of excellence with Shadow of Death...Karen's ability to weave a tale full of rich history and vibrant prose...I love this series and cannot wait for Ms. Dales to get in front of her computer and deliver more tales of The Chosen."
- *Bitten By Books* (5 Stars)

Also by Karen Dales

THE CHOSEN CHRONICLES

Changeling
Angel of Death
Shadow of Death
Thanatos

The Flower and The Sword (forthcoming)

thanatos

BOOK THREE OF
the chosen chronicles

karen dales

This book is a work of fiction. The characters, incidents, and dialogue are drawn from the author's imagination and are not to be construed as real. Any resemblance to actual events or persons, living or dead, is entirely coincidental.

Thanatos:
Book Three of the Chosen Chronicles

Copyright © 2014 by Karen Dales

ISBN: 978-1-928104-02-5
eISBN: 978-1-928104-03-2

Cover Art, Design and Author Photo
© 2014 by Evan Dales
WAV Design Studios
www.wavstudios.ca

Dark Dragon Publishing
313 Mutual Street
Toronto, Ontario
M4Y 1X6
CANADA
www.darkdragonpublishing.com

For more information on the Author,
Karen Dales and The Chosen Chronicles
www.karendales.com

thanatos

book three of
the chosen chronicles

karen dales

Dark Dragon Publishing
Toronto, Ontario, Canada

*In Memory of Roxane Parton, Jane Estelle Trombley,
and Shannon Neprily, my biggest fan.
All were taken too soon from this world.*

prologue

He stood upon a precipice he could not see and stared out into an immeasurable void. Some sense of self told him his jaw hung slack and his eyes rounded at the sight before him. He had never witnessed such beauty, such serenity, such love in all the years of his existence. There before him, lighting up the darkness of space, a resplendent golden white sphere radiated brilliant pulsations in perfect symmetry with each other as the light danced around, illuminating the darkness. A part of his mind immediately thought he saw the sun, or any star for that matter, but the beauty and the emanations of light reminded him more of a lotus flower—a lotus flower of a million resplendent petals.

Awestruck he watched this beautiful celestial flower. His spirit craved to be enfolded into the loving petals of light, yet he remained rooted to his unseen escarpment. A flicker of movement appeared, and he widened his attention to the darkness around the luminous flower. If he had breath it would have caught in his throat, instead tightness encircled his being at what he witnessed.

Countless upon countless pin point lights sparkled in rows as if they were pollen, but instead of floating outwards into the black void, these lights flickered towards the centre of the star-flower. He had never seen such a sight and he watched the hundreds, perhaps thousands, of rows meander their way until, at the touch of a petal, the singular light dissipated and seemed to become absorbed into the gentle resonating orb. He could not comprehend what he witnessed and curiosity focused his sight upon a small smattering of lights as they floated in its oblique path.

Closer and closer, larger and larger, these individual pinpricks of light became until each became a pulsating blue-white star that reminded him of will-o-the-wisps. He focused further, apprehension growing as curiosity pulled at him. The lights became more defined, as if he were standing right beside them, floating with them, towards the star-flower, until the circle of light that he had originally perceived changed form. Each light was in fact the illuminated outline of—he could not believe what he saw—a person! The closer he examined them the more he saw of their features. It was almost as though they were drawn with sparkling chalk on a black chalkboard, but he knew to the depths of his core this was not the case.

He stared in wonder at the cragged face of an old man, his eyes sparkling with awe, his face slack with desire, and a smile of pure bliss adding to his serenity. Baffled by what he saw, he turned his attention to another of the lights. Surprise filled him as the outline and then form of a child of about twelve coalesced before him. The girl was bald and wore what appeared to be a hospital gown. The outline of a teddy bear was clutched in her arms and on her face was sad resolution that slowly blossomed into peacefulness as she moved towards the star-flower. In her place a new form floated. A confused looking man, in what appeared to be torn or burnt clothes, led a procession of similar individuals, many had shock, fear and sadness marring their appearance until they floated closer to the beautiful pulsating flower. He watched the throbbing light envelop them, succoring them, and lifted them up until their faces filled with wonder and love.

"What is this?"

The thought punched him hard in his center and he found himself back on the precipice staring at the solar-lotus and the thousands of lights that floated to its core. Shaken, he lifted his hands to brush back his long hair in an effort to gain some semblance of self, only to have his hands halt before his face. Fear gripped him as he turned his hands over and back, examining them, for they appeared to be made of the same light and translucency as the dots streaming to the flower. Panic struck, his focus went to his body. He knew, before he saw, what he would find. He could not gasp. He could only stare dumbfounded.

"Am I dead?"

"Do you wish to be?"

The strange voice spun him away from the brilliant pulsating sunflower to find a weathered old man sitting cross-legged on a higher point upon the energy outlined crag, his features indistinguishable. Like the orb-people and like himself, this old man was defined by lines of light and illuminated translucency. The only demarcation to the old man's race was the oriental styled robes he wore.

"Who are you?" he asked.

The old man opened his eyes, revealing a brilliance of light akin to the star-flower, and gently smiled. "The real question you need to ask is; 'Who are you?'"

He opened his mouth to answer, but found he could not utter a word. The question had stunned him to the quick. His whole life he had wondered, as had others, as to *what* he was. Never had he truly considered *who* he was. Who was he? Images of the Three Ladies and his first meeting floated to mind and he recited, "Blessed be he who is Chosen. Blessed be he who is the One."

"Really?" The old man's smile widened to include surprise, his brow raising as he grunted and groaned to his feet.

Doubt pulled his lips into a frown as the old man came to stand beside him. A part of him felt surprised at how short the old man appeared, barely coming up to his waist.

"And do you know what that means?" asked the old man, the smile still on his face.

Confusion flowed through him. He did not know. They had never told him. He had assumed They meant that he was Chosen as Fernando was Chosen, as Bridget was Chosen, as Notus was Chosen.

A stab of pain at the thought of his Chooser doubled him and he fell to one knee, his face held supported by the old man's warm hands. He could not help but to gaze into starry eyes.

"Such pain, it clouds." The old man shook his head sadly. "It is through the attachments in one's life that suffering is created."

He had heard these words before, long ago in another life.

"Another life for me, yes. The same life for you."

Recognition dawned and he raised his hands to take the old man's in his. "Master?"

The old man shook his head, his smile returned. "No. No. No titles here. No names either."

He could not believe who was before him. It was not possible. He had been dead for almost a thousand years. "How? How is this possible?" he asked, his eyes roaming from one sparkling old eye to the other.

"Do you not remember your teachings?" The old man canted his head, deeply studying the one before him. "Ah, I see; lack of experience for the once born-forever living. It is no wonder you are here and not there."

"There?"

"With them." The old man gazed up to the pulsating lotus and pointed at the myriad of lights that flowed into it.

He stood and followed the grizzled old finger before it lowered. They stood in awe of the sight. "Why aren't you there?" he asked.

"Ah, a true question," beamed the old man. "Follow."

In silence, he followed the slow pondering steps of the old man, the one who had once saved his life, the one who had been with him, taught him, and cared for him when Notus could not, the one who had married the warrior's path with that of the spiritual. He watched the old man before him and felt surprised to see the figure before him waver and flicker through a myriad of familiar forms until one stunned him into stillness.

"Come, boy," said the figure that was Geraint. "You asked a question." The figure turned forward along the path, flickering once more between forms.

On leaden feet he followed the man who had once abandoned him, who once had trained him, who had once cared for him as if a father. The one who had set him upon the warrior's path. The one whose sword he cherished because he *was* his father.

"A tricky definition," said the now old man as he continued down the unseen rocky path. "Is a father one who gives his physical building blocks to his progeny or is a father one who chooses to care for another, younger, person? One who loves that younger person regardless of a biological connection? One who is loved in turn by that younger person? Is love the real connection or is it something tangible, quantifiable?"

Confusion filled the spaces around the pain, lapping at the hurt until he closed his eyes and turned his head away.

He felt a hand on his arm and he opened his eyes to see the old man looking up at him, a sad smile on the wrinkly wizened face. "You must decide."

The old man turned and pointed into the blackness. "There."

From the new vantage point on the precipice he could see the star-flower at a new angle. It appeared more on its side and the pulsations of light lit up the rest of the darkness until it washed over them. He closed his eyes as the sensations of love, acceptance and warmth flowed over and through him. He had only felt this way with one other. With each swell of light sound erupted in an ethereal chorus unheard before to his ears. The chord undulated and vibrated, filling him with the sense of peace and love that he knew the pinpoints of light had felt and all he wanted was to stay there and bask in its glory.

A hand alighted on his arm and he opened his eyes.

"Look there," said the old man, his arm still pointing.

Still reeling from the music and the light he followed the old man's arm and saw past the star-flower. A single tendril of light flowed from the center back of the golden white orb. It led past where they stood on the precipice and into the darkness until it was caught by a brilliant blue white orb in the distance. It glimmered and glowed like a sun. He noticed that this white path of light was sparsely made up of individual orbs of light similar to those that flowed into the star-flower, but these orbs no longer held any shape except of a tiny pinpoint of light. Peering closely at the star in the distance he could make out a scant few other trails of light flowing towards it from faraway places.

"I go there," replied the old man.

The answer surprised him. "Now?"

"Soon." The old man groaned as he sat down to stare out into the spaces.

"Why not go there?" He stayed standing as he pointed to the star-flower.

"Because I have only one thing left to do before I become."

He gazed down at the serenity on the old man's face. "What is that?"

"To help you help them."

"I don't understand." He sat down beside the old man.

"That is the problem, is it not?" The old man turned his head to face him. "They did a poor job in preparing you properly, but I guess it is their nature. Their detachment from the world left them ill equipped to truly help you be a benefit to them.

"Look over there." The old man pointed to a place that was devoid of any light, but it was not dark. In the space wisps flowed. "You know that place."

Indeed he did.

"You have been there many times. Only you have been allowed to penetrate it. Only you have been able to bring hope to those in the centre of its shrouded light.

"A grave mistake was made, based upon the hubris of those who made it," continued the old man. "It was hoped that you would be the one to correct it."

"Correct what?"

"Sometimes detaching oneself too much can lead one away from the path as attaching oneself can create suffering. It is the middle path that must be walked, but before that path can be traversed one must mark the way."

"I don't understand." He closed his eyes, afraid that he might know what the old man wished of him.

"Love," whispered the old man.

"What?"

"Do you love?"

The question shook him. "Yes," he susurrated before he could stop himself. He loved Jeanie.

"And so many others," stated the old man.

He nodded, though a part of him wished he did not.

"Then you know what to do." The old man stood up and offered a hand.

Taking that hand, he stood to stare down at the old man.

THAΠATOS

"I love you, boy," said the old man, his form flickering to that of Geraint and then back.

"I—I love you too, father."

The old man smiled as he stepped off the precipice.

A flash of light blinded him and then he saw a brilliant orb flying to the distant blue white sun. When it was gone a sense of peace and purpose filled him as he turned his attention to the Void and what it contained.

He stepped off the precipice.

Í

Thanatos watched the club, its patrons flowing in and out from the wide open black doors, from his position across the street. He sat in the comfort of his chauffeured limousine, the window rolled down to allow a greater chance of catching telling words in his sensitive hearing. Despite the sonorous snoring from Godfrey, Thanatos was able to pick up conversations from *Beyond the Veil's* patrons. It was difficult because of all the traffic that tended to act as a barrier between him and them, but if he closed his eyes and concentrated intently he would discover that it was mortal trivialities that engaged the black clad individuals who partook of the city's polluted air.

He glanced at his wrist watch and sighed. He had already spent a few hours in surveillance of the place to no avail. His run in with the Angel hours ago and the unfortunate misunderstanding had almost made Thanatos give up on trying to convince the Angel to return to Britain. Toronto was not safe for the Angel. It was clear when Thanatos had given Corvus his warning to leave the Angel alone, and a part of him wished that Corvus and his Vampires would have heeded his advice, but Thanatos knew better. Over twelve thousand years amongst man proved how predictable they were, even when gifted, or cursed, with the longevity that required blood feedings. It was a very rare occurrence for Thanatos to be taken by surprise by what mankind did. The last one hundred years were the only ones that offered any real origi-nalities, and those that did he could count on one hand.

Allowing the plush leather interior to cradle him, Thanatos closed his eyes and focused once more on the goings-on at *Beyond the Veil*. One group, young by the timber of their voices, yammered about how Brian was the most gorgeous thing on the planet. A snigger escaped Thanatos. If only those children knew the reality of the one they had a crush on. Then again Vampires were now the trendy thing—at least in fiction. If they knew that Vampires were not things of fairy tales or the imaginings of lonely house wives sitting at their computers pumping out sex filled fantasies, maybe then they would flee to the safety of their homes and hide under their beds. Or worse, come out with torches and stakes ready to commit genocide. The boogie man did exist and he had a name—Vampire.

Godfrey's soothing snoring caught and was interrupted as Thanatos' human servant endeavoured to find a more comfortable position than that of reclining in the driver's seat. It took a moment before the gentle soughing of Godfrey's breath filled the limousine's cabin. Thanatos smiled at the back of Godfrey's corn blonde head. He had made the right decision in taking in the young lad from the streets.

Thanatos remembered early on the scared child who had al-lowed others to take their advantage with one desperate enough to succumb for the promise of food. Of course Godfrey no longer held these memories, having had them carefully removed from his psyche by his new benefactor. In all the years Godfrey had been with Thanatos, knowing what he was and caring for him anyways, Thanatos never doubted his servant's loyalty or love. It was that which made it so difficult to watch Godfrey age and then die when the time came.

Thanatos shook himself out of his melancholy and sat straight backed at the edge of the black leathered bench. *Enough of that,* he admonished and turned back to watching and listening to those across the street.

Glancing once more at his watch, it explained why so many people were leaving the Goth club. Dawn approached and *Beyond the Veil* began shutting down for the night to allow its undead staff prepare themselves for their death at sunrise. Soon the trickle of mortals came to an end, but instead of the doors being closed and barred for the night, they remained open as several Vampires, in ones and twos, made their way back to the club. Thanatos frowned. *Would they not be going to their own homes?*

Cold fear gripped him when he witnessed Stephanie, Domina of Seattle, and Michael, Dominus of Victoria, enter *Beyond the Veil.* It was not so much that they were both so far from their own domains, but rather that they had come at their Dominus' calling and Michael had brought his fabled limestone war hammer *Subtle Persuasion.* Corvus was up to something.

Once the front doors to the club were closed and barred, Thanatos' anxiety heightened. Waking Godfrey from his much needed nap, Thanatos ordered the car started. Whatever Corvus had planned would not take place in such a public place, but at the same time, with sunrise so close, he could not take things into a remote area. With the early morning hours there was only one possibility and he indicated for Godfrey to drive around the back of the building.

Straightening his black driver's cap, Godfrey did as ordered.

"There. Park there," ordered Thanatos once they were at the back of the strip of two storied buildings that provided domiciles for Queen Street West's businesses.

Godfrey nodded and pulled the limousine into the back alley between the buildings and the city parking lot, shutting off the engine. They parked close enough to the back of the club to see what was going on, but far enough that hopefully they would be ignored.

In the dark quiet of the car, Thanatos and Godfrey watched as a flood of Vampires came out of the back to take up positions the ringed the back entrance to *Beyond the Veil.* A slim female with long blonde straight hair came to lean against the side of their limousine oblivious to the passengers within. It took Thanatos signaling through the rearview mirror to Godfrey to keep perfectly quiet. He knew what Godfrey would have done and it would have jeopardized their position.

It did not take long before they watched the Angel walk down the opposite end of the laneway to enter into the small parking area for the employees of *The Veil*. What transpired between the Angel and the Vampires tensed every muscle in Thanatos' body. Corvus defied him, but the manner in which he did made Thanatos' gorge rise. A whimper of fear emanated from Godfrey and Thanatos watched as a wall of fog began to grow around them, but before they could bear witness to the creatures that were part of the Angel's Dragon's Breath the mist dissipated into nothingness.

In silence they watched Corvus bring out his young protégé. Rose held the Angel's sword between her two hands. Maybe there would not be a war between Chosen and Vampire in the Americas, hoped Thanatos, but these wishes were dashed away at the reaction of the Angel to Rose.

It could not be possible! The Angel knew this Vampire? Realization struck and Thanatos put a hand to his mouth as Rose bit deep into the Angel's neck while at the same time impaling the Angel with his own sword. It took all his effort not to cry out, not to rip the car door off its hinges to fly over to them, and not to go over and kill all the Vampires that stood snickering over the wounded Angel as he bled black blood.

Anger welled up through Thanatos but he quelled into check as he watched Rose stumble back from her meal, the last remnants of the Angel's red blood dripping from her chin as confusion and insanity widened her green eyes.

Corvus' order snapped Thanatos' attention back to the Angel as Michael, wielding *Subtle Persuasion,* smashed the heavy limestone hammer onto the flat of the blade that protruded from the Angel's back. The resulting scream deafened the night as the blade broke.

Stunned, Thanatos and Godfrey could only watch as Corvus ordered his Vampires into the club, taking a moment to gloat over the prone figure of the Angel and to talk to Rose, who sobbed bloody tears as she clutched the Angel. It did not make any sense why a Vampire would do this, especially Corvus' protégé, but when Corvus and Brian left her alone to the sun Thanatos released the breath he did not realize he held.

The substance of the air shifted with the onset of dawn, still Thanatos watched through his protected windshields as the

Vampiress pulled the fractured blade from the Angel's body before succumbing to the death that dawn created. Stunned and furious at what he had witnessed, he ordered, "Drive up to them, Godfrey."

"Yes, sir," replied Godfrey, his voice shaking. He turned on the engine and put the vehicle into gear to roll the limousine to the fallen Angel and the Vampire who slew him. The sound of crunching loose stones beneath the tires echoed in the cabin of the stretch limo until the car rolled to a halt next to the fallen figures. Throwing the gear into park, Godfrey let the car's idling rock them.

There were bare moments before the new born sun's rays would fall upon the two, but would that be enough? Thanatos did not care. He had waited lifetimes to discover the answers he craved. *I would not end like this.*

"What do you want me to do, sir?" asked Godfrey, turning in his seat to stare worriedly at his master.

Thanatos met his fatigued servant's gaze with determination and released a shuddering sigh. "Bring them in, Godfrey," he ordered.

"Both, sir?" queried his servant.

For the briefest of moments Thanatos contemplated the wisdom of saving the Vampiress as well, but her reaction to having drunk the Angel's blood cried out for answers to unspoken questions. Thanatos gave a quick bob of his head and Godfrey was out of his driver's seat and onto the concrete, his driver's door wide open.

Diffuse early morning light splashed across the limo's cabin as Thanatos opened his door. Eyes tearing and skin prickling he assisted his man-servant in settling the Angel's flaccid form supine onto the cabin's floor. Thanatos could not bear to step outside and had to wait as Godfrey passed the Vampiress to him. She was light, lighter than he expected, as he placed her dead form onto the calf hide leather seat that backed against the driver's station.

By the time the full strength of the morning's sun splashed to the ground around them, Godfrey had slammed the passenger door shut before taking his position behind the wheel, closing his door with similar aplomb. If it were not for the specially treated windows of the limousine, Thanatos would have joined the Angel and the Vampiress in a true and permanent death. Trembling hands did not help with the task of getting the car moving. Godfrey had forgotten he had left the car's engine on, the screech as he turned the key making him jump. Throwing the gear into reverse, Godfrey backed the car up, out of the club's parking lot, before tossing the gear into drive. Tires spat stones as he heavy footed it out of the back lane.

Bending over the vampiric corpse as the limousine sped down the road, Thanatos gave a cursory glance at the Vampiress, noting the slight burning smell that rose from her limp form. He and Godfrey had just gotten her into the safety of the limousine before the sun could do any real damage to her. The most, if he let her live, that she would have to deal with was a new hair cut.

Thanatos turned his attention to his true concern and knelt beside the pale figure of The Angel. Fear choked him with the possibility of what he could lose, but he shook his head. This time he would not let anything happen.

Dread turned into determination and Thanatos allowed centuries of medical practice to calm him into detached professionalism. Smoothing the Angel's black stained white hair from placid pale features, Thanatos sucked in a shocked breath. There, branching up from the collar of the Angel's black cotton dress shirt, streaks of black beneath paper white skin reached up through the veins and arteries, marring the perfect whiteness.

Thanatos laid his fingers upon the silent carotid artery in hopes for a sign, but nothing. He pressed his ear against the slim, muscular chest in hopes to hear what his fingers could not feel. Again, nothing. Frustration built. Rising up, Thanatos pulled out the little pen-light he tended to carry on the inside of his dress jacket, next to the fountain pen Godfrey had bought him for their first Christmas together. With a punch of his thumb the light flickered on as Thanatos lifted the eyelid of the Angel. Flickering the light back and forth, he prayed to see some sign of life from the Angel. He nearly dropped the pen-light and whooped for glee when he saw the Angel's dark red pupil contract when the light hit it.

Karen Dales

Without a thought, Thanatos clicked off the pen and stuffed it back into his inside jacket pocket. Time was running out and he had to do whatever it took to keep the Angel alive.

Ripping open the Angel's shirt, Thanatos gasped at the blackened maw in the upper left quadrant of the Angel's abdomen—the site of the sword's impalement. Black ropes and tendrils serpentined all across the pale scarred torso, hinting that the iron's poisoning had been effective in its spread.

Thanatos did not understand why they continued to grow, to consume, burning the Angel's body from within. Did the Vampiress not pull out the broken sword? Chewing on his upper lip, he did not know what to do and he closed his eyes in recollection of what he had witnessed.

Two pieces had been pulled from the Angel. Thanatos' dark brown eyes popped open in realization. What if the sword had shattered into more? It would account for the growing effects of the poison.

He palpated the cauterized wound, finding nothing. Time was running out. If there was a piece of iron sword still inside it would have to come out now. Waiting until they returned to his home where he had some of the tools necessary would not be possible. By then the Angel would be dead and Thanatos would have lost his one chance.

With no other recourse, Thanatos shrugged out of his dress jacket, tossing it wherever it landed, and rolled up his shirt sleeves. Shaking his head with what he was about to do, he braced himself with one hand on the Angel's slim waist and gentled his right hand into the charred ruins of flesh. Desperately wishing for the tools of the surgery that made the twentieth and twenty-first century medicine so much neater, Thanatos closed his eyes so as to concentrate on what communication his fingers sent him.

Heat encapsulated his hand as he felt around, the iron's poison eating away at the Angel. All around his fingers he could only feel burnt flesh over laying soft tissue soon to char. If he could find what remaining piece there was and remove it, then he would have a chance to save the Angel's life.

Gritting his teeth, Thanatos felt something that should not be there. It was hot and smooth and radiated such a heat that his fingers jerked at the sensation. It had to be it. Carefully, so as not to slice his own cold flesh against the sharp iron sliver, he gentled the piece out of the Angel's ruined abdomen until he held the palm length shard before his wide surprised eyes. Blackened blood dripped down from the poisonous metal to mix with the gore staining Thanatos' hand. A shudder ran through him at the sight and he placed the sword shard on the limousine cabin's floor, uncaring of the stain it caused in the beige carpeting.

Despite the size of the shard Thanatos knew the possibility of others left behind and stuck his hand back into the wound, feeling around for any other pieces of the shattered sword. Closing his eyes in concentration his fingers told him that the wound was clear and he pulled out his hand once more, noticing for the first time the sucking wet sound as he did so. A glance out of the polarized window told him that they were not far from his home, but there was still not much time left.

Uncaring that his gored hand left prints on the Angel, Thanatos checked again for a heartbeat. Again, there was nothing. No breath. No pulse. He opened the pale eye and looked for any sign of life, but without his penlight he could not discern if what he saw was real. It did not matter. He had to try.

A shift in his position and Thanatos tilted the Angel's head back. Modern medicine came up with so many wonderful practices and this one was the best in his opinion. Thanatos began the simple procedure of CPR, praying to whatever benevolent Gods there were, to save the Angel. In Thanatos' experience death was the ultimate healer, and he believed himself to be such, but he would not let the Angel experience this form of healing if there was anything he could do.

The last five minutes of the drive were the longest as Thanatos shifted from chest compressions to breathing life giving air into the Angel's lungs. He wanted to swear at the Angel, to yell at him to live, not to give up, but it was not his place to do so. Instead he found his eyes blurred with unshed tears.

The passenger car door opened within the safety of a spacious garage.

"We're here, sir," stated Godfrey. Worry mingled with fear

marked his tired face.

Thanatos gazed up at his servant, his large brown eyes imploring help, as he continued with this round of chest compressions.

Without a word, Godfrey nodded and slipped into the back cabin to kneel beside the Angel's head. He stared at the Angel's slack features in fear.

"I need you to help me, Godfrey," said Thanatos, his eyes catching blue. "*He* needs your help."

Taking a shuddering breath, Godfrey leaned over to apply his mouth to the Angel's and was surprised at the heat radiating from what appeared to be a corpse. Together master and servant, God of Death and creature of life, worked to bring a spark back to the Angel.

By the time Godfrey became dizzy Thanatos ordered him to back off so as to feel for a pulse from the carotid artery. With closed eyes, he pressed his cold fingers to hot flesh, his stained fingers leaving further marks of drying black blood on the Angel's skin.

A flutter ran beneath his finger tips, catching him by surprise and halting his own breath. Thanatos placed his fingers lightly on the artery. There it was again! Releasing the faint and fluttering pulse on the Angel's neck, he laid ear against a pale chest ribboned with black. Did the Angel's chest rise slightly before lowering? Thanatos dared not to hope too much, but a smile split his face at the whisper sound of an awakening heart.

"Sir? Is he…"

Thanatos sat up, releasing his breath and nodded, his eyes bright as his smile touched them. "He is, Godfrey. Barely, but he is."

Godfrey's eyes closed as his shoulders slumped in relief mixed with exhaustion. "Thank God."

"No, Godfrey, thank you." Thanatos reached over to pat the young man affectionately on his shoulder. "There's still so much we have to do. The Angel is not out of danger."

Nodding, Godfrey eased his way backwards on his knees out of the vehicle until he was standing on the concrete pad of the garage. "What do you need me to do, sir?"

Thanatos peered up at the young man. "Get my instruments from my laboratory in the basement and bring them to my room. I'll need whatever gut you can find in my desk."

"What about sutures?"

"Oh." Thanatos followed Godfrey's gaze to the black tendrils marking the Angel's whiteness. "Bring what I have of those too," he said somberly. Worry flashed through Thanatos. To introduce more of the poisonous iron in an attempt to close the wounds could ruin everything, but they could not remain open. A thought popped to mind and he glanced back at Godfrey. "Do you still have that antique bronze sewing set?"

"Yes, sir, I do," nodded Godfrey.

"Bring it to my room. I'll meet you there."

"Yes, sir." Godfrey turned to leave through the door that led into the mansion but turned back at the last moment. "Sir, what about the Vampiress?"

Thanatos, now outside of the limo, glanced back at the forgotten presence lying on the leather bench. "Leave her there. She's safe." He did not see Godfrey's nod, but assumed it had occurred before he heard the door unlock and open to allow his servant to enter their home to follow his orders.

Returning his gaze to the Angel, Thanatos gently lifted the one and only person who could possibly save him, if only he could save the Angel first.

II

xhausted, Thanatos sat at the kitchen's cherry wood table. Noon day sun leaked around the edges of the shuttered window over the sink while heavy brocade drapes eradicated sunlight from the sliding glass doors which lead out to the patio and sculpted back garden. Blood encrusted hands supported his weary head, his elbows propped on the table. He had done all that he could to save the Angel and prayed it would be enough. What meager skills he possessed to patch the wound felt inadequate and destined to fail. The bronze sewing needle had saved the Angel, but how much damage had the sword done? Even as Thanatos stitched the wound the evidence of the sword's poisoning still wound its way through flesh.

Leaning back in the chair, the cool wood pressing against his back, Thanatos reached under his collar and pulled on a silver chain until an elaborately decorated silver phial came free to dangle from his rusty fingers. He pressed the pendant to his lips with both hands and closed his eyes. *Please, please, don't let him die. I've come so close. Please tell me what needs to be done.*

He pulled the phial away from his lips and stared at it. It was not the container that he cared for, but rather the contents. Through millennia the container had changed, ever growing smaller and smaller until its last use almost two thousand years ago. Now this was all that remained. He had sworn, when he had last used it, resulting in such devastating consequences, that he would never use it again. But this time was different. Was it not?

Releasing the pendant to dangle above his splattered white dress shirt, Thanatos leaned forward once more, his hand rubbing his mouth, his other arm resting forgotten on the smooth table. He had sent Godfrey to a much deserved rest after helping to remove the Angel's gory shirt and long leather coat. One could be repaired and cleaned; the other was left for the garbage. Thanatos had never seen Godfrey turn so pale, but the sight of the Angel's many scars, especially those of obvious torture on his back, worried Thanatos that his servant would faint, or worse. He would not have blamed him, the evidences of abuse sickened Thanatos. With a declaration that he could handle the situation he dismissed Godfrey with the hope that the young man would find solace in sleep.

Thanatos leaned his elbows on the table and buried his face once more in his hands. What was he supposed to do? The Angel lay in a coma in his bed. Corvus had defied him. After so many centuries of non-interference Thanatos found himself plunged into the middle of a war. He had to do something, but what?

The silver phial dangled heavily against his chest and he took a deep breath. There was no doubt that Corvus had to be punished. Had his beautiful Bastia been still alive that responsibility would have fallen to her. He wanted to laugh. Bastia wanted the Angel's death, and the death of all the Chosen. It had been the Angel who had punished her. Now Thanatos had to deal directly with Corvus and his personal war against the Angel and the Chosen. It was not something he ever wished to do. He had naively believed Corvus would let go of his hate and his need for revenge. Thanatos shook his head. How could he have been so blind?

Pushing back from the table, the chair grinding against the tile, Thanatos stood and walked out of the kitchen through the swinging mahogany doors, across the marble tiled black and white floor, past the large brown stained oak front doors to ascend the grand staircase that branched off into two to a second story.

Feet dragged against the carpeted runners as his hand trailed along the polished banisters that matched the front door until he halted a brief moment at the top of the left side of the staircase. A sigh escaped as he made his way back to his suite where the Angel lay unconscious on his bed. Corvus would have to wait. His destiny would be determined upon the fate of the Angel. Thanatos prayed he could be lenient.

Trepidation filled him as he came to the end of the hall. His door lurked as if a stranger's. Not one in which he had entered and exited as a friend. Lowering his hand in the realization that knocking would do no good, Thanatos pushed down the handle and entered. The door made no sound save for the gentle click behind him as it closed into the frame.

Peace filled the room, a precious peace of one who could yet be drawn into Death's embrace. Thanatos would not allow it.

Over the plush carpeting, Thanatos made his way to the bed. He closed his eyes. Despite all his efforts the black tendrils of iron poisoning still gripped the Angel. Carefully, Thanatos sat beside the sleeping Angel and raised the bone white hand snaked in black in his own black encrusted one. The heat that came off of the Angel was startling. Not willing to be distracted Thanatos felt for a pulse in the wrist and closed his eyes in relief. The beat was thready and weak but it was still proof that a heart beat in the black veined alabaster of the Angel's chest.

He sat there, staring at the Angel, his eyes brimming with unshed tears. How could he have been so stupid as to allow fear to keep him from approaching the Angel for so long? He wiped his eyes with the back of his hand and shook his head. Thanatos knew the reason. He was terrified that the Angel would say no. Now it could be too late. His fear of denial had paralyzed him for so long that sitting here, beside the one who could possibly hold the answers to Thanatos' questing, seemed childish and idiotic.

Leaning forward, Thanatos brushed an errant white lock from the placid pale face of the Angel, the softness surprising to his fingers. After all these centuries to behold the face of the Angel was bliss mixed with despair. *So young.*

"Please don't leave me," he whispered; his voice rough with controlled emotion. Laying his hand on a shoulder of fevered flesh, Thanatos leaned back so as to rise and caught himself.

The phial did not pull back with him. It pulled at his neck as if it were a piece of iron and the Angel was a magnet. He leaned back further in the hopes to disengage the pendant but the chain only cut deeper into the back of his neck. Confusion contorted Thanatos' features as he raised his hand to encapsulate the silver phial. Intense heat flared through his grasp and he released the pendant, his brown eyes widening. In all his millennia he had never experienced this effect with the contents of the phial, for it could only be that. His silver ring on his right hand did not pull towards the Angel.

Slowly, he stood, moving backwards from the Angel until the phial rested normally upon his breast. Curiosity and a scientific mind prompted Thanatos to step closer until he felt the tug of the silver and he could see it straining against its leash. Taking the necessary steps backwards, Thanatos tentatively picked up the phial between thumb and forefinger and was surprised to find the silver was cool.

Standing by the door, Thanatos cocked his head to the side, his eyes studying the Angel as if he were an experiment with unexpected results. "Is this what you need?" he said glancing at the pendant in his grasp. The silver began to warm.

Comprehension slammed him, causing him to inhale. Hope swelled as he turned to flee out of the room and down the stairs. He almost found his feet sliding out from him as he turned too quickly around the end of the stairs in his excitement. The suite of rooms that were Godfrey's was off to the right, his ringing footfalls crashed into silence as he ran down the carpeted hall. Despite his own fleeing fatigue he ignored the twinge of guilt as he pounded on Godfrey's door.

Through the mahogany Thanatos listened with growing impatience as his servant stumbled his way to the door. On well oiled hinges the door opened to reveal a sleep deprived young man in blue pajamas, his short blonde hair pillow tousled. Thanatos did not wait for permission to enter the dark room; his excitement eradicated all politeness as he quickly took in the sight of Godfrey's messy bed before turning back to gaze on Godfrey's pleading blue eyes.

"I'm sorry to do this to you, Godfrey." The words flew out of his mouth as he stepped up to the taller young man, his hands resting on cotton covered arms. He felt his servant wilt and was surprised to see Godfrey close to tears. Guilt tugged at Thanatos to drop his arms. In a softer tone he explained, "I need you to find Notus, Godfrey, and bring him here."

"Now, sir?"

"Yes," insisted Thanatos. Had Godfrey whined?

Godfrey glanced at the green glowing numbers on his bedside table and closed his eyes. "You want me to go and bring one of the Chosen back here, now? It's one o'clock in the afternoon."

Surprised at the time, Thanatos turned to see the clock and was about to debate the issue that it was almost a quarter after when the real fact to Godfrey's statement rang true. Returning his gaze to the mortal man, he almost apologized. Godfrey had been awake for far too long with too little sleep. "Go before sunset and bring him right after."

A sigh of relief filled the space between the two. Godfrey nodded, his eyes closed. "Yes, sir, I'll find out where he is staying and bring him here. Now, please sir, may I have a few more hours to rest?"

This time Thanatos apologized, walking past his servant, his hand resting on the door's handle, he turned. "Yes, Godfrey, please. I'm sorry to have disturbed you."

A faint smile lifted Godfrey's lips as he walked to his bed. "Unnecessary, sir. I understand," he said, sitting on the mattress.

"I guess there's no need to tuck you in like I used to, eh?" Thanatos smiled.

A soft chuckle warmed the atmosphere. "No, sir. I'm no longer haunted by bad dreams."

Thanatos exited the servant's quarters. "You are the lucky one," he murmured as he returned to sit by the Angel.

III

otus sat on the black leather couch; his bruised eyes stared into the dark space of the empty condo. Time stilled until motionless, the only indicator that life resumed its normal cadence was the building brilliance lining the brocade drapes. Part of Notus wanted to fling the heavy swatches open to dash searing pain through his being until nothing remained except for ash, but he could not move. Stunned shock staked him to his seat, immobilizing him in a repeating loop of what he had done.

Dried tears stained salty tracks down his face. How could he have done what he had to the only child of his immortal heart? Closing his eyes, a shuddered breath escaped as he repeated the horrific events of the previous night. In his mind's eye he could see the boy, wounded in body, receive the killing emotional blow that only Notus could have ever given.

How could I have been so stupid?!

For a moment Notus thought more tears would flow, but there were none left to feed the tsunami of his self loathing. For all their lives together Notus had kept Eira's confession and never mentioned to anyone the true relationship she had with the boy. In the span of one evening the revelation had destroyed everything, sending the boy fleeing from him, Bridget and Fernando, into a night ruled by those who would do anything to avenge themselves upon the Angel.

Too late. It's all too late.

Notus' shoulders slumped. Fernando and Bridget had been furious at him, and rightly so. A part of Notus had almost wished that the Master and Mistress of England had exacted their justice on him. Instead they had ordered Notus back to his condo, dropping him off and walking him to his door sure in the belief that Notus would try and do something foolish. They had not been far wrong. He had been so tempted to open those drapes. Instead he tottered into the boy's room and slept in the scent of his Chosen child.

Dreams had wracked him through the sunlight hours, burning fevered nightmares of his last hours as a mortal man and the re-birth as a Chosen. In the dreams he did not see his little children's faces. Instead each of the slaughtered held the visage of the boy. His white beautiful face marred by splattered black blood, his crimson eyes staring at nothing. It was a relief when he fled the bed at twilight, exiting the condo to race up to the roof of the building.

He had to get away.

The sun's remnants itched his skin, distracting him for a moment until he recalled why he had fled their temporary home. Crashing to the stone pebbled roof, Notus had released the tears he had held at bay as the most brilliant of stars winked into the dusted velvet of the sky.

He had lost everything.

Loneliness filled his being for the first time in millennia.

Time had passed in a blur of tears. It was only of the prickling of his skin that informed him of day's approach. On rubbery legs, his body guided him back down the stairs and to the empty suite, his mind left far behind to sing the reality of what he had done.

Staring at the darkened room a stabbing pain grasped him, nearly toppling him over. His grief soaked mind cleared for a brief moment to realize that it was too late to heal the wounds between them.

*   *   *

The sofa felt as rocks beneath him as he gazed into nothingness. He did not know how long he had sat there until a knock rang through air. He had no time for distractions from his grief and ignored the gentle tap.

A firmer pounding alighted his door, eliciting a groan. "Go away," he managed before closing his eyes once more. He wanted to melt into the couch and disappear.

"Father Paul Notus?" a voice called from the other side.

Notus opened his eyes, frowning at the door. No one knew him here by that name save Fernando, Bridget and...and...He could not bring himself to think of the boy. Curiosity wiggled into the cracks of his grief and he stood and walked to the door, halting before he could turn the latch. Memories of being tricked into torture moved him to seek the peep hole. Through the fish-eyed view he saw a young man dressed in a black suit and tie, his head capped with wavy blonde hair. Turning away from the sight, Notus walked away from the door, determined to ignore the individual on the other side.

The knock came again, this time more insistent.

Annoyance exhaled his breath. "What do you want?" he called so as to carry through the door.

"Please, sir," came the muffled reply. "It's about the Angel."

Elation was quickly squashed by suspicion. There was no denying what he had felt before. The Angel was gone. The boy was lost. His son was dead. His breath caught in a sob. "Go away!"

The pounding came away. "Please, sir, let me in. I've come to take you to him."

The image of standing over the cold corpse of the boy leaked new tears from the corners of his eyes. "The Angel is dead," he gasped.

"No, sir, he is not."

How could the man on the other side have heard that?

Notus wrenched open the door. The young man stepped back at the baleful glare, his face paling. Notus did not care how he appeared to this young mortal. How dare he come here with lies?

The young man fumbled with the hat he held in his hands. "The Angel is not dead, sir." His voice trembled. "I was sent to bring you to the Angel."

The words resonated between Notus' ears without comprehension. Shaking his head, Notus stepped back to allow the man to enter. If the situation was not so confounding he would have noted the man's wide eyed visual tour of the boxes that created a maze down one side of the living room. Without a second thought, Notus closed the door and locked it, the click causing the man to startle around to face him.

"Who are you?" demanded Notus. He crossed his arms, standing before the locked door. There was no doubt that the one before him was mortal. Vampires became dead during the day. It did not preclude the concept that the one before him worked for Vampires.

The man glanced down at his hands that still twirled the hat between well manicured fingers. "I...um...I'm Godfrey de-Morte—"

"That's an interesting name," stated Notus. The sight of the young man's discomfort chipped at the ice numbness of his earlier shock.

"Oh...well...I..."

Notus sighed. "You said you were sent to bring me to the Angel," offered Notus. "But he is...he is..." He could not bring himself to say the word. The wound still wept.

Godfrey looked up, green eyes matching hazel. "No, sir," he shook his head. "The Angel is not dead. He's—"

"What?" Notus could not believe what he heard. He took a step closer towards the mortal, ignoring the retreating step, to place his hands on the young man's arms. Hope and fear warred within him. "He's...he's...alive? I felt...He can't be..."

"Yes, sir, but just barely." Godfrey's eyes widened at the contact. "I was told to bring you."

Notus dropped his arms, confusion abounding and turned away, shaking his head. "How did you find me?"

Godfrey slipped his hand into his inside jacket pocket and pulled out a leather billfold. It was Notus' turn to be stunned. It was the boy's wallet. He took the proffered item, his hand trembling as if it were an antiquity, and opened it.

"The address is on the ownership papers for his motorcycle," stated Godfrey, a slight smile on his face.

Relieving the wallet of its green paper, Notus' hand shook as he opened it and nodded his head. "You say my boy's still alive."

"Yes, sir, but barely."

Notus placed the form back into the wallet and turned his attention to the young man. A part of his mind screamed at him not to go with him, that it was a trap laid by the Vampires who ruled the city, but his heart told him differently. If there was a chance, even a slim chance, to save the boy and possibly mend things, then he would do it, his Oath be damned. He would do anything to have his son back and God had seen fit to give him a second chance. He would not make the same mistake again.

"Okay. Let's go." Notus placed the wallet down on the coffee table and turned to leave, the young man in tow. "One thing though," he added as he held the door open.

"Yes, sir?"

"We have to make a stop on the way."

"Yes, sir." Godfrey gave a curt nod and followed the Chosen out of the condo and into the hall.

ÍⱰ

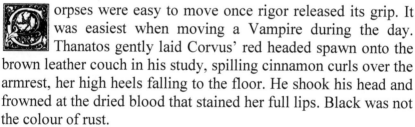orpses were easy to move once rigor released its grip. It was easiest when moving a Vampire during the day. Thanatos gently laid Corvus' red headed spawn onto the brown leather couch in his study, spilling cinnamon curls over the armrest, her high heels falling to the floor. He shook his head and frowned at the dried blood that stained her full lips. Black was not the colour of rust.

Exhaustion weakened his body and he hid a yawn behind the back of his hand as he sat heavily onto his matching reading chair. No warm cup awaited him. No paper brought in. No fire in the hearth to warm the chill. Godfrey was gone to find Notus and bring him back. A shudder flared through him at the thought of seeing Notus. What was done was done; there was no time for regrets. The only thing that mattered was the Angel.

He lowered his eyes to his hands resting on his lap and brought the blackened digits closer. He had forgotten to wash them in the rush to save the Angel. Both the Vampiress and he were stained. Leaning forward until his elbows rested on his knees, he allowed the weariness to consume him as he meditated upon the girl. He replayed the early morning's events. It made no sense why she would at first be eager to kill the Angel and then turn around after doing so, bleeding him into her being and onto the ground, then cry out mourning him. It made no sense.

Corvus' reaction was even more puzzling. Was this girl not one of his coterie? One of his oldest and dearest? Why then did Corvus and Brian leave her for the sun? Questions upon questions ravaged his mind. It made no sense.

A sound startled him from his dozing, snapping his eyes open and straightening his back as he witnessed renewed life return to the Vampiress before him. A flutter of eye movement beneath nearly translucent lids foretold their opening. It was then that Thanatos noticed the emerald green of her eyes. In silence, he watched her extract herself from the chrysalis of undeath. Slender pale arms reached heavenward as she stretched, her back arching. She appeared as if waking from a deep sleep, but Thanatos knew it was not Orpheus' grips she stirred from.

In patient silence, Thanatos observed the Vampiress' consciousness return to the here and now. A content smile lifted her lips a fraction before crashing into an open mouthed silent scream. Her emerald eyes saucer wide, she bolted to a sitting position, a hand covering black stained lips as she took in the sight of her host.

"Where is he?" she demanded. Pearls of red pooled in the corners of her eyes.

Blinking back his surprise at the sight and unexpected thick Highland Scottish accent, Thanatos leaned back and folded his stained hands on his lap. Her question proved intriguing as most that wake in unknown surroundings would normally ask where they were. The Vampiress did not ask anything selfish. This pulled a frown on his face as all Vampires he knew were narcissistic creatures.

"Who do you mean?" asked Thanatos as he studied the creature before him.

He could hear the answer before she stuttered, "The Angel."

Thanatos watched in horrified amazement as the Vampiress dissolved into gut wrenching sobs. Tracks of blood tears streamed down her pale face, making her appear a survivor of some tremendous accident. It was not her gruesome transformation that stunned Thanatos, but rather the evidence of tears and grief displayed by a Vampire. In all his long existence he had never witnessed its like and it played to his sympathy for this creature.

"I—I kilt him!" she hiccoughed through her wails. Her arms wrapped over her abdomen as if in great pain. A new wash of blood flowed from her eyes.

Shaken by her admission, as well as her guilt, Thanatos left his chair to kneel before the Vampiress and cradled her face in his hands. "Tell me what you remember," he demanded from the depth of her being, his brown eyes locked onto her blood stained ones.

Thanatos felt her relax as he pressed his command, but she tensed as she told him more than he could have known until all he could do was sit back on his haunches, arms dangling at his sides. The girl before him had been raped into a Vampire by Corvus, and she remembered it all: her life before the forced rebirth, the unlife as the Vampiress Rose who gladly stabbed and drank from the Angel, to the confused and distraught Vampire who now held mortal memories. The greatest revelation was who she had been. It also explained the Angel's reaction and compliance.

Released from the bonds to Corvus, Rose regained her mortal self. She was once again Jeanie, the lover of the Angel of Death, and her mind reeled at what her Rose-self had been and done.

A flutter of a question tickled the back of his mind, but he pushed it aside. No, he could not ask what the Angel's blood had tasted like. Rising up from his kneeling position on the ornate antique rug, Thanatos frowned. Blood-tears were imminent stains in the carpet's design. Determined to avert that disaster, he fished into his pockets for anything to stave off the inevitable and was rewarded with a crumpled and torn tissue. With a flick it snapped open and he knelt on one knee before the Vampiress, patting away the blood-tears from her face.

"The Angel is not dead," he gentled, dabbing the corners of her eyes.

"But—"

"I understand," he cut in. Her cool hands reached up to take the red stained tissue. Relinquishing the task, Thanatos stood and than sat back down on his chair, opposite the girl. "I assure you that he is well cared for."

"Then where is he?" she asked. Her eyes darted around the room as if by some miracle the Angel would be there.

"He's upstairs." Thanatos studied the Vampiress for any sign of malicious intent. From her convincing performance he doubted that she would make another attempt on the Angel's life, but it was better to be cautious than sorry. If necessary, he would extinguish this creature before more harm could be caused. "He is safe."

The Vampiress swung her supple legs over the side of the couch and pushed to stand before Thanatos could halt her.

"Please," she begged. Her fingers twisted the tissue, threatening to rip it in twain. "I need to see him. I–I need to know he's still alive."

A frown pulled at Thanatos' face as his legs pulled him to stand. The fleeting observation that they were of height was waylaid by a new rush of blood-tears. Despite his better judgment, he nodded. "On one condition."

"Anything," she blurted, excitement and expectation replacing the tears.

Thanatos took a step closer to the Vampiress until their faces were only inches away. "Do you remember my visit to your maker?"

The girl nodded. Her face paled beneath the trails of blood.

"Then you know who I am," he stated harshly. He had to ensure she knew who dominated the situation.

Another nod and her eyes widened.

"Who am I?"

"You—you're the m—m—maker of Corbie's maker," she stuttered.

Fear threatened to fell her, but Thanatos grasped her by her upper arms. "And do you remember what I promised Corvus if he did anything to the Angel?"

If she had been mortal Thanatos had no doubt that she would have soiled herself. *Thank the Gods for small mercies.*

"Aye," she exhaled.

"If you attempt to finish what you started in that driveway you will wish you never rose from that grave so long ago," stated

Thanatos through clenched teeth.

"I wish I never had," she whispered.

Her honest sincerity and the conviction in which she said it stunned Thanatos. Despite being a Vampire, the girl portrayed characteristics that were incongruous to them. Stepping back, Thanatos released his grip and dropped his hands to his sides. "Follow me."

Out the door and down the hall, he led the Vampiress through his home, into the front foyer with its marbled tile and wrought ironworks on dark oak double doors that led to the outdoors and freedom. Thanatos marked her slight pause as they ascended the ornate stairs with balustrade of grey stone. The open expanse of its landing, with a portrait of a meadow painted in sunset towered over the two, provided the crutch of the two wings of the building, outstretched in opposite directions.

Turning to the left, Thanatos walked the well worn Turkish runner in loafers of equal worth. Behind him, in bare feet, the Vampiress whispered over the finely woven wool. For a fleeting moment, he worried for the state of the antique carpet. Blood was impossible to fully remove from fibres. Luckily, the Vampiress had ceased her tears, for the moment.

The door to his suite loomed before them and with a practiced hand Thanatos turned the crystal knob and pushed inwards. Without a sound the door swung open, revealing a grand room with a mahogany king sized bed jutting out from the centre of the far wall. Tucked into the folds of white cotton, the Angel lay as Thanatos had left him.

In a flash, Thanatos found himself knocked into the door, surprise and anger vying for attention as he turned around. How could he have been so stupid as to trust the one who almost had killed the Angel!

Recovering his composure, Thanatos was struck by the sight before him.

There, on the bed, the Vampiress had climbed in next to the Angel and cradled his head to her breast. New tears dripped red onto silken white hair and a black lined face. Held dumb by the vision, Thanatos could only stare until her blood filled eyes glanced up at him.

"Why won't he wake?" she asked, pressing her cheek against the Angel's crown. "Why won't he heal?"

Thanatos tore his eyes away from the pitiful sight and stared at the floor for a moment before meeting her pleading gaze. Slowly, he made his way over to the bed and sat on the edge. The mattress dipped ever so slightly under his weight.

Unsure of what to say, he frowned. Gazing at the Angel, he followed the ribbons and strings of black that radiated from the abdominal wound that was now carefully stitched up. Underneath his shirt, Thanatos felt the small silver phial yank at his neck.

"It is because he is not Chosen," sighed Thanatos. He raised his right hand to quell the tugging.

"He is the Angel. He *is* Chosen—"

"And how did he feel? What did his blood taste like?" snapped Thanatos. He had not meant to say that, but there was no denying it. He was angry at this girl.

He stood up and walked towards the window. Not for the first time, Thantos was pleased he had installed external light sensors to automate his black out blinds. Gazing out at the manicured backyard, arms crossed over his chest, he continued, "Shall I tell you? He was warm. His blood was unlike anything you've ever tasted." He turned around to face her stunned expression but saw only his distant past. "He tasted like magic," he whispered.

Her delicate hand flew to her mouth, shocked agreement widening her eyes.

She knows I am right, thought Thanatos.

A distant sound of a garage door opening swiveled his attention. Godfrey was back, hopefully with Notus. "Can I trust that when I return I will find the Angel in better or similar health?" he asked.

"Aye, ye hae my word on it," she replied, stroking the Angel's face with graceful fingers.

Thanatos' dark brown brow rose. "You appreciate what will happen to you if you do not keep your word."

The Vampiress nodded solemnly.

Trusting his long developed instincts, Thanatos turned his back to the scene of the Vampiress cradling the Angel, and walked out of the room. Without closing the door behind him, he returned to the first floor, hovering by the bottom step to await his visitor.

His nerves fluttered butterflies in his stomach, something he had not experienced in centuries, as he heard the lock tumblers turn in the front door. Godfrey followed his instructions perfectly, opening the door to admit...

Who are these two Chosen? Thanatos silently queried his servant as a handsome swarthy Iberian man and a beautiful blonde woman of obvious Norman descent entered his home.

Godfrey returned the questioning look with a knowing smile and held the door for one last person to enter.

Heart in his throat, Thanatos watched as a man with grey salted brown hair and sad hazel eyes stepped over his threshold. A shy smile pulled at Thanatos' features. "Hello, Brynydd."

Notus looked up and met his host's eyes. Hazel eyes widened before rolling back. Notus collapsed to the floor, unconscious.

υ

hrough a pink haze of tears, Jeanie cradled the Angel's head against her breast. Thick droplets of blood pooled in the corners of her eyes only to overflow down her pale face, collect once more at her chin, and then drip onto an alabaster face marred by spider tracts of black poison. A part of her knew she had to cease crying lest she grow hungry due to blood loss, but gazing at her lover's comatose form only served to increase the deluge.

She remembered *everything* despite the fact her Rose-self knew she should not be capable of doing so.

Jeanie closed her eyes, sending a new wash of red down her face. They had agreed she should wait beneath the lamp post while Fernando, Bridget and her love went in to free Father Notus from the Mistress' clutches. Bridget had insisted that Jeanie stay behind at the whorehouse, but Jeanie needed to be near the Angel. She knew, without telling the others, that the Angel needed her with him. After the torture he suffered at Violet's hand, the Angel was still weak, even though he tried to hide it.

A sob tore through her chest and she laid her cheek against his burning forehead. Everything they had planned, as they had laid in Bridget's bed, fell apart. Through days before the confrontation between the Angel and Katherine, she lay with her love, gently touching his ravaged body with healing fingers. Once he brought Notus home, the Angel would Choose her, with or without Notus' blessing. She did not understand her lover's concern about the Good Father's possible reaction. In Jeanie's mind, Father Paul would be thrilled, even agreeing to perform a wedding ceremony for the two of them. Jeanie believed Notus would be happy that she and the Angel would share eternity together.

Her dreams were shattered beneath that lamp post so long ago.

A shudder ran up her spine.

Corbie Vale, her once captor, had found her standing in a pool of light that dimmed to black as he stepped forward to take his revenge. Dark brown, almost black, hair framed an ashened face twisted with malicious intent. Dark brown eyes seared fear into her soul before he sank his teeth into her neck.

There was no exquisite pleasure as he gulped her life into his, only intense pain. She had wanted to scream, to shout, to cry out for help, but no words could escape her mouth frozen wide in terror. Tears of salt wept down her face at the realization that she would die to the sound of obscene slurping. The Angel was inside the courtroom. He was not there to save her. He was saving the Good Father. This was NOT how it was supposed to be!

She had tried to struggle with that thought but was clutched in an iron embrace. She was supposed to be with the Angel—with Gwyn—her lover. He was the one who was supposed to drink her blood, because she loved him and he loved her, to change her, Choose her. Now this vile creature, this Vampire, was killing her!

With each gulp of her blood, she felt herself weakened until her heart began to skip and falter painfully in her chest. She tried to gasp for breath. Dots of black filled her vision as her heart stacatoed its requiem painfully through her chest, up her arms and neck to pound through her ears.

A blast of pain shot through chest as her heart crescendoed its finale and a curtain of black filled her being.

Inky darkness so complete that she could not see her hands an inch before her face filled the tiny cramped space. No sound stirred. Panic would have normally crashed between her ears, instead there was profound silence.

She did not know where she was, and worse, she had no recollection as to *who* she was. This, coupled with a growing claustrophobia, made her squirm. She needed out—NOW! Each kick, each punch, each smack met silk cushioned wood. The more she panicked the worse it grew until she stopped.

Distant sounds flitted to her ears. Muffled thumpings, each to its own tempo, ignited a burning within the depth of her being. She did not know what those sounds were, but they called to her. Focusing only on the cacophony of muffled percussion, the burning in her centre erupted into a tremendous need to quench that fire. The only way to do so was to reach the drums, and to do that she had to free herself from the box.

Patiently at first, her fingers ripped away the soft fabric until smooth wood caressed her palms. No matter where she moved her hands, all she felt was the silky texture of polished wood. There was no purchase for her fingers to grip so as to pull apart the wood. It was then that the full implications of her predicament slammed into her consciousness.

She was locked in a coffin!

Renewed panic welled her eyes, and an explosion of exquisite scent filled her nostrils. With the silk cloth removed, her fists pounded against wood. Her cries for help rang only in her ears until the sound of wood splitting snapped her attention.

Trembling in terror, she carefully felt around the coffin lid. The smoothness gave way to a ragged seam. It was enough to dig her finger tips into the wood.

Hiccoughing back her tears as wood bit into her flesh, she pulled at the broken lid. Each successful piece spurred her to move faster until she felt something solid and cool and damp on her chest. The scent of fresh earth exploded in the coffin's confines.

Stunned to the quick, she halted her explorations.

Oh my God, I've been buried alive!

Sense and reason were replaced by the primal need to escape, to survive.

Karen Dales

She did not remember much of her frantic tearing at wood and dirt as she sought freedom from her entombment. At some point in her ascension a scent so pure and divine assaulted her through the pungent loam. She did not know what it was, save only that it beckoned her to continue. Up through the earth she climbed, following the delicious scent that ignited a burning hunger in her centre.

Crazed by her ordeal and the need to devour what produced the beautiful bouquet, she barely noticed her freedom from her grave. All that consumed her was the appearance of a small child dangling from the outstretched arm of a man.

It was the child that had called to her.

Famished and fatigued, new instincts kicked in. Without a second thought, she pounced, ripping into the small unwashed neck with elongated teeth. If the child had screamed she had not noticed.

Her life as a Vampire was born that night. Her father, Corbie Vale, bestowed her her name—Rose. He and his other child, Brian Haskell, took her from the morbid graveyard, leaving the child's corpse to decorate the space between tombstones, but not before slitting the child's throat so as to hide the marks. There would be time enough later to teach her how to hide her trail.

She had never known such exquisite bliss until the child's thick hot blood washed over her tongue, filling the burning in her centre with an explosion of life. All that mattered was to keep that life force aflame, and to do that required more, much more.

The first few months under Corbie's wing were blurred, punctuated only by moments of clarity when the blood of her victims danced across her lips to slide down her tongue and pool in her centre, refueling the life force that animated her. Nothing mattered during those weeks and months of her infancy except to delight in a sea of blood and revel in her father's attention.

The years following her Vampiric birth witnessed her blossoming into a Vampiress of sadistic tastes as they moved from one European city to the next. She paid no mind that each move was done in extreme haste. Despite the fear and rage that twisted Corbie's Romanesque features when they fled their homes to find new ones, she did not care. Only to bathe in the blood of her victims brought her true joy and sparked smiles on her father's constantly concerned face.

It was the eve of their voyage across the Atlantic that sent real fear and panic through her. Weeks, maybe months, of being closed up in a wooden shipping box was too similar to that of her time buried in that coffin. Corbie had promised she would again blossom under a red rain, but fleeing to the new country was the only way to ensure that the Angel of Death could not find them. It was the first she had ever heard of the creature that hunted their kind.

Jeanie gazed upon the Angel's ravaged face. How she was about to forget his beauty she could not comprehend, but if she could forget herself for over a hundred years…New blood tears pooled in her eyes. Which was she really? Jeanie, mortal lover of the Angel, or was she Rose, a Vampire who reveled in blood and death? She shook her head. Her Jeanie-self refused to think of the atrocities her Rose-self had committed through the decades, culminating in her attempted murder of the Angel.

She closed her eyes against the torrent that realization released. She remembered everything. His capitulation as her Rose-self bound him down, even as he called her Jeanie; the succulent taste of his flesh before sinking her teeth into his neck; the taste of his blood, so unlike anyone else she had imbibed; the feel of his sword piercing his abdomen; and finally, the purification of his iron assaulted blood that forced her to retreat from draining him dry.

Oh, how she could have! Never before had she tasted blood so pure, so intoxicating, so invigorating! There was no doubt in Jeanie's mind that it had been his blood that awoke her to herself, but at what cost?

She opened her blood stained eyes and studied the black tendrils that marbled his pale face. "Oh Gwyn, my love, how could it hae gone so wrong?"

ʊí

hat the fuck did you do to him?" roared the dark haired Chosen. He grabbed Thanatos by the shirt collar and gave a violent shake.

Thanatos placed his hands over sun darkened ones and pried off the offending appendages, his welcoming smile replaced with indignant anger. How dare anyone lay hands on him!

"Fernando!" shouted the woman from her crouched position next to the slumped Notus. One delicate hand rested on Notus' shoulder, steadying her, while her other hand pressed against the monk's face and neck. "Paul's fine. He's only fainted."

"Fainted?" inquired both host and guest in unison.

Fernando rubbed the ache from his hands. He could not believe the strength in the short, dark haired man before him. Brown eyes narrowed as he reassessed their host, new found respect finally relaxing his facial features, but not his stance.

"I guess I can understand the reaction," said Thanatos. Sad sympathy filled his voice even though his expression hardened at the rude glare from the Chosen called Fernando.

"What do you mean?" demanded the female.

Thanatos watched the blonde Chosen gracefully rise to her feet, smoothing her indigo cotton skirt so that it hung wrinkle free to her just above her supple knees.

"Before we continue this further, may I suggest that we save Father Notus the continued indignity of lying across my threshold?" Thanatos' cold question was more an order. Without waiting to receive agreement from his two unwanted guests, Thanatos knelt down on one knee, slipped his finely tailored arm beneath the monk, and hoisted to stand, Notus unceremoniously flung over his shoulder.

Ignoring the two, Thanatos turned to walk to his study which was becoming more of a recovery room than a place of quiet contemplation. He would have shaken his head in annoyance had it not been the realization that here, in his home, over his shoulder, was Father Paul Notus. The last time Thanatos had held him like this Notus was called Brynedd two millennia ago.

Behind him, he heard the two Chosen follow as Godfrey closed and locked the front door, before he too followed. Down the hall and to the left, Thanatos entered his study, careful not to hit Notus' head against the frame. It had been easier when he had brought in the Vampiress.

Laying Notus supine on the same couch she had lain on, Thanatos' eyes fluttered to the abandoned black high heeled shoes haphazardly placed on the floor beside the couch, a clear reminder of who had been there moments before. Turning around, Thanatos' eyes caught indignant dark eyes before resting his gaze on a furious icy glare that belied the visualized gentleness of the lovely lady before him.

"Is there anything else, sir?"Godfrey stood in the doorway, his hand on the crystal doorknob. Tension vibrated off of Thanatos' servant; hopeful pleading filled his blue-green eyes.

Thanatos thought for a brief moment to ask Godfrey for a cup of refreshment but thought better of it. Clearly, Godfrey was extremely uncomfortable with having these strange Chosen in their home. "No, Godfrey. That will be all," said Thanatos. "If there is anything, I will get it myself."

"Yes, sir," exhaled the servant in relief. "Thank you, sir. Good night, sir." With a last nod of his head, he closed the door behind him as he fled the room filled with immortals.

"Impressive," commented Fernando as he walked to the

newly closed door to lean his back against it.

"Shut up, Fernando," snapped the blonde. She gracefully knelt beside the unconscious monk, worry clouded her eyes.

"What?" sneered the Iberian. "I was just commenting on the help."

"Right." The woman rolled her eyes, her attention on Notus.

"It's hard to find good mortal help," stated Fernando.

Thanatos witnessed the exchange with some amusement before cutting in. "I do not know who you are or why you have come to my home with Notus, but I would appreciate an explanation before my *invited* guest revives." He stepped closer to the kneeling woman, who gracefully stood. Her matching indigo patent leather pumps raised her only slightly above his five-four stature. *She must have been considered tall in her time,* mused Thanatos.

"Forgive me." She extended her hand. "I am Bridget, Mistress of the Chosen of Britain."

Thanatos accepted the proffered hand, noting the softness belying strength. "Enchanted."

"And this—" she waved with her other hand towards the Iberian leaning petulantly against the door "—is Fernando, my—"

"I am Fernando de Sagres, last heir to the Fidelgo de Sagres, Master of the Chosen of the United Kingdom." Fernando lifted off the door to come and stand next to Bridget. His dark brown eyes bore threateningly. "And you are?"

Thanatos did not like the impudent tone, stiffened his back and took Fernando's hand in his own, noting the young Chosen was only an inch taller than his Chooser. "I am your host and you are an unexpected guest in my home." He glanced at Notus' unconscious form, frowning at no sign of stirring. Pulling his attention back to the couple before him, he took his hand back to cross his arms over his chest. "Notus is invited. You are not."

"Please forgive us." Bridget laid a hand on Thanatos' forearm. "When Notus arrived at our hotel suite shortly after nightfall, he said that the Angel was still alive. Of course, we didn't believe him. We both know what we felt—"

"Wait." Thanatos raised a hand, interrupting Bridget in midsentence. "You felt the Angel die?"

THAⴖAⵜOS

The question surprised the two Chosen. They stared at each other, confused, for a moment before returning their attention to Thanatos.

"Yes," replied Bridget, cautiously.

"Even though he is not Chosen?" Thanatos studied the two. Clearly they had not considered that. It was further confirmation of what he believed the Angel to be.

"How could you know that?" queried the Noble.

"I am not without my means." Thanatos turned to sit down in his reading chair and stared up at the Chosen. "Suffice it to say, the Angel is alive and in my care."

"Where is he?" demanded Fernando.

The same time, Bridget cried, "I want to see him."

"All in due time. All in due time." Thanatos raised his voice to brook no further interruption. "He is in good hands. Trust me."

"And why should we do that?" retorted the Noble.

"Because," groaned Notus as he raised himself to sitting. Swinging his legs of the edge of the couch, Notus ignored Bridget and Fernando to stare directly into their host's mocha eyes. Hurt vied with anger, turning Notus' usual warm tones into frozen tension. "Because he is my Chooser."

"Wha—"

"Holy F—"

"Hello Seddewyn," said Notus. The chill in the room dropped to sub-zero.

"Jesus Fucking Christ!" swore Fernando, his eyes wide as saucers.

Bridget stood still, a doe caught in head lights. Her mouth opened and closed in an effort to find the right words, gazing at the ancient immortals in the room. Unable to say anything, she sat on the vacated couch cushion beside Notus, while Fernando began to pace the room, a panther caught in a cage.

"Hello Brynedd," said Thanatos, quietly. After centuries apart, he knew their meeting could turn sour. He had hoped for better, but hope was a fleeting mistress and it was clear she had already left the room. Now he had to deal with the consequences

43

of his abandonment. "It's been a long time. Too long."

"You could say that," replied Notus, tersely. "I am now known as Paul Notus."

"Ah yes," a fleeting smile touched Thanatos' full lips. "You are now the Good Father."

"I wouldn't say that," muttered the monk, wincing. He continued in a stronger voice. "I expect you left Seddewyn behind long ago and became someone new."

"Actually, no." Thanatos broke eye contact with his Chosen to stare at a spot on the floor. "I took back what was my identity before I came to the Blessed Isle millennia ago."

Bridget sucked in a shocked breath, at the same time Fernando halted in his tracks, both stunned by the revelation.

"I am once again Thanatos."

Oppressive silence threatened to crush everyone in the study. Notus sat back, exhaling a shuddering breath. He had never known. The God of Death. He shook his head, dismissing the possibility and returned to the familiar. "After all these centuries—nay, millennia—you call me to your side, now, on the pretense that the Angel is still alive?" The hurt of betrayal and abandonment strained his features.

Bridget placed a soothing hand on Notus' arm in an effort to calm the rising conflict that caught Fernando in rapt attention, a smirk lifting his lips.

"And how the hell do you know about the Angel?" Notus' voice turned deadly, protective, although he felt he had no right to be so.

Thanatos took a deep breath and let it out slowly. This was definitely not going as he had hoped. "I surmise that you were still under the effects of your swoon when I explained to your friends that the Angel is alive and in my care. Yes, I know you felt him pass, even though he is not Chosen. What you failed to recognize is that he did not die. For the Angel, those are two different things."

Confusion washed over all the Chosen.

"I don't understand," admitted Notus, the anger evaporating. He had felt the boy die, did he not? Was that not his fault because he refused to Choose him again even though the boy begged for it? Notus lowered his eyes. The idea that there was still hope humbled him.

Thanatos settled further into his chair and explained in dispassionate tones how he witnessed the Angel's capture by the Vampires. He went on to describe how the Angel was felled when the sword ran him through before being left for the sun to finish, as the Vampires returned to their lair. Thanatos ignored the crystal clear tears that ran down Bridget's face and welled Notus' eyes as he continued his narration of how he and his mortal servant pulled the Angel into the cabin of their black stretched limousine. He described, in great detail, how he removed the shattered sword fragment from the Angel's iron poisoned body. Thanatos watched Fernando grip the back of the couch and lowered his head as the tale continued onto the successful resuscitation of the Angel. All the while he edited out the Vampiress' involvement. He could not say why he did so, but followed his well practiced intuition.

His narration finished to a stunned audience. It took a moment before Fernando cleared his throat. "Where is he?" he asked, his voice strained with emotion. "Where's the Angel?"

"He's upstairs, in my suite."

"C—can we see him?" asked Bridget, hope glittering the tears in her eyes.

Thanatos gripped the cushioned armrests of his chair, preparing to rise. "Of course, but I wish to warn you that he is still deeply under the effects of his wound."

Worry tightened their features. They knew what iron did to their friend.

Nervous apprehension twitched Notus into action. "One thing."

Thanatos rose to his feet, a questioning expression pinching his olive features. "Yes?"

Notus broke eye contact with his Chooser to stare at his clenched hands. "Actually two things. Why now? Why after all this time have you come back into my life? Was it only because of the Angel?"

Thanatos stared down on the man he had once known as Brynedd—Bard, Ovate, Druid, father, husband and Chosen—and marked how little changes had crept into his visage. "How much do you remember of your apprenticeship with me?"

"Before or after?" countered the monk, looking up.

A sigh escaped the God of Death. "Before."

Breaking his gaze from his Chooser, Notus gazed at a distant bookcase. "You were searching the skies for some important event."

"A series of events," corrected Thanatos.

"And you found it," added Notus, returning his Chooser's gaze.

"The first only." Thanatos watched curiosity blossom on his Chosen's face, noting confusion in the other two. Clearly they were close to Brynedd, but not so close as to know everything about the monk. "I was searching for the one who could reunite me with the one who Chose me."

Bewilderment infected Notus until he sat back, the chocolate leather creaking behind him. "The Angel."

"Yes." Thanatos stepped towards the study's door. "But first he needs your help."

Fernando rounded the corner of the couch, intercepting his host before he could reach the door. "What do you mean? You're not making any sense. You say the Angel is alive—"

"He is," cut in Thanatos, matching the Iberian's cool look. "But that does not mean he is out of danger."

Bridget bolted to her feet at the same time as Notus decrepitly rose to his.

"So you didn't come for me," he muttered, hurt and confused.

The room fell silent at the hushed declaration. Thanatos turned his gaze to his Chosen and sighed. "Do you really feel the need to do this? Now?" Renewed tension thrummed the answer, and he walked over to stand before the man he once knew as Brynedd. "Fine." Cold frosted his voice. "Yes, I came back because of the Angel. I Chose you because I knew you would find him. I left you because you wouldn't find him with me in your life. You are the one that's important to the Angel. Not I. I didn't know why for a long time, but I do so now."

Notus lowered his eyes, humbled and hurt by the truth. "Why?"

"Because I can't save the Angel's life, only you can."

THANATOS

Thanatos turned on his heel and strode to the study's door, ignoring the stunned expression on the other two. "Do you wish to see the Angel, or not?"

Notus felt as if he had been placed in a centrifuge left on high: dizzy, confused, nauseous and directionless. Never in his wildest imaginings had he expected to ever be in the presence of his Chooser again. After everything he had gone through in the last few days, seeing his Chooser had been the last straw to his eroding psyche, snapping it in twain. He should be embarrassed for having fainted. He had never done that in his entire life, but standing face to face with his Chooser after so long had been the final straw. Now he stood in Seddewyn's—correction: Thanatos'—home with the wounded Angel somewhere in this grand house.

Hurt by Thanatos' confession, Notus numbly followed last behind Bridget. She gave him a sad shake of her head, her blond hair bouncing as she passed. For everything he had gone through these past few days, witnessing her admonishing glare was the tip of the iceberg. He did not know if he could sink any lower, but he had been proven wrong on so many things lately that he would not be surprised to what depths he could slide.

Eyes lowered, he exited the study, followed Bridget's heels down the ornate hall runner, across marble tile, their footfalls echoing off mahogany paneling and oak doors. Silently to the gallows, he ascended the stairs, his stomach bottoming deeper with each step upwards. He almost breathed a sigh of relief at what he believed to be the last step, but it was only the landing. Butterflies took flight again. Their brief rest disturbed to an even greater frenzy.

Notus bit back a whimper, the tortuous stairs carving deeper into his abdomen. What vision of the Angel would he be met with? He knew that the boy was grievously wounded. It was his fault. Tears welled in his eyes but did not fall.

The last step came and went. He vaguely noted the paneled hallway. So intent on Bridget's feet, he almost ran into her stationary form. It was enough to lift his head.

Before him, the Master and Mistress of the British Chosen stood before his Chooser. None said a word as Thanatos turned the crystal knob.

The door swung inward.

Across the Master suite, in a king sized bed laid the Angel in the arms of a fiery read head. Notus' eyes widened at the sight, his mouth filled with ash. Bridget spoke the name he could only hear in his head.

"Jeanie!"

ʊíí

orbie stared out the front windows of the second story building. No music pounded in the background, only the clank of bottles being restocked and the clink of glassware slipped into their holders to dangle above the bar. The shush of damp cloths over floor and table mingled with metal scraping floor, all the natural sounds of preparing *Beyond the Veil* for another night of frivolity.

His arms crossed over his chest, chin resting in the palm of his hand, Corbie stared onto the busy street. Electric lights of white, yellow, amber and red brought the neighbourhood alive. Normally, the sight of the growing line-up outside his front doors would twist his thin lips into the semblance of a smile, but not tonight. Instead, Corbie watches as more patrons, elaborately dressed in their individual Gothic styles, joined the line.

Several of them he recognized as regulars. A few of those that he personally knew looked up and found him. This time a smile curled his lips but did not fill his dark brown eyes. He did this intentionally. They may be wolves among the sheep, but they were nothing to Corbie except pawns to command.

In everything he did, Corbie ensured that those he ruled knew he saw them as the same as they regarded humans. Corbie Vale was Dominus of Toronto, but since Bastia's murder at the Angel's hands, Corbie worked to be more than she. In over a century he took advantage of coming to the colonies to increase his power. Now with the Angel dead, nothing could possibly hold him back from consolidating that power and becoming Imperator of all Vampires. Well, almost nothing.

Turning his back to the outside view, Corbie walked through the front of the club, past steel tables and red padded matching chairs that sparkled in the studio lighting. Normally, he would nod at the bartender polishing the counter. He noted the smile on her China Doll face, but continued walking past the well stocked bar, past gruesome metal statues that lent to the ambiance of the place, and into the cage lined back of the building.

No multicoloured lights flashed or whirled. Held stationary until the music would force them to gyrate; they created rainbow puddles on the thick worn hardwood dance floor. Quiet movement whispered around Corbie as employees prepared for those who would dance in *the Veil*.

"Mr. Vale," called a voice, turning him to face the direction he had come.

The young human girl who tended the bar ran towards him, her comfortable Doc Martin's clunking against the floor. Her black tights and leather bodice accentuated her slim Oriental build. Thick black eye make-up and fake blue contact lenses made her eyes appear larger over full lips painted blood red.

She halted a few feet away from him, her small breasts heaving in time with her panting breath. Cora had been working for him for the last four years, her beauty yet to diminish. She knew what her employer was, but it did not matter. She was his slave, and one of the few of his human employees he supped upon. If Cora was lucky, he would take her downstairs, past the private rooms where humans fucked and Vampires fed, down another set of stairs, past Brian's suite of rooms and another set for Rose. He would lead Cora through his sitting room and his office, leading her into his sanctuary. It would be there where she would experience what a Vampire can truly do. When next she woke she would be Jasmine, but tonight she was still Cora, bartender of *Beyond the Veil*.

"What is it, Cora?"

"I haven't seen Mr. Haskell tonight. I needed to talk to him about the inventory," she said, her hands grasped behind her back.

"Corbie ignored what the stance did for her small breasts, but appreciated its militaristic nature. He had trained her well. "What about it?"

Fake blue eyes fluttered, clearly not expecting her Master to take an interest. She dropped her gaze, uncertainty slouched her crisp stance. "Over the last three days I've noticed a bottle of Jack, three bottles of house Merlot and two bags of pretzels have gone missing."

"Have you seen anyone behind the bar who shouldn't be there?" He frowned. This was Brian's responsibility as Manager.

"No, sir," said Cora. She tentatively fluttered her gaze up at her employer.

"Thank you, Cora." Corbie turned to continue towards the back of the building. "I'll study the surveillance videos."

"Mr. Vale?" came the querulous reply.

He turned back to face his bartender, annoyance tightening his features.

Cora pulled a rolled newspaper she had been holding behind her back, proffering it.

Plucking it from her grasp, Corbie turned and continued walking towards the back fire exit, the newspaper tucked under his arm. Brian should have delivered it to his office.

The door slammed open at the touch of the bar, admitting Corbie into the long dark hallway. Black light caused the fluorescent graffiti on the black walls to jump out. It was not the door ahead of him that he walked towards. He had no desire to go outside and stand on the fire escape. Instead he rounded the low wall on his left to descend the stairs to ground level.

Pinpoint halogen lights, widely dispersed, gave off enough illumination for humans to see, but left it dark enough for Vampires to take advantage of the shadows. The black painted hall opened wider. A lone Vampire employee swept the floor. She did not glance up as Corbie walked past hangings of shimmering black fabric that served as doors to rooms decked out with plush couches, tables, and even a St. Andrew's Cross. Each play room would be used by Vampires and human alike.

A quick sniff revealed the scent of blood, sweat, semen and vaginal fluids. He would have to call in a professional cleaner later this week.

At the end of the wide hall a green exit sign glowed above another black metal door. This one did not lead outdoors, but to a landing where two doors led in different directions. One was to the outside and the other to the basement where he and his Vampires died each morning and rose each evening.

Corbie ignored the first door and punched in the cord on the number pad beside the basement door. A click informed him that the door was unlocked and he descended a steep set of rickety stairs. Once the club was opened, the door would remain unlocked. One could not entice flies without spinning a web.

There was more activity in the basement. Members of his coterie and guests from out of town had risen and were preparing for the night. He passed Orchid as she left one of the guest rooms, her remaining coterie member in tow. Secretly pleased at her diminished ego, Corbie offered her a nod. Her male companion continued to stare at the long flowing blond hair that swung back and forth, brushing her rump, as he trailed two large suitcases behind, his own duffle thrown over a shoulder. Soon the two would be off to New York City to rule and Corbie wondered once again if it was still wise to have Orchid as Domina of New York.

Arriving at the last door, Corbie opened it to reveal his elaborate sitting room. Yellow light warmed the space. Golden frames surrounded horrific and dark images, works of Goya being the most prominent. Gilded settees and chaise attempted to make the room appear comfortable.

Corbie took no notice as he opened another door, one that led to the heart of his operations – the White Room. In stark contrast to the rest of the interior of the building, the White Room was wide, spacious and brightly lit. Fluorescent light flooded over a bar at the back, a white and steel couch, chairs and his white oak desk. Even the computer monitor and phone on his desk where white. Behind the desk, flashing multiple images, an array of monitors, housed in the white wall, recorded everything going on at *the Veil*.

Removing the newspaper from under his arm, Corbie went to sit at his desk. The high backed, padded white leather chair tilted back as he placed his feet on the desk, crossing his legs at the ankles. The paper gave a snap as he unfolded it. Every evening Corbie would ritually peruse the news. Knowledge was a powerful weapon in the right hand, and one which he ensured to keep primed.

The first few pages were filled with regular inanity—the Provincial Election. It did not matter to Corbie who won. The new leader of Ontario would become his slave, too, though it would be easier if the current dolt was re-elected. Further into the newspaper he halted, removed his feet from the table and sat up. Laying the paper flat on the desk, he smoothed over the folds, his anger rising. There, in black and white, for millions of readers to see, a headline boldly stood out:

DRAINED!

Three bodies found. Blood mysteriously missing.

Anger locked his jaw. *Whoever did this would be staked to the roof to await the sun!*

Grabbing the phone's handset, Corbie punched a few numbers. He heard the other end ring once before the other end picked up.

"*Beyond the Veil,*" answered a seductive voice.

"Has Brian returned?" clipped Corbie.

"No—ah, wait," answered Cora. "He just walked in."

"Tell him to get down here right now," he ordered, anger filling his tones.

"Ye—"

"Corbie slammed down the receiver, his eyes scanning the article.

It did not take long for Brian's knock on the door to herald his entrance. Corbie picked up the offending article and threw it at his servant. "Who did this?" he roared, rising from his chair. "I'll have that Vampire's head on a spike adorning my office and their ashes in a jar under it!"

Brian barely managed to catch the flying newsprint before it smacked him in the face. Ignoring his Dominus' rage, he opened the paper and read aloud, "Blue Jays lose 7 – 6 against New York—"

"Not that," snapped Corbie. "The other side."

Lips pursed in annoyance, Brian turned the paper over without taking his blue-grey eyes off his maker. Corbie jerked his chin upward, indicating for Brian to read.

Corbie waited the few moments for Brian to read. "Well?"

"What do you want me to say?" snapped Brian, crumpling the newsprint into a ball.

"Who did this?" countered Corbie, rising from his seat.

"How the Hell would I know?" Brian walked towards the desk and tossed the crumpled paper in front of his Dominus.

Corbie glared at the ball and then back to Brian before retaking his seat.

"I was with you last night and I just got back from driving Michael and Stephanie to the airport."

"Who would have done this?" demanded Corbie. To drain a human to death was a clear violation of the laws to ensure Vampiric anonymity, but worse, it was an affront—a challenge—to his authority.

"The article stated there were no wounds on the body." Brian swept his short dirty blonde hair back from his face.

Silence crashed down between the two. They did not need to speak the words to know the truth.

"Where is de Sagres and his whore?" Anger pinched Corbie's face.

Brian picked up Corbie's phone, punched the numbers and waited. On the fourth ring a male voice answered. "Speak to me."

"Where are the Chosen?" asked Brian.

"You put Marcus on them?" asked Corbie, impressed.

Brian nodded to his maker as he listened to Marcus' report. "After their visit here last light, I followed them as they drove around. I think they noticed me because I lost them—"

Corbie growled his displeasure.

"—but I managed to pick up their trail after an hour or two of driving."

"You don't know where they went during that time?"

"No, sir," replied Marcus. "But I found out where they are staying."

"Where?" chimed Corbie and Brian together.

"At the Hyatt across from the museum."

"Are they still there?" asked Brian. A large part of him hoped the Chosen took his threat seriously and left to fly back to England. If they stayed and were the ones who killed the three humans, then there would be repercussions on both sides of the Atlantic. He halted that line of thought. With the Angel as ashes, the Chosen would once again be vulnerable.

"No, sir," answered Marcus. "Shortly after I arrived, a limo showed up. Notus and the driver exited to go into the hotel. They were gone for about twenty minutes when they arrived back with de Sagres and the whore. They all got into the limo and drove off. I followed them to a mansion in the Bridal Path."

Brian's wide eyes met with his sire's closed pinched expression. "Tell him to stay where he is," ordered Corbie. "Do not, and I repeat, do not attempt to engage."

"I heard that, my Dominus," said Marcus. "Your will is my command."

Brian hung up the phone. "They're at Thanatos'."

"But why?" queried Corbie, his black eyes narrowing. Without a second thought, he swiveled in his chair, pulled out the rolling shelf from under the desk, and tapped a few keys on the keyboard. A few clicks of the tracking mouse tightened his thin lips. Spinning around on his chair, he looked up at the array of monitors.

Images of *the Veil* in full swing blinked out to be replaced by a composite picture of rolling video of the parking lot behind his building. Together, in silence, they watched themselves leave Rose and the dead Angel for the sun. A smirk raised Corbie's lips as they watched Rose remove the shattered sword, the video becoming brighter with the oncoming dawn. Expectation filled both Vampires for the upcoming conflagration. Their faces fell into shock at the sight of a black stretch limousine roll up and Thanatos' human servant exit the vehicle to carry Rose's dead form back to the car. Corbie's chair creaked as he leaned back, stunned at the sight of Thanatos accepting Rose before the servant went to retrieve the Angel. Corbie spun around in his chair to face Brian. He did not need to see the rest of the video.

Brian broke his gaze from the monitors, his expression matching that of his Dominus'. "Thanatos has the Angel."

Corbie could not believe it. The Angel must still be alive, and Rose with him. Worst of all, Thanatos had him and had summoned the Chosen. Everything he worked so hard for over the last century was in peril.

Thantos had warned him to leave the Angel alone, that the Angel was his. Corbie had dismissed the threat. Now, he could not. "We have to kill him," he muttered.

"Kill who?" asked Brian, worry painting his rugged features.

Leaning forward, resting his elbows on the wood, Corbie clasped his hands together. "Thanatos."

"Are you fucking kidding?" Brian threw his arms up and began to pace. "We've been together for nearly fifteen hundred years; this is the most insane thing I've ever heard! Kill Thanatos?" He walked back to the desk and laid his hands on it, bending down to face his maker. "Is there some magic number when Vampires go crazy, because you've past it?"

"Don't push me Brian. I'm not in the mood," warned Corbie.

"Why not?" demanded Brian. "I am to you as you were to Bastia—"

"Brian," growled Corbie.

"—but I'm not going to stand idly by while you try and kill the God of fucking death!" Brian's voice rose until he was shouting.

"Enough!" Corbie slapped the desk and stood up, his chair rolling behind him to bang into the wall of dark monitors.

"No." Brian stood up and crossed his arms over his chest. "I'm not going to let you ruin everything we've worked for. Bastia blew it. She made an enemy of the Angel."

"And I've made an enemy of Thanatos by killing the Angel."

"What if the Angel's still alive?"

Corbie locked his jaw, waiting as patiently as his anger would allow.

Anger leaked out of Brian. Corbie was listening. "If the Angel's alive, then no harm, no foul, and Thanatos has what he wants."

"And if you're right, what about Rose? She knows my plans."

Brian tapped his chin with a free hand. "Marcus is there. I'll have him recon the place and we'll find out if the Angel's alive and what's happened to Rose."

"Once we know if the Angel's alive or dead, I'll know what to do," remarked Corbie. "Call him."

"Yes, sir." Brian reached to pick up the phone.

ᴠᵢᵢᵢ

xcruciating agony gripped him, flaying his flesh. Fire flowed through veins, arteries and capillaries, feeding the rapacious beast that threatened to devour him.

He did not know the creature, except that it permeated every cell of his being, filling him with sensations that curled him into a ball in an effort to escape. He would gladly suffer a lifetime of torture rather than to experience this agony.

Curled tight in a fetal position, he took neither note of the soft grass beneath him, nor the warmth of the light on his body. Eyes tightly shut against the sight of the garden; every physical wound was renewed and compounded by the injuries to his heart. The worst was the damage wrought by those he loved most.

Discovering Jeanie to be a Vampire had been the cap stone to his guilt, having failed to protect her, his oath to see her come to no harm now broken. A part of him accepted the retribution of that oathbreaking. The burning in his gut flared brighter and he groaned.

He could see her. Fiery locks flamed about her head as she stepped forward, his sword lying across both outstretched hands. Her voluptuous form swayed with each step, the slight breeze tugged at the looseness of her green silk blouse. Beautifully formed legs, held steady in stilettos, were wrapped in a black leather miniskirt. Everything screamed to him that this Vampire before him was his love, except for her glacial green eyes.

His heart split in two at his inability to save Jeanie which had birthed the Vampire that sank her fangs into his neck, fulfilling the prophesy of his oathbreaking. He wept at his failure to the one woman he had given himself to completely. He loved Jeanie and he had betrayed that by failing to save her.

Hot tears streamed down his face to drip and sizzle in the grass. Thoughts of Jeanie slipped to another, heart wrenching truth.

It had been Notus' betrayals that set all his limbs trembling in agony. To have given so much to the man who saved him from a lonely existence, only to have Notus deny him to become Chosen again. Worse was discovering that Notus held the secret to his family. That Geraint had not only been a beloved mentor, but his father in truth, which made Eira his sister. The revelation of that truth and the betrayal of the trust he held for Notus, ripped sobs from his throat and burning tears from his eyes. He desperately wanted for all the pain to vanish, for everything to cease, but even those desires fanned the flames of his agony.

How could he? he cried. A spasm of pain curled him tighter. "I loved him," he muttered in his crossed arms over his chest.

Long dead memories assailed him, each one cleaving further chunks out of his battered heart. When had Notus discovered the truth? Had it been that first night when Eira and he first met? A flash of her tall slim stature, framed by a waterfall of raven black hair, filled his mind. Her jet eyes flashed with happiness, under-coated by sadness.

She had known they were siblings! Yet still she held her tongue. Had she know the truth of their shared bloodline even on that day, so long ago, in the glade that had transformed his life? He wept harder, his cries wracking his body.

Notus had known and still took him away into a world of night and blood where even there he was denied due to his differences.

Why? He convulsed as another sob tore at his chest. So many unanswered questions rioted through his mind, flaying his heart.

All those he loved knew the truth of his origins, his family, and yet all denied him that familial bond. Even Auntie, who he now knew to be his true great-aunt, held all these truths from him. Ah, the charade she and Geraint played! Burning tears carved their tracts and he succumbed to the tortures of his heart and the agony of its poisons flowing through him.

"It was never my intention to cause you pain." An old, familiar voice flowed over him.

He could not block out the sorrow filled tones. He wanted to flee the pain the confusion tore at him. *Why didn't you tell me?*

Silence.

Had she gone away, leaving questions unanswered as she had when she died? A cynical corner of his heart believed it to be so, but the tiny flame of hope opened his tear filled eyes. His whole life he searched for the reasons for his differences. Fifteen hundred years of silence, clues, disappointments and betrayals had carved their marks upon his body, raising further questions.

Trembling, his eyes slowly came into focus. Before him burbled the grey stone lined spring. On a flat stone, at the back, a silver chalice sat chained by silver links to a short cairn made from similar stones. He had drunk from that cup, but it had been untethered. He wanted to drink the spring's energizing waters. Burning questions and the miniscule hope that she would answer them turned his back to the tranquility that the sacred spring offered.

He uncurled from his tight fetal ball, his body screaming in the process, eliciting further tears of pain until he was able to roll onto his back. The cool green grass barcly eased the fires that flared up and down his spine. The warm radiant light ignited and renewed the wounds carved into his body.

Panting, he squinted, the light burning his pupils to pinpoints, and rolled his head in the direction from where the familiar voice had originated.

His eyes widened.

Countless centuries passed, yet still he could never forget the visage of the woman who took him in, cared for him, and loved him. Though he clearly recognized her, Auntie appeared as she must have in her youth. Kneeling on the green grass, a robe of earth brown cloaked her form. Dark curling hair cascaded over her shoulders to rest lightly on the tops of her large firm breasts. No longer opaque with age, her eyes glittered a shade darker than her hair. Crevasses born from wind, sun and strain, no longer marred her features. Her cheeks and eyes bore the weight of youth in their plumpness. Sadness tampered with her smile.

Shock suppressed the fires running through his body as he attempted to leap to his feet.

He realized his mistake too late and he collapsed to all fours as the inferno roared through him. His long white hair draped in sweat filled ropes about his head to brush against flattened and browned grass.

A soft hand alighted on the top of his head as if to comfort. "Oh, my dear, precious boy," soothed Auntie in a voice untouched by age. "I am so sorry. Can you ever forgive me?"

Forgive you? The thought came unbidden as he panted down the pain. *I was the one who caused your death!*

"I should have told you the truth, but I believed we had more time. What a fool I was." She dropped her hand into her lap.

Trembling, he lifted his head to peer at her tear streaked face.

"If I had told you," said Auntie through a breaking voice, "then you would never have suffered as you have done."

Her hand came up and brushed the white strands from his face. He gasped as lightning agony dropped him to the grass. Images upon images of his lifetime of pain and torture wracked his body, and still Auntie's hand lay on his head.

He could hear her crying through his tears. He had never desired to cause her pain despite the omissions of truths her silences had set into motion. Visions of his life before her death needled his mind; of the brutal beating in the grove while his sisters watched; of the loss of his father, Geraint; of Auntie's brutal murder because he was not careful enough; of the discovery of the bear in the cave that rent skin from flesh, nearly killing him; of Notus' attack that changed him forever.

"I wish I could have spared you the rest," sobbed Auntie.

New images flowed through him, each as excruciating as if the incident replayed itself in whole. His murder of the rapists and, later, their brigand cohorts; the experience etched into his upper right arm, marking him as other. His unwilling submission to the Master and Mistress of the Chosen. Had they witnessed what their servants' weapons had done, he would have been Destroyed. Through the centuries of slaughter and death, cleaving people from the lives they fought so hard to sustain, until one unlucky happenstance sent him into an unending nightmare from which he awoke, unable to walk. More deaths of friends and foes, the guilt piling higher than any midden until he finally fought for life, only to lose his Jeanie and receive the worst for it.

Pain closed his eyes and curled him into a ball once more. He never wanted to kill, never desired to cause pain, yet his life was that—Death. He never realized how much he hated his role. What could Auntie possibly have told him that could have changed all that suffering?

"Tell him," came a different feminine voice.

"Show him," another, yet similar, voice spoke.

"We thought he was lost," said a third.

"We did not comprehend our error until it was too late," chorused the three voices.

"A chance—"

"—to repair—"

"—what now is."

Opening his tear filled eyes he could see the Three Ladies standing tall and regal far behind Auntie, near the edge of the glade. The Lady in White rained tears onto her milk pale face from eyes as devoid of colour as the snow pigment of her knee length hair. Her ivory hand gripped her sister's sunburned stained hand. The Lady in Red shed no tear. Her beautiful red eyes, so much like his, held only fear tinged regret as a breeze played with crimson hair identical in quality to her sisters. Her other crimson tinted hand held the last of the three, ruby and obsidian intertwined. Coal black eyes spoke to the resolution set in her midnight face. The Ladies did not step closer.

Once more he tried to untangle himself from the pain, only to be halted by Auntie's hand sliding to his stinging shoulder.

"Please, do not," pleaded Auntie.

He gazed at her, confusion blending with the pain. "Why?" he rasped.

"Look."

For the first time, he became aware of the veins of black that ran through his body. He stared at the blossoming bands of black that encircled his wrists and sent tendrils up his arms to connect with others that were rooted in similarly black seared wounds on arms, chest, legs and abdomen. He held no doubt about how his back must appear. It still did not explain the Ladies' trepidation.

"The poison that flows through you would spread," explained Auntie. "It could rend this realm's tenuous connection to the earth as no other calamity ever accomplished."

Another bone-wracking spasm shuddered through him, distracting his questioning mind for but a moment. Fighting back the pain, he gazed once more onto Auntie's face.

"They thought you lost," she continued, brushing stray strands of white from his face. Sorrow etched her youthful features. "They—we—knew our mishandlings. Never did we believe you would find your way back, but you did. And now we are here." She sadly smiled.

"Tell him," repeated the White Lady.

"Show him," reiterated the Red Lady.

"Daughter of our blood, rectify the error," stated the Black Lady.

Auntie lowered her head in reverence. "Yes, my Lady."

Closing her eyes, she took a deep breath and placed both of her hands over the crown of his head.

ix

ou know this Vampire?" Thanatos spun to face the Chosen now in the room with him. He could not believe the twists and turns of fate.

His declaration, at first, elicited the same stunned expression in the three, before comprehension twisted their visages into other emotions.

"Vampire!" exclaimed Fernando the same time Bridget exhaled, "Oh, no."

Tears filled Notus' sad eyes.

Movement in the corner of Thanatos' eye brought his attention around to witness the Vampiress gently extricate herself from cradling the Angel, to stand beside the bed. Shocked revelation glittered from her eyes. What she did floored Thanatos.

Unsure steps towards them, hands wringing the red soaked tissue, the Vampiress appeared caught in a dilemma that broke as Notus stepped into the room and opened his arms. "Oh, my dear, sweet girl."

It was invitation enough. In a flash, she fell into Notus' embrace, both collapsing to their knees, sobbing.

"I'm so sorry," repeated the girl, her bloody tears soaking into the dark brown cotton of Notus' shirt.

A nervous knot twisted in Thanatos' gut. Fate had the upper hand and the control Thanatos assumed he held proved an illusion. Left out of the loop, he did not know how to proceed, but chose to watch as the situation played itself out.

"We believed you dead," murmured Notus. He brushed the girl's cinnamon curls from her forehead to lay a kiss on her pale skin. "We saw you under the lamp post. I had you buried."

A shudder ran up the Vampiress' spine. Thanatos knew she recalled her human death and her vampiric rebirth.

"Whatever could you be sorry for?" Notus hugged the girl tighter.

The question tightened the knot in Thanatos' gut. Notus appeared to be disregarding the fact that the person he knew as a mortal now existed as a Vampire.

Releasing the embrace, the Vampiress glanced into Notus' love filled visage before her face fell under the gazes of those standing.

"How?" Fernando cleared the strangled shock from his throat. "How is this possible?"

Thanatos felt the Iberian's cold glare before he saw it.

Thanatos knew the answer to be complicated and dangerous to reveal. "There will be time for answers," he evaded. "I believe this is a time to answer earlier asked questions."

He found himself curious, despite his apprehension. Questions of his own percolated. In his long life, Thanatos had witness and experienced many feats of fate, but never had he found himself so entangled. The confluences staggered him; giving greater credence to what he prognosticated two millennia earlier.

"I believe you desired to see the Angel?" His query brought everyone back to the situation at hand.

Rising to their feet, Notus held the Vampiress with one arm around her shoulders, while her arms ringed his waist. The mutual need for consolation surprised Thanatos. He had never seen Chosen and Vampire lovingly embrace one another. Maybe it was a start.

In unison, the two walked to the side of the bed. Trepidation trembled through Notus' frame. Bridget, Fernando's hand tight in hers, walked to the other side of the king-sized bed. Thanatos followed the procession alone. The expected tug around his neck was his only comfort as Bridget's gasp rang in unison with Notus' groan. The tightening of Fernando's grip on Bridget's hand belied the hard expression on the young Chosen's face.

All stood in silent horror of the black tendrils suffused through the Angel's pale torso, arms and face. Some threads appeared more pronounced, thickened, the closer to the old scars now filled with solid black. An erratic web extended out from the newly stitched belly wound.

"He's alive?" ventured Notus. His susurrant voice spilled into the silence.

Thanatos understood the doubt. Seeing the Angel so wounded he had felt the same. He came to stand at the food of the bed, his hand holding the straining phial through his shirt. "Yes," he nodded, "but barely."

With tears shimmering down her cheeks, Bridget let go of Fernando's hand and lifted the edges of the pristine white sheet and crimson coverlet to tuck them around the Angel's shoulders. Kneeling one knee on the bed, she brushed blood dappled white hair back from his face and glanced up at the Vampiress' red stained face. Understanding softened Bridget's features and she offered a small smile to the girl who had captured the Angel's heart before she leaned over to lay a kiss on the Angel's forehead.

Bridget snapped back to stand beside Fernando, her hands flying to her lips. "He's hot!"

"His body is fighting the iron poison, but I'm concerned that it may have been too much," replied Thanatos.

"What do you mean, "too much?"" demanded Fernando. "He's survived worse."

"But that was when he was Chosen," stated Bridget. "He's mortal now."

Thanatos felt the urge to correct them, that the Angel had never been Chosen, nor mortal, but now was not the time. He would let them have their illusions, for the moment. "It does not matter." He faced the Iberian. "I'm afraid he may not wish to live."

The statement stunned them all and they returned their attentions to the Angel.

The Vampiress' eyes glittered with fresh ruby tears. "It's all my fault," she sobbed, relinquishing Notus' embrace to cover her face with her hands.

The knot slicked tighter in Thanatos' gut. He wanted to lie, to falsely console the girl that it was not her fault, but he could not. Instead, fear of the revealed truth immobilized him.

"How could it be your fault?" soothed Notus. His arm tightening around her shoulders, turning the Vampiress so that she could lay her head on him. but she would have none of it. "If the fault lies with anyone, it lies with me."

"No. No." The Vampiress shook her head as she backed away, sending fiery locks flickering. "Ye dinna—Ye're—"

"Rose!" snapped Thanatos. He broke from his fear to halt her.

At the mention of her Vampiric name, she halted. Green eyes flickered to Thanatos, unable to defy him.

The Chosen stared dumbfounded at the girl they had once known.

"But—" The Vampiress trembled, pain and self-loathing reflected in her eyes.

Thanatos halted her words with a shake of his head. The fuse for her violence hung precariously close to the flame. He had to do something lest the war between Vampire and Chosen explode in his bedroom. "It is not your fault. If one is to lay blame it would land on the one who turned you into a Vampire."

Anger suffused with irritation flowed off Fernando as he pushed past Bridget to stand beside Thanatos. "Enough of your convoluted statements," demanded the Master of Britain. "What the hell do you mean, and why did you call Jeanie Rose?"

Thanatos pulled his attention from the Noble and glanced at each of them in turn. He needed to spin-doctor the situation before it completely grew out of hand. Landing his gaze on the Vampiress, he sighed. "When one is turned into a Vampire there are a few things that occur that you need to know, since their transformative experience is so different than how one is Chosen.

"It is not a matter of an exchange of blood as the mortal nears death," explained Thanatos. "The Vampire feeds on the mortal a number of times. The time between feedings could be days, weeks, even months. At the final feeding, the Vampire kills the mortal."

"That—that is what happened under the light-post," gasped Notus.

"But Jeanie hadn't been fed on before,"

"I was," came the Vampiress' small reply. "The night Notus was taken and again by Violet when she captured us."

Sympathy for the girl flared in Thanatos. She had no understanding of what had been done to her. "Once killed by that final feeding, it can take hours, days, even months before the fledgling Vampire claws her way to this existence from the grave. Whether it is due to the death, the trauma or the so-called rebirth, or a combination thereof, the Vampire no longer recalls who they once were. Not even their name. Usually, their sire is there to provide a first feeding and a new name. Eventually a new persona arises, one that is guided and controlled by their sire. In Rose's case, her sire is Corbie Vale."

Thanatos watched in as shock and horror crossed the Chosens' faces. Only Notus' softened with compassion.

The Vampiress took a halting step away, unable to bear the brunt of their stares. The rest of the truth hung over the room, ready to cleave and damage the fragile peace.

Notus broke the tension. "But she's Jeanie."

"Now." Thanatos lowered his gaze, the guillotine ready to fall. The irregular shape of the Angel's feet beneath marred plush blue and white spiral designs of the comforter. Sighing, Thanatos lifted his eyes to meet forest green rimmed with red. "Do you wish to tell them, or shall I?"

She frowned, her gaze returning to the Angel. Thanatos knew she could defer back to him, but maybe she would take the responsibility and seek repentance. It could prove to help heal the rift between immortals that should never have occurred. If the Chosen knew the truth, but it was tied to what the Angel was and that question still required answering, hopefully from the Angel.

The Vampiress slumped her shoulders in defeat. "I was the one who stabbed the Angel with—"

Thanatos watched in horror as the ax fell in the form of Bridget grabbing Rose by the front of her blood stained shirt and knocking the Vampiress back against the wainscoting. Fernando came to stand beside Bridget, not to stop his Chooser, but to add his own threatening figure. Menace radiated off of them, promising a true death to the one they had known in Rose's mortal life.

"Stop!" demanded Thanatos, moving to intercept before more violence could explode. "All of you, stop!"

"Why should I?" cried Bridget. Tears of rage and sorrow mingled on her glistening cheeks as she held the Vampiress against the wall.

Thanatos' gaze flickered to the pinned Vampiress and witnessed the internal fight raging in her green eyes. He sucked in a breath as Jeanie succumbed to Rose. In a blink of an eye, Rose had thrown Bridget to the floor and straddled the Mistress of Britain, her hands at Bridget's throat and fangs bared.

All three Chosen stared dumbfounded at the sudden change of the girl they had once known.

Unaffected by the sudden violence, Thanatos stepped forward, hands outstretched. "Rose?" he susserated.

The Vampiress turned to face her host, her hands clenching tighter around Bridget's neck in response to the Chosen's struggles. Rose caught sight of Fernando readying to defend his Chooser. "Don't, or I rip off her head," she promised, the Scottish inflection absent.

Fernando's eyes widened, taking the threat seriously.

"Jeanie," ventured Thanatos as he drew closer, waving the Iberian back.

Trembling with bridled rage, Fernando crossed his arms over his muscular chest.

Confusion lit in Rose's face, as something within her reasserted itself. She glanced down at the Chosen beneath her, realization dawning. Snapping her hands off Bridget's neck, she scrabbled off the Chosen.

"Oh my God!" cried Jeanie. Horror of what she had done backed her into a corner. "I'm so sorry, Bridget. I'm sorry."

Clearing her throat, Bridget stood with Fernando's assistance. Both glared at the girl. Thanatos lowered his hands, crisis averted. There could no longer any doubt that though Jeanie had been the Angel's love, she had been a vampire for much longer.

"Jeanie, is it true?" Rising from his seat next to the Angel,

Karen Dales

Notus took a step towards the girl. "Did you do this to him?"

"Aye," sighed Jeanie, lowering her head in shame.

"You fucking cunt," sneered Fernando. He turned his rage onto his host. "How could you bring her here?" He tried to take a step towards Thanatos, but was halted by Bridget's grip around his arm. "She fucking admitted to trying to kill the Angel and you left her alone with him? Are you fucking nuts?"

Thanatos bore the brunt of the Iberian's rage. His eyes fell to Notus' downtrodden features. "I did not bring you to the Angel for this. I've already explained about Jeanie. You've seen it yourself. I will let her explain. If that is not good enough for you, then you may leave. I will not suffer violence in my home again." He glared at the two younger Chosen. "Do I make myself clear?"

"We will honour your wishes," stated Bridget, her voice tense as her fingers gripped deeper into Fernando's arm. "Apologies."

"Accepted." Thanatos inclined his head and turned to face the Vampiress. "Jeanie?"

She stepped from the corner, head still lowered, her voice small. "I was given the task of returnin' the Angel's sword. I was so excited. All I remembered and knew about the Angel was what my fath—Corbie and Brian told me. I dinna remember anythin' from before I dug myself from the grave. I dinna know why Corbie chose me until after. All I knew was here was the one who kilt so many of my kind—"

Notus winced.

"—and ran the few who remained across the ocean.

"I was overjoyed at the honour Corbie gave me. He instructed me on what t'do and I did. What I dinna ken was the Angel's reaction on seeing me. I dinna know why he kept callin' me Jeanie. I am—was—Rose.

"I—I...gave him back his sword by stabbin' him through. I also bit him." Jeanie's narration fell off to silence as her fingers touched her lips in remembrance of the act. Lowering her hand and lifting her gaze to meet Thanatos', she continued. "I had never tasted anyone like him. So pure, until the iron poison tainted him. It was then that I remembered everythin'. From my time with him, with each of ye, when I was mortal, and my name, to all the things I'd been and don as Rose. Everythin'."

Silence crashed down again.

"Do you now understand?" asked Thanatos, breaking the quiet.

Notus gazed at the young Vampire, unshed tears filled his eyes, and held out his hand to her. Jeanie ran into his embrace to weep on his shoulder.

"So what you're saying is that it wasn't Jeanie's fault, but, rather, Corbie's," frowned Bridget. The marks on her neck faded as if Jeanie's attack never happened.

Thanatos gave a curt nod.

"Hold on a second." Fernando raised his hands, his arm released from Bridget's grasp, palms facing outwards. "You said Vampires forget who they were when they are made, and now you're saying that she remembers."

Thanatos nodded again. "That's right."

"How is that possible?"

"The Angel's blood," stated Thanatos matter-of-factly.

"That doesn't make sense," replied Bridget. "He's no longer Chosen, and Chosen blood doesn't cause that effect." Her voice became mournful, "We know. We've seen enough during our war against the Vampires."

Thanatos sighed. Doubt filled him. Would they believe him? More important, would they help him to help the Angel? "That would be true if the Angel had ever been Chosen."

Denial and outrage filled the room until Notus' voice cut through. "He was Chosen. How else—"

"Please. I'll explain everything. I promise," stated Thanatos. "But first I need—no, he needs—your help."

His plea silenced the others.

Jeanie turned to face Thanatos, but did not break from Notus' embrace. Thanatos noted the significance of that and hope blossomed in his chest.

"What can I do to help?" offered Notus.

"Your blood," answered Thanatos. "The Angel needs your blood."

X

Marcus hung upside down, his hands gripping the solidly fastened eaves while his lower body lay across the cool black roofing tiles. It had not been as difficult as he had expected to get this close. The only thing he had to ensure was not to be seen by anyone in the large bedroom beneath. He did not need to see the scene unfold beyond the large paned windows, but he had to be ready lest someone inside yank the drapes further apart.

A smile tugged across his thin lips at the chaos that ensued. Corbie would be displeased by his report that the Angel and Rose still lived. All Vampires knew not to encourage Thanatos' involvement, but Marcus knew better than most how the Ancient's threat unnerved his Dominus into defiance.

Brian had been Corbie's Celtic body slave, but Marcus had been the head of Corbie's personal guard, a duty that he continued despite the lack of necessity into this day and age. He was grateful that he had been allowed his mortal memories. It made it easier to do what needed doing. Now he worked in the shadows to ensure calm and order. Already the mortal thief from Beyond the Veil decayed in a ditch far north from his Dominus' city. No more bottles and bags meant for mortal consumption would go missing.

Yes, Marcus' Dominus would be displeased to discover the Angel held onto tenuous life. He may be happy to learn of Rose's continuous existence, but Corbie would not be pleased to hear that the Master and Mistress of Britain, as well as the Good Father, stood at the Angel's bedside.

Pulling himself back onto the roof, Marcus drew up into a crouch, a hand on the shingles to keep his balance. His cellular phone in his front jean's pocket pressed into his hip, inviting him to call his Dominus, but he would not, not yet. Someone could overhear. With careful steps close to the roof's edge, and keeping low, he retreated to the back of the mansion and leapt off to a rolling landing on the grass at the cornerstone.

Dew soaked into his black long sleeved shirt and dotted his pants. Slapping away shards of cut grass and decaying leaves, Marcus took off towards the neighbouring fence and climbed. He did not wish to rely on luck. Through the neighbouring yard Marcus evaded security sensors to walk nonchalantly down the stone driveway and onto the street. Hand slipping into his left front pocket, he hit the button on the key fob and slipped into the dark embrace of his black Camero. Tinted windows obscured any curious passer-by's eyes as he pulled out the phone from his other pocket. A few buttons pressed elicited a ringing tone and then Brian's bored voice.

"Thanatos has Rose, and the Angel's alive, but barely." Marcus switched hands to slip the key into the steering column, igniting the engine with a roar. "The Chosen are there."

"What?" barked Brian.

The sound of the fumbled phone announced Corbie's demand. "Notus is there?"

"And the Master and Mistress of Britain." Marcus' cold monotone met silence. He waited and was about to inquire what to do next, but Corbie cut him off.

"Get back here," ordered his Dominus. His voice filled with rage.

"Ye—"

"No. I've changed my mind." His Dominus' tones cooled to that of the general he had served when they were mortal. "Stay on the Chosen, especially de Sagres and his whore."

"And if they stay the day, sir?"

"I'll send Cora to keep watch. Make sure you're back by dawn."

"Yes, sir." Marcus shut down the engine. "What if de Sagres and Bridget stay the day?"

Silence flowed through the receiver, the real issue unsaid. Corbie had ordered the Master and Mistress out of his domain. If de Sagres and his whore stay, instead of returning to England, then the doors leading to renewed conflict would open. It would be a declaration to a war Corbie was not yet ready for, yet. Marcus' Domunis spoke quietly. "If they do, we'll be ready for them. Afterall, they can't stay in there forever. They'll need to feed."

"What of Notus?" asked Marcus.

"Let him alone," remarked Corbie. "He's no threat. I want you back there right after nightfall. Do not get noticed. I'll have more for you later."

"Sir, what of Thanatos?"

A huff of exhaled breath indicated his Dominus' irritation. "I'll deal with him when the time comes."

Marcus could hear the uncertainty in Corbie's voice and chose not to react to it, but it made him nervous nonetheless. "Yes, sir."

He tapped the red button, ending the call. In the silence of his car, Marcus reclined his black leather seat and watched.

XÍ

otus blinked, Thanatos' request unexpected. He had been wrong to deny the boy, believing that his oath never to Choose another took precedence over his own desires. Now Thanatos presented another chance, and despite every instinct honed for nearly two thousand years, the opportunity to Choose the boy again—could not be denied. "Of course," he exhaled.

"Now you agree?!" snapped the Noble. Incredulity widened his dark eyes as anger tightened his jaw. "What of your precious oath?"

"I was wrong." Notus lowered his gaze. He could feel Fernando's accusatory gaze burn into him, but it was Bridget's head shake that brought him low. So much pain would have been averted had he agreed to the boy's request in the first place. "I'll Choose him, but I don't know if he would want me to do it after everything that's happened."

"You won't be Choosing him, Brynedd." Thanatos walked up to him and laid a hand on his shoulder. "He was never Chosen—"

"That's preposterous!" Fernando's frustration exploded into the room. "He's always—"

Thanatos spun around. "I will explain everything, but not

now." His cold tones chilled the growing tension.

Notus remembered the imperious tone of his teacher and Chooser, and was glad he was not the target.

"If you would cease to interrupt me, you may receive the answers you are rudely demanding," reprimanded Thanatos.

Fernando's eyes widened in surprise before his face flushed with contained anger.

Bridget laid a hand on Fernando's arm, shaking her head to forestall any further outburst of her Chosen.

"Fine," spat the Noble. "But answer me this question first."

Contained annoyance flickered across Thanatos' visage.

Receiving no answer, Fernando matched Thanatos' gaze. "You say that the Angel was never Chosen—which is preposterous—then what the hell is he?" The Noble's voice rose in pitch until he shouted the last.

"A God."

Thanatos' dead-pan answer struck the room into silence.

"That's per—"

Fernando halted his tirade as Thanatos raised an open hand.

"I've answered your question," stated Thanatos. "That is enough for now. When I had Godfrey bring Notus here, I did not expect him to bring two other Chosen. Since he has, the chance to save the Angel's life is increased."

Thanatos walked over to stand before the Mistress and Master of Britain, his dark brown eyes boring into theirs. "Notus has acquiesced. I ask you both, as the Angel's friends—since it is obvious that you care deeply for him—will you offer your blood so that the Angel will live?"

"Yes," exhaled Bridget without hesitation. Anticipated worry mixed with relief on her pale face, as hope flushed her cheeks.

"No one's ever had more than one Chooser. It can't be done," retorted Fernando. He pulled out of Bridget's grip on his arm and walked across the room to stare through the opened sliver of drapes, arms crossed over his chest.

"The Angel is not—"

"I heard what you said." Fernando spun around to face Thanatos. "I won't do it."

"The more Chosen blood he receives, the better is his chance for recovery," said Thanatos, surprised at the Noble's answer.

Notus stepped from Jeanie's embrace towards the Noble. "If I'm willing, after wrongly denying the boy, can you not—"

"No," snapped Fernando. "One other voice in my head is too much."

"Please, Fernando." Bridget stepped toward her Chosen. "This is the Angel—Gwyn—our friend. He needs us."

"And you believe this man?" Fernando shook his head. "We've only known him for—what?—an hour and you're willing to believe his insane ideas about the Angel? There's only one God and He forsook us a long time ago. No. No more unwanted voices."

Bridget deflated and turned away from him.

"That is a shame," commented Thanatos. "The Angel would have a greater chance of survival if you participated. I took you for a man not motivated by fear."

"Hold on. That's—" Fernando bore down on their host, clearly insulted.

"That's exactly what your decision means." Thanatos' cold statement halted Fernando toe-to-toe.

The challenge to the Noble's honour could not be ignored as they glared at one another. Notus could see the affront take its toll on the younger Chosen, as his sun kissed hands opened and clenched in desire to hit someone. Whether aware of the Noble's reigned in emotions or not, Thanatos stood relaxed, reflecting calm challenge.

"Fine," snapped Fernando. "You want my blood so badly, you can have it."

"Thank you." A smile washed over Thanatos' features, making him appear more youthful.

"What about me?" chimed Jeanie. "I'd be happy to give the Angel my blood." Hope filled her green eyes.

Thanatos walked over to her and lifted her hands in his. "Your offer is very kind, but he needs Chosen blood."

"Oh...well, then..." she muttered as he dropped her hands and took the few steps to the intercom on the bedside table.

"Godfrey?" He bent over to speak into the device as he pressed the button.

"Yes, sir?" came the distorted reply.

"Please bring up three sets."

"Three, sir?"

"Yes, please."

"Yes, sir."

The distortion cut to silence and Thanatos stood straight. "Godfrey will be up shortly."

It did not take long for Thanatos' servant to arrive with assorted medical paraphernalia.

"Aren't we just going to allow the Angel to drink from us?" asked Bridget, coming to stand beside Thanatos as he separated the empty blood bags and I.V. tubes on the bed beside the comatose Angel.

Thanatos shook his head. "He's too weak for that."

"An I.V.? Do you think that's wise, considering the state he's in?" remarked the Noble, coming to stand beside his Chooser.

"It's the only way." Thanatos connected three lines to the bags and turned to face his guests. "The faster this can be done, the better."

"I've never given blood this way before," smirked Fernando, rolling up his black shirtsleeve.

"It's not often a Chosen experiences something new," remarked Notus, following the Noble's example.

"I don't know about this," commented Bridget, her face going green. She rubbed at her nude arms, feeling naked in the blue string top dress. "This was not how I imagined..."

"You're afraid of needles?" Fernando turned to her.

"Shut up," she snarled.

"There's nothing to worry about," offered Godfrey. A gentle smile lit up his blue-green eyes in pride. "Thanatos knows what he's doing."

"Oh, he does, does he, mortal?" Bridget's finely sculpted blonde brow lifted, crashing Godfrey's full lips into a frown.

"He's a physician," said Thanatos' servant, recovering some of his confidence.

"You are?" Notus turned to face his Chooser. He could not have been more surprised, yet somehow this disclosure seemed apropos.

"He's a coroner for the city," replied Godfrey. A perturbed look from his employer lowered his head and he placed the needles neatly onto the metal tray. "If you no longer need me, sir."

"That's fine, Godfrey. You may go." Thanatos picked up one of the hollow needles and attached it to a clear plastic line. "Please take several packs out of the freezer as I'm sure our guests will require refreshments afterwards."

"Yes, sir." Godfrey turned and left.

"A coroner?" asked Notus once Thanatos' servant was out of earshot.

Thanatos grunted in reply, dismissing the obvious and held up the needle and line. "Who's first?"

Three bags full of Chosen blood lay on the bed. Bridget rubbed the inside of her elbow. "Well, that wasn't too bad."

"Really?" drawled Fernando. "If Thanatos hadn't brought over that chair when he did, you would be sprawled on the floor, passed out. Who'd ever heard of a Chosen afraid of needles?"

"Shut up." Bridget leaned back in the leather seat. "You looked green about the gills, too."

"I was picking that up from you."

"Right." Bridget closed her eyes and sighed, disbelieving him.

Thanatos watched the two snipe at each other as he worked to attach the blood-filled bags to the corner of the tall mahogany headboard. Despite their constant bickering, the two Chosen loved each other. A part of him felt jealousy at their luck. He had never found someone to walk through eternity with. The one who had Chosen him, making him believe they would be together forever, left him when the others of her kind departed. He was left desolate until he met and fell in love with Bastia. He shook his head at how that had turned out.

"Is everything alright?" queried Notus.

His Chosen came up beside him, concern radiating off of him. The sound of the shower in the en-suite bathroom turned off. The Vampiress would be out shortly. "I was just thinking, Brynedd."

"I don't go by that name anymore, Seddewyn."

"*Touche.*"

Thanatos pulled out the silver phial that strained against the chain around his neck, clutching it in his hand. "It was never my intention to hurt you."

"But you did, and you did so when you knew I still grieved for my family," sighed Notus.

"It is something we both have in common."

Thanatos opened his hand. "Do you know what this is?"

Notus' hazel eyes widened at seeing the finely crafted silver piece of jewelry fight against its owner. "No. I don't."

"It's not the container that's important, it's what's inside." Thanatos turned the base until it came free in his hand. Both chain and silver cap relaxed to dangle naturally around Thanatos' neck, but released from the chain, the pressure the phial exerted in its attempt to reach the Angel grew. "It is the last of my Chooser's blood."

Lifting a syringe with what appeared to be a plastic needle, Thanatos dipped the tip into the phial and drew back on the phalange. Old rust coloured blood filled the tube, draining the phial dry. In the joining of the three lines from the blood-bags, he inserted the catheter to join the blood from the three Chosen.

Loathe to use the surgical steel needle, Thanatos took the Angel's flaccid left hand and fitted the end of the plastic tube into the vein. The motion was quick enough, enhanced by immortal abilities, that the Angel's body had no time to react. Black blood flowed a couple of centimeters up the line, proving its viability. Taping the thin plastic tube to the Angel's hand, Thanatos opened the plastic valve at the juncture. Red filled the lines as he held his breath. Down the fine plastic, immortal blood flowed to mingle at the junction, mingling with the ancient blood, before it continued its journey into the Angel's body.

"What now?" Jeanie's whisper cracked the tense silence.

They all broke their gazes at the trickling blood. Thanatos could not recall her arrival. Though the Vampiress wore the same outfit of a black leather skirt and blouse, her face appeared clean and her red curls hung in damp waves.

"Now we wait, hope and pray," replied Thanatos.

"And?" said Fernando, black brows rising.

"You get your answers.

"If you'll follow me back to my study." Thanatos turned to

leave.

"I'd like t'stay with the Angel," stated Jeanie.

"Of course."

"Do you think that wise?" interjected Fernando.

"She's Jeanie," replied Notus, as if that were answer enough.

"She's also the Vampire who landed the Angel in this predicament and nearly ripped off Bridget's head," snapped Fernando.

"I promise I wilna hurt him." Jeanie stepped closer. "I ken what I am, though I despise it. Please, ye can trust me." Her forest green eyes beseeched them all.

"It would be best for someone to keep an eye on the boy," offered Notus.

"Jeanie was fine with him before," nodded Thanatos. A niggling of doubt still gnawed at him, but she had done nothing to harm the Angel since the return of her memories. He turned to face the Vampiress. "Stay with him. If anything changes, call us immediately."

"I will," she replied. Ignoring the protestations from Fernando, she went to sit by the Angel's side.

Thanatos could not eradicate the beansidhe-like image the Vampires displayed. Her rust coloured streaked face and wild curling copper hair had sent a shiver up his spine, and he hoped he was right to trust in his instincts. Turning from the grim sight, Thanatos exited his bedroom, the Chosen following.

XII

Darkness encapsulated him, buoying him in a silent void. The familiar experience gave comfort when long ago it had evoked terror. He relaxed, trusting his lack of visual stimulus would be relieved by the diaphanous beings that had once fed on him in their search to taste life, but nothing came. No demons of white floated towards him. Concern at their absence turned him around—or at least he believed he did—in hopes of discovering their whereabouts.

No splash of white marred the dark. He frowned. Not even the pinpoint of brilliance where the Ladies resided broke up the monotony of black. The absence of everything set his heart trembling.

A caress fluttered along and across his body. He spun to see where it had come from, but nothingness met him. Another breeze ticked his face and body, pressing against him until a sensation of moving backwards roiled his stomach with vertigo.

Arms flung out to catch his balance did nothing to help the spinning nausea. It added to the pressure from the unseen breeze turned wind. Bringing his arms in, he spun around in hopes that facing the direction he moved would alleviate the dizziness. It did not.

THANATOS

The sense of acceleration stole his breath, once facing what could only be forward, and tightened the muscles of his face and body. Some rational part of his mind informed him to relax as he moved through the void, but the sensations from the strange experience refused to relinquish control.

The tactility of movement increased, adding pressure to his eyes until he did not know if they were open or closed. Where the winds took him remained a mystery, eliciting a fear he had not felt since his first venture into this place as a child. He wished he could cry out, to make it stop, but he could not. Opening his mouth filled it with the tempest and stole away any sound he could utter.

Pressure continued to build, accelerating him through the darkness. Fear grew into a terror that pounded between his ears, adding its staccato to the whistling, unseen wind. He did not know how long he continued to travel, accelerating through the void. He tried to count the seconds until they became minutes, leaving off when hours seemed inevitable. Time held no meaning except to his dizzied mid.

A new worry inserted itself into his fear, adding its own unique flavor into the terror. At some point, he must arrive wherever he was being taken to. Would he decelerate in time? The pressures on his body amplified and the whistling crescendo pitch stabbed his ears, piercing his head with spikes of hot pain until he did not care what happened to him. He wanted to scream, to place his hands over his ears to halt the torture, but the pressures of the wind immobilized his body. Unable to do anything, he did the one thing he could. He surrendered.

His ruby eyes widened at the sight of the grove of his childhood. The same place where his first encounter with Eira and the other three older children had left him scarred and heart-sore, opening the gates to the white-faced demons.

How did I get here?
Why here?

The glade appeared no different from that fateful day. The old oak dipped its leaf laden branches, cutting shadows into the dew coated grass. Nudged against the ancient guardian a hedge of Mayflowers coated in fragrant white flowers scented the air. Petals released to dance in the breeze came to rest upon the tintinnabulate creek, adding to the glittering as clear water cascaded over a riverstone bed. All the while, silver-scaled fish leaped through their watery world into the realm of air to catch buzzing morsels, as a rainbow of wildflowers watched from the riverbank. The perfection of the visage evoked memories of a childhood washed in innocence.

He took a step towards the ribbed trunk of the oak and the protective shade its branches created, and halted. The noonday sun did not burn his bare shoulders and nor did the brilliant daylight sting his eyes. Confused, he glanced down. Shock filled his mouth with ashes and he clicked his jaw shut.

Raising his hands, he stared through their translucent forms to the greenery beyond.

"This is the past."

Startled, he spun to see Auntie, the woman who had found him and raised him in secrecy, standing beside him, young, pretty and pellucid. The woods beyond showed through her visage.

"Did you think that I did not know of this place?" She turned and smiled.

Surprise silenced him.

"I, too, used to come here as a girl," she continued. She took steps towards the blooming hawthorn, her fingers reaching to touch the velvet petals only to pass through without so much as a whisper of disruption. She turned to face him, a sad smile touching her eyes. "This is a sacred grove. One in which the Ancient Ones set their stones. Of course, those stones are either buried by centuries of deadfall or hidden in the lush woods.

"It was here that my great-grandmother taught me the Ancient Ones' ways and how best to honour them. It was also here that I found you as a babe."

He could not believe what he heard. The revelation constricted his throat to whisper, "Why did you never tell me?"

Llawela lowered her gaze to the grass between them. "What could I say?" She raised her head, setting long brown curls swaying, and met the hurt in his eyes. "I loved you. I still love you. All

I wanted was to protect you, but I could not. I made an error in judgment and it followed me to my grave. Now I have been given a chance to tell you everything I should have when I was alive."

"I don't understand." He stepped towards her, his unscarred arms outstretched and imploring.

Llawela sadly shook her head. "I did my best to teach you, to keep you from harm's way. I did not do as well as I should have and it cost you so much. I thought we would have more time together. I was wrong. I'm so sorry."

Silence crashed between them. No birds chirped, no bugs buzzed, only the tinkling of the stream filled the space. Hearing Auntie's confession evoked ancient memories from when she was beaten, broken and left to die in his arms. Swallowing down the ball of sorrow, he dropped his gaze. "I know," he said huskily, "but I failed you. I did not listen. I was caught, found out." He raised his grief filled eyes to meet hers. "It's my fault that you were killed."

She came and laid her hand on his forearm. "No, it is not."

Surprised at the warmth of her touch, he covered her hand with his, capturing the sensation. Tears welled, creating glimmering jewels of his eyes. Oh how he missed her touch, her warmth, her love! Guilt broke the banks, flooding his face. No matter her declaration of his innocence, it could not contend with a millennia and a half of self-recrimination. "I'm so sorry," he cried.

Somehow, he found himself on his knees, his head pressed against her breast as she held him close. Between his catching sobs, he heard her sing the lullaby she had sung to him when he was a child. He did not know how long she held him as he released the buried guilt.

Gradually, the tears abated and he pulled away to gaze into her hazel eyes. Tears shimmered and ran jeweled tracks down her face. They both sat on the grove's green carpet, gazing at each other.

Small warm hands reached up to brush away the moisture on his face. "I've missed you, boy." A smile lit her face.

"No more than I've missed you." He took her hands in his own, marveling at the difference in size and structure.

Rising to her feet, she pulled him up with her until he towered over her once again. "It's time I show you the truth."

Curiosity tinged with trepidation filled him as Auntie led him through the greenwood. They followed the same trail that he had taken when a child. He had believed, when he had first found it, that animals had carved their passage brown into the green undergrowth. Clearly, he had been mistaken.

Branches decorated in new growth passed through their ephemeral forms. Sunlight dappled the low underbrush, breaking up the perpetual twilight of the forest floor in radiant beams. Unseen animals conversed and called out to each other from the canopy above to the shrubbery below, their natural music a cacophony to his ears.

On they trod, he following her. He did not need to ask where she led until they emerged from darkness into the light of the flowered expanse that led to the roundhouse they had shared. New thatch glittered golden and the brown hide door swayed in the breeze despite being tacked open against the wattle and daub wall. A flicker of movement beyond the threshold caught his breath, halting him in his tracks. He felt a tug on his wrist and gazed down into Auntie's smiling eyes.

"You have waited so long for the truth," she said. "There is no point fearing it now."

"I'm not afraid," he said, affronted.

"Then why do you tremble?" She arched a brown brow in amusement.

It was the same look that she made when she would catch him doing something he knew better than to do. He opened his mouth to deny the truth, but closed it with a click, realizing how easy it was to fall into childish habits. For his whole, long life, he has sought the truth of who he was, and now, having those answers so close, set a conservatory of butterflies fluttering in his gut. Releasing the breath he did not realize he held, he lowered his scowl to the patch of path between them. "I guess I am as ready as I can be."

She patted the back of his hand, lifting his gaze to meet hers.

Across the painted, beflowered landscape they walked hand in hand to the entrance of Auntie's hut, and the only place he ever called home.

THAПATOS

"You promised me!" shouted the tall young woman with long, straight raven hair.

"I said I would train you to honour the Ancient Ones, and if you proved yourself worthy, I would teach you Their secrets as they had been to me by my own great-grandmother."

He stood transfixed in the roundhouse. There was no sign of his existence in the living space, but seeing who stood arguing confounded him. He glanced to his right, seeing the young, ephemeral Auntie still grasping his right hand, and back to the solid, old woman who raised him. His mind reeled at the sight of the two versions of Auntie.

"This is the past," whispered the younger version. "It is easier this way."

"I'm not asking for all Their secrets," simmered the raven haired woman. Her anger slipped away at Llawela's cross-armed stance.

"Can they—you—I mean..." He shook his head, confusion making his mind throb.

"No," answered his Auntie. "We are shades of things to come. Now, be silent, and watch." She gave his hand a comforting squeeze.

Releasing a huff, he returned his attention to the past.

"Please, Auntie," begged the woman. She ran the few steps to fall on her knees before Llawela, to clutch at the older woman's grey homespun robe. "I'm getting older and have born no son."

"You and Geraint have two lovely daughters," snapped Llawela, ignoring the younger woman. "Can that not be enough? Daughters bear the lineage, the power..."

He could not believe his ears. Comprehension of who knelt before Auntie ran goosebumps over his skin and negated any ability to hear the rest of his mother's pleading.

"Get up, Enid," ordered Llawela. She plucked her niece's hands from her robe and forced the younger to stand. Frustration warred with sympathy across the old woman's face as she glared up at the tall woman.

"But he has no heir." Sadness choked Enid's voice.

"Do you wish this for your father or for you?" The anger

came back.

"Both!" cried Enid. She tried to grasp at her Auntie's arm, but Llawela had moved beyond her reach.

Llawela sat down on the edge of her raised palette, the furs and woolen blankets dipping under her weight. She shook her head, sending grey and white wisps flying. "Have we fallen so far from the tree that gave us birth?"

Confusion stole into Enid's pleading eyes. "I – I don't understand."

Llawela turned to gaze sadly at her oldest niece. "No. I guess you do not. Even after all I have taught you." She sighed in defeat. "I will give you what you ask for. I will give you the rites necessary to conceive a boy, but it must be done on the full moon of Beldan."

"That's three nights from now!" cried Enid. "Geraint's away with my father. He won't be back in time."

"That is when it must be done." Clouding hazel eyes bore into the young woman.

Silence crashed into the roundhouse, the only break being that from the music of nature intruding from outside.

"He will find you," stated Llawela. She refused to take her piercing gaze away.

Lowering her head, Enid nodded.

"Understand this, my niece, that the child you seek comes with a heavy price. If you choose to go through this rite, the son you bear will become more than your father's heir, more than your husband's heir. He will be more than any who have been born to woman since the Ancient Ones walked with us, for our blood is their blood." Llawels's voice grew more resonant, filling the roundhouse with her prediction until it spilled out the door to silence nature with her pronouncement.

Enid stood wide-eyed and shivering, and slowly nodded. Her straight, midnight locks draped her ashen visage.

If it had not been for young Auntie's hand holding onto his, he would have fled the cottage. He recognized the voice that had taken over the older Auntie. The chorus of the Three Ladies chilled him to the core.

"Then I will teach you."

THANATOS

Old Llawela slumped, suddenly deflated of presence. Enid rushed to her Aunt and caught the old woman before she could fall to the rush strewn, mud packed floor.

He stood in the center of the glade, his hand still in Auntie's unyielding grip. The sun had set some time ago, leaving the stars to be outshone by a pregnant moon. His mind spun at the knowledge presented to him, and he glanced at the young Llawela, his great Aunt, unable to voice the multitude of questions that filled him.

A rustle of foliage and a snap of dried deadfall announced Enid's entrance into the grove. Moonlight washed the scene in blue, colouring the circles beneath her dark eyes and tingeing her pale features stark. Her hand held a large wicker basket covered with a green cloth. He felt a tug and he allowed Auntie to lead him to stand before the Mayflowers. He knew what he witnessed. He did not require an answer to his unspoken question.

With the sound of distant drumming accompanying the nocturnal animal calls, Enid placed the basket down beside her and stripped off her green gown, leaving her clad in moonlight. Silver scars marked her flat abdomen and topped her full breasts as she folded the fabric and left it by the oak. The haunting sounds lent their air as she carefully extracted the objects from the basket and placed them around the grove. Once completed, she stepped into the fast running stream, its cold bite strangling a gasp from her full lips. With words unuttered beyond memory, Enid began the rite.

He watched his mother move through the sacred grove, weaving words and action, chant and dance, invocations and beseechments. A fervor captured her eyes and twisted her tresses until she appeared to be a mad woman. On she went, and with it, the sound of drumming crescendoed until her call crashed through the grove's boundaries.

Silence descended.

Even her bosom's breath could not be heard.

Sweat dripped off her shivering body, and she clutched her arms across her chest as she stared up at the moon now directly overhead.

A soft, steady beat flowed into the grove, and yet still the animals remained silent. The slow, low heartbeat reverberated off tree and brush. Enid continued to gaze upon the moon.

Euphoria mixed with fear, twisting Enid's features. He studied her face and bit his lower lip at the resemblances he found there. Tension thrummed through him. He did not know if was because of his tumultuous emotions or the rising drumbeat.

Without warning, Enid's face hardened to her purpose and she lifted her arms to the moon. The words that fell from her lips shocked him.

"No!" he cried. He tried to race to her. Anything to halt the spell of summoning from spilling off her lips, but Auntie's strong hand held him fast.

"There is nothing you can do," remarked Auntie. Sympathy softened her features. "This is the past."

"But the sp—"he implored.

"Did you think only you were given such knowledge?" Auntie sadly shook her head. "Do you not remember that it was I who taught it to you?"

"But they will come!" Fear tinged his words.

Auntie sighed. "What Enid summons is not what you have summoned. Now, be silent and watch."

He turned his attention as bid and halted his breathing at the sight of a finger of mist appearing to float down from the moon. Around and around the thread spun slowly about the grove, encapsulating Enid and her observers within its beclouded walls until even the moon became obscured.

No diaphanous beings swirled in the vapours. No skeletal faces stared maliciously. No razor sharp maws stretched in gruesome grins. The bizarre mist appeared exactly as it did, except that it did not fill the grove. It encircled and cut off the sacred grounds from the rest of the world.

Enid stepped into the center, her arms stretched out to the unseen moon. Once again, she called out the spell.

The flowing mist lost its smooth texture as it serpentined the glade. Its turbulence became akin to boiling storm clouds. Still, nothing formed in the grey-white cloud.

Chest heaving, Enid screamed the summoning a third time,

tears flowing down her face to drip and mingle with the sweat on her chest. As her last words disappeared into the silence of the grove, she collapsed to her knees, the cool, damp grass buoying her despite her fatigue.

"Why?" she sobbed, hugging herself against defeat. "Why won't you come? Please. All I ask is for a son—a son to continue the line."

He could not stand to see this woman—his mother—in agony. Tears welled in his eyes with the realization of how desperately she wanted him. Why, then, did he end up abandoned? His turbulent emotions reflected in the mist. No answer presented itself and Enid collapsed to the ground, her hiccoughing cries filling the grove.

"You cannot go to her." Auntie's hand gripped harder.

A shuddering sigh pulled him back to being an observer. He did not know how long they stood there watching Enid pour her tears into the earth, but as her cries became whimpers, he noticed that the barrier by the ancient oak appeared to rip apart. His breath caught at the sight of a long, slender leg, clad in silver cloth, emerge from the rift. It was followed by a tall figure of a man, despite his soft androgynous features and long flowing argent hair. A shimmering silver tunic covered skin a shade lighter.

The rent in the mist closed behind the strange man. It took every effort to remember to breathe. A part of him felt the fool for having assumed that only the Three Ladies existed in that otherworld. Now, in this earthly glade, stood a male version, as stunning as the Ladies themselves. Red eyes caught his. Did the Silver Man smile at him for a flickering moment before turning his attention to Enid? Despite that flutter, cognizance gripped him. The man stood a silvered mirrored image of himself!

The Silver Man stepped towards Enid's prone, weeping form. Every movement more graceful than a dancer's, he knelt beside her and laid a delicate hand on her shuddering shoulder. "Do not weep, for I have come."

His words, spoken in the ancient tongue, raised her head. Wiping tears from her eyes, Enid gasped at the sight of the man before her. Numb from shock, she allowed the Silver Man to raise her to her feet. She had to tilt her head back to stare open-mouthed at him.

The Silver Man ran his thumb across her cheek until he cupped her face in his sterling hand. Long, delicate fingers of his other hand played with strands of her raven hair. His mellifluous voice filled the grove. "It has been so long since I touched the earth."

Lowering his head, he pressed his cheek to Enid's, whispering something in her ear. She shook her head and attempted to take a step backwards, but halted as the Silver man straightened. Mild disappointment flickered over his face before replacing it with a recondite smile.

"Do you comprehend the recompense you will be asked to pay?" His silver tongue became harsh.

Enid nodded.

"Will you pay willingly?"

Again, she nodded.

"For a third and final time, do you concede that in exchange for a son of the line you will pay whatever is required?" The Silver Man took a step back, taking in her full view.

Shivers ran rampant over Enid's body. "Yes," she replied in the same language.

"So be it."

The softly spoken statement rang gunshot through the grove, staggering Auntie and he with its concussion. She did not let go of his hand.

He could not believe what he had witnessed and it's implication. In dumb silence he watched as the Silver Man knelt before Enid. Tenderly, argent hands ran down the length of her trembling legs, and he bent low to place a kiss on the tops of each of her feet, while murmuring words only Enid could hear.

The hands rose up, caressing gooseflesh until the Silver Man placed two more kisses upon her knees. Enid would have buckled had it not been for his steel grip. Once she stood steady, he raised his hands over and around her buttocks. More words were spoken as he kissed her below her bellybutton.

A long, drawn out moan exhaled from Enid's lips as she relaxed into the Silver Man's ministrations. He caught her before she could collapse. His head between her breasts, silver lips uttered unheard words before placing suckling kisses upon each nipple.

It was too much for Enid. She fell to her knees and was ensconced in the Silver Man's embrace. Even in this position, he towered over her. Bending towards her impassioned face, the Silver Man breathed words into her parted lips before covering them with his own.

A tug turned on his hand turned his attention from the seduction to a new rift forming by the oak. Through it stepped a figure similar to that of the Ladies. Nude, her skin appeared as pale as moonlight. Her delicate features were draped in a midnight cloak of hair bedecked with glimmering jewels as argent as the Silver Man's flesh. Opalescent eyes glanced about the grove before landing upon the two on their knees in the center. A smile hit her beautiful face and she stepped towards the two.

Gracefully, she lowered herself to her knees behind Enid. The Silver Man pulled back from the kiss and his eyes caught those of the newcomer. A smile twitched the corners of his lips. "It has been too long."

The words were not meant for Enid, and it appeared as though she had not heard.

"Have her speak the words." The Starry Woman's voice fell upon the grove in a smattering of starlight.

The Silver Man nodded, his hair becoming a curtain as he bent to whisper in Enid's ear.

Wavering on her knees, Enid tilted her head back, and with eyes closed, spoke the ancient words. Her voice sounded rough and abused against the other two. When their sound no longer filled the space, the Starry Lady moved forward, capturing Enid's collapsed form.

Disbelief filled him as the figure of the Starry Woman dissolved into Enid. Once she was gone, Enid opened her eyes. A contented smile lifted her lips as she stretched her arms above her head. As she lowered her hands to flow over her body, a doubled image appeared, as if the Starry Woman superimposed herself over Enid.

"My love," spoke Enid in the voice of the Starry Woman. She lowered her body until she lay supine with the Silver Man kneeling between her legs.

"Let me worship at your altar." A gruffness entered into his voice that sent a shudder through Enid's body.

"As it was from the beginning," sighed the combined form of Enid and the Starry woman.

"And so will be for eternity," replied the Silver Man.

With a gesture of his hand, the Silver Man's clothes vanished, leaving him naked and unadorned, his passion rigid. Leaning over Enid, he kissed above her triangle.

"It is time to leave."

Auntie's words shocked him from the developing scene and he turned to face her. Without his acquiescence, the tug on his arm propelled him into the darkness.

XIII

orbie stared at the white cordless phone sitting idle on his cream oak desk, its single red light the only indication that it still worked. Behind him, the bank of monitors exhibited the closing operations as another night of business ended. He did not need to watch Brian flit from screen to screen, ensuring that everything flowed in an orderly manner.

A hollowness in Corbie's gut clutched at him. Maybe there was a straggler at the bar that could be sent down to him. He turned to pick up the receiver to call Brian, but let his hand drop. So what if he was hungry? He had been hungry before. It had always brought clarity of thought, especially when he needed to be ruthless. The question was whether such thought was required, since Thanatos had hung his threat over him.

Leaning back in his chair, he raked back his lanky black locks and sighed. Thanatos had the Angel, and Rose was with them. To top the worst-case situation, the Chosen Master and Mistress of Britain also made themselves guests. Notus, too, presented a problem, but to a lesser degree. Corbie was not ready for the war he planned to wage. Unfortunately, more often than not, one rarely chose both the time and place of battle. The advantage of having the home field was one he had not calculated into his machinations. It was the superior general who could see advantage within adversity. Killing the Chosen, who clearly violated the tenuous peace by stepping into his realm, would open the door to all out war between Vampire and Chosen. He would be justified. The Chosen could blame no one by themselves.

Yes!

A smile tugged his thin lips into a satisfied smile. Let the Chosen come to the Americas. It would be easier to defend against aggressive invaders than to be the one perpetrating the offense. Regardless of their probably lower numbers, the Vampires could only win, eradicating the Chosen Bastia had endeavoured to destroy.

Yes, it would work.

Picking up the phone, he dialed Brian's number.

"Yes, sir?"

Corbie spun around in his chair to witness Brian standing before the bar, phone in one hand and his other tapping the wooden surface. "Contact those who haven't left the city and tell them I'm ordering them to meet me here tomorrow night, an hour past dusk," ordered Corbie.

"But some of them are already at the airport," replied Brian.

Corbie scowled at the defiant tone that seemed to be creeping more and more into his fledgling's voice. "Then take yourself out there and bring them back," snapped Corbie, his patience wearing thin.

"Yes, sir," said Brian, curtly.

Corbie watched Brian stab his phone with his finger, disconnecting the call, before storming out of the club. Placing his quiet receiver back into his base, Corbie turned to his desk. They would come. They had no choice. He was their Dominus, no matter that each held the title in their own right.

Relaxing into his white leather office chair, his hands resting on his lap, he knew that only one thing stood in his way of becoming Imperator of the Vampires. Thanatos must die.

It was crazy—inconceivable!—but despite the Ancient's threat, it became clear on whose side the God of Death stood. That in itself would be the kindling to ignite the idea in the minds of his Vampires. Kill the Angel and the God of Death, destroy the

Chosen they supported, and begin the conflagration that would eradicate the Chosen, placing the mortals in their proper position in the food chain.

If all fell into place as the plan formulated itself, then by the end of tomorrow night Corbie would be Imperator.

It all hinged on one question: Can the God of Death die?

XIV

The scent of warmed blood filled Thanatos' study. Ninety-eight point six degrees Fahrenheit; Godfrey knew how to return frozen blood to a more mortal state. Thanatos relaxed into the chestnut brown leather chair as the three Chosen did the same on the matching sofa across from him.

"I still don't like leaving Jeanie alone with him." Fernando scowled as he took a bone Chine cup and saucer from the cherry tray Godfrey offered.

Bridget and Notus took theirs, Bridget turning the finely crafted cup to admire the gold-filigreed roses. "I have to agree." She took a sip. Surprise flashed across her face before she took a larger gulp.

"I appreciate your concern, but I believe the Angel is in good hands." Thanatos took the last teacup and looked up at his servant. "That will be all, Godfrey. I'll call if needed."

"Yes, sir," bowed the young man. Neatly tucking the empty tray to his side, Godfrey nodded and turned to leave the room.

Once Godfrey's footfalls fell beyond mortal hearing, Thanatos sighed and settled the untouched cup onto the round mahogany side-table to his right. "Now, to the answers to your questions, but be warned that some of the answers may not be to your liking."

"I have a question." Bridget settled her empty teacup and saucer onto the coffee table between them. "I've Chosen quite a number of people through the years and never once did the process require more than the blood of one Chosen. Upstairs you required mine, Fernando's and Notus', not to mention the powdered blood of your Chooser, yet you did not use yours. I think I can say—speaking for Fernando and Notus when I ask—why? What the hell is all this about?"

"Though I rarely admit it," interjected Fernando, shaking his head, "I'm with Bridget."

Master and Mistress turned to face Notus, sitting at the end of the couch, cup and saucer resting on his lap. His hands cupped the warm China, his head held low. With a sigh, he placed the untouched contents and container beside Bridget's empty teacup, and leaned back into the soft cushion. "I've made many mistakes in my long life. The worst led to my boy lying upstairs, hanging onto life by a thread. The other is not learning the truth about the man who Chose me."

Hazel eyes locked onto brown until Thanatos nodded, conceding the point. "Fair enough," stated their host. "In our time together I perfected the illusion of Seddewyn. That's all I allowed for you to know.

"I've made my fair share of mistakes, all of them accumulating to this place, this moment of time." Thanatos raised a hand, halting the inevitable questions from the three. "Please understand, this is incredibly difficult for me. I ask that you hear me out in full. What I will speak of has been unspoken for over ten thousand years."

"Ten thousand!" sputtered Fernando. Bridget's elbow in his gut precipitated a whoosh of breath, silencing the Noble with a muttered apology.

Thanatos nodded his acceptance of the apology, but this did not abate the sudden case of nerves that shuddered through his body. He had envisioned revealing his secrets only to Notus, but having the other two Chosen in his study added a greater uncertainty had not expected to experience. Standing, he took a couple of steps to halt behind his high backed chair. Thanatos closed his eyes and exhaled in an attempt to calm his nerves. He laid his hands on the back of the leather-clad cushion and opened his eyes to stare at his guests. Curious and confused gazes met his.

Where to start? Where to start? His mind groped, the answer self evident despite his denial to reveal the truth. "The name my mother gave me was Ta'ano, and she held the respected position of—what's the best way to describe it?" He bit his lower lip, searching for the right word until he found it. "She was a High Priestess, set apart to serve as handmaiden and hierodule to the Gods.

"I grew up amongst them, one of the sacred children conceived by a God, raised to become a High Priest and servant of the Gods, as my mother and my forbears did upon the arrival of the Ancient Ones.

"There was no place in all the world that lived as we did. Some might say it was the first city to exist. I know that Catal Huyuk was modeled on our fair city, as were others. I know, for I visited them often after I was Chosen. I watched them grow, and I watched them die.

"The name of the place I lived is lost to the annals of time, as its location and the language I grew up speaking. Roughly, it translates as 'Where Gods and Men Meet.'

"You mean a temple?" asked Notus.

Thanatos shook his head. "It was the place where the Gods walked with us, taught us, and transformed human beings into something more—the Chosen."

Collective gasps drew his attention from the past back into present for but a moment before continuing. "My mother was blessed into this state when I entered my apprenticeship at nine years of age. I no longer saw her, for she now served my sire as one of His Chosen."

Thanatos caught sight of Bridget's hand lifting in preparation to ask a question. It appeared that his request would be ignored. Huffing out his annoyance, he nodded.

"Are you saying that the Chosen were servants to aliens?" asked Bridget, cautiously.

Floored, Thanatos could only blink his astonishment until recovered enough to response. "Aliens? Gods, no! They were Gods.

THANATOS

They moved from our reality into others, transporting from one place to another at will. Even by today's standards they performed great feats and wonders by what could—even now—be called magic. They took a primitive species and taught us how to capture seeds and grow our own food. They taught us skills and trained those with an aptitude in specializations of creation. They nudged us into new discoveries and knowledge, guiding us as we grew."

"What was the catch?" asked Fernando.

Thanatos frowned, disturbed at the closed off posture of the young Chosen. The black shirt strained across Fernando's broad shoulders as his arms crossed against his chest. "There was no catch. Without them, humanity probably wouldn't have even discovered agriculture. No—" He cut off further interruption. "Let me explain in my own way."

He had to try a different tactic. "I was born over ten thousand years ago." He ignored their incredulous expressions. Plowing ahead, his voice grew louder as he dove into the telling.

"The city I grew up in was situated on the south-west side of a fresh water lake that would eventually become the Black Sea. A city ancient when I was born…"

"Ta'ano!" cried the woman standing in the centre of the stone circle. Her wavy, black hair played in the breeze. A central fire illuminated her white tunic, embroidered with symbols of her office outlining her breasts. In the silver moonlight her sun touched skin seemed to shimmer with heat, but it was her smile, lighting up her amber eyes, that summoned Ta'ano into outstretched arms.

"Oh my Ta'ano. My dear little boy," cooed the High Priestess as she hugged him to her chest, brushing back his long curling locks.

Ta'ano gazed up into his mother's watery eyes, his own tearing at the sight. He did not want to let his mother go. He knew what would happen and the end of his happiness tore at him.

"Remember that I will always love you," whispered his mother. She kissed the top of his head. "Be good and study hard. If you are lucky, we will see each other again."

"I don't want you to go, mama," cried Ta'ano.

"I know, sweet one," murmured his mother. "But we always knew it would be this way." She unhooked their embrace, forcing him to step back as she knelt before him. Cupping his face with delicate boned hands, she gazed into his eyes. "Now stand with Appe and the others."

He nodded and wiped the tears from his eyes before turning to join the seven other children at the eastern curve of the circle. Ancient Appe, Loremaster and Teacher of apprentices, took his hand. The old man's gnarled and leathery talons gave Ta'ano's a reassuring squeeze.

Through shimmering eyes, Ta'ano watched his mother rise and stretch her arms to the heavens. Priestesses and Priests ringing the rest of the circle began a low thrumming chant. Ta'ano had never witnessed a rite before, coming quickly under its spell. Before his eyes, his mother became the High Priestess, the one who served the Gods, the one destined to be Chosen.

A thrill of fear and awe rooted him to the green earth beneath his bare feet as she turned to face the children. "You who have been blessed by the Gods to learn Their Mysteries, come forth and swear the Oath." The High Priestess' voice rang through the sacred site, pitched perfectly above the growing thrum.

One by one, each of the children stepped forward to stand before the High Priestess. In an ancient language, each swore service to the Gods. When it came time for Ta'ano to step forward, he no longer recognized the woman who had given him life. She appeared taller, her voice more resonant and there, in her eyes, appeared a loving stranger. Her graceful hands lowered onto his head and he repeated the words, the language of the Gods flowing naturally over his tongue. A thrill of power raced through his body and he knew it was done. The woman before him smiled and he returned to Appe.

The vocalizations from the others dropped to a low five part harmony that vibrated the cool night air and set Ta'ano trembling. He knew what would come next and he watched in awe as his mother used the Summoning. Slender arms rose to catch the full moonlight, she implored the Gods to heed her call and descend upon Their children. Three times, she spoke the spell and as the final syllable cracked across the grove, the chanting, too, suddenly ended.

The deafening silence numbed Ta'ano's ears and he gasped. Around the circle, a fog lifted from the ground, spiraling and thickening, as it grew taller. Appe's hand firmed its grasp on his. Ta'ano had not realized he was trying to escape, but it was too late. The mist now encapsulated the worshippers, severing them from the rest of the world.

Motion in the northern portion of the circle drew Ta'ano's attention away from the heaving bosom of the High Priestess in religious ecstasy. Older Priestesses and Priests dropped to the dew soaked earth in prostration as a rift tore the mist.

No one seemed to breathe as a God, in splendid golden beauty, stepped forward. Gracefully, he appeared to float across the ground. Sun coloured trousers and a resplendent tunic of grain yellow set off the God's smiling honey eyes. Long sand coloured hair played with the breeze.

Ta'ano stood awestruck, ignoring Appe's insistent tugs to join the others in prostration. Ta'ano knew he should lower himself to the earth, but this God, who approached his mother, could only be the one who had sired him. As if reading his thoughts, the God turned to gaze at him, the beautiful smile widening until Ta'ano could see the sharpened teeth that the Chosen would be blessed with. No malice touched the God's visage, but at his wink, Ta'ano gulped down his pounding heart and fell to the ground with the others.

A muffled conversation between the High Priestess and the God floated to Ta'ano's ears and he found a kernel of courage to look up. There, in the centre, the God stood tall over the High Priestess, as if she were a young child and he the parent. Loving hands reached to each other, but it was the God, bending to capture his mother's lips with his own, that widened Ta'ano's eyes.

The embrace seemed to go on forever before they broke apart and bid everyone rise. Ta'ano slowly rose to his feet, assisting ancient Appe to stand.

"The time has come to announce a new High Priestess as I leave to serve the Gods." Ta'ano's mother's voice filled the Circle. "Cha'kata, come forth, for in due time, if the Gods will, at the turn of the cycle, you will be Chosen."

A woman of about eighteen years, her long brown hair in thick rope braids, came forward. Dark eyes sparkled in awe as she knelt before the High Priestess and the God. Her thin muslin tunic could not hide the explosion of goosebumps that spread across her bronze skin.

With head lowered, the High Priestess laid her hands on the young woman's head. "Cha'kata, you have proven yourself countless times. In the years of your apprenticeship and subsequent initiation, you have served the Gods with loving sacrifice, and served the people with honour and humility. Cha'kata, is it your will to take the Oath of the High Priestess and serve your office with the qualities you have proven over the years?"

"I will." Cha'kata's voice rang with fear. All knew that in nine years she would be accepted as Chosen or be sacrificed to the Gods in accordance to their desires.

The question was asked twice more, each time the retelling was slightly different. Once Cha'kata answered for the third time, the High Priestess nodded.

The Golden God leaned forward and whispered in Ta'ano's mother's ear. She smiled, lifted her hands from the benediction and backed away so to allow the God to assume her position. For the first time, Ta'ano heard a God speak and it weakened his knees. Never before had he heard anything so beautiful. He had no comprehension of the words He spoke, but Ta'ano could not tear his eyes away as the God administered the Oath to Cha'kata. The young woman's melodic voice sounded flat and hollow in comparison as she repeated the words phrase by phrase.

The Oath complete, Cha'kata rose to her feet, assisted by golden hands. She accepted his kiss, and would have swooned had He not caught her. He whispered something in her ear and she smiled.

The end of the rite approached, the realization gripping Ta'ano's heart. In a moment, his mother would be gone. Tears sparkled in his eyes.

A new rift formed in the swirling mist, setting off murmurs from those in the circle. The Golden God turned to face the newcomer. Much smaller than the God who stood in the grove, a figure approached with tentative steps. Gasps rang round the sacred site. A Child-God, clothed in moonlight, gradually made his way to stand by the Golden One. Head lowered, long silver hair draped to cover nervous features. Ta'ano could not tear his gaze away from the self-conscious Child-God.

Once in the centre, a golden hand came to rest on the young one's trembling shoulder, giving him a reassuring squeeze. The Child-God stood by the new High Priestess and Ta'ano took in the small size of the Child-God. So similar, yet so different from the Golden One now whispering into Cha'kata's ear.

Cha'kata's grown eyes widened as she glanced from the silver child to the Golden God. Ta'ano could not mistake the increase of tremors playing across the young God. Curiosity stole Ta'ano's stinging loss, and heightened as the new High Priestess' voice silenced the growing murmurs

"It is the will of the Lady that the People be blessed with the care and rearing of one of Her own." Cha'kata's eyes brimmed with unshed tears of joy. "Never before have the People been so honoured, so blessed." She turned to face the Golden One, hands clutched to her breast. "The People accept the trust and charge She has placed upon us. We will do all in our power to take care of him."

The Golden God nodded in acceptance and patted the Child-God's shoulder to indicate he should go stand with the others. The silver child shook his locks and stood his ground. Ta'ano's jaw dropped at the glittering tears on the Child-God's pale face. In the language of the Gods, the child begged the Golden One. Graceful pale fingers clutched sun dyed cloth, the act drawing a firm line from the once smiling bronze lips. Ta'ano watched the God lower himself to bended knee, coming to a height with the moon-touched Child-God. Whatever passed between the two sent a new wash of tears down the youth's face before he turned to come and stand between Ta'ano and Appe.

Ta'ano's eyes were on the silver boy. Taller than Ta'ano by a head, it became clear that the Child-God was of a similar age. Appe attempted to lay a comforting hand on the silver child's shoulder, but unsure of the protocol, allowed his twisted hand to drop in concert with his grizzled frown.

Not so tied to unknown etiquette, Ta'ano tentatively reached out and took the Child-God's chill hand in his own. The act surprised the silver boy and their eyes locked. Never before had Ta'ano seen eyes the colour of blood.

Cha'kata's voice filled the grove. The ritual words of parting came easily to the new High Priestess, as the Golden God led Ta'ano's mother to the rift. With a final glance to her son and the soundless words "Be good" riding her lips, she disappeared into the swirling mist along with the Golden God.

A sun darkened hand and a moon touched one gripped each other as both broke into sobs in the midst of joyous jubilation.

XV

ou need to understand that the relationship between the Gods and humans were more direct, more visceral, if you will." Thanatos hid the amusement from his face, the expressions of dumb shock on the Chosen surprising him. "The Child-God had been sent to learn our ways, but his true purpose for being with us revealed itself later."

"What happened," whispered Bridget. Caught in the spell of the storytelling, her blue eyes widened.

She reminded Thanatos of a child being told a bedtime story, and he smiled. "Now that I and the other children were initiated, we were moved to another building where we were to live, study and work together for the next three years."

"What happened to the boy?" interjected Notus.

"He came to be housed with us. The High Priestess ordered he be treated the same as any of the other children. Of course, theory could not translate into practice, especially with awestruck children…"

Ta'ano's tears had left streaks on his face. The bundle of belongings clutched in his arms as he followed the other new initiates at a distance. He could not join in the celebration, nor the musings as to who would become High Priestess or High Priest after Cha'kata. His heart mourned his mother.

A few paces back, the Child-God shuffled, following the others to their new life and responsibilities. Clad only in the shimmering silver tunic and trousers, the youth walked with arms crossing his chest. No items filled his slender, pale arms.

A hiccoughing sob caught Ta'ano's attention and he slowed his pace until he walked side by side with the Child-God. In the torch lit hallway, long argent strands reflected bronze. Ta'ano wondered what the Child-God would look like under the light of day.

"Come on, children," called Appe from far ahead. He stood by the wood-lintled door, the heavy lid tacked back against the white washed clay walls. A torch trembled in his hand. "We do not have all night. Tomorrow is a new day and it is quickly approaching."

Ta'ano sped up his pace, but at the Child-God's lack of speed, Ta'ano slowed down to keep abreast of the silver boy.

One by one, boys and girls entered through the door until Ta'ano halted by Appe, in concert with the Child-God.

"Go on in and find a place for your bed." Appe lifted his grizzled chin to indicate the two should enter.

Without glancing up at the old man, the Child-God stepped across the threshold with Ta'ano at his heel, and winced.

The large rectangular clay formed room flickered between light and shadow as sconce torches illuminated the room. A single, well-worn path led from the door to the back of the room. On either side, delineated by hip high clay walls, cordoned off sleeping quarters filled with excited children settling into their new home. Three rooms at the back remained unoccupied. With a resolute sigh, Ta'ano walked to the first available space on the right and placed his items on the slight rise meant for his bed. He ignored the other children's glances as he set up his pallet.

"Good night, children," called Appe as he left, swinging the hide door closed behind him.

With nowhere else to go, the Child-God walked to the end of the dormitory and into the empty room next to Ta'ano's.

The room settled into silence as all watched with unease as the silver boy leaned against the white wall and slid down to hug his knees to his chest. As Ta'ano slipped into his bedroll, he tried to keep his eyes from the Child-God. Clutching the grass doll that his mother had made him, Ta'ano quietly cried himself to sleep as the torches guttered out.

The sound of sobbing drew Ta'ano from the murky depth of sleep. At first, he thought he made the cries, but as sleep fled, he realized it came from someone else. The abject cries wrenched Ta'ano's heart, the misery evoking his own. Slipping from his bed, Ta'ano used the dull light filtering from the edge of the door to guide him to the room beside his own.

His eyes widened at the shadowed sight of the Child-God weeping uncontrollably, in the same position as before. Tears filled Ta'ano's eyes. He had lost his mother, but his people had exiled this Child-God. The thought stunned Ta'ano and moved him to action.

Quietly, he stepped over to kneel in front of the silver boy. Laying a hand on a pale arm, Ta'ano was shocked at how cold the boy was. It dawned on him that the silver boy had no bedding and none had been provided. Frowning, Ta'ano decided to take matters into his own hands. He wiped the tears from his face before taking a cold pale hand in his and stood.

Surprise lifted red rimmed blood coloured eyes.

"Come on," tugged Ta'ano, lifting the Child-God to his feet.

In the darkness, Ta'ano led the tall, silver boy to his pallet. He slipped in between the furs and motioned for the silver boy to join him. Slim shoulders slumped and Ta'ano helped the boy into the bedding until they both were on their sides, their bodies spooned together.

The Child-God said something in the language of the Gods, and squeezed Ta'ano's hand encircling the silver boy's slim waist.

Ta'ano could not believe what he had done. The petal softness of the tunic and the scent of flowers from the argent strands resting near his face chased Ta'ano into sleep.

*   *   *

"Well done, my dear boy," said Appe. His twig-like form, clad in a simple sand coloured robe, stood in the doorway to Ta'ano's cubicle. A smile increased the crevasses in the old man's features and displayed the gaps in his teeth. Brown hair hung in ropes, framing a bald pate.

Blurry-eyed, Ta'ano tried to roll onto his back, but found he could not. The silver boy's mellifluous breath warmed against his neck. Sometime in the middle of the night, the Child-God had turned around, curling his body around Ta'ano's.

"Wake up." Ta'ano used his free hand to shake the Child-God's pale shoulder and winced as the silver boy rolled onto his back, eyes fluttering open. Arm pinned beneath the taller boy's head, Ta'ano tried to pull his numb limb free. The motion startled the Child-God, bolting him into a sitting position. Crimson eyes wide took in the surroundings.

Freed from his bedmate's heavy head, Ta'ano grasped his tingling arm to his chest and grimaced as he wiggled feeling back into red digits. With the covers pooled at his waist, Ta'ano sat up, worry clenching his stomach with what Appe must think.

"I'm sorry, Appe," he stuttered. "He was—"

"It's well and good." Appe waved the apology away and directed his next words to the disheveled silver boy. "Good morning, Blessed One."

The Child-God looked up at the old man, clearly not understanding, and squinted. Light from the morning sun flowed in through the windows unnoticed from the previous night. Tan coloured leathers, pulled back and tacked away from small square holes in the wall opposite from the dormitory's entrance, revealed the light of morning. Ta'ano rubbed the sleep from his eyes and sat up. All around stood the other children, their eyes wide at seeing their friend sharing a bed with the Blessed One.

In the dust moted light of day Ta'ano took in the features of the Child-God. What he first thought was moon coloured hair, now took on a shimmering quality similar to the scales of a fish, and the Child-God's skin appeared even paler. Glittering eyes, the colour of spilled blood, teared in the miniscule radiance.

"It's time for first meal and then to your lessons." Appe clapped his hands and turned, shooing the onlookers to make their morning ablutions.

Ta'ano carefully extricated himself from the bed and stood up. Shaking feeling into his hand, he was about to turn and join the other new initiates when he noticed that the Child-God still sat in bed, shoulders slumped in dejection. Ta'ano knew he could not leave him there alone.

Returning to the bed platform, Ta'ano knelt before the silver boy and bent to gaze up into the beautiful forlorn features. "It's alright," he said with a smile. "I'll take care of you."

Poppy coloured eyes met his and Ta'ano took the Child-God's cold hands in his own, lifting him to stand as he rose to his feet. Despite the constriction around his heart at the loss of his mother, Ta'ano knew she would be happy to know he cared for the Child-God Appe called Blessed One. Taking care of someone else also would be a distraction from his sore heart.

Still dressed from the night before, they wound through the maze-like complex. Ta'ano, hand in hand with the Blessed One, made their way to the kitchen where Ta'ano picked up two pottery bowls from a stack beside the cook-fire burning in the corner of the building. Hanta, Mistress of the Hearth, smiled at him as she knelt beside the glowing embers, stirring the contents of the cook-pot. Sunlight from a hole in the roof above the cook-fire spilled down to wash her dark curling hair and sun bronzed skin in brilliance.

"Good morning, Ta'ano." She bowed her head. "Congratulations on your initiation. Your mother must be pleased." She scooped a dollop of boiled cracked oats and dried berries into one bowl. "Oh, don't cry. Be proud. Not everyone is Chosen. It is a great honour. You'll see her again. If that weren't true, her body would have been discovered in the fields."

Ta'ano sniffed back unbidden tears and wiped away the moistness on his face. He had not meant to burst into tears at the mention of his mother, and his embarrassment reminded him why he held the second bowl.

Turning around, Ta'ano saw the silver boy standing in the

corner beside the door. His pale arms crossed his chest and his head turned away from the awe filled visages of the other breakfast goers.

"May I?" asked Hanta, taking the empty bowl from Ta'ano.

Before Ta'ano could offer an answer, Hanta filled the bowl, walked over to the Child-God and prostrated herself before him while holding up the steaming bowl to the silver boy.

Panicked scarlet eyes sought out Ta'ano. Surprised at the Child-God's lack of understanding, Ta'ano motioned that the silver boy should take the bowl. With unsure hands, the Child-God took the bowl and quickly moved to stand slightly behind Ta'ano.

Hanta rose and sat back on her feet. "Did I offend the Blessed One?" Worry drew downward lines across her forehead.

Ta'ano glanced over to the silver boy and back to the Mistress of the Hearth still on her knees. "I don't think so," ventured Ta'ano. It dawned on him that the other boy did not understand their words.

Ignoring the onlookers and Hanta's querulous gaze, Ta'ano led the silver boy out the far door and into the large courtyard filled with soft green grass, fig and date trees, their fruits already picked. Small children ran about while the new initiates sat together in twos and threes, their dark eyes flickering over to Ta'ano and the Blessed One. Appe sat beneath an olive tree, licking his fingers clean and conversing with older initiates. Though never Chosen to be High Priest, Appe was venerated for his Elder knowledge. At over sixty summers, Appe was the oldest member of their magnificent city.

About to join with a couple of his friends sitting in the sun in the middle of the courtyard, Ta'ano noticed their wide-eyed stares. Turning to face the Child-God, he could not deny the fear reflecting back at him. Not fully understanding the silver boy's trepidation, Ta'ano took him by the free hand and pulled him from the shadowed darkness of the kitchen into the brilliance of the late autumn morning.

The boy gasped, the light bringing immediate tears to his eyes. Silence detonated across the courtyard. Even Ta'ano halted at the sight. What Ta'ano saw beneath the diffuse sunlight from the dormitory paled in comparison. The shimmering cloth of the boy's tunic and trousers rippled and reflected like sun dancing on the big water, but it was his waist-length straight hair and fair skin that drew everyone to prostrate themselves. Never before had one of the Gods come down to stay with them, and never had they seen one so young as the Blessed One.

Ta'ano stood beside the silver boy, awestruck at the Child-God's astounding beauty. Shaking himself from his reverie, Ta'ano led his charge to a fig tree. In its welcoming shade, Ta'ano sat down, pulling the boy with him. The sound of shuffling and the return of voices indicated that all had returned to a semblance of normalcy. Ta'ano kept his eyes on the silver child as he lifted his bowl and dug into his breakfast with his fingers. It was the same first meal as all the others, but it could have been sand for all the attention to taste Ta'ano gave it.

Back against the cool bark and knees raised to his chest, the silver boy sniffed the contents of his bowl and placed it down on the dew dotted grass beside him. Encircling pale arms around his legs, the Child-God buried his face into his knees. Ta'ano's shoulders slumped at the boy's despondency.

"A word, Ta'ano?"

Ta'ano glanced up through the speckled sunlight to see Cha'kata resplendent in the robes of her new station. Rising quickly to his feet, bowl still in hand, he followed the High Priestess a few paces away to a secluded corner of the quadrangle. Gazes from the others burned into Ta'ano's back as if he did not wear the soft tanned leather tunic. Never before had he felt so naked, so exposed.

"I see you have shown the Blessed One great kindness," remarked Cha'kata. Her gaze lingered a moment on the Child-God under the fig tree before swiveling her attention back to Ta'ano. "I am happy you have done so. Do you plan to care for the Blessed One?"

Ta'ano glanced to the soft grass between their bare feet for a moment. Is that what he wanted? The tension in his gut relaxed as the answer came to him. Lifting his head to catch the High Priestess' brown eyes with his own, he nodded.

Cha'kata smiled. "Your mother would be proud. Since you've taken on this great responsibility, you need to know why he is here."

Ta'ano's eyes widened.

"Will you swear upon your Oath to the Gods that you will never reveal what I tell you? For if you do, I will order your blood to flow to nourish the fields."

Ta'ano's eyes felt as though they would jump from their sockets, his mouth open nearly as wide. Closing his mouth in surprise, he quickly blinked the sudden dryness from his eyes. What had he gotten himself into? Doubtful that he could back out now, he wondered what would become of the argent haired boy if he did. Slowly, he nodded. "I swear."

Cha'kata's smile widened to show perfect white teeth in her dark bronze face. Placing her slender, warm hands on his shoulders, she leaned down to whisper in his ear. "He is a gift, a promise between the People and the Gods. Through him, those Chosen will be able to walk beside us in the daylight *and* beside the Gods. It has been foretold that as our kind spread and take over this world, the Gods will retreat into theirs. When They do, he will be the one left so that the Chosen remaining can live in the light."

The news stunned Ta'ano and he turned his head to view the frightened child under the tree. *Him?*

A gentle hand touched Ta'ano's chin and he turned his face back to view Cha'kata's brown eyes a hand's span away from his. "This means we will all be blessed by the return of those who were Chosen, including your mother."

Could this be true? Did this mean he would see his mother sooner than originally believed? He glanced back at the Child-God. The sight evoked his sadness and loss. He would take care of this silver boy, but not for the reasons Cha'kata believed. He would do it because, in his heart, Ta'ano wanted to see how beautiful the boy could be if he smiled. "I'll be his friend," he whispered more to himself than to answer the High Priestess.

Cha'kata patted his shoulder. "Your mother would be so proud."

Ta'ano did not hear her as he turned to walk back to his new, lost friend.

*   *   *

Ta'ano's concern about the Blessed One continued to grow throughout the day. Whenever possible, the silver boy avoided being out in direct sunlight, always preferring the shade trees and buildings provided. When the new initiates were given a finger's breadth of time to play and swim in the freshwater lake, the Child-God trembled, shook his long shock of silken hair, and fled to the shade of a fisherman's lean-to.

By the time the sun lowered to the western horizon, the Blessed One had refused all meals and drinks, growing more sullen as the day headed towards its death. The only instance that appeared to catch the silver boy's interest was Appe's first lesson teaching the new initiations the language of the Gods.

Upon noticing the Blessed One's attentiveness, Appe had tried to engage him into assisting with the lesson. Unfortunately, it had the opposite effect, driving the silver boy into reclusive shyness.

When it was time to retire for the balmy night, Ta'ano slipped out of his still damp tunic and crawled into bed. The sounds of the other children following suit and the buzz of night insects from beyond the closed windows, tugged at his drowsy head. Before the last torch guttered out, Ta'ano watched the silver boy remove his shimmering tunic and trousers. Red touched the Child-God's exposed skin, making the pale flesh seem the colour of snow. Turning on his side, Ta'ano welcomed his new friend into bed.

The following three days continued the same course, driving Ta'ano's concern further with each meal and offered drink that was denied by his friend. How long could a God go without sustenance? The question drove home a more important one: what did a God eat?

The evening held the bite of upcoming winter, the chill held at bay by the three evenly spaced fires in the courtyard. Initiates and apprentices mingled, pottery bowls filled with nourishing stews and flatbreads to soak up the juices in hand. Ta'ano walked from the warm kitchen out into the indigo canopied quadrangle, the light from the sconce torches and the fires leading his way. Rounds of flatbread under each arm and bowls held in both hands, Ta'ano walked over to the silver boy sitting under what had become their fig tree. Tonight Ta'ano would make the Child-

God eat.

Placing the bowls down on the grass in front of the silver boy, Ta'ano sat. Again, as always, the Blessed One rested his back against the tree with legs drawn up to his chest and arms circling long legs.

Ta'ano released an annoyed huff. "You have to eat," he stated. Lifting a round of bread, he broke it in half and shoved one half into a silver hand.

Red eyes glowered over knees and the Blessed One let the bread fall to the grass.

Frustration built, puckering Ta'ano's face. Picking up the half round and taking a cool delicate hand in his own, Ta'ano shoved the bread back into the silver boy's hand. "You need to eat." Anger seeped into his tone.

The Child-God scowled and tossed the bread, sending it spinning over a group of young apprentices, to land against the back of a young man enjoying his meal with a pretty young woman. Silence thundered across the courtyard as all eyes turned to watch the spectacle evolving with the Blessed One.

Ta'ano, fully aware of their prominence on the green, tried to ignore the stares. Embarassment flushed his face as he stood, hands on his hips, to glower down at the silver boy. "How dare you throw and waste food!" he admonished.

A collective gasp rode a wave of disbelief through those in the courtyard. Never before had one of the People taken such a tone with one of the Gods.

"You have to have something or you're going to die!" Ta'ano did not realize his voice had risen in frustrated anger until he heard the last syllable bounce off the walls and back to him.

Angry crimson eyes glared up at Ta'ano. Rising to stand, the Blessed One took in the shocked visages of those around. Fury fled to be replaced by mortification. Eyes welling, the silver-haired boy fled the quadrangle, knocking Hanta back from her perch in the doorway to the kitchen.

Surprised at the speed and the reaction of the Child-God, Ta'ano could not hinder a burrowing of fear.

Go after him, a voice cried out in his mind.

Without further instigation, Ta'ano dashed after his friend.

Through the brightly lit corridors of the complex, Ta'ano followed as fast as his feet and the architecture would allow, until he knew where he was being led. It came to no surprise when he crashed into the dormitory.

Skidding on bare feet, Ta'ano saw that he had blocked off the only exit and relaxed as much as his anger would allow.

In the centre, moving to the back, the silver boy looked for an escape and found none. Turning, he faced Ta'ano, eyes wide.

Ta'ano did not notice the thick rising mist enveloping the room and it's now hidden contents as he stepped forward to deal with his petulant charge. Anger shook Ta'ano. He had failed his task. Worse, he had done so in front of everyone. Tears of frustration and shame trailed down his face.

By the time he stood in front of the Child-God, Ta'ano still had not noticed that the vapours had risen to his waist, his brown eyes locked onto red.

"How could you do that?" bellowed Ta'ano. He came within a hand's-breadth of the silver boy. "After all we've done for you— after all I've done for you! Do you realize what you've done to me?"

Red rimmed Ta'ano's sight. Here was the reason why his mother was taken away from him. Standing before him was a God who did nothing to ease his aching heart, especially after all Ta'ano had done for this silver child. With a roar, Ta'ano raised his hand, eyes a blur with tears, and threw a punch at the beautiful boy's face.

His anger evaporated as the Child-God caught the fist in his hand and yanked Ta'ano into an embrace.

Ta'ano did not know what happened. One moment he and the Blessed One stood in their dormitory, and then a wash of vertigo gripped him. When it released, he stumbled back from the Child-God to find they were in the middle of an expanse filled with tall, wild grass, the city nowhere to be found. Under the broad canopy of the clear night, brilliant stars illuminated the Child-God, lighting him up in silver. In the distance, the sounds of leopards and a herd of large deer gained prominence over the buzz of insects and the calls of fellow nocturnal creatures.

Terror gripped Ta'ano as he spun around to face the darkness, pounding the blood through his ears. Panic stricken, he turned back to face the Blessed One. Where were they? Was this punishment? New tears filled his eyes. "Please! Please! I'm sorry. So sorry," pleaded Ta'ano, hands coming together in supplication and tears flowing down his face. "I didn't mean to get so angry. I didn't mean to try and hit you. Please. I want to go home."

Ta'ano could not see through his tears, but felt a brush of silken hair flutter against his shoulders as the Blessed One leaned down to rest his cool forehead against his. Supple chilled arms came up and around Ta'ano, the comforting gesture releasing a torrent of grief and misery from Ta'ano.

He did not know how long they stood there, his hands clutched onto the soft fabric of the Child-God's tunic, weeping and held in the silver boy's embrace. Gradually, Ta'ano's cries became hiccoughs as the fit came to an end. He felt the Child-God's head come to rest on his shoulder. Even the Blessed One's breath felt chill as he sighed onto Ta'anos neck.

Instinct or intuition shocked Ta'ano to stand perfectly still as the Child-God nuzzled his neck. Unsure and more than a little afraid, Ta'ano's breath came faster, his eyes widening at the sensation of icy soft lips playing across his neck.

A sharp pain, as if something cut into his throat, drew a hoarse gasp from his lips. What was the Blessed One doing? The thought fled at the fierce sucking pressure on his neck that sent shocks of pain tinged pleasure through Ta'ano's body.

High above, the stars twinkled as they stood witness, but Ta'ano could not see them as their brightness faded from sight. The sound of suckling chased him into a dark void.

Over dry, crusty eyes, Ta'ano's heavy lids opened. The attempt to swallow the bolus of dust in his mouth failed as he took in his surroundings.

He was back at the dormitory, on his palette, lying on his left side. There was no sign of the silver boy. Had everything been a dream?

He tried to rise but his listless body would not respond. A cool hand reached around Ta'ano's midsection as a mellifluous breath sussurated a shushing sound into his ear. A body pressed him from behind, the comforting embrace lulling him back to slumber

"Careful with the bowl."

Appe's quavering baritone pierced the silence, shocking the darkness into throbbing pain. The warm lip of pottery pressed against Ta'ano's mouth and he opened his eyes as the meaty taste of broth danced across his tongue. Despite the stinging torchlight, the flavor of the soup exploded his thirst and he raised his hands to grip the bowl.

"Slowly. Slowly, lest he sicken."

Ta'ano moaned his displeasure as the pottery left his lips, dribbles of broth trailing down his chin. He gazed up to see Appe standing above him. Who cradled him and held the bowl?

Turning his head, Ta'ano could make out the worried features of the Blessed One. The pounding between his ears roared to life and he could not catch his breath. Vertigo chased him into darkness.

It was not the thirst or the gut gripping hunger that pulled Ta'ano from unconsciousness, but the deep ache that permeated every fibre in his body. Opening his eyes, Ta'ano pushed himself, with trembling arms, up to sitting, the bed coverings slipping to his lap. Goose bumps blossomed across unclad skin and he pulled the warm covers as high as they could.

No sounds came from the dormitory and Ta'ano turned his aching body and nearly jumped out of his skin. Beside the palette, on the floor, sat the silver haired boy, his legs pulled tight to his chest. In a rush, the memory from the night on the plains slammed forward. He slapped a hand to his healed neck, brown eyes wide.

"You bit me!" The words flew from Ta'ano before he could retract them.

Blood coloured eyes peered fearfully over bended knees.

Ta'ano ignored the distressed expression on the pale boy's

face. "You fed off my blood!"

The Child-God winced as Ta'ano's voice rose until the last word rang off the stone walls.

A grumbling sound filled the awkward silence that followed. Ta'ano gripped his midsection. When had he last eaten? He glanced back at the watery crimson eyes, understanding eliciting nausea. If Blessed One's fed on blood, then when had the Blessed One last eaten? It suddenly made sense to why the silver boy refused Hanta's delectables. It also begged the question as to what became of his mother.

Swiveling around, the Child-God brought forward a covered clay fired pot and a strangely shaped stick. Shifting to a cross-legged position, the silver haired boy laid the items on the floor before Ta'ano. "S—sorry."

The proclamation stunned Ta'ano, but it was the sound of the Blessed One's beautiful voice that dropped Ta'ano's jaw. Never before had he heard anything so alluring and rich, and the Blessed One was a child.

The silver boy pushed the bowl and the strange stick closer to Ta'ano. His long, straight hair hid the abashment on his exquisite face. "S—sorry," he said again.

"You speak our language?" Ta'ano glared at the Child-God once he recovered his shock. "Why didn't you say som—"

The silver boy shook his head, clearly not understanding. Tears overflowed down his pale face and he made a move to retrieve his offering.

Ta'ano closed his eyes and groaned at his stupidity. Reaching over, he opened his eyes to meet blood coloured ones, his hands coming to rest over the Blessed One's. "I'm sorry."

The pot warmed Ta'ano's hands once silver-pale ones relinquished the item into Ta'ano's care. Placing it onto his lap, Ta'ano lifted the ceramic lid. An explosion of scent tore a growl from Ta'ano's stomach and set his mouth watering. Thick, rich meat stew wafted steam to his nose. Juice soaked grains puffed, vying for space with the slices of softened root vegetables.

Without ceremony, Ta'ano lifted the bowl to his lips and was about to shovel the meal into his mouth, willing to burn his fingers so as to enjoy the taste, but halted. The silver boy had

THANATOS

elevated the strange stick that had a small bowl carved into one end. Curious, Ta'ano lowered the pot, cradling its warmth against his stomach with one hand and took the stick with the other.

It was light, and the rounded end with the shallow bowl looked peculiar, but the intricate carvings along the shaft widened Ta'ano's eyes. Images of flowers and vines rose from the round part to the hilt, spiraling white heartwood against dark bark. Ta'ano glanced back at the Child-God's expectant expression.

"Did you make this?" Ta'ano could not keep the awe from his voice.

The Blessed One frowned, not understanding.

Worry washed through Ta'ano. If the Child-God had made this for him, then Ta'ano did not want to hurt the silver boy's feelings. No doubt remained about the Child-God's repentance, but what was this stick?

Long, cool fingers took the stick from Ta'ano as the silver boy came to kneel before Ta'ano. Ta'ano watched the Blessed One dip the rounded end of the stick and lifted sauce and meat in its bowl. Ta'ano's eyes widened. He no longer had to eat with his fingers. Taking the food-laden stick, he popped the food into his mouth.

"Thank you." Ta'ano smiled around the mouthful.

"Our friendship grew," continued Thanatos, having finally sat down in his chair. "The Blessed One learned our language, our ways, and I learned his. Numerous times others would attempt to get to know him, to become his friend. After all, who wouldn't want to befriend a God, but he never allowed it. In the end, I spoke for him, very similarly to what I'd see a Blessed One do with the High Priestess. He'd whisper in my ear and I would have to repeat it. I was the only one he'd allow to hear his voice.

"This also took me outside the relationships I had made before he came and my mother was Chosen. At first, I minded, grating against the growing void between my friends and me, but before too long I relished this strangely elevated position and the close bond he and I developed.

"I was the one who he pulled with magic from the city every

Karen Dales

so often so that he could hunt to feed, always bring back his kills to Hanta to cook. He never once fed on me.

"Years went by. He taught me how to hunt, and after the kill, we would bathe in the lake. It must have been the same lake, but we were far enough away so as not to see the torchlights from the city. Only I was privy to see the Blessed One smile, laugh, and to hear his voice. He became my best friend, and on the night he fed from me again, we became lovers."

XVI

T a'ano's back arched against rough sand. He could not hear the soughing of the beach, only the blood rushing through his body, igniting tingles of pleasure. Cool lips pressed once more against his, and he opened his mouth in invitation as his hands raked up a supple, chill back. Shocks of desire ran down his spine, his tongue caressing the invader's.

Forcing the hungry mouth from his, Ta'ano gasped for breath, his eyes opening to smile up at the Blessed One. The flickering light from the campfire beside them tinted the dangling silver braids orange, his lover's face more beautiful than the night sky.

"I do need to breathe," smirked Ta'ano.

Crimson eyes fluttered from gazing at Ta'anos, to his lips, and back again. "No, you don't." The Blessed One's lust filled growl precipitated another hungry feeding on Ta'ano's more than willing mouth.

Hips rising in an attempt to reach up and press his body against pale flesh, Ta'ano moaned, his erect, throbbing rod desperate for release. He knew that his lover teased him. Ta'ano had no doubt he would pay him back. The Blessed One's stiffened member pressed against Ta'ano's thigh, a pale promise of what awaited.

Karen Dales

"I want you," gasped Ta'ano between kisses.

He felt the Blessed One shift, pressing his tall form against Ta'ano. His rod trapped and pressed between them was almost too much to bear.

"I need you," growled the Silver God, his mouth nuzzling Ta'ano's neck.

The sound pulled a gasp from Ta'ano's throat, his hips pressing up, his staff threatening to burst from the sensation of cool, hard flesh. He wanted,—no, needed—the Blessed One to take him, consume him. The chilled mouth sucked at Ta'ano's neck, the scrape of sharpened teeth promising more.

"Please," begged Ta'ano, his hands reaching to pull the Blessed One even closer. The sensation of strong, supple muscles added to his desire and he pumped his hips again.

So close. He was so close.

The Blessed One shifted and Ta'ano sighed as his lover entered him. This was bliss, and he gazed up at the most beautiful creature in the world.

Poppy coloured eyes remained closed as the God moved, taking pleasure in Ta'ano's body. The expression on his pale face sent tremors racing from Ta'ano's centre, his member throbbing in anticipation of what was yet to come.

The Silver God drew out and forcibly pounded in, tearing a cry from Ta'ano as sun browned legs wrapped around slender pale hips. Again, the thrust came with almost painful force. Ta'ano did not try to hold back his cries, his hands grasping the Blessed One's stabilizing arms. Another thrust threatened to consume Ta'ano, his back arching with each blissful intrusion. His staff was so hard, it was almost too painful to bear.

Ta'ano did not know how long they moved together. All that existed was sensation, inside and out, but there was one thing missing. The thought of his lover sinking his shell white teeth into his neck loosed what little control he had. His orgasm thundered through and over him, spasming his body as he screamed his pulsating release.

Past the pinnacle, his body still shuddering out its seed, the Blessed One's body pressed against his. Teeth bit deep into Ta'ano's neck and pulled a renewed thunderous orgasm.

A throbbing not his own, coupled with the pressure on his neck, caused Ta'ano to moan. Shudders ran under Ta'ano's fingers, the Blessed One taking his pleasure from Ta'ano's willing body. Time stretched out until the Blessed One pulled out to lay beside Ta'ano's languor filled form, his seed staining them both.

"You taste sweet," smiled the Silver God. His head propped on his hand. Rows of long, thin braids mingled and lay on the sand.

"You taste salty," grinned Ta'ano, mischievousness pinching his brown eyes. Oh, how he loved those blood coloured orbs.

"I was talking about your blood." The God lifted a handful of sand and slowly spilled it on Ta'ano's belly below his navel.

"I wasn't." Ta'ano's smile widened.

The fall of sand halted. It was signal enough. Ta'ano rolled over on top of the God, his face a hand's breadth over the stunning features, gazing into twin pools of blood. "I love you, *kreidad.*" Ta'ano used the God's word for 'beloved,' his expression serious.

A sparkle ignited the Blessed One's eyes and he lifted his head, planting a kiss on Ta'ano's lips. "You are mine," replied the God in his own language.

"Again?" grinned Ta'ano, alluringly.

"Can't you give a God a rest?" teased the Blessed One.

"I wouldn't imagine a God would require rest, especially from this," beamed Ta'ano.

The ravishing Silver man rolled his eyes before becoming serious. "There's only so much I'm willing to take. I won't endanger you."

Cool arms wrapped themselves around Ta'ano, and he lowered himself to rest atop his lover's supine form. His ear pressed to the silky smooth skin. The slow pulsation of the God's heartbeat invoked a lassitude through his body.

"I don't want this to ever end," muttered Ta'ano. His warm breath blew the pale nipple before him erect.

"I don't think there's a chance of that," sighed the Blessed One.

Ta'ano raised his head and found sad eyes staring back at him. "What do you mean?"

"Tomorrow night. Have you forgotten?"

Brown eyes widening, Ta'ano's gut clenched. How could he have forgotten?

Cha'kata had served as High Priestess for nine years. Tomorrow the Blessed One would come to Choose her, but not before she picked her successor. Rumor whispered that Ta'ano would be picked, but it was gossip, and such things were often untrue, he hoped.

"I won't be picked," mumbled Ta'ano. Laying his head back down on his lover's chest, surprise caught him as the Blessed One slipped upwards to sit. Rocking back on his knees, Ta'ano sat between two long, sensuous legs, the Silver God's rod flaccid in a nest of argent silk. If it were not for the serious expression on the Blessed One's face, Ta'ano would have tested his lover's desires.

"How can you not be picked?" The Blessed One brushed waist length argent braids away from his incredulous face.

"I don't want to hear this." Ta'ano tried to turn away, but halted at a touch on his arm. A sinking feeling threatened to pull him under.

"Ta'ano you are the son of a High Priestess, Chosen by the one who sired you." Pools of blood bored into watery brown. "You were the only one willing to befriend and care for an out—a lost child of the Gods. You excel at every task, and others naturally look to you for leadership. Who better to serve than you?"

Ta'ano's shoulders slumped, hating the truth ringing his ears. "It'll change everything."

"I know." The Blessed One pulled in his legs to sit cross-legged.

Ta'ano gazed up hopefully. "Maybe you can—"

"No," said the Blessed One, a little too harshly before quickly softening his tone. "I'm too young, and the wrong sex."

The realization that part of the duties as High Priest would be to lay with a Goddess to establish his position, not to mention, to share his seed with willing priestesses at the appropriate rites, stunned him.

"No! I won't!" He rose to stand and walked to the other side of the fire. The constant lapping of the water against beach roared discordantly in his ears. Spinning around, he faced his love. "I love you. I want only you."

The Blessed One rose to his feet, the dying firelight flickering off his moon touched flesh. Standing head and shoulders over Ta'ano, he took Ta'ano in an embrace. "I love you too, but we both have responsibilities and duties to our peoples."

Ta'ano's tears dappled the pale chest as he clung tightly. "Promise me one thing."

"Anything, *kreidad*," answered the Blessed One.

"Promise me that you'll be the one to Choose me when my time comes."

"There's never been any doubt."

"I served as High Priest for nine long years. I did the best I could. When I beheld the Blessed One, her wavy chestnut hair falling to her knees and her large verdant eyes stunning me to the quick, I knew then what it was to be in the presence of a Goddess. Never before, and never since, had I seen such a beautiful woman. I went with her reluctantly, the pain in the Silver God's eyes following me.

"I can't tell you wonders I experienced in her arms. Cha'kata went through the veil and my beloved witnessed it all, trying to be happy for me even though I knew is heart was breaking.

"Cha'kata's body was discovered in the fields the next morning. Her passing hit all very hard. Only Appe could recall the last time a Choosing failed. Many of the elder priesthood weren't surprised. For Cha'kata's nine years as High Priestess the yields from the fields diminished each year. Cha'kata, herself, bore no children. A fallow High Priestess meant fallow fields.

"It was a day of great celebration when copious green shoots blossomed in the fields after the first planting in spring. Even more cause to celebrate was the finding of my daughter from the Goddess amongst the shoots. Da'ana was taken to be raised to become High Priestess, as I had been taken to become High Priest. I was her sire, because of the rites, bestoing many siblings upon her.

"If my heart had not been given to the Silver God, I'm sure I would have reveled in the visceral duties I performed, as well as my clerical. Regardless, the obligations put a heavy strain upon

Karen Dales

our relationship. More often than naught he would go out to hunt alone. The times I joined him were filled with hurried passion, the obligations of my station hanging guillotine over us. We knew it would be so, but living the reality proved more difficult.

"My Blessed One became more distant over the years, our only time together being when we shared our bed in my private quarters. Many a night I had energy enough to lay in his arms, falling asleep during my retelling of the day's events. I knew this added to the tension between us. He had great difficulty sharing me with the people and the Gods I served.

"Nine years rolled by. The harvests out did each from the previous year. The People grew fat for the first time in generations, and in each furrow I planted my seed new life sprung. The people were rich and there was talk of breaking tradition so as to keep me in office for another nine years.

"I watched my beloved walk out of the courtyard where this discussion was made formal. Witnessing the hurt in his eyes and feeling the boulder in my gut was enough. I gave the priests and priestesses the reasoning that tradition must be followed or what we hold dear and sacred would become meaningless. We couldn't break from our pact with the Gods. It was enough to end that discussion."

Ta'ano nervously paced his lamp-lit chamber, the Blessed One sitting on the bed, watching without a word. Tonight Ta'ano would pick someone to replace him before being taken away to be Chosen by the Goddess, if she did not allow his Silver God providence over this. The Silver God issued a defeated sigh and slumped his shoulders. The sound halted Ta'ano and he turned to face his love. This should be a happy time, but Ta'ano felt trepidation. After tonight, there was a distinct possibility he would no longer be with his beautiful God. The thought gripped his stomach, churning his watery gut.

"It's time."

The young initiate stood in the open doorway, his long white robe brushing past his knees.

"Thank you, Amuno. We'll be out presently." Ta'ano

dismissed the handsome young man and turned to face the Silver God. "We should go."

The mist thickened around the assembly at the holy site outside the city. Ta'ano allowed his gaze to flicker onto his daughter, Da'ana, before skimming across the other children. How many of them had he sired? He shook that thought away. Mothers maintained close ties with daughters and sons. Fathers became teachers, and for Ta'ano, as High Priest, he had to oversee all the young ones' education, amongst many other responsibilities. It meant little to no time to become close to any of his children, let alone his lover.

The Blessed One stood, shoulders hunched, beside Appe's age stooped form. The dejection on the Silver God's face nearly caused Ta'ano to forget his place in the ceremony. Turning to face the children, he followed the protocols long established and was not surprised as the Goddess stepped from the rent in the north.

Long flowing chestnut hair hung in a waving cloak down her back, accentuating her curvaceous form. The green of her diaphanous robe brought out the colour of springtime in her eyes. Ta'ano stifled a shudder as she came to stand by him, his sudden erection pressing tight against his belly, a traitor to his heart. Ta'ano glanced at his lover and found jealousy in those blood red eyes, enough to weaken lust's grip.

Throughout the ceremony, Ta'ano felt his lover's gaze caress his body. Even the Goddess noticed the stares, but ignored them, keeping her voice to Ta'ano's ears only.

Fear gripped Ta'anos gut. It was time to pick his replacement, and afterward he would depart with the Goddess to become one of the Chosen, leaving his beloved behind.

The next part moved in a haze with Ta'ano going through the ritual and selecting the religious leader of the People. Amuno would make an excellent High Priest part of him thought, but his eyes never left the Silver God even as he bestowed the oath.

"It is time to go," whispered the Goddess, her voice the sound of birds on a summer's breeze.

Despite all his years preparing for the moment, Ta'ano could not deny that he would give it all up to spend one more night in his lover's arms. What was his life in the pale expanse of his love's denial, and what of the Silver God? What would become of him amongst the People, all alone? Ta'ano shot the God a pleading look.

Red eyes widened with surprise before determination took over his pale features as he straightened his back. "No."

His voice shocked the assembly into silence. No one, except Ta'ano, had ever heard the Silver God speak. Stirrings of awe forced mutters from sun darken lips as the God stepped forward to face the Goddess standing shocked next to Ta'ano and Amuno.

"I will Choose Ta'ano," said the Silver God in the language of the Gods. He stood a hand's width taller than the Goddess, forcing her to look up at him.

"This is unprecedented," replied the Goddess, her voice a whispered hiss in the hopes to keep their voices low. "You are too young."

"Age does not matter," stated Ta'ano's lover, through clenched teeth.

Ta'ano could not believe it. His heart soared that his beloved wanted to bestow the gift upon him, breaking tradition to do so, and keeping his promise from that night so long ago.

"You are—"

"I know who and what I am." The Silver God cut the Goddess off. His features softened as his gaze fell upon Ta'ano. "I am the light in the darkness so that the Chosen can live in the world in service to the Gods. I am the one to end the service of those Chosen no longer meet to serve. I am the one, the only one, who can move from this world to the others with my will alone. Most importantly, I am the beloved of Ta'ano, High Priest of the People. Please. Allow one who loves Ta'ano to Choose Ta'ano." His crimson eyes pleaded to green.

A broad smile split the Goddess' stern features as she threw a hug around the Silver God. None were more stunned than Ta'ano. Amano, sheepishly grinning, had to tap Ta'ano on his chin to make the former High Priest close his mouth.

"Yes, my child," cried the Goddess. She stepped back, took

Ta'ano's hand and the Silver God's in hers. "We are so proud, for this is what being Chosen truly means. You have both Chosen well."

The rite concluded with the Goddess returning through the veil, leaving everyone stunned at the turn of events. Ta'ano did not register that Amano had left, dismissing the mystical fog and shooing all away so that the two lovers stood in the grove illuminated by glittering firelight. The setting full moon vied to tint them blue.

He was no longer High Priest of the People, and nor had he been taken to the realms of the Gods. All expectations fled into uncertainty that did not matter. His beloved Silver God stood beside him once more.

"Are you angry with me?"

Ta'ano stared up into the worried pale face. "Never, *kreidad*." His hands reached up through long, braided locks to grasp the cool neck, pulling his lover's lips to his own.

They lingered, tongues exploring one another until Ta'ano broke away to catch his breath. "What will happen now?"

"We go back to the city." Cool moon touched hands came to rest on Ta'ano's shoulders. Ta'ano could not mistake the seriousness in his lover's tone. "We pack, and we leave."

"Forever?" Ta'ano sucked in a breath. No one Chosen had ever returned to the People, but no one to be Chosen had ever stayed in the world of the People at the end of the Rite.

"I don't know," replied the God, solemnly.

"This is the place?" asked Ta'ano as he stepped from the mists.

"I could think of none better." The Silver God dismissed the vapors, revealing a rocky outcrop overlooking an expanse of water as far as the newborn sun could allow. Without further comment, and with his leopard skin bag over his shoulder, he climbed the white rock facing and disappeared.

"*Kreidad!*" called Ta'ano, scampering after his lover. The sun would soon scorch the pale God's skin. It was that thought which sent his heart a flutter in worry until he saw the tall form standing under the protective lip of a dark cave.

"Had you worried?" smirked the God.

Shaking his head, Ta'ano let out a huff and walked into his lover's arms. His head rested against the Silver God's bare chest. "I worry because I love you."

Ta'ano heard the deep rumbling chuckle and smiled. "Do you trust me?"

"Of course," replied Ta'ano, listening to the God's slow heartbeat.

They stood in each other's arms as the sun rose over the waters. "I would never have let her or any other Choose you," murmured the God.

Ta'ano tightened his embrace around his lover's waist, his heart soaring at the proclamation.

"You were mine the first time I fed from you."

"Don't you mean that you were mine," teased Ta'ano.

Another of the God's chuckle shook Ta'ano. "We were meant for each other."

Ta'ano stepped from the embrace to gaze up into his lover's eyes. "What happens now?"

A cool, pale hand caressed Ta'ano's sun darkened cheek, as intense blood coloured eyes bore into brown. "Go. Enjoy your last day, but make sure you're back by sundown."

A thrill of fear ran down Ta'ano's spine, but he quickly quashed the feeling before it expanded. Ta'ano trusted his God, his lover. Raising a hand, he captured the Silver God's hand as it slipped lower, pressing his face into cool flesh. "I want to stay." The husky words left his lips, desire dropping his tone.

Chill lips encapsulated his, igniting a need for more. Before Ta'ano could press the advantage, the Blessed One pulled back, a grin pulling at his full lips. "Not yet." His voice strained with desire. "I have much to prepare."

Ta'ano released a resigned sigh and lowered his gaze. There was no way he could win. Tonight his beloved would Choose him and, in the end, that was all that mattered. "I'll be back."

Heading to the exit of the cave, Ta'ano halted at the chill grip on his upper arm.

"Ta'ano, you know I love you," stated the Silver God.

Ta'ano nodded, turning back to gaze up at his lover.

THANATOS

"I want everything to be perfect for you."

Recognizing the Blessed One's desire, Ta'ano smiled. "I know. Don't worry. As soon as the sun touches the horizon I'll be back."

The frosty grip released him, and Ta'ano headed into the brilliant outdoors.

The sun had dipped below the horizon, streaking the sky in magenta and hews of blue, when Ta'ano climbed the white rocks leading to the cave. He had not meant to arrive so late. Bright stars pinpricked the overhead tapestry, heralding smaller, less luminous stars that splattered out from the thick belt marring the plum mottled indigo.

The moon had yet to rise, causing a tightness of worry in Ta'ano's gut, , but the yellow gloaming spilling from the cave's mouth gave ample illumination. Heart speeding in a mixture of trepidation and excitement, Ta'ano climbed the lip of the ledge and stepped into the cave.

His breath caught at the sight and tears welled in his cycs. Fresh cut flowers dotted and decorated the crevasses of the cave. Small clay pots sat on the floor and ledges, their fragrant oils scenting the space, while wicks flared and flickered. The transformed space's beauty struck Ta'ano dumb.

In a far corner of the cave, the Silver God turned from having lit another lamp. "You're back," he exclaimed, shaking the fire from the twisted grass taper.

"It's—this…this is beautiful," stammered Ta'ano.

The God stepped forward, careful of the small, flaming pots on the ground, a smile showing his perfect white teeth. "You like it?"

"I—I love it!" Ta'ano walked forward to meet his lover and raised his arms up to draw cool lips to his own. "Is this part of becoming Chosen?" asked Ta'ano once released from the kiss, but not the embrace.

Pleasure fell into concern on the Blessed One's face. "I don't know. I've never chosen anyone before and I've never seen the process either. I only know the mechanics."

"The mechanics?" Ta'ano cocked his head to the side.

"Before I was left with the People, I was told by the Lady…" The worried expression grew. "I was told what I could do and what I was not allowed to do."

"I don't understand."

The Blessed One released a sigh. "That first time, that night on the plains when I was so hungry that I almost killed you?"

"I remember." Ta'ano's voice softened with the memory.

"I was forbidden to feed on the People, Ta'ano." Crimson eyes bore into brown. "The People were not to find out what I hungered for, and thus what the other Gods fed upon."

Horror lit Ta'ano's visage. "Are the Chosen—"

"No!" The Blessed One turned away, his back straightened with indignation until broad pale silver shoulders slumped in defeat. "And yes."

"So my mother is dead?" exclaimed Ta'ano. Ne stepped around his lover, to face him.

"No. She's Chosen," he said, refusing to meet Ta'ano's eyes.

"I don't understand."

"Ta'ano, the Chosen are ones who serve the needs and the desires of the Gods. In return, they are given a great gift."

Ta'ano took a step back, nearly knocking an oil pot over. "What kind of gift?"

Their eyes caught.

"Immortality."

The word struck Ta'ano dumb.

"Not everyone the Gods take to be Chosen can accept the gift."

"Like Cha'kata," whispered Ta'ano, his voice strained.

"Like Cha'kata," nodded the Silver God.

"But what about me?" implored Ta'ano. "You've never Chosen anyone before. I don't want to die." Panic dried his mouth, pounding his heart between his ears.

"I would never let that happen." Cool hands landed on Ta'ano's shoulders. "You said you love me. Do you trust me?"

The statement sobered Ta'ano and he nodded. "With my life."

Relief washed over the tall, slender form of the God. "Then trust me now," he said, holding out his hand.

THANATOS

Ta'ano took his lover's hand in his and allowed himself to be led to a palette made of cured animal skins, their fur adding to the comfort, and woven blankets. Gentle hands removed Ta'ano's simple yellow woven tunic. Despite the burning lamps, Ta'ano hugged his naked form against his shivering nerves.

The Blessed One lowered to his knees beside the makeshift bed, drawing Ta'ano down with him. "Lie down."

Ta'ano did as bade, and once he lay supine, he gazed up at his lover, trying to still his nervous trembling.

In silence, the Silver God pulled out a lidded pot from beside a large, flaming lamp. "First to prepare your body," he said. "You will not change after this night, therefore this is important."

Ta'ano lay there, wincing every so often as his lover used the sticky substance from the jar to remove most of Ta'ano's body hair. Time moved slowly through the process until every part of his body tingled. He had never experienced such discomfort, but knew that many women—and some men—of the People engaged in the practice.

Sticky from the procedure, Ta'ano sat up once his lover indicated and stared down at his now hairless chest. All that remained was a dark nest between his smooth thighs. It felt strange. The breeze from the cave's mouth felt odd against his clean flesh.

A flash to his right caught Ta'ano's attention. A flint knife glimmered in a pale hand and he closed his eyes. Cool breath whispered for him to relax and he felt the blade against his throat. Slow, deft movements of the blade removed nearly two days beard growth. Not once did the stone blade bite deep enough to draw blood.

"I'll be almost as hairless as a boy," mused Ta'ano.

A clink of flint against stone declared the shearing complete. Ta'ano moved to stand, but halted as graceful fingers began to unplait his dark hair. The sensation sent shivers up and down his spine. Bolts of bliss shocked from his centre, stiffening his member to bob in need for attention.

"Not yet, beloved," teased the sultry voice behind him.

Ta'ano groaned. A splash of waist length hair, freed from its bond, caressed Ta'ano's back.

"How long do you want it?" queried the God.

ॐ 135 ॐ

"As long as you can become," growled Ta'ano.

"I meant your hair, silly," laughed the Blessed One.

Opening his eyes, Ta'ano turned to face his lover. "Why ask?"

Beautiful red eyes smiled. "Certain things cease growing when you become Chosen. Such as body hair. For some strange reason, head hair continues to grow, but extremely slowly. If you want it short, it will take many, many turns of the seasons before it is this length again."

A provocative curve lifted Ta'ano's lip. "Which would you prefer?"

"Long," replied the Silver God, huskily.

"Then leave it," smiled Ta'ano.

The Blessed One nodded, swallowing down his growing desire.

"What happens now?"

"I make you Chosen."

"Will it hurt?" The thought of the unknown procedure relaxed its hold on Ta'ano's rod and tightened his chest.

"Only if you want it to," replied his lover, playfully.

Ta'ano's eyes widened in surprise and he was about to say something when his lover's cool lips encapsulated his own. Opening his mouth, the God took the invitation and thrust his tongue into Ta'ano's mouth, greedily feeding desire.

Too early, his lover broke from the embrace. "Tonight you will experience mortal passion for the last time. Savour it well for tomorrow night we will experience each other in a new way."

Chill lips descended onto warm, devouring Ta'ano's passion with his own. The caress of fridgid limbs intoxicated Ta'ano and he gasped as cool lips trailed down the side of his mouth to tease the sensitive spots of his throat. Each sucking kiss pounded desire through his body. He wanted—no, needed—more.

Somehow, Ta'ano found himself on his back, eyes fluttering. Without the protectiveness of his body hair, each lick, each suckle, each kiss of his lover's cold lips send riots of need to pull through his body, stiffening his rod until it strained and throbbed.

He did not know how long his beloved's sharp teeth teased his neck, but nothing could compare to those lips, that tongue, that mouth, as his lover worked lower. Gentle kisses, plied against his bare chest, sent shivers racing and Ta'ano moaned as his beloved traced around each hardened nipple with cool lips.

The God made love to him and Ta'ano could not believe the sensations that sent his throbbing member to near painful rigidity. Suckling pressure worked down the centre of Ta'ano's abdomen, his lover carefully ensuring only his lips caressed Ta'ano.

Hands teaching to the silver braided tousle, Ta'ano attempted to guide the Blessed One lower, hips straining, his rod pulsating with the need to be touched, enveloped and released. His lover's deep throated chuckle against his upper abdomen sent a shock of pleasure to vibrate from the base of his shaft to its straining pinnacle.

So close to release, yet so far. Ta'ano cried out, hips straining to be taken. His lover worked his lips lower and when Ta'ano believed he would be encapsulated in the God's cool, moist mouth, the lips skirted to the inside hollow of Ta'ano's thigh.

A sob of desperate frustration brought tears to his eyes. How many times have they made lover over the years? None could compare to the attentiveness and shocking pleasures Ta'ano now experienced.

Kisses skirted so close to his stones, now drawn tight to his body. A glancing caress of his lover's cool cheek as he teased Ta'ano's throbbing shaft caught Ta'ano by surprise. He cried out, needing more. Tongue and lips halted their ministrations. So close, oh so close. Ta'ano panted from denied release.

Opening his eyes, Ta'ano watched his lover crawl up his body until the God supported himself to stare, face-to-face, over Ta'ano.

"Turn over," ordered the Blessed One. His voice filled with bridled desire.

In the lamp light, Ta'ano gulped. The naked lust on his lover's face quickened his breath. Glancing down between the space between their bodies, Ta'anos' rod reached up on its own accord to touch his lover's rigidity. He did not need to be told again. Tonight the God would ride him.

Turning over, Ta'ano raised up on all fours. The cool skin of his beloved ached the flesh along his back and with a quick thrust, Ta'ano cried out, impaled, filling him with the Blessed

One's need, and then they moved. Drawing apart, the warmth of the cave caressed his back as his lover reared up on his knees. Cold hands braced on Ta'ano's hips and pulled Ta'ano back onto his lover's rod, the pleasure forcing a cry from Ta'ano's throat.

Each thrust from his beautiful God threatened to send him to oblivion. Sweat slicked his body, their rhythm increasing, their cries and grunts growing more urgent. Ta'ano did not know how long he could last. The God played his body with expert precision.

Faster they moved, and Ta'ano found that he too now knelt, seated and supported by his beloved's arms. A cool hand encapsulated Ta'ano's engorged shaft and moved in opposition to the thrusting. Ta'ano could not last much longer. Eyes closed and head lolling back for a moment's rest before they pulled apart, only to drive together, Ta'ano sobbed.

"Now, Ta'ano. Now." His lover's voice growled, vibrating down his neck to resonate along his shaft.

His body rocked, the explosion of pleasure tearing a cry from his impassioned rough voice. The stinging sensation of his lover biting deep into his neck heightened the pulsating waves that continued, threatening to turn him inside out and leave him a dry husk.

A growl and a tug on his neck announced his lover's release deep inside his body. The sensation set off another orgasm that rocked Ta'ano. The sound of sucking continued, each draw of his blood into his lover's mouth pumped more seed from his weakening staff.

Vertigo snuck up, stealing the remaining pulsations, darkening the edges of his now open eyes. If it were not for the cool arms encapsulating him, Ta'ano would have slid bonelessly to the pallet. Weakness crashed over Ta'ano. A part of him feared what would happen if his lover did not halt his feeding, but another relished the fact that his beautiful God devoured him. It was that thought that followed him into the darkness.

He floated.

Darkness encapsulated Ta'ano and succored his weary self.

He did not care if he lived. All became bliss as he floated in an atramentous void.

A pin-point of light glittered in the darkness until the sight became all encompassing. Within the sphere, a garden of immense beauty prickled tears from Ta'ano's eyes. Nothing in his life had prepared him to witness such a vision. He wanted to go into it, to feel the lush grasses beneath his feet, the breeze along his skin and smell the scent of a riot of flowers.

Somehow, his desire translated into movement towards this heaven and halted as a white wispy object swam between him and the green expanse. Quizzical to the addition of other diaphanous creatures coalescing, Ta'ano moved forward once more.

"Come back, Ta'ano." A familiar voice called from everywhere. "Come back to me. Please."

Ta'ano recognized his beloved's desperation. Go back? Back to where?

"No. Please, don't leave me," sobbed the voice.

Leave? Where was he going?

Ta'ano returned his attention to the beauteous green garden, trying to ignore the strange white figures beginning to swarm around him.

"I need you," cried the voice.

The admission furrowed Ta'ano's brow.

The white creatures appeared to float closer to Ta'ano. The sight sent a chill of fear through him and he tried to spin away towards the voice.

"I can't live in this world without you," sobbed the voice.

The white creature floated closer, attempting to touch Ta'ano.

Ta'ano fled towards the voice.

"I love you," wept the Blessed One, cradling Ta'ano's placid form to his chest.

Consciousness poured into Ta'ano a moment before his body thundered a gasp, sending his silent heart pounding. Eyes popping open, Ta'ano scrambled out of his lover's embrace to all fours, limbs quivering.

"Easy. Easy."

A warm hand stabilized his trembling shoulder. Each breath became less ragged, regulating his fibrillating heart and easing the tingling pain from his fingers to the side of his head.

"Take slow, easy breaths."

Ta'ano followed his lover's instructions until his body calmed and he sat back on his haunches. Red rimmed the pools of crimson, the evidence of their flooded banks still glistening on pale skin. The realization that the Blessed One had been crying dried Ta'ano's mouth.

Shifting to sit on the floor, Ta'ano's eyes widened at the sight of the illuminated cave. What had appeared dull and uninteresting grey stone now glittered a billion stars. Each reflected flames that once glowed only orange, but now flickered a rainbow of colour. The deep dark of the back of the cave no longer hindered his sight.

Mouth hanging open and eyes wide, Ta'ano slowly rose to his feet, arms outstretched to take in a myriad of sensations. Tendrils of heat from flickering lanterns competed with cool sighs of the breeze gaining entry to their abode. A soughing from outside tickled his ears and he realized he heard the lapping of the water against the beach. Closing his eyes to concentrate, sounds he would never have heard mixed to create a new music.

Warm hands rested on his shoulders and he opened his eyes and smiled. His silver lover stood before him, affection glittering scarlet eyes. A braided length of argent hair caught Ta'ano's attention and he grasped the strand, his fingers flowing over the texture. What had once felt soft now ran silken, and what had appeared to have one colour now displayed many shades Ta'ano had never witnessed. He met the beauteous petals of his lover's eyes, mesmerized.

A shiver ran through Ta'ano as warm, gentle hands slid down his arms to grasp his hands. Warm thumbs caressed the back of his hands and Ta'ano's eyes widened further. "You're warm!"

Full lips pulled into a smile, announcing a chuckle that resonated through Ta'ano.

"Come."

A tug at both hands and the Blessed One led him out of the cave to stand at the entrance, midnight illuminated above.

"Look."

Ta'ano stared out across the expanse of the great water. Silver jewels danced upon the smooth surface. No longer black, the sea ran indigo, and the beach…Billions of granules shimmered from an unknown light. Small animals, crustaceans and insects filled the tract with life Ta'ano had never noticed before.

A spark of bright light streaking in the corner of his vision spun Ta'ano to gaze upwards. "Oh my…" gasped Ta'ano.

Nothing in his life had prepared Ta'ano for such a sight and he fell to his knees at the awesome, multi-faceted jewel that was the sky.

Stars that once had flickered in pinpoints now glowed and pulsated in colours he had never seen. The wash of milk that ribboned across the expanse had become a treasure trove of sparkling jewels. Every so often, a streak of fire heralded the ascent of new souls to the heavens. Never had Ta'ano witnessed such beauty.

The sight of the night sky became obscured by the argent brilliance of the Blessed One, his beautiful face lit with love.

"Am I Chosen?" whispered Ta'ano.

The silver smile widened to reveal perfect white teeth, upper incisors and canines long and pointed.

Ta'ano's hand flew to his mouth and felt similarly pointed teeth. The reality of his transformation stunned him. In all his years as an acolyte and then as an initiate, the honour of being Chosen by one's God remained a theory of possibility. No one knew what being Chosen truly meant. N one Chosen ever came back to the People. Ta'ano stood, his body inches from his beloved God, and gazed up at him. Questions swirled in his mind.

His lover's hand came up to run down the sides of Ta'ano's face, his forehead leaning to rest against Ta'ano's. *I have waited so long for this.*

The sound of his lover's voice resonating through his mind stunned Ta'ano and he pulled away as he stepped back. "How?"

The smile returned to light up the Blessed One's face. "You're Chosen," he explained. "My blood has given you new life, connecting us." He stepped forward, embracing Ta'ano. *I love you. Even had you not been chosen to be High Priest, I still would have Chosen you.* Warm lips descended to encapsulate Ta'ano's. *There is so much for you—and me—to discover.*

Ta'ano yielded to the intensity of the kiss and the emotions that rolled over him. Whatever he had thought of their previous lovemaking paled in comparison to the fearsome need they filled in each other, on the ledge between the night sky and the luminous cave.

XⅧ

The hut appeared as it had when he had lived there, except that his bed was not on the floor next to Auntie's palette. In fact, there was no sign of his existence in the place he had called home. The small, flickering fire in the hearth along the curving eastern wall held the only indication of life.

"This is before your time."

He spun around to find Auntie, still young and beautiful, sitting at a wooden table silvered with age. She appeared haggard, almost run down with her dark hair frazzled over top a face beset with exhaustion. Hands wrapped around a steaming wooden bowl did not provide comfort.

"Please, sit down." She relinquished the bowl and motioned for him to sit on the wooden bench opposite. "I had hoped that being in this place would put you at ease."

Sliding into place, he noticed that he no longer had an insubstantial form. His alabaster arms carried the scars and wear of centuries, the silvered starbursts on either sides of his wrists proving the testament of time.

A sun touched hand enclosed over his, bringing his attention to the woman who had raised him.

"I wish I could have seen you grow into the man you've become," said Llawela. She smiled sadly before lowering her gaze to the table between them. "How I wish I had found the courage in life to tell you what I now must, in death. Had I been unafraid of the truth, I could have spared you much pain. Now, the Ladies have given me another chance to set things right between us, between you and your heritage."

He frowned. For so long the truth remained a mystery. With what he most desperately wanted within arm's reach, uncertainty and fear tightened his chest. Releasing the breath he had not realized he held, he glanced down at the same spot on the table. "I had thought that Geraint was my father."

"For all intents and purposes, he was," replied Llawela. "By our laws, any child born to a married woman maintained her husband as the rightful father, regardless of who sired the child."

The knowledge humbled him, pulling the corners of his mouth down and he lifted his gaze. "What of what you showed me?"

"Ahh, I knew we'd come to it sooner rather than later." She relinquished his hand to grasp the steaming bowl once again. "Enid, my brother's daughter, bore you, but she was a vessel, nothing more."

He opened his mouth to question, but halted all sound at Llawela's raised hand.

"Please, let me explain in my own way," she said. "This is hard enough."

Closing his mouth to purse worried lips, he nodded and ignored the roiling butterflies in his abdomen. So close. He was so close to the truth and though it thrilled him, terror could not be held at bay.

"Our family is an ancient one," began Llawela. "The stories handed down to me from my great-grandmother were told to her by her grandmother and her grandmother before her, to even further back to a time when this island was still connected to the rest of the world and my ancestors resided in the east. Don't ask me what that means. I don't know, but it is part of the story."

The butterflies turned to rocks and gooseflesh erupted across his scarred flesh. He did not need to ask. He knew. Centuries of being with Notus in museums and libraries taught him much. He could not have uttered a word had he tried.

"Our ancestors came to this land, servants to the Gods before the sleeping giants took to their perpetual dance," continued Auntie. "Not much has survived from that time except their language and their gifts of love by procreating with my ancestors.

"It was they, my forerunners, who were chosen to be lovers, priesthood and servants to the Gods. Our blood mixed with theirs, and no more so heavily co-mingled than with my ancestors.

"Before the accursed Romans came to our land, my forebears had done all they could to continue the teachings from the Gods and maintain the exalted bloodlines. The *Derwyddon* and the *Gwyddon* worked both sides of the Gods gifts. Only those proving their bloodlines would be chosen to train, to serve. My ancestors served the Gods and brought law, healing, and lore to those of the land who supported us, until the Romans destroyed *Ynys Mon*.

"They brought foreign Gods, but they also brought bloodlines from their Gods to mingle with ours, strengthening what has become unknowingly diluted. My grandparents' great grandparents recognized this, and though many considered them traitors to the people, the results of co-mingling their daughters with Rome's highest sons brought renewed strength to the bloodline.

"With the destruction of *Ynys Mon* and the Romans bent to eradicate the *Gwyddon* and *Derwyddon*, the teachings became secret. Often my great grandmother would take my siblings and me to special places in the woods under the pretext of gathering herbs and firewood. Out there, surrounded by verdant life, she taught us many things and told us many stories of our people and our Gods before the Romans came.

"I loved these times until, eventually, only I joined her.

"I didn't realize that she was training me. Of my parents' eight surviving children, their seventh proved to carry the desire to serve the Gods. Of course, I had no knowledge of what was being instilled in me.

"During the harvest festival when I was nine, our village received a rare and potentially dangerous guest, had the Romans found out. A *Derwyddon*—a seer—had come.

"My great grandparents—nay, the whole village—believed

that all the *Derwyddon* had been eradicated, but here came a young man into our midst proving everyone wrong.

"I remember being so excited as I brought the news to my great grandmother. At first she didn't believe me, then my little brother came in to her hut, full of excitement. The *Derwydd* had arrived during the night, choosing to travel at the sun's setting for fear of his survival if the Romans saw him.

"Swept up in the commotion, great grandmother and I followed my brother to the chieftain's hall—My home! The *Derwydd* was in my home, and there he sat at the high trestle, my father and my mother seated to either side of him.

"I remember, as I entered the hall, that I came to stand still to stare at the large, smiling brown eyes turned onto me. Power exuded from this man and I trembled beneath it.

"My great grandmother was similarly affected, especially when he smiled, but she regained her composure quickly enough. My hand in hers, we walked towards my parents and the *Derwydd*, the villagers opening a path.

"Rising from his seat, the *Derwyd* came to meet my great grandmother and me. What transpired in that greeting surprised us all. Bowing, the *Derwydd* greeted my great grandmother with the sign accorded to one of high rank amongst the *Gwyddon* before he knelt in front of me.

"Despite his youthful and friendly appearance, I shuddered in fear and awe. I had never met a *Derwydd* before. There were supposed to be all gone.

"'My name is Seddewyn,' he said."

"Seddewyn?" he interrupted. His back stiffened straight and his eyes widened in shock.

"You know this man?" Llawela blinked her surprise.

Know? No. He shook his head, sending long white locks to sweep over his bare arms, but he knew the name. He quickly did the math and asked, "Was there another with Seddewyn?"

Llawela frowned, thrown off her narration by the boy's seeming recognition. "No. He came alone."

Dejected, he slumped his shoulders. How was it possible for Notus' Chooser to have also known Llawela? The chances were astronomical, and he feared it had everything to do with him. "Go on," he said. He needed to know the rest of the story.

Llawela nodded, suspicion pinching her eyes. "'My name is Seddewyn,' he said," she reiterated. "'What's yours?'

"I told him and his smile broadened until I could see his strangely pointed teeth. He then asked how old I was. Again, I told him, my fear slowly turning to curiosity.

"He reached out to push a curling lock behind my ear. 'I came here because of you, Llawela,' he said.

"My shock echoed in the gasps of those around and the platter sized eyes of my parents.

"'The Gods sent me a sign and I found you,' he continued. 'Do you love the Gods, *cariadfab*?'

"I nodded and told him that I loved hearing the stories great grandmother told me.

"With that, he stood and spoke to my great grandmother in whispers until it appeared something was decided. Coming to stand beside my great grandmother, Seddewyn addressed my parents. 'Your daughter fulfills the prophesy I have read in the stars,' he proclaimed. 'She is the seventh child of a seventh child, born to the bloodline of those who serve *Dôn*, and who has recently turned nine. I would like the blessing of her parents—and her Chief—to initiate her into the mysteries of the Gods her heart already serves.'

"The *Derwydd* had come for me. Being only nine, I wasn't sure of what he was talking about, but whatever it was brought tears of joy to my father's eyes. He gave his immediate blessing.

"How long ago had someone last been chosen to serve the Gods? No one knew. The *Derwyddon* were supposedly gone, but here stood one and I was to become one of the initiated.

"No longer would I sleep in my father's hall. My great grandmother would take over my rearing and further training.

"For three days I was made to fast. Special drinks made to cleanse me only were allowed. Each day I bathed in herbal scented water. On the evening of the fourth day, I was taken to a grove deep in the woods—the same grove where Enid conceived you.

"Seddewyn was there, and my great grandmother stood by his side. It was all very mysterious to me. In the cool of the night, standing naked before their robed forms, I was put through many trials. It was after being given a specially concocted beverage that I lost all sense of space and time. I escaped my body, and that's when the Ladies took me to Their sanctuary.

"They told me many things, all that came to pass in my later years, but were forgotten when I awoke at dawn, my head in my great grandmother's lap and my woman's blood between my legs. Seddewyn was no where to be found with the sun cresting the horizon. Nor did he show himself to us or any within the village. He had left, but gave my great grandmother his final prophesy. 'Llawela will herald the return of the Blessed Ones.'

"She did not understand the meaning and neither did I.

"My life had been turned upside down. Had I known what I was getting into, I probably would have fought to keep my life the way it had been. No longer living with my brothers and sisters under my parents' roof, my days became quiet, but it was more than that. My childhood friends no longer saw me as one of them. I wasn't an outcast, more that they no longer knew how to relate to me. I was *Derwydd*, and I now out ranked them.

"It was hard. I missed my friends. I missed my family. Mostly, I missed being a child. Everyone bowed to me, even my parents, when all I wished was to be held in their arms.

"A lonely life, to be sure, but my great grandmother kept me busy. The nights were worse. Don't get me wrong, I loved my great grandmother, but at nine years old I missed my old life.

"My great grandmother taught me much in the years I lived with her. She taught me the healing arts, the ability to listen to the spirits and, most importantly, how to entreat the Gods in Their own language.

"Over the years, I was shaped by my great grandmother. My childhood friends came to me for help in healings and matters of the heart. They were no longer friends, but rather, those to whom I ministered to. My father became more Chief to me than a parent as he would come by to discuss important matters with my great grandmother and me. To my mother, I was the priestess who sang her to the Summerland when her last pregnancy and labour took her from this world. For nine years I lived and studied under my great grandmother.

"It was when she contracted the wasting disease that she arranged with my father to have me married to a man of her choosing. She did not want the line to end with me. Powerful children would come from my loins if I coupled with a man of strong standing. My father agreed and I was married to the son of a neighbouring Chief whom I met only a handful of times before.

"I knew what my great grandmother expected. As the one to herald the God's return, she believed, with the right match, I would become the vessel in which They would return.

"Oh how wrong she was. Young as I was, I got caught up in her delusion and though I did not love my husband I lay with him as often as possible. My reward for this was a womb where no child grew.

"My great grandmother was devastated and passed away shortly before my husband was killed in a raid. The prophesy no longer seemed possible.

"I retreated from the world, a widow and a failed priestess, to this hovel.

"My family believed I had shamed them. My oldest brother's disillusionment stung the worse, especially since he had become Chief after our father died. Of course, as Chief, he could not let his sister go without. He did his best to care for me, but at arm's length.

"For years I lived upon the good graces of those who were my kith and kin. To others, I became the strange woman who lived alone, a woman to entreat for help when all else failed. I was known to be the last daughter of *Ynys Mon* and as such I was treated with a mixture of fear and respect.

"I lived that way for many years, and thought, at first, I railed against my self imposed isolation, I learned to treasure it. From a distance I watched my oldest brother's children be born and grow. It was Enid, beautiful, fay Enid, who captured my attention, reminding me much of myself when I was young. Her desire to learn the old ways came naturally, as if all I need do was remind her of something she already knew.

"My brother attempted to discourage his eldest daughter, but she met his stubbornness with equal might. At last, I had found someone to pass my knowledge to, and I asked her father if I could initiate Enid as I had been. His answer devastated us both. Shortly thereafter she was married to Geraint.

"You know the rest of the story," sighed Llawela. "What Seddewyn had prophesized came true." She lifted her gaze to meet his.

The burning need in her hazel eyes set him back, but it was the implications her words and what she had shown him that begged him to deny the truth.

He stood up, breaking eye contacted and causing the bench to slide back on the dirt floor. Stepping around the bench, pent up energy forced him to pace the small living quarters. If it were true, the realization he was never—

Spinning back, he faced Auntie, his breath coming in short gasps. "You—you're saying—" He could not bring himself to finish the preposterous thought.

Llawela rose from her seat, cooling bowl forgotten and untouched, to stand before him. "You are one of the Blessed Ones, the Old Gods, if you will." She tried to take his hands in hers, but he spun away.

"That's impossible!" He swung back to face the woman who had raised him.

"You are," she insisted, taking a step forward.

"No. I am Chosen." Every denial came to mind, waging war against the truth.

"Are you?" she challenged, arms crossing over ample bosom. "You may deny what I have shown you. You may even decide what I told you is a just a fanciful story, but let's lay this out plainly."

Inwardly, he cringed, not wishing to hear, but having no choice.

Llawela ignored the fear in her charge's ruby eyes and barrelled on, ticking each point off on her fingers. "You were sired by a God onto my niece, who has ancient blood ties to the Gods, and by a Goddess who rode Enid during the act.

"You were born *three* moons early, fully formed and healthy when any other child born so soon would have died.

"Raising you, I had to keep you from the sun lest you burn, and even after that fateful night, you could tolerate no sunlight.

Even your appearance and growth defied the norm.

"All lessons I, and Geraint, taught you seemed more an awakening of memories. Even those who hunted in our woods recognized you for what you are."

"I am not a God," he protested.

"Say whatever you wish, my boy, the truth is plain and marked across your body."

He glanced down to take in the silvered lines that scarred his arms and torso. The modern black trousers hid others. "They came after I was Chosen," he said, hopeful to have found a loophole.

"But you weren't Chosen when you received this." She pointed to the charred horizontal line below his left ribs.

Slapping his hand to cover the offending wound, his breath came faster. The truth bled into him. He shook his head in vain denial. "I *was* Chosen," he said, weakly.

Compassion filled Auntie's stance. "Were you?" she said softly. "Or had you finally come into your power?" She took a step closer and laid a hand on his arm, never breaking eye contact. "You are the psychopomp, bringing souls to the realms beyond the world of the living and allowing a conduit for those of the Otherworlds to connect with those of the living. You already have caused this to happen on more than one occasion."

"Bur that was when I was Chosen." The protestation rang weak in his ears.

Llawela shook her head. "It happened before, when you were nine, and it happened several times before your last wounding. My dear boy, try as you may to fight it, the truth is the truth. To prove this to you, wake up."

Fine white brows furrowed. "Wake up?"

"Wake up!"

XVIII

rian gripped the steering wheel of Corbie's black Cadillac Escalade, causing the finely tooled leather to squeak in protest of the rough handling. The early morning roads glistened from a light rain that had begun as he pulled away from *Pearson's International Airport*. It had ended as he arrived at the hotel, dropping off those he managed to catch before they flew home. If it were not for the fact that Corbie expected him back before dawn, Brian would have happily stayed with his fledgelings at the *Sheridan*.

The Escalade seemed to know its way home, coming to a halt behind the club. Engine purring, Brian sat on the heated leather seat, his mind a-swirl with what had transpired in such a short time.

Turning the key, the vehicle settled to sleep. Brian leaned back in the seat and closed his eyes. He did not want to go in and face his Dominus, and that realization surprised him.

Bastia's obsession with the Chosen had killed her and sent their kind into a war that made them refugees in a new world. Now, Corbie's fixation on the Angel rang with a similar insanity. Brian had tried to deny it, but witnessing Corbie's reaction to the failed revenge niggled that worm of doubt even deeper.

It took Michael's bluntness to point out what Brian failed to recognize. Why else had Brian collected only his vampiric progeny when there were others of Corbie's get waiting to fly home? Why take them to a hotel rather than back to *Beyond the Veil*?

Brian raked his dark blond hair back from his face with both hands. He had not meant to stay, but Stephanie invited him into her room where all the others waited. He was their Dominus and as such they were his responsibility. What caught him off guard was their vehemence against Corbie's desires. Worse was Brian's sudden joy at hearing this.

Almost fifteen hundred years as a slave had blinded Brian to the truth that his fledgelings had hammered home. Brian had sired more surviving vampires, thus creating a larger coterie, than Corbie. It was Theodore's statement that Corbie's power was based solely on Brian's coterie that had stolen his breath had Brian needed to breathe. Clearly, his progeny had been speaking to each other about the situation, leaving Brian unaware, until now.

"I will not bend knee to that man," stated Nikolas. He stood with arms crossed against his chest, covering the blue and green argyle sweater, the single king sized bed to his right. The black out drapes were pulled back to allow the light polluted night to spill across him and the two who sat at the bottom of the bed. "He is not my Dominus."

"He's not anyone's Dominus here," remarked Lenore. She leaned back in the burgundy lounge chair beneath the window, her slim ankles crossing daintily below her flowing green skirt.

"He's mine," snapped Brian. How foolish. They all knew this.

"We know," stated Theodore. His sweet, young face belied a remarkable intelligence. He always appeared energetic, even to his bouncing leg as he sat at the end of the bed, closest to Nikolas. "But Corbie is bent on a path that will lead us to destruction."

The others in the room nodded.

Brian could not stifle the grip the statement had on his gut.

"His obsessive behavior towards the Angel is a minor issue," continued Theodore. "We understand—and some of us even respect—the need for revenge against the Angel and the rest of the Chosen, but they did not start this conflict. Bastia did."

Murmurs of agreement filled the emptiness. Brian stood still, awaiting the inevitable.

Theodore continued once the rumblings died down, his attention focused on his Dominus. "Bastia was our Queen, our creator, and through Corbie, ruled us all, and we allowed it. Corbie now tries to emulate Bastia's illusion. I, for one, am tired of having others lord over us."

The last statement prickled Brian into loosening his tongue. "If you have any complaints about me being your Domi—"

"We don't," interjected Stephanie. She rose from the floor beside the second chair where Michael sat and came to face Brian. "You are our Dominus, but never have you used that power. You've always given us freedom to be as we are. It is for that freedom that we wish you to be free of Corbie before he does something to destroy us all."

"After all, did Thanatos not issue a warning—one which Corbie broke—about leaving the Angel alone?" Michael's quiet statement pointed to the root of the current situation. Michael stood, his presence seeming to fill the room. The Angel appears to have survived Corbie's revenge and now lies within Thanatos' estate, the Chosen with him.

"Don't feign surprise, Brian," continued Michael. "The walls have ears at the *Veil*."

Brian smoothed his features into a mask of indifference. The knowledge from his progeny had surprised him. "What do you want of me?"

"Stand with us against Corbie," said Vincent. He uncrossed his legs and allowed them to dangle next to Theodore's nervous leg, his hand reaching to still his neighbor's fidgeting.

Brian's eyes widened at the incredible statement. "You would have me turn on my Dominus?"

"We would have you stand up to save us against Thanatos' wrath," said Nikolas.

"Which will pale against the Angel's," said Michael.

Brian frowned, allowing his gaze to fall to the brown broadloom at the foot of the king sized bed.

"We would have you be free as you have allowed us our freedom," added Lenore.

"This is rebellion," muttered Brian.

"No," stated Nikolas. "This is a matter of survival. When Thanatos comes, as we know he will, stand with him instead of Corbie."

"And what do you think that will achieve?" snapped Brian.

"Our freedom to rule as we individually see fit." Michael sat back down, pulling Stephanie onto his lap. "Feudalism failed with the mortals—"

"What you're proposing is a different kind of feudalism," shot Brian.

"To a point, yes," replied Theodore, his leg bouncing again. "The difference is self determination without bending knee to one who would rule all."

Brian closed his eyes and took a deep cleansing breath. How similar it was to the system he grew up with before he was captured and sold as a slave. It came with its own problems, ones in which were often solved in bloodshed, but freedom had its price. He opened his eyes and allowed his vision to fall on each of his progeny. "What if I refuse?"

Theodore's shoulders slumped. "After this meeting, we would have to kill you."

Stunned at the unfortunate truth, Brian could only blink. Recovering, anger overrode surprise. "You're not giving me a choice."

Lenore scooped a length of dark brown hair to settle behind her right ear. "Be that as it may, we would not have brought you to this if we did not believe you'd side with us."

"We've seen how Corbie has treated you over the centuries," stated Vincent. He resumed his cross-legged position. "Enough is enough. How much longer before you're pulled into insanity?"

"Corbie's toxic to our survival," interjected Michael. His hand absently caressed the swell of Stephanie's hip. "Had Bastia been victorious against the Chosen our lives would be quite different now. What Corbie is attempting not only places us squarely against the Chosen again, but risks our exposure to the mortals. Neither is acceptable. Bastia started a genocidal war and the likelihood of our eradication is high if it continues here on this continent."

"I, for once, am well pleased with my life and do not wish it threatened," said Stephanie.

The others nodded in agreement.

Silence descended as Brian digested their words.

"To do as you wish," said Brian, the words flowing slowly, "indicates Corbie must be killed."

"Yes," agreed Theodore and Nikolas in unison.

"And you expect me to do the deed?"

"No," replied Michael.

Brian frowned. "Then what do you expect of me?"

"To do nothing," stated Nikolas.

"I don't understand." Brian crossed his arms over his chest.

"We'll do as Corbie requests—"

"Up to a point," interrupted Lenore.

"—to a point," continued Nikolas, inclining his head to the seated Vampiress. "When Thanatos comes to make good on his promise, we do nothing."

"Are you so sure Thanatos will kill Corbie?" Brian shook his head at the audacity of the plan. He had met the God of Death less than a handful of times through the centuries. Not once did Thanatos appear to be the kind to soil his hands so directly. Then again, with the near fatal attack on the Angel...Brian did not know what to expect.

"If Thanatos does not kill Corbie," explained Michael, "then we will kill him and any other of his coterie there, and attribute it to Thanatos' vengeance."

"You seem so sure of yourselves," snapped Brian.

"Yes. Yes, we are," said Theodore.

"We could not do this without the fact you allowed Corbie's coterie to fly home when you kept us here," commented Stephanie, snuggling Michael.

"Corbie's supporters are dispersed," stated Michael. "Yours are consolidated."

"We cannot lose," beamed Vincent.

"And what of me when this is done?" A worm of worry flared in Brian's gut. If they can plan to rid the world of Corbie, who was he to say they would not attempt the same on him, eventually.

"You become Dominus of the Greater Toronto Area," answered Lenore.

"And?" Brian's blue-grey eyes pinched in suspicion.

"And each Dominus or Domina over a city or region is left to rule as he or she sees fit," grinned Lenore.

Nikolas stepped forward to stand before Brian, hand outstretched. "What say you?"

Lips pressed into a line, Brian gradually uncrossed his arms. The plan appeared solid, but the long term repercussions could lead to even more conflict between the Dominii. "I'll agree on one condition."

Nikolas scowled and dropped his hand. "What?"

"That what we've begun here tonight continues." He glanced at all his co-conspirators before returning his attention to Nikolas. "That council, begun with us, continues with each one of us as equals."

"A republic," snorted Nikolas before a wry grin pulled at his face. "So long as we never have a democracy or an autocracy."

Brian slipped his hand into his progeny's. "Agreed."

The rest of his coterie swarmed around him, the deal struck.

Brian glanced up at the sliver of sky he could see over the club. Unlocking the Escalade, he stepped out and onto the gravelled parking pad and noticed the dried blood at his feet. Twenty-four hours seemed so long ago.

Slamming the car door shut behind him, Brian turned to enter *the Veil*. Half an hour remained until oblivion. Too much time to get tangled in his lies. Pressing the button on the key fob brought the gratifying honk of a car locked up for the day. Brian closed the steel door behind him, hearing the mechanism click tight as he descended the stairs.

XIX

hanatos allowed the silence to fill the room. The expressions on his guests' faces told him everything he needed to know. Despite the incredible tale that lent more to fantasy than reality, they believed him.

"It's so hard, yet so easy, to accept the truth of your story," said Bridget. Her bright blue eyes confounded. "Your story is fantastic."

Thanatos nodded. Had he been on the receiving end of the tale he would have difficulty believing it.

"So the Chosen were actually servants of ancient Gods?" Fernando's tone belied his continued disbelief. Bridget's left hand came to rest on her Chosen's right thigh in warning.

"There are stories—legends and myths, if you will—in almost every culture of a higher race, or gods, that have left our world to go to another one which mankind can't reach," said Notus, his voice quiet. He glanced up as he Chooser. "You're saying that these stories are true?"

"Somewhat," replied Thanatos. "They are based upon the earliest of the Chosen and those they served."

"I don't understand." Bridget's statement voiced Notus' confusion. At the same time, Fernando threw up his hands in frustration before coming back down to slap his thighs. Bridget moved her hand just in time.

Thanatos sighed and glanced at the platinum Omega on his left wrist. No wonder he felt exhausted. He had been awake for nearly thirty-six hours.

"How does this relate to the Angel?" asked Bridget.

"Because he is one of those who the Chosen originally were picked to serve. One of the Blessed Ones," said Thanatos.

"That's not possible." Notus' voice took on strength. "He had a father, a mother and sisters. All of which were human. I knew his sister."

"Tell me, Notus," Thanatos leaned forward, "did his sister look like others of her ilk? Did she carry an air of power around her? Did she have a sense of natural leadership? Did she look like him?"

Notus frowned, knowing the answer.

"Remember, the Gods coupled with mortals producing children, some which were Chosen. Many were not. I don't know the reasons, but this is true even to my parentage and progeny," explained Thanatos.

"But after so many thousands of years, why now?" queried Bridget.

A small smile tugged the edges of Thanatos' lips. One of the three believed him. Despite his desperate need for rest, he knew the rest of the story required telling. "It's nearly dawn, and though you must be tired, I think it would be best if I continue. If you wish to take a break, you are all welcome to stay and rest. I have rooms aplenty."

He watched as the three shot glances at each other, looking for agreement, until Bridget turned her blue eyes back on him. "I, for one, want to hear the rest," she stated. "I don't think I'd be able to sleep knowing there's more."

Thanatos nodded. "Sleep can wait."

"My beloved and I left that cave beside the sea to travel a world we never imagined. Most of the time we did not come across any people. Life abounded. When we met up with welcoming bands, we would listen to their stories, learning their language and their ways if we chose to stay with them for a time. In every case, my Blessed One left me to mediate, never speaking directly to our benefactors, much like it was before he Chosen me.

"The world was one incredible adventure after another. We would leave one place to explore sights never even imagined. The massive walls of ice far to the north were spectacular, even though I had heard such tales in my childhood. Of course, these tales were dismissed as ridiculous and impossible by my people, when my beloved and I stood at the base of such magnificence, its chill biting even into our immortal flesh, we knew we had to search for other wondrous lands.

"We were both young and the seasons passed by in blinks of the eye. I don't recall how much time had flown by before home-sickness settled over me. I wanted—no, craved—a sense of per-manence. Bands and tribes we had visited were our time keepers. Friends grew old and died, leaving children and grandchildren to do the same, until our presence in the past became legend and then myth. When we returned, they no longer received as friends, but venerated both of us as gods.

"I think it was that, more than anything else, that grew the sense of urgency within me, to return home. My beautiful Blessed One saw my misery and through his incredible powers we stepped through the mist and fell into a salt water sea."

Ta'ano sputtered, taking another wave of salt water in the face. Despite having the strength of the Chosen, the weight of the ruck-sack threatened to pull him below the surface. Shucking off the straps that had bitten into his shoulders, his belongings sunk into the black waters.

Treading easier, Ta'ano spun around in search of his beloved.

Not far away Ta'ano found his God struggling to keep his head above the surface. The waning moon illuminated silver on his soaked face.

"*Kreidad!*" exclaimed Ta'ano, as he swam unfettered to the God he loved. Regardless of their immortality, Ta'ano did not want to test it against drowning.

"Stop panicking!" shouted Ta'ano. He came up behind the trashing Blessed One and dug his fingers into water expanded straps.

The Silver God's flailing increased, sending pulsations of terror and nausea to wash through Ta'ano. It took every ounce of self control not to fall under the spell and succumb to fear. Clearly, his order had gone unheard.

Stop panicking, he sent. *You'll drown us both!*

Ta'ano! The Blessed One tried to turn and face his Chosen but a wave crashed over them.

Fingers entwined his lover's rucksack straps, Ta'ano managed to pull his beloved back up, the God gasping as he resurfaced. Throughout their years together and still his beautiful God still did not know how to swim. He would have to rectify that if they got out of this situation.

Treading water for the both of them, Ta'ano miraculously loosened the straps digging into moon silvered skin until the sack floated free. It bobbed once before it sunk below black waves to join its compatriot at the bottom of the sea.

No longer weighed down, the Silver God still struggled to keep his head above the waters, his fear lessened under better control.

Move your arms in circles at your sides, sent Ta'ano, demonstrating. *Like this.*

The Silver God mimicked the movement and the anxiety flowing from him decreased further. *Where are we?* Fear mingled with concern flowed with the thought.

Another wave lifted and then plunged them down, washing cold salt water over their heads.

"How should I know?" sputtered Ta'ano, spitting the taste from his mouth. *You were supposed to bring us home.*

Beneath the riot of newly risen stars and full moon, Ta'ano watched confusion wash over the Silver God.

I did. I mean... The frown on his beloved's face appeared strange to see, igniting a knot of anxiety in Ta'ano's gut.

The Silver God raised a worried gaze from the black waters between them, meeting equally concerned brown eyes. "This is the spot. I can feel it."

Ta'ano frowned and then spat as another wave rolled him. *We can discuss this later. We need to get to land.*

Karen Dales

Treading around in a circle, Ta'ano gazed into the distance, his search hampered by the undulating waves. All around them desolate waters appeared to go on forever. How his beloved managed to send them into the middle of a sea baffled him. Never before had the Silver God sent them astray, his godly senses always sending them to solid land even if they had never been there before.

Despite being in foreign waters, another concern began to build. How long did they have before sunrise? They had to come ashore sooner rather than later. He had to protect his beloved.

Eyes searching, anxiety grew. Ta'ano did not know if the feeling was his alone or exacerbated by the Blessed One. It did not matter. Apprehension spurred Ta'ano.

"There!"

The Argent God's exclamation surprised Ta'ano and he spun about. Beads of silver dripped from his beloved's face, his loose hair a-swirl on the surface. Blood coloured eyes fixed upon something far in the distance. Ta'ano turned to look, but could not see what his God saw.

I don't see anything, sent Ta'ano. Nothing but black water reflecting star and moonlight filled his view.

There's land, responded the Blessed One. *I can see it.*

Trusting his beloved, Ta'ano nodded. They had to swim for it, and that meant his silver haired lover had to learn how to swim. *Let's go.*

Ta'ano, I can't swim! Anxious red eyes turned on him.

You're treading water just fine, replied Ta'ano. *You can do this. All you need do is mimic my movements.*

The Silver God shook his head. *You don't understand.*

Ta'ano frowned. Fear, nausea and a general malaise that sapped energy flowed through their connection. It was the same whenever they had to cross running water.

He swam closer to the God he loved, his brown eyes locking onto stunning features. *I won't leave you. I will do everything in my power to get you to land. I love you.*

The Silver God nodded, the corners of his full lips lifted slightly. *Let's go.*

*   *   *

Coughing water, Ta'ano fell to his hands and knees on the rocky shore, the Blessed One supine beside him, gasping for air. The strength of the Chosen had been their saviour, but it came at a great cost. Hunger surged through Ta'ano. Halfway to shore, the Blessed One's strength departed and Ta'ano had to swim for the both of them, which considerably slowed their progress. The moon had been climbing to its zenith when they started. Now it hovered above the western horizon. Night had grown short and soon the stars would be blotted out by the sun.

Ta'ano spat the salty taste from his mouth and sat back on his haunches, hands on his lap as he stared up at the trees ahead. No shelter presented itself save for whatever shade their leaves could offer. It would have to do.

Climbing to his feet on unsteady legs, the weight of his doe hide tunic and leggings threatened to pull him back down onto the rocky shore. Water cascaded down his body, his feet squishing in water tightened boots.

"We have to go." Ta'ano stared down at his lover and offered a helping hand.

Long, pale fingers wrapped around his and Ta'ano heaved. The Blessed One stood, the weight of his waterlogged clothing staggering his squishing steps.

"How are you feeling?" asked Ta'ano.

Hands on thighs, the Silver God spat onto the once dry rocks, his hair draping argent ropes to the ground. Slowly, he stood. What usually was beautiful pale features now revealed dark circles around eyes and a greyish tinge cast onto silver. "I can honestly say I have been better, but I improve."

On unsteady legs, Ta'ano turned to face the black sea, it's dark waters lapping at rough hewn stones mere feet away. His beloved had sent them into the middle of the deep waters when home should have been their destination.

A hand gentled onto his shoulder. "It's there," said the Silver God, searching the darkness. "I can feel it."

A shuddering breath brought tears to Ta'ano's eyes. "What happened?" The knowledge that the home he grew up and served in now existed at the bottom of an ocean boggled the mind. His beloved would not lie.

We've been gone a long time," susserated the Silver God.

"Surely we haven't been gone so long as to see the end of my people," proclaimed Ta'ano. He spun about to glare up at his beloved's tired features. The movement knocked the pale hand from his shoulder.

He could not believe this. He did not want to believe it. Tears welled in his eyes to mingle with the drying salt water on his cheeks. Arms wrapped themselves around Ta'ano, drawing him against his God's damp chest.

"The world changes, my beloved, but you are the same," whispered the Blessed One as he held Ta'ano. "It is a curse of being Chosen."

Ta'ano pulled away, thinking of his childhood friends, his students, his children. Their bones now lay at the bottom of a sea when they should have rested next to a fresh water lake. "Then why do the Gods Choose us if we are to suffer so?" A sob caught in his throat, the immeasurable years weighing down.

"Because our hearts would break to lose those we love." Sad crimson eyes fixed onto Ta'ano.

Ta'ano welcomed his lover's lips onto his, his hunger consuming him. The loss of his people drove his need to feel that he still lived. All fatigue vanished, his mouth opening to drive his tongue to explore his lover's despite knowing the Silver God's body as intimately as his own. Equally famished, the Blessed one returned the desire to revel in their love's survival.

Gripping the back of his lover's neck with one hand, Ta'ano struggled to disentangle the water logged laces of the Silver God's tunic. Their tongues abandoned their caresses long enough to push the heavy doe hide from pale flesh.

Under the fleeting moonbeams, Ta'ano imbibed in the beauty of the Blessed One's slim muscular form until passion's flames erupted a greater need. Ta'ano grasped at the growing outline of his beloved's arousal. Desire pulsated through him, their passions mingling and enhancing each other.

Throwing off his tunic as if it were made from thistledown, Ta'ano closed the distance and found his lover's mouth once more. A prize awaited. His body, pulsating and rigid, demanded release as he kissed, sucked and bit his way down the soft salt-touched skin until his lips met the waistband of the saggy trousers.

Warm hands pressed him lower and he knelt, rocks digging into his knees. Yanking down the pants, Ta'ano's rod jumped at the sight of his God in full erect splendor, a sight he never grew tired of. Licking his lips in anticipation, Ta'ano kissed the tip of his lover's rod. The soft silkiness urged him further and he opened his mouth, sucking in the full glorious length. Sea salt spiced the flesh as Ta'ano wrapped an arm around his lover's thigh. His other hand reached up to cup and caress the God's tightening stones.

Slowly, Ta'ano drew back, his tongue spiralling around the solid shaft, to take in each sensation. The need for release poured through him and Ta'ano knew this could not be a time for prolonged lovemaking. His own pulsing rod could not wait.

A hip thrust from the God buried the pale shaft in Ta'ano's mouth and he moaned. Sucking, Ta'ano worked his lover's rod, the soft flesh over solid rigidness driving him as his hand worked the stones. Moans from above and in his mind told him that it would not be long, but Ta'ano needed more.

Relinquishing the solid shaft, Ta'ano sent an image of desire to the God. Crimson eyes widened in surprise and the Blessed One lay down on his back with Ta'ano between his knees.

Hunger burned hotter as Ta'ano lowered his breeches, releasing his shaft into his hand. Nowhere near as soft as his lover's, Ta'ano ran his hand down his firmness, the pulsating need drumming against his palm.

The Blessed One moaned at the sight, his glistening member jumping in need. Ta'ano gripped his lover with his other hand, pumping them in unison, but still he required more. The sight of the Silver God arching his back told Ta'ano all.

Releasing his lover, Ta'ano guided himself in and gasped. Long legs wrapped around his waist. On knees, Ta'ano gripped his lover's thighs as he began to thrust, driving himself deeper and deeper still.

Together they moved, their passions twining until neither knew where the other one started or ended. A hand—Ta'ano believed it was his—encapsulated a rigid silver rod, working in time with each thrust.

Ta'ano watched his beloved God undulate and cry out with each intrusion. Never before had Ta'ano seen his lover so beautiful.

A wash of seed spilled over Ta'ano's hand, but it was the sight of his lover's shuddering orgasm that pulled his own climax. Together they rode waves that threatened to leave them empty husks. A final convulsion stole Ta'ano's strength and he collapsed into the Silver God's embrace.

Their bodies still conjoined, the Blessed One lifted his wrist to Ta'ano's mouth. "Drink."

Ta'ano canted his head back and gazed onto his lover's face. Blood exchange tended to be part of their lovemaking, but not this time. The need to reaffirm life drove the need for blood away. Ta'ano shook his head.

"You're exhausted. Take it."

So much more was sent with those words. Above all, the Silver God's love for Ta'ano. He could not reject the gift. Kissing the inside of his beloved's wrist, Ta'ano could feel the racing pulse of the after glow and bit as gently as he could.

Succulent blood poured into his mouth, ambrosia igniting renewed energy and stiffening his well used staff.

The God moaned and writhed, sending renewed passion through them.

Ta'ano relinquished the wrist and kissed the fading marks. He glanced up at the sky before gazing down at his beloved, sheathing his staff deeper. *We have some time before the sun comes up.*

Pale hips lifted to welcome the greater intrusion and pressed a returning rod against Ta'ano. *And when night falls, we will search out the People and discover what happened to the other Chosen.*

Renewed tears spilled down Ta'ano's face with each thrust. This time they overflowed from happiness. He would find them because his Silver God loved him.

XX

We decided that traveling by foot was the safer method. The world was in a state of flux and neither one of us wanted to find ourselves in a similar situation. It also afforded us chances to talk with other travelers. Each time we shared a campfire I would ask about others like my beloved and me. Most often we would receive fantastic tales that hinted that other Chosen walked the land.

"Northward we went, following others and their news of great dwellings of mud and daub. Trepidation mingled with hopeful anticipation as each story became more and more alike with another's until my beloved and I stood outside a flourishing city nestled in the centre of a verdant marsh.

"It was so similar to my home, for a brief moment I imagined this to be the city of my birth. Of course it could not be. Each building was built upon another, connecting each hovel by terraces and wooden ladders. We followed the dry track to an opening that stood invitingly to newcomers.

"It became clear in that predawn that early visitors were unexpected. Soon the rooftops teamed with groggy-eyed on-lookers whispering and pointing. The commotion our presence caused compared to nothing upon the arrival of a resplendent delegation that came down to meet us.

"A woman of great beauty stepped forward. Her black curling hair hung long, framing a heart shaped face. Green eyes widened before she bent knee and lowered her head.

"Never before had we received such a welcome. I then realized that her obeisance was directed to my love. Hope blossomed in my chest and was rewarded when she lifted her head, a beatific smile illuminating her face. She was Chosen!"

"Welcome, my Lord," she said in the language of the Gods. "Your coming has been foretold."

Ta'ano stood dumbstruck beside his equally stupefied beloved. Silence crashed down between them, the only sounds being the distant murmurs of those observing from the rooftops.

"May I rise, my Lord?" inquired the woman, a wry smile lifting her full lips.

"Ah...of course," replied the Blessed One. Confusion mingled with disbelief marred his features.

Ta'ano shot wide eyed shock to his beloved. Never before had his lover directly responded, always going through Ta'ano to make his thoughts and needs known.

The beautiful woman stood. "Please, come and retire at my humble abode. It has been a long time since either of you have been in the presence of another Chosen and, frankly, our words are not for the common people."

The Blessed One looked to Ta'ano who frowned but nodded.

"Wonderful!" She clasped long, delicate hands together. Her grin widened to expose her elongated teeth. "Please follow me," she added, turning to lead them away.

Ta'ano walked before his beloved and climbed the ladder after the Chosen woman, the processional falling in behind. Through, up and over, they followed her between homes elaborately painted with frescoes of animals. Over solid rooftops and through other more public buildings they climbed until they were led down into a large rectangular room more lavishly decorated than any other Ta'ano had seen along the way. Their followers halted at the opening before being dispersed by the woman.

Bull heads made of clay and painted to make them as real as possible lined the two longest walls. Frescoes of leopards, vultures and people illuminated the walls. The majesty of the artistry captured Ta'ano so that he did not notice the step to the sunken floor. The Chosen woman caught him before he could make a greater fool of himself.

Straightening himself, Ta'ano lowered his eyes in embarrassment and went to stand next to his Silver God.

"Please, join me." She turned to step up to what appeared a massive bull head at the end of the building, opposite from the other where the ladder stood. Bright paintings coloured the walls around the bull head. Under the head, small statues of heavily pregnant women in different poses, many on birthing thrones, stood a hand's breadth high.

The Chosen woman sat on a reed mat laid before the bull head and indicated that they should sit before her.

"Please allow me to introduce myself," she said in the language of the Gods, once Ta'ano and his beloved sat. "I am Ta'rha, Chosen by the Lady Herself."

Ta'ano's eyes widened. Never had he heard of the Lady Choosing one to serve Her. He glanced at his Silver God and found the same awe on his pale face.

Ta'rha smiled at their obvious astonishment. "I pray you do not hold that against me."

"No. Of course not," recovered Ta'ano. "It's just that…"

"You're never heard of Her Choosing someone," finished Ta'rha.

Ta'ano grimaced. "That and in all journeys we've never encountered another Chosen."

"Yes, well, the world is changing," observed Ta'rha, lowering her eyes, smile gone.

A vast expanse of uncomfortable silence divided them until the Blessed One bumped Ta'ano's arm with his. Mortified at the his lack of manners, Ta'ano cleared his throat. "I apologize. You have welcomed us into your home and gave us your name, and we have not reciprocated. I am—"

"Ta'ano," interrupted Ta'rha, her smile returned. "And my Lord, the Blessed One of the People."

The title took the Silver God aback, his posture straightening.

"Your story is legendary," Ta'rha quickly explained. "When I was a little girl, I often heard about the Blessed One who came to live with the People, and the High Priest who loved and was loved by Him. A beautiful story of how my Lord swept the High Priest away to Choose him so that they could be together forever."

Ta'ano could only blink in shock.

"The story inspired us in the hopes that one day, if we were lucky, we would be Chosen by a God or Goddess who loved us." Ta'rha's green eyes turned to penetrate Ta'ano's brown, her smile replaced with seriousness. "Your example became the expectation for future priests and priestesses."

"That was never our intention," said Ta'ano once he recovered, somewhat.

"I know," her smile returned, "now. As a little girl, the love the two of you shared became larger than life to those left behind."

"You seem to have us at an advantage," said Ta'ano.

"Then shall I tell you a bit about myself?" Ta'rha cocked her head to the side, the action adding to her beauty.

Ta'ano and his beloved nodded in unison.

"As you must gather, I come from the People. In fact, I am the last to have been Chosen. By the time I was born to the High Priestess and her Chooser, the lake had turned to salt and lapped at the buildings closest to it."

Ta'ano gasped and shot a look at his frowning Silver God before returning his attention to their hostess. "We attempted to go home, but found ourselves in the middle of an ocean."

Ta'rha sadly nodded. "It was a difficult time for our people. The waters were rising and nothing we did to appease the Gods halted the change. My mother implored the Gods and on the night of her Choosing the Lady, in all Her splendor, stepped through and took me as Her new High Priestess even though I was only to be initiated. She had heard the cries of Her people and declared that She would work through me to save all They had created.

"For the next nine years I became a vessel for Her. The Chosen who had gone before now came again, helping to arrange what needed to be done.

"Those years were filled with hectic desperation. All that had been created which could be taken, left with our people. Families went with different Chosen while I stayed to work Her will and watch the sea enclose over our home.

"In my eighteenth year She came to me and Chose me. In that rite She told me that it was time for the People to grow and expand, and that the Chosen were the vessels of that change. The Chosen would serve the Gods now by caring for the People.

"I stood with Her as the first waves washed over our home. Our diaspora had come. I led the last remaining people here. A long journey, as you well know, but we've been here for about seventy generations."

"I didn't realize we had been gone so long," whispered Ta'ano. His lowered eyes gazed at the reed mat. If Ta'rha had been here for so long, how much time had passed before them? The numbers staggered him.

A hand alighted on his knee and he looked up at Ta'rha.

"I know it is hard to hear this, but the People have flourished," comforted Ta'rha. "There are more Chosen in the world now, helping to bring civilization and peace to the People by teaching them and connecting them with the Gods.

"Look around," Ta'rha gestured to the opulent room. "Her presence fills the People with love and peace. In return, they honour and worship Her as their Great Goddess."

"What of the other Gods?" asked the Silver God.

Ta'ano saw and sensed worry in his beloved.

"They, too, are honoured," replied Ta'rha. "Shrines and temples, like this one, abound in this city."

"And you are able to call the Gods from them?" The frown on the Blessed One's face grew.

Noticing his disquiet, Ta'rha's green eyes tinted with fear. "No, my Lord. Not here, but in the fields where the people grow their grains."

The Silver God nodded in relief. *So They still come.*

Ta'ano took a pale hand in his and gave a gentle, reassuring squeeze. "You mentioned that you were expecting us," said Ta'ano in an effort to redirect the conversation.

Karen Dales

Ta'rha nodded. "She wants to talk to you, my Lord."

The news stunned them and they both looked at each other for answers before returning their attention to their hostess.

"Why now?" croaked Ta'ano's beloved.

"I do not know, my Lord, but She requests your presence."

Ta'ano, what should I do?

Fear and worry flowed into Ta'ano. No amount of gentle hand holding would calm his beloved. *Meet with Her. See what She wants.*

"When?" asked the Blessed One.

"Tonight," replied Ta'rha, relieved. "I would be honoured to have you stay the day here with me. I'm sure your journey was tiring, so please, sleep here. When you wake I will take you to the sacred site."

Ta'ano inclined is head, agreeing for the two of them.

The marsh at night teemed with nocturnal life as they walked the well worn tract. The drone of mosquitoes and other insects worked a counterbalance to the chirps, calls and cries of restless waterfowl. Shoulder high reeds of green cloaked the croaking creatures. Above, a clear sky littered with stars swarmed around the hair thin waxing crescent descending into the west.

Ta'ano slapped at a bug that landed on his forearm as he walked. The heat of the humid evening made it impossible to wear anything but light weight woven kilts. Even Ta'rha wore the garment, her large breasts exposed to the warm elements, the biting bugs appeared to ignore her.

No one from the city walked their path through the marsh. The only indication of others faded into the distance behind them. Soon they had the stars and the grinning moon to guide them, the gloaming torchlight from the city devoured by the night.

Each footstep took them further into the darkness, neither one of them interrupting the songs of nature that rolled over them.

Hundreds of questions ran rampant in Ta'ano's mind. It had been so long since he was in the presence of another God. The last was the night he chose his successor and his silver lover spirited him away to be his Chooser. With no contact for so long,

 172

fears composed many of his concerns, the primary being what if She wanted his beautiful Silver God to go back with Her, leaving Ta'ano alone. The notion of no longer sharing his body, his heart, his life with his Blessed One shot stabs of hot agony through his gut.

"Ta'ano, are you alright?"

Ta'rha knelt in front of him, but appeared to be of the same height. It then occurred to him that he too knelt on the earthen tract, his arms gripping his midsection. Ta'ano had no recollection of how he had ended up on the ground.

With Ta'rha's gentle assistance, Ta'ano stood on shaking legs, the anxiety passing. Never before had he experienced anything like this. "I'll be alright," he managed.

I'm sorry, flowed the apology from the Silver God.

Ta'ano turned around to face his lover.

Abashment coloured the Silver God's face before he turned away to stare into the darkness. *I didn't realize I was—*

It's alright. I understand. Ta'ano went to stand in front of his beloved. The feelings of apprehension melted into embarrassment and he knew where those mind numbing fears had come from.

"We should get going," interjected Ta'rha. "We still have a fair distance to go."

Ta'ano watched her turn and continue down the path, and smiled. She had given them the privacy they needed. Taking a pale hand in his, they followed at a distance, sharing their feelings until hope supplanted fear.

Time passed slowly as they travelled to the sacred site. The Cheshire moon slipped further until it vanished, leaving the stars to illuminate their path. Questions popped to mind, but Ta'ano kept quiet, enjoying the feel of his lover's hand in his.

The marsh dissolved behind the path, taking the stinging insects and riotous sounds with it. Dry mud warmed each step as fields of wheat, barley and lentils created a sea of plenty. The magnitude of the farmland astounded Ta'ano. Their journey to the city had been from the other direction.

He had seen fields of agriculture in his youth, but never on this scale. The production had to be more than enough for the citizens, and he commented so to his lover.

Ta'rha turned and smiled. "We do produce more than enough," she explained. "At the harvest, many people come from all around to trade for our bounty. It's a harmonious way of life for the People. Those in the city grow and create things that others need and want, and those not of the city provide the people what they need and want. It becomes a festival that lasts a full turning of the moon. I hope you'll be able to stay long enough to experience it."

Ta'ano canted his head and shrugged his shoulders. Everything could change by the rising of the sun. To move from this uncomfortable line of thought, Ta'ano pointed to what appeared to be a grouping of leather tents near the edge of the prolific fields, a banked fire in their midst. "Who are they?"

"They are the guardians of the land. They live here during the growing season. It's a great honour, for without their care, there would be no harvest."

"Where is the sacred ground?" asked the Blessed One, fearting his voice.

"It's in the centre of the field," replied Ta'rha. She continued down the path until it and she were swallowed by the growing wheat.

Releasing a nervous breath, Ta'ano and his beloved followed her in.

A perfect circle, borded by a wall of wheat and barley, their heads reaching to the heavens, not yet burdened so as to bend, enclosed the sacred site. Short green grass carpeted the space, the perfect green marred by a large fire pit rung with rounded stones. Ta'ano estimated that at least a hundred people, if not more, could stand the circumference comfortably. The sacred site appeared larger than the one that now sat at the bottom of an ocean. The cool grass dampened the sound of their entrance as Ta'ano and his beloved went to stand across the ashen fire pit.

"Are you ready to proceed?" asked Ta'rha. No longer the articulation of a friend, her tone took on the timbre of a well trained High Priestess.

Not trusting his voice to betray him, Ta'ano nodded. A gentle squeeze of his hand gave him a sense of reassurance, but Ta'ano wondered if it was for him or for his lover. It had been so long since he had participated in such a rite.

The slight incline of Ta'rha's head was the only indication of her commencement. Words as ancient as time flowed from her full lips, filling the grove with their power. In his mind, Ta'ano recited the spell with her, surprised that after all these years he still remembered.

A breeze swept over the tops of the grains, the shushing of their shafts adding their music to the spell. Ta'ano glanced around at their dancing heads. He should not have been surprised at the sight of white wisps flowing in from all around. Usually his Silver God would call so as to transport them from place to place, but this was different. A shiver erupted gooseflesh along his body. He tried to ignore the sudden chill, and was grateful when his Blessed One came up behind him, pulling Ta'ano in an embrace to his lover's slim form.

With the second repetition of the invocation, the white mist began to swirl sunwise around the circle site, connecting with each other to form a rising barrier between them and the agriculture. Higher it went upon the third iteration until the thick fog encapsulated them in a dome of white mist.

In the northern section of the barrier a rift formed. With the final words of the chant intoned, the breach opened and out stepped three of the most beautiful women Ta'ano had ever laid eyes upon.

Standing taller than his beloved, Their slim bodies clad in diaphanous veils the colours of their being, white, crimson and ebon. Youthful in appearance, they radiated an ancient wisdom that permeated the circle. Though Ta'ano could not gaze long upon their countenance, their exotic allure felled him to his knees.

"My Lady, we have come as You have decreed." Ta'rha sunk to the grass, kneeling on one knee with head lowered in reverence.

"My beloved daughter," chorused the three as They came to stand before Ta'rha. A scarlet toned hand delicately descended onto Ta'rha's dark curls. "You have done Us proud."

"Thank you, my Lady." Ta'rha choked back a sob at the praise from the Goddess.

As one, the trinity turned and walked sunwise around the circle until They came to stand before Ta'ano. Ta'ano quickly averted his gaze to the ground. Even Their bare toes that peeked out from under Their silken robes appeared beautiful.

"Rise, Ta'ano," They chorused.

On shaking legs, Ta'ano did as bid but refused to raise his head.

"It has been far too long—" said the White Lady.

"—since last you stood—" continued the Red Lady.

"—in a circle such as this," concluded the Ebon Lady.

"Have you never thought to call the Gods since you were Chosen?" They asked.

"Or has our son been more than enough for you?" added the Red Lady.

The playful tone snapped Ta'ano's attention to Their teasing smiles. He did not know how to respond. His mouth dried in the heat of his embarrassment.

Their chuckle increased Ta'ano's discomfiture, his face burning. Despite having lived for so long, it surprised Ta'ano at how They managed to reduce him to an awkward pre-initiate.

Before Ta'ano could find the courage to reply, the Lady turned Their attention to the Silver God standing behind Ta'ano. "It has been a long time, my son," They intoned, Their playfulness replaced by seriousness.

They frowned at the silken and his sad visage. "Too long, perhaps?" queried the Red Lady.

"I thought that—" started the pale God.

"Once grown you would be welcomed back?" asked the Ivory lady, a slight smile on lips so similar to Ta'ano's lover.

"You were never gone from us," They stated.

"You know your purpose," stated the Red Lady.

"That has never changed," said the White Lady.

"You are the gateway—" said the Black Lady.

"—so that—" continued the Crimson Lady.

"—the Gods can remain," concluded the Alabaster Lady.

"Without you none of our Children can live, laugh, feast and make love all in Our presence," They chorused.

"Without you, how will they be able to move between the

realms?" asked the White Lady.

"Without you, how will they be able to beseech us directly?" asked the Ebon Lady.

"Without you, how will the dispersed People remain connected, not only to themselves, but to us as well?" queried the Ruby Lady.

"You were able to do so before I came to be," stated Ta'ano's beloved, his courage returning.

Sadness darkened the Lady's features. "Before—" began the White Lady.

"—in the early days—" continued the Red Lady.

"—when the People were little more than animals—" said the Ebon Lady.

"—their connection with the earth, the spirits, us, came naturally," explained the Crimson Lady.

"We decided to teach the People," said the Dark Lady.

"We saw something in them akin to us," said the Pale Lady.

"We fell in love with the People," said the Red Lady.

"As the People grew," said the White Lady.

"As our seeds mingled," said the Crimson Lady.

"As our blood flowed from one to another and back again," said the Black Lady.

"We thought the rift between us would vanish," They chorused.

"Instead it grew," said the Silver God.

The three nodded.

"The more the People learned," said the White Lady.

"The more the People innovated," said the Red Lady.

"The more alike the People became to us," said the Dark Lady.

"The more they drew away from us, making the rift larger," They intoned.

"So you created the Chosen," said the Silver God, comprehension widening his ruby eyes.

Again, the trinity nodded. Ankle length hair caught in the breeze.

"Now the People are dispersed," explained the Black Lady.

"Now the People mingle their seed, their blood, their

innovations, with others," said the Red Lady.

"Now the Chosen must become the conduit," said the White Lady.

"So that the People may continue with their connection to us," said the Dark Lady.

"And us to them," said the Crimson Lady.

"The Chosen were chosen so that when this time came, they could serve us and teach the People without anything lost," They intoned.

"That time has come," stated the Ebon Lady.

"So I was created for what?" asked the Blessed One. Hurt constricted his voice.

"To guide the Chosen," answered the Ivory Lady.

"To ensure the Chosen do not stray," said the Ruby Lady.

"To teach and remind them of whom they serve," stated the Dark Lady.

"To enforce, to judge, to reap, so that the connection between us, the Chosen and the People continue to do good," They chorused.

The enormity of the task horrified Ta'ano and he turned to see that his lover's face had ashened.

"You grew up among the People," stated the White Lady.

"You fell in love and Chose one of the People." The Red Lady smiled at Ta'ano.

"Who better to serve them as a reminder of our real presence?" said the Black Lady, her face set in a serious mask.

"But how? How am I to do this?" The Pale God could not keep the tremor of horror from his voice.

"Kneel before me, my son," The chorused, a gentle smile on each of Their faces.

Ta'ano's beloved shot a worried glance at his love. Ta'ano did not know what to say. The enormity of what the Lady revealed stunned him, but his lover needed some sort of reassurance and so Ta'ano nodded his encouragement.

The surprise on the Blessed One's face turned to determined resignation and he lowered his tall form to one knee before the Lady. Their smile grew and together They bent around him; the White Lady to his left ear, the Red Lady to his forehead, and the

THANATOS

Black Lady to his right ear.

Ta'ano could not see through the curtains of long hair, but Their sussurated word, "Awaken," tickled the edge of Ta'ano's hearing. A kiss from each of Them, before They straightened, left the Blessed One still kneeling on the grass, his pale chest heaving.

A grimace twisted Ta'ano's beloved's face before he cried out and fell on his side, gripping his head.

Never having seen his Silver God in physical pain, Ta'ano found his courage. Dropping to kneel beside his love, Ta'ano apprehensively touched his beloved in an effort to offer aid and comfort. Throbbing pain jumped up his arms to take pounding residence in his head. Teeth gritted, Ta'ano could only imagine the full extent of what his lover endured.

"What did you do to him?" demanded Ta'ano. His fear of Their power gone in the face of his lover's agony.

"He will be fine," answered the Sable lady.

"Make them stop!" cried the Silver God, curling into a foetal position on the grass.

Furious, Ta'ano rose. If necessary, he would physically confront the Lady. He halted his action as all three knelt around his beloved, querulous expressions on Their exotic features.

"It should not be like this," said the Pale Lady.

"He fights," observed the Crimson Lady.

"He must surrender," announced the Sable Lady.

"To what?" demanded Ta'ano. Impotent in the face of his lover's pain, he stood while the Lady knelt.

"He must surrender to his power," They answered, rising to their feet to gaze down at one of Their own curled and sobbing.

The sight of his beloved in such a state scrambled Ta'ano to the dew coated grass once the Lady backed away. Gathering his lover so as to rest the silvered head against Ta'ano's breast, Ta'ano brushed the hot tears from the beautiful face. Fear and concern mingled with helplessness in Ta'ano's gut. *"Kreidad,* I am here. What can I do to help?" implored Ta'ano.

Eyelids with long silver lashes fluttered open. "Make them stop," he pleaded. Another cry tore from his full lips.

The throbbing headache that thundered through Ta'ano nearly

made him swoon. Swallowing down his gorge, he glanced up at the Lady. "What does he mean?"

"Our son is now connected to all Chosen, as all Chosen are now connected to him," explained the Ebon Lady.

"He hears and feels all that the Chosen think and feel," continued the Red Lady.

"In this way the Chosen cannot be lost to us and us to them," stated the White Lady.

"In this way he will be the light in the dark times to come," said the Dark lady.

"In this way he will be the darkness in the times of light," said the Ivory Lady.

"In this way he continues the bond between the People, the Chosen and Us," They intoned together.

"But that doesn't help him now!" Ta'ano winced at the level of his own shout. He did not know how much more of the migraine he could take, and if what he experienced was this intolerable, Ta'ano could hardly comprehend what his beloved underwent.

A frown pulled at the Red Lady's lips, the other two turning to face Her.

"We must, or all is lost," sighed the Crimson Lady.

The other two nodded, slight frowns on the intractable features.

The Red Lady lowered herself to sit on Ta'ano's left. The surprising proximity knocked the migraine to a headache and he watched with eyes wide in wonder as She whispered into his beloved's ear. "Focus. Focus on your breathing. Focus on each inhalation and each exhalation. Nothing else exists except breath."

The Silver God shuddered a sigh and Ta'ano felt the headache slip further away.

"Listen to my voice," continued the Red Lady. "Feel the cool earth beneath your body. Feel the gentle breeze across your flesh. Fell the dampness of the grass. Feel the starlight on your head.

"Above you are the stars. Below you are the stones. You exist between them. You encapsulate everything: the earth, the moon, the sun the stars."

The pain melted away, replaced by contentment. Ta'ano

lowered his head to rest on his lover's and closed his eyes, falling into the spell the Crimson Lady wove.

"There is no sound except for your quieted thoughts," she whispered. "There is no feeling except for your settled feelings. Now reached out to your Chosen, to your beloved, to your Ta'ano. Allow yourself to once again feel his feelings, to hear his thoughts. Gently now. You are safe. You are loved. Feel Ta'ano's love for you. Hear his heart beat for you. Hear his thoughts only for you.

"Now reach out—no, not that far. See Our beloved Ta'rha in your mind. Remember you are safe, you are loved. Now open yourself to feel her feelings, to hear her thoughts. No pain comes. Know you can close that off as easily as you can with Ta'ano. Know that you can open that connection with Ta'rha as easily as you can with Ta'ano.

"No reach out father."

Ta'ano's beloved whimpered and the pain returned. Ta'ano shushed him, holding closer.

"Sense all the Chosen," continued the Red Lady. "I know it is a lot and that it hurts, but you will be alright. Now, focus on one. Sense her. Feel her. Let her know you are there. Open yourself to her as she opens to you. Let her know she is not alone. Let her know who you are. Now close yourself from her and move to another. Sense him, let him hear you as you hear him…"

Ta'ano held his Silver haired God, listening as the Red Lady gently awakened his beloved to his new abilities until the lightening in the east heralded dawn's approach. The longest night in Ta'ano's life came to a close as the Red Lady finished and stood once again between Her sisters.

"It is done," They chorused once Ta'ano and the Silver God stood before Them.

"Thank you," said the Silver God, bowing his head. "I will do as you have bidden."

"You can be nothing more than our son," They intoned. "That in itself is much."

The Lady turned to face Ta'rha sitting on the dew dropped grass. Their attention sent her scurrying to her feet.

Arms encircling his lover's waist, Ta'ano did not pay

attention to Ta'rha as she sent the Lady home. Pale arms surrounded him in a tight embrace. His beloved had changed, but he would always be Ta'ano's.

A kiss landed on Ta'ano's crown. *And you will always be mine,* sent the Silver God.

XXI

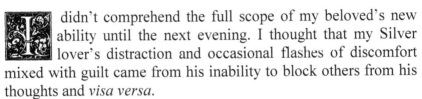 didn't comprehend the full scope of my beloved's new ability until the next evening. I thought that my Silver lover's distraction and occasional flashes of discomfort mixed with guilt came from his inability to block others from his thoughts and *visa versa*.

"He was like a man used to holding a cup of water, but now he had to balance so many more, always trying to keep the liquid from escaping.

"I was partially right. What I didn't realize was that proximity affected his ability to lock out the thoughts and feelings of other Chosen. This meant he had the greatest difficulty with Ta'rha.

"The situation didn't come to a head until he and I were alone in Ta'rha's home. She had been called away earlier to attend a birth. I presumed we had time. I was wrong. Ta'rha came back while we were...well, you know.

"I guess the sight of us, coupled with the proximity to one another, sparked her desire. Before too long the three of us were together.

"Initially, both he and I were uncomfortable and unsure, but with Ta'rha's understanding we became a threesome.

"The centuries we three spent together were some of the

happiest and most pleasurable for me. With her love and compassion she showed my beloved how to master his awakened abilities. With me, she taught me that sharing my Blessed One didn't diminish the love he and I felt for one another.

"Eventually, the city became more and more deserted as the land could no longer support the People. Ta'rha, my beloved and I had a difficult decision. In the end, she decided to follow her people.

"My beloved and I could not. He had put off for so long his connections with other Chosen. It was time to find them and let them know in truth that he walked the world alongside them.

"Our parting with Ta'rha was bitter-sweet. We knew we'd find one another again, and that she'd always be able to communicate with us through my beloved.

"He and I took to wandering the world again. This time he led. We met many Chosen since we sought them out, staying with them for periods of time before moving on.

"We went north and west to lands once under the great ice. We met up with my daughter, De'annu, who had been Chosen. Our reunion was filled with great joy. It was she who led her People to create great circles of stone to help amplify the powers needed to call the Gods.

"It was then that the Lady's prophesy appeared to be taking hold. It was becoming harder for the Chosen and the People to communicate directly with the Gods.

"Disturbed by this, my beloved and I continued our travels to see if this was indeed the case. We heard of great cities rising back east. What we found was a land filled with large urban centres, the capital dedicated to my mother!

"We found her in the central temple. The reunion between Da'annu and I paled in comparison to the one between my mother, Inish'anna, and me. I was a grown man and Chosen of the Silver God she had last seen as a child. We were feasted and celebrated.

"Inish'anna showed us many innovations of the People - particularly writing. She taught me and my beloved. What disturbed us the most was her news that she could no longer call upon her God. We stayed for a while but the People's reverence for my mother disturbed us.

"We eventually left with a caravan travelling east to a land bordered by desert on both sides. It was there that we met with Aset and Asar…"

"My Lord Anapa!"

Ta'ano turned at the call from his attendant running down the hall. Lips twisting at the boy's lack of decorum, Ta'ano crossed his arms over his bare chest. It did not take long for the fifteen year old to halt in front of him, bare feet squeaking against stone.

"What is it, Djaty?" asked Ta'ano, irritation lacing his words.

He watched the boy place sun browned hands on similarly coloured knees as he attempted to catch his breath. His black hair peeked out from under his white *knat*. Ta'ano needed to have a word with the lad about his sloven appearance before someone complained to the chamberlain. Ta'ano liked Djaty's boyish charms and did not wish to see him replaced.

"My Lord," gasped Djaty as he managed to stand straight. "The Lady Aset and Lord Asar have asked that you meet them."

"Now?"

Djaty nodded, sending tails of his *khat* bobbing.

Ta'ano huffed. "Where?"

"They request your presence in the temple of—"

"Not again," interjected Ta'ano.

"They said if you don't come—"

Ta'ano walked off in the direction that Djaty had come. "Go to my chambers and right yourself before someone sees you in such a state."

"My Lord," replied the boy.

Ta'ano barely registered the sound of Djaty's fading footfalls as he followed the maze of halls out of the building.

Did you get the call? sent Ta'ano.

Anger tinged with annoyance flowed into him.

Yes, replied the Blessed One. *I am on my way. If you get—*

I'll stall them, if I can.

Ta'ano felt the connection shut down as he raced as fast as he dared through the underground complex. He had always trusted his beloved's intuition. How could he not since his lover was a God?

Their arrival two centuries ago had placed both Ta'ano and his beloved in a most awkward position. Aset and Asar had welcomed them with open arms, declaring to their People that they were blessed to have more gods descend to walk among them.

Ta'ano's lover had set his jaw in anger at the proclamation. Whatever concerns and suspicions he had to drive them both to this land were placed before them without apology. The only thing that caused Ta'ano's Chooser to go along with the charade was the People's reaction of pure joy at the arrival of Imn and Anapa, the names Aset gave them in front of the People without Ta'ano's and the Silver God's permission.

Corruption of the old ways ran rampant. Never before had either of them met a Chosen who masqueraded a god until now. It explained why there were so many Chosen in the land. Aset and Asar had set things up brilliantly, leaving them completely in charge of a prosperous and thriving people.

The unfortunate result of their delusion was that they believed they could become Choosers. No one but the Gods could do such magic.

Ta'ano followed the secret underground tunnels that connected their temples until he found the steps leading up to Aset's inner sanctum. Only the Chosen, their mortal attendants and the Silver God knew about and used them. Taking the steps two at a time, Ta'ano arrived to find his beloved in a heated argument with Aset and Asar. Sutekh leaned against the back wall, his arms crossed over his muscular chest, a smirk lifting his thin lips as he watched.

Ta'ano frowned at the sight. There was no love lost between he and Sutekh. Sutekh not only made it clear to all that he believed that he was a God, but that he should also rule over all the Chosen in Kemet.

Subtle waves of anger washed through Ta'ano as he came to stand beside his beloved. "Enough!" he shouted. "This is not how you speak to the Blessed One!"

He glanced up at his lover, unhappy to see his pale jaw locked and grinding. This was not how he ever wished to see his beloved, but Aset's constant badgering made Ta'ano wish they had never come to this land.

Ta'ano turned his attention to the couple, ignoring Aset's glare. There was no doubt to her beauty. Large brown eyes lined in khol accentuated her glamour. Long black hair spilled waves down her back and front, covering ample breasts and the straps of the impeccably white *kalasiris* hugging her curvaceous hips to hang down to the tops of her feet.

Her husband, Asar appeared to wish his wife would leave well enough alone. Dressed similarly to Ta'ano and Sutekh, Asar stood with hands on his hips, khol lined dark eyes closed, clearly exasperated. Ta'ano thought the Chosen counted silently at the subtle movements of his full lips.

"You asked me to come." Ta'ano addressed the statement to his hosts. "If this is another attempt to convince the Blessed One—"

"Du'mezi is dead."

The harsh statement from Aset's lips stunned Ta'ano. When he had left his mother, she was happily in love with fellow Chosen, Du'mezi.

"What? How?" sputtered Ta'ano. He had never heard of a Chosen dying, let alone be killed.

"Word came from Ur this morning." Sutekh stood up and walked over to join them. His deep voice sent shivers down Ta'ano's spine. "It seems that we are not as nearly as immortal as we were led to believe." Black eyes narrowed menacingly on the Blessed One. "Ishi'anna has proven to be a jealous woman. Du'mezi was caught in their marriage bed with a number of nubile young mortals. In a fury she cleaved his head from his body."

Ta'ano gasped. He could not imagine his mother ever doing such, but millennia of living changes a person.

"What does that have to do with your request?" asked the Silver God, his voice cold.

"We need to know how to create more Chosen," stated Aset. "You of all people—"

"The Blessed One is not a person. He is a God. One of those who we serve and were rewarded by," interjected Ta'ano. "He deserves the respect and reverence all of his kind should receive."

"We are all Gods now," defied Sutekh. "None of the Chosen can call upon the Old Ones anymore. Believe me, we've tried."

"That does not make the Chosen Gods," stated Ta'ano. He could feel anger flush his face.

"That in itself does not, but it is the Chosen who now bring agriculture, architecture and many new innovations to the People. Of course, the People will worship us. We are stronger, smarter and longer lived than they."

"And now they can kill us," rounded Asar.

"Between both issues, the Chosen will eventually fade into the past as the Gods of *our* People have." Aset glared up at the Blessed One. "Unless you teach us the secret to create more Chosen, we will all become stories eventually to be forgotten and the Ancient Ones will truly be lost to the People."

"Are you saying that the Blessed One's presence upon the land is not enough for you?" shot Ta'ano.

"In the time since he Chose you, has he Chosen others?" Sutekh's black brow rose up as he canted his head to the side, arms still crossed over his bare chest.

Ta'ano pursed his lips. There was no need to answer the question.

Ta'ano's beloved let out a sigh and dropped his arms to his sides. "What you say is true. The Lady indicated this eventually when Ta'ano and I stayed with Ta'rha and her People."

"And where is Ta'rha now?" asked Sutekh, smugly.

The Blessed One turned his red glare on the impudent Chosen. "She went east into lands no Chosen has sent foot in."

"How does that have anything to do with the matter at hand?" demanded Ta'ano.

"It proves that the world is much larger than originally believed," said Sutekh. "As such, the Chosen will become spread too far apart, becoming vulnerable."

"And alone," added Aset. "If we are not taught this magic, you condemn all Chosen to an immortality of loneliness, destitute and bereft of their connection to the Ancient Ones."

"I am still here," countered the Blessed One.

"But for how long?" snapped Aset.

The question slapped both Ta'ano and his lover across the

face.

"What?" exclaimed Ta'ano, spinning to face the wide eyed shock of his lover. A fall of dread plummeted in his stomach.

"I am *not* going anywhere," protested the Silver God. His eyes locked onto Ta'ano's. "I would never leave you."

The lump dissolved at the surety of his lover's words and the sincerity that flowed with them. He smiled at his beloved before turning to face the others.

"You may never choose to leave Anapa, Imn, but eventually the Lady *will* call you home." Asar's gentle tone sent a shiver of foreboding down Ta'ano's spine.

Tears welled in Aset's eyes. "Do you know how long it has been since I was able to call my Chooser—my Blessed One? Or when the last time Asar stood in the presence of his?

"The People do not know of you and the Gods," said Asar. "They know us."

"How can we go on knowing that one day our solitude will be overwhelmingly complete?" asked Aset. "How can we go on without Choosing those *we* love as the Old Ones Chose us?"

"You are the last. Even you cannot fulfill all the needs of all the Chosen," said Sutekh.

"You do not know what you ask of me." The Blessed One's shoulders slumped in defeat.

Ta'ano frowned. He knew the toll that would be exacted from his lover. More Chosen meant more minds and hearts forced upon his beloved.

Aset fell to her knees before the Silver God, hands clasped between her breasts as she gazed up with pleading eyes. "Please."

The Blessed One closed his eyes, his face pinched in pain for a long time. When he opened his eyes, he nodded. "I will teach you," his quiet voice filled with gravel, "but on one condition."

Wide hope filled eyes shimmered up at the Blessed One. "Anything, my Lord."

Ta'ano locked shocked gazes with Asar before noticing Sutekh's triumphant grin. Something was wrong. He needed to confide with his beloved, but the wall was secure.

Unaware of Ta'ano's concern, the Silver God continued, "Once I teach you, only certain Chosen will be able to call me. I will state who, and those who cannot call upon me must go through those I choose to remain in contact with. Understood?"

"So you would set some Chosen above others?" inquired Sutekh.

"Yes."

"Do we have any say in whom you will set above the others?"

"No," replied the Blessed One.

Anger sparked in Sutekh's eyes before being quickly extinguished. He bowed to cover his fury.

Aset rose to her feet, her lovely face beaming with gratitude. "When can you teach us?"

"I take it that you have someone in mind?" asked the Silver God.

"Yes," nodded Aset.

Ta'ano took an involuntary step back at the hurt in Asar's eyes.

"Then I will show you before dawn."

Aset clapped, bouncing in glee. "Tonight we will hold a great banquet and before the sun rises you will teach us to become Choosers."

Asar spun on his heel, storming out of the sparse chamber. Sutekh followed with the same briskness. Ta'ano walked beside his beloved out of Aset's halls, the niggling of worry growing more pronounced with each step.

Music, torchlight and laughter filled the cool night air as Aset's guests enjoyed the food and drink provided on long ebony tables. In the eastern edge of the courtyard, settled atop a rise of stone cut stairs, Aset sat on an ebony throne, gold leaf highlighting the artistry.

Eyes bright with happiness, Aset appeared the Goddess she claimed to be. Newer, thicker khol outlined her glittering eyes, making them appear larger than they were. The sunset coloured *kalsiris* covered her curvaceous form, tucking under the elaborately beaded necklace of gold, turquoise and red stones that sat over her collar bone down to her bosom. Bare feet peeked out from beneath the hem of the flaxen cloth.

Ta'ano stood off to the side, far down the garden, and watched her as he sipped from a ceramic mug. Misgivings and doubt soured the taste. He did not want to come to the party, but his lover thought it best. One of the two had to make an appearance. Ta'ano frowned as the flavour of his drink flowed over his tongue.

Other Chosen had come to celebrate the event. Nyftys and Pasht talked quietly beside a long table across from him while Re took his enjoyment from one of the prettier women as he sat on a chair at the end of another laden table. Ta'ano wished he could have stayed with his beloved in his chambers, or at the very least kept to his own.

A gong sounded, turning Ta'ano's, and everyone else's, attention toward Aset.

With the grace of a cat, she stood resplendent in her majesty. Her crown stood high on her head, black hair framing her heart shaped face. A cloak of feathers rested on her shoulders, giving the appearance of wings whenever her arms moved. A knot tied itself in Ta'ano's gut.

"My fellow Gods. My beloved People," she addressed the party goers. "Tonight we celebrate a wonderful event." The crowd of about a hundred quieted. Re removed the girl from his lap and stood. "Tonight I will become a mother to a new God."

Whispers broke the silence.

The gong sounded again. Aset stood, as did everyone else, until whatever was supposed to happen did not. With the flick of her fingers Aset summoned a female servant to whisper in the girl's ear. Message received, the maid turned to do her Goddess' bidding.

Ta'ano watched as the servant came to a halt. Two guards met her at the side of entrance to the garden.

"What is the meaning of this?" asked Aset.

The two guards bowed low before their Goddess, grips on perpendicular spears tight. Straightening, the guard on the right kept his eyes focused forward and far away. "My Queen, there has been an incident."

Aset's eyes widened in worry. "Of what sort?"

Ta'ano stepped forward to join Aset, taking note of how agitated the two guards appeared despite their stony features. "I think they would prefer if we went with them, Aset."

Red painted lips turned down. Clutching the feathered cloak tight around her body, Aset descended the steps and waved to the guards that they should precede her. Without an invitation Ta'ano followed in Aset's wake, as did Nyftys.

It did not take long to arrive at a set of tall doors, the scent of blood heavy in the air. At Aset's nod the guards opened the doors. The smell did not prepare them for the sight splayed before them.

Aset and Nyftys paled, struck dumb at the bloody and dismembered remains of Asar. Comprehension of what lay before him sent Ta'ano into action, yelling to the guards to accompany Imn to the murder scene while sending a message to his beloved to come.

In a fog, Aset wandered across the blood splattered floor before dropping to her knees beside the dismembered head of her husband. Uncaring or unaware, cooling red blood seeped into her *kasiris* and the feathers of her cloak. Carefully, she lifted Asar's head to cradle it in her arms, its lifeless eyes staring up at her.

Ta'ano's breath caught as Aset began to wail her grief. Tears flooded his eyes and he watched as Nyftys too became overwrought. It did not take long before Ta'ano's beloved entered, halting abruptly as his bare feet landed in a red puddle next to a disembodied arm. Ta'ano had never seen the argent God turn ashen.

"How?" gasped Ta'ano's lover. He turned to face the guards. "Who has done this?"

The two guards trembled under the imperious red glare of Imn before dropping to the stone floor in prostration, their spears clattering beside them. "We do not know, my Lord," said the guard on the right, his forehead pressed to the ground.

"Sounds of an altercation called our attention, my Lord," trembled the one on the left. "When we arrived, we found... we..." The guard's voice caught in terror.

"There was no one here," said the first guard. "We found..."

"Leave," stated the Blessed One, compassion softening his tone.

The guards did not need to be told twice. Kowtowing, they

backed up. Upon reaching the corridor, they stood and all but fled.

The Silver God returned his attention to the murder scene, a worried on his face. Ta'ano took quiet steps to stand beside his beloved. *Who did this?* sent Ta'ano.

He watched his beloved close his eyes, take a deep breath and quieted. Ta'ano knew his Blessed One searched the Chosen. *Sutekh is not here*, sent the Silver God, his eyes snapping open at the revelation.

Ta'ano glanced up at his lover. *Not here? Where is he?*

I am uncertain. He is blocking my efforts to find him.

Do you thin—

I am afraid so, answered the Silver God. *We will have to deal with him later. We have more important concerns to deal with now.*

The Blessed One stepped forward until he stood behind Aset. At the touch of his hand on her shoulder she came to a hiccoughing halt to her wailing and turned to gaze up at him, still holding Asar's head to her bloodied chest.

Her beautiful face shimmered with the trails of tears down her cheeks and she glanced down at the head of her husband, placed a kiss on the cold, blue forehead and laid it back down on the congealing floor. Rising to her feet, the Silver God caught her before her shaking legs caused her to collapse. Embraced in his pale arms, she clung to him as a new wash of tears trailed down her face.

A twinge of sadness tightened Ta'ano's chest as he watched his beloved comfort Aset. He could not begin to imagine the pain she suffered. A part of him was grateful that it was her, not him, who mourned the loss of a beloved. He knew it was selfish, but the sight of Asar's murder shattered his illusion that the Chosen were impervious to death, leaving him shaken to the core.

"Apana."

The soft calling of his name in this land brought Ta'ano's attention to his beloved still holding Aset.

"Please, if you will, make arrangements for Asar's burial."

The request seemed so alien, but unfortunately necessary. Ta'ano nodded. "All the p—pieces need to…" He could not bring himself to finish the sentence.

Aset pulled away from the Blessed One and stood, wiping her face with her hand. "I will do it."

"I will help," said Nyftys, stepping forward. Glistening tears dripped from her face to mingle with the cooling blood on the floor.

The four stood in silence. The macabre scene laid around them. In one horrific moment their world had been shattered.

Aset's gasp turned their attention to her. Not knowing what else could be wrong, Ta'ano frowned.

A body part is missing, sent his beloved.

Turning back to the scene, Ta'ano's eyes widened and his stomach lurched with the revelation.

XXII

orty days it took to painstakingly prepare Asar's body for burial. A gruesome task, Ta'ano did the best he could to reattach the mutilated sections together, the stench of death assaulting him as he worked.

A thankless task, Ta'ano did it because his beloved requested it of him, but mainly to keep Aset from further pain. Occasionally, Nyftys would help him. In this matter no one not Chosen could attend Asar's burial preparations. The funeral would be a different matter.

Ta'ano stepped back from his handiwork. Laid out on a long wooden table Asar's body was ready for its sarcophagus. Sewn together, the body now lay wrapped in layers of linen with jewels, prayers stamped into gold and Asar's jewelry snug between the layers. There was one thing missing. One that Aset and Nyftys could not find despite their searches.

A sound far off to the back of the underground chamber turned Ta'ano to watch as several mortal servants descended the dark steps. One carried a flaming torch which stung Ta'ano's eyes. The other six carefully brought down the sarcophagus.

"Put it on the table over there," ordered Ta'ano, pointing to the work bench he had cleared for this purpose.

Karen Dales

"Yes, Lord Anapa," bowed the man with the torch.

Ta'ano watched the men gently place the elaborate coffin down. In silence they left, taking the light with them. Only a small splash of illumination descended the steps to provide Ta'ano the ability to see the intricate details the artisans carved and painted into the wood.

Drawn to the beauty, Ta'ano trailed his fingers over the etched hard wood until he stood by the centre, both hands flat on the lid. There was one duty left to him. With careful movements, he lifted the gilt lid and placed it standing against the wall. The image of a stylized Asar stared at him with blank eyes. Repressing a shudder, Ta'ano went to the body. He lifted the linen wrapped corpse and carried it to the coffin. The sight of its dark depths caught his breath and for a moment Ta'ano hesitated to place the dead Chosen into its final resting place.

How snug the fit with no room to move, but Asar need never do so again.

Asar's death had stunned the Chosen. Word rapidly spread. The Chosen were more vulnerable than believed.

Ta'ano placed the staring sarcophagus lid back, shutting out the image of the dead Chosen. Ta'ano wished the scars from that vision would leave, but they were carved too deep.

The Chosen were vulnerable.

The funeral at sunset was beautiful, thought Ta'ano as he trailed after the other Chosen into Aset's private chamber. Ta'ano should not have been surprised, but the attachment of a phallus onto the coffin at the appropriate place seemed a tad gauche. Part of him understood her reasoning. They never found Asar's phallus, nor the perpetrator of the crime.

All eyes turned as the Blessed One came into the room. Ta'ano wanted to rush to his beloved's side, but such an emotional display would undermine the severity of the situation.

"Before Asar's murder a case was made as to why I should teach you the secrets of how to Choose another." The Blessed One stepped into the centre of the sparse room. "I had agreed, and now I clearly see the need." He turned to face Aset. "Bring forth the one you wish to be Chosen."

Aset bobbed a nod before leaving the room.

Do you think this is wise? sent Ta'ano. He glanced from face to face of the Chosen waiting to have this mystery resolved. Nyftys stood closed to the bed at the far wall, her hands wringing in nervousness. Sutekh was nowhere to be found, still. Pasht and Re stood sullen by the opposite wall across from the bed.

Wise or not, the need has been made evident, responded the Silver God.

It did not take long for Aset to return with a young man in tow.

Ta'ano's eyes widened at the handsome youth. Long black lengths of hair flowed past his broad tanned shoulders to tease a smooth, well muscled chest. Large brown eyes gave the young man an innocent appearance, but it was his full lips and high cheek bones that accentuated his beauty. For a moment Ta'ano desired to discover what remained hidden beneath the plain white *shenti*.

Standing beneath the scrutiny of his Gods, the young mortal kept his head lowered in reverence and fear.

"This is Heru," introduced Aset. "He has served me well since he entered into my service as a boy. I wish to make him my son, to become one of us."

No emotion played upon the blank pale face of Ta'ano's beloved as he walked over to stand before Heru. "Do you comprehend what Aset wishes of you?"

Heru dropped to the floor, his forehead pressed to the polished stone. "My Lord Imn," he muttered. To have the Hidden One gaze upon him, let alone speak to him, sent the young man trembling. "My Lady Aset told me I would become a God."

"No. You will not become a God," corrected the Silver God. Aset's sharp intake of breath remained ignored. "You will become Chosen, one who serves the Gods. Do you understand what that means?"

Heru shook his head.

"I will teach him," said Aset.

The Blessed One turned to face her. "If he survives. He is not of the People."

"The People are dispersed," said Pasht. "The seed of the Gods now flow into a larger number of people. One need only gaze upon Heru to see that the blood of the People and the Gods flow strongly within him."

"That, and many others, are reasons why I wish to Choose him," said Aset, standing beside the prostrate young man. "In any case, you have made a promise."

Ta'ano felt the sting of Aset's final words, even bringing his hand to his reddening face. Displeasure darkened the Silver God's features.

Aset, realizing her mistake, fell to the floor beside Heru. "I–I am so sorry, my Lord," she stammered. "I am—"

"Enough," stated the Blessed One, his voice stern yet understanding. "You forget that I feel all you feel. All that you think, I can hear."

"Thank you, my Lord." Aset laid a gentle kiss to a moon touched foot before rising. This time she kept her head demurely lowered.

"I will teach you," said the Silver God, "but be warned, never before has a Chosen become a Chooser. It may not be possible."

"I accept this risk so that I may be with my Lady Aset for all time," said Heru, rising to his knees.

"You may die," stated the God.

"I would rather die in the attempt to be with my Lady than to grow old in the knowledge that my cowardice drove me from her service."

"Well stated, boy." Re clapped his hands as he stepped forward. "Let them try, Imn. The worst is that the mortal dies and we learn that only the Gods can be Choosers. The best is that we can become alike to the Gods if the mortal is successfully Chosen."

Ta'ano did not like the other potential downfalls that could affect his beloved.

The Silver God frowned before nodding. "Heru, if you do become Chosen, you will have your youthful body forever."

"My Lady Aset had me prepared, my Lord Imn," blushed Heru.

Amusement lifted pale lips and set a spark in blood red eyes. "Aset, if you are ready, take Heru to your bed."

Heru rose to his feet, and Aset led him to the linen wrapped straw bed that was supported by four marble white pillars. With a graceful sweep of her hand Aset pushed the sheer muslin drapes aside, allowing Heru to sit on the edge.

Aset turned back to face the Blessed One. "What do I do?"

Ta'ano and the others drew closer. An air of anxious expectation vibrated through the chamber. Heru's large brown eyes landed on Ta'ano who tried to offer a reassuring smile. The alarm on the young man's beautiful face told Ta'ano he had failed.

"You must drink him until his heart struggles and is about to stop," answered Ta'ano's beloved.

Panic set in and Heru jumped to his feet. It took Aset's strength as a Chosen, and the other gifts, to sooth and calm Heru enough so that he sat back down. Tilting his head to expose the leaping artery in his muscular neck, Aset sat, pulled Heru to her and bit deep.

Ta'ano watched as she fed and imagined his beloved sinking his teeth into him. A stirring beneath his *shenti* made him turn his attention away from Aset's gentle feeding and found Pasht standing near him, her dark nipples tightened into buds. Embarrassed, Ta'ano took the couple of steps to stand beside his Silver God.

Sensing Ta'ano's proximity, the Blessed One took Ta'ano's hand in his. Together they watched Aset take Heru's life into hers, the labouring sound of the mortal's heartbeat becoming more prominent.

It did not take long until Heru's heart began skipping. Aset lifted her mouth from his neck and gently laid him back. Bluish in tone, eyes slightly open, Ta'ano knew it would not be long before the mortal passed through the Western Gate.

"Bite your wrist and feed Heru your blood," instructed the Blessed One.

Aset did as bidden, biting deep, wincing at the self-inflicted pain. Chosen blood splattered on her *kalsiris* and dripped across Heru's *shenti*, up his abdomen and chest, to spill into his slightly opened mouth.

"Drink, my beloved," encouraged Aset, as she lowered her bleeding wrist to press against his purple lips.

A sucking sound filled the quiet as mortal lips sealed over the wound, causing Aset to gasp in pleasure.

"Do not let Heru drain you," said the Silver God. "I wish I could say how much he should take, but in this situation I think more is better."

Aset nodded, her eyes closed, focused on the feeding.

Ta'ano had never stood audience to something so erotic. When he and his lover spent time with Ta'rha, he was an active participant every time the three made love. Standing there, fingers entwined with his beloved's, watching Heru feed from Aset hardened him to painful rigidity.

Glancing at the others proved he was not the only one affected. It took every scrap of willpower not to have his way with his beautiful Silver God right then and there.

Later, my love, sent the Blessed One. He gave Ta'ano's hand a gentle squeeze. *I will have you once this is done.*

Ta'ano barely contained his moan, his rod leaping and caressing against the *shenti*. The image of them entwined was a tortuous promise.

Aset's gasp drew his attention to her and her intended Chosen. Flushed with pleasure, Aset leaned over and laid a gentle kiss on Heru's blood stained lips. Rising, Aset turned to face the Silver God. "What happens now?"

"Now you wait," said the Silver God, his voice rough with lust insatiate.

"Wait?" inquired Re.

"Heru must make the Choice," answered the Blessed One. "The same Choice all of you had to make."

"To live," whispered Pasht.

"Or to die," said Ta'ano.

"Birth is a painful process," said Ta'ano's beloved. "So too is this. Be with him, Aset. Give Heru reason to Choose life." He turned to leave.

Aset scrambled off the bed and came to stand before the Blessed One, worry etching her features. "Wait! That's all? There's nothing left to do?"

Ta'ano's lover looked over his shoulder, long silver strands swept forward to hang down his naked chest. "The hard part is to come."

All Chosen turned at Heru's cry of pain, his body convulsing on the bloodied bed. Aset fled to Heru's side, tears filling her eyes.

Come, sent Ta'ano's beloved. *I wish to remember less disturbing times.*

Hand in hand, Ta'ano let his argent lover lead them away from the sounds of pain. *Was it like that for me?*

A shudder brought the Silver God to a halt in the corridor. "Yes," he said, turning to face Ta'ano. "I thought I would lose you."

Unshed tears glistened red eyes. It was enough to send Ta'ano into his beloved's arms. "I remember white faced creatures pulling me to stay with them."

"They are those that Chose wrong."

"You mean that was the Land of the Dead?" Ta'ano pulled away enough to gaze up at his lover.

The Silver God shook his head and pulled Ta'ano back into their embrace. "They are not in the Land of the Dead, and nor are they in the Land of the Gods. The blood of the Gods, coupled with their wrong choice, led their bodies to die, but their spirits to linger between realms, hungry for what their wrong choice cost them."

Ta'ano trembled at the thought that he had nearly become one of them.

My chambers are closer, sent Ta'ano's beloved.

Yes, sighed Ta'ano.

Their wish to feel and celebrate their life and love in each other's arms nearly drove them to couple in the hall. When his beloved finally rode him, they were safe behind closed doors. In a tangle of cast off clothing Ta'ano cried out his release.

X X III

hen the sun set that evening Heru emerged as one of the Chosen," continued Thanatos. "The ramifications and implications were too broad to fully conceptualize. The Chosen could now become Choosers. One thing my beloved had to instill, or at least try, was that not everyone could be Chosen. Only those whose blood ran thickest with the essence of the Gods could be successfully Chosen, and that one must Choose out of love. The second reason became evident when Aset and Heru realized they could speak mind to mind and heart to heart like my lover and me. What my beloved did not reveal, at least not right away, was that he now heard Heru's thoughts and felt his feelings along with all the other Chosen. That meant that as the Chosen multiplied, so did it increase the number of Chosen he could hear and feel.

"Over the years others were Chosen. Word spread, partially because my beloved and I travelled to teach others since, as time flew by, it became near next to impossible to call the Gods as the People once had. Only those on a small island to the north could claim this gift. My daughter, Da'annu had found a way and in their land they created circular monuments to facilitate their connection.

"My daughter was a genius, but there appeared to be something special about the land and its People."

"Whoa. Hold on a second," interrupted Fernando. "You're saying that the Chosen built Stonehenge?"

"And Avebury, and all the other stone circles?" asked Bridget. Disbelief widened her blue eyes.

Fatigued, Thanatos nodded. "I, myself, stood on Silbury Plain and assisted in marking out the ditch and ring. Of course, that was long before the stones were set. The Chosen were assisted by many of the People dedicated to keeping the lines of communication between them and the Gods."

"I don't believe it," exclaimed Fernando, standing to pace.

Thanatos sighed. "It doesn't matter if you believe it or not. It doesn't change the truth. You continually forget how long I've walked this earth."

Slowly, Fernando lowered to sit once more. His tongue fell silent.

"What happened in Egypt?" Notus' quiet voice filled the void.

Thanatos smiled at his always inquisitive Chosen, thankful for the redirection back to the story. "Not long after Heru was Chosen, Sutekh brought forth an army from the south, intent to take power. His guilt over Asar's murder was solidified in Aset's and the other Chosen's minds.

"Intent to take power, Sutekh set himself up as a God. Those that followed him fought for him. Aset could not let this stand, and Heru, her Chosen, met Sutekh with their own army of the People.

"The fighting was fierce. My beloved and I watched in horror as the blood of mortals soaked the earth, pooling like puddles of rain. Something had to be done otherwise Chosen would fight Chosen. My Blessed One intervened.

"Through his link, he brought Sutekh to his knees, allowing Heru the victory required. Of course, this was not enough to ensure peace between the Chosen. My beloved would not acquiesce to Aset and Heru's demands that Sutekh be executed by decapitation. What my beloved did was establish Aset as Mistress of the Chosen of her lands. Heru became her consort-child. He also removed the rule of the People by the Chosen. If the Chosen were to be perceived as Gods, then to curb their power a mortal would rule over mortals, but would always be guided by the Chosen through their direct voice or by those servant-priesthood that served the Chosen."

"It sounds like he attempted to recreate what was established between your people and those you call the Gods," remarked Notus.

Thanatos nodded and smiled. "Yes. With the help of the Chosen, a new structure was born. The Chosen would be seen as Gods by the people of Khem and those with the blood of the People would become the Chosens' priesthood. Aset's mortal seneschal, Narmer, was picked to rule the People of the northern and southern lands."

"The first pharaoh." Notus' hazel eyes widened.

"Yes." Thanatos' grin grew. "Well under my beloved's heel, and somewhat mollified that he would have some sort of power, Sutekh acquiesced and he and Aset found a tenuous peace.

"My beloved and I made Khemet our home—our base of operations, if you will—while we traveled for extended periods of time." Thanatos took a shuddering breath, unwilling to move into the next part of the story, but knowing he must. "Everything changed for me, and for the Chosen, when Rameses the Second waged war against Muwatallis for Qadesh."

Ta'ano stared at the beads, small knife and arrowhead made of strange silver-black metal that lay on the map table in Rameses' tent. Frowning in cautious curiosity, Ta'ano nudged the beads with a forefinger and watched them roll a few finger widths before coming to a halt. It was the knife and arrowhead that concerned him the most.

"What are these made from?" Ta'ano looked up to face the Pharaoh standing on the other side of the table, his tanned arms supporting his muscular bulk as he leaned on the wood.

"They were found on the two *Shasu* that were captured," replied Rameses, his voice deep and resonant. The manner in which he uttered every word commanded attention.

Ta'ano glanced up at his beloved beside him. A frown marred

the beautiful pale features as long, slim fingers picked up the knife by its wooden hilt. "I have never seen its like before," commented the Blessed One as he turned it this way and that, catching the strange metal in the lamplight.

Rameses' shoulders slumped at the revelation. Standing straight, he reached over the table and picked up the arrowhead. "There has been word that the Hatti have found a new metal, something stronger than anything ever used before," said the Pharaoh. "If this is it and the Hatti are equipped with such weapons, then we may be at a great disadvantage."

Unsheathing the bronze sword that hung from his golden belt, Rameses held the blade point down on the table. Ta'ano and his beloved watched as the Pharaoh brought the arrowhead against the flat of the bronze blade. Using the arrowhead's edge, Rameses slivered off a tiny portion of bronze.

Ta'ano could not hold back his gasp. It joined the clatter of the knife as the Silver God dropped it as if burned.

"If you will excuse me." Ta'ano's lover turned, pulling up the cowl of his white cloak over his head. "I need to…"

"Of course, my Lord Imn," bowed Rameses.

Ta'ano frowned at his beloved's unexplained retreat.

"He goes to inform Sutekh, Re and Ptah what we've discovered," explained the Pharaoh.

Ta'ano doubted that was the case. Concern drove his desires to quit Rameses' presence. Turning back to the handsome mortal, he asked, "Is there anything else?"

Rameses nodded. The gold striped white *khat* brushed his broad shoulders. "The *Shasu* who had these" —he dropped the arrowhead onto the table and resheathed his sword— "have revealed that Muwatalli has pulled back his forces. The way is clear for us to continue our advance."

"Is that wise, Rameses?" challenged Ta'ano. "We are already so far ahead of Ptah's, Re's and Sutekh's divisions."

"Muwatalli is a coward," stated Rameses. "Why else would the Hatti flee to Aleppo?"

Despite Rameses' assurance, Ta'ano could not quash the sense of unease that roiled his belly. "I do hope you are right." Ta'ano turned to leave. "The truth will be found in the light of day."

Ta'ano walked out of the Pharaoh's tent in search of the one he shared with his beloved. Infantry and charioteers sat around cook fires, eating their evening meals and drinking beer. The sounds of boisterous merry making, libations to the Gods and song competed against the tension that soon they would engage in battle. Tonight they celebrated life with their brothers-in-arms.

In the deepening twilight, Ta'ano could see sentinels set at equal distances around the encampment. Regardless of Rameses' positivity, there was reassurance in seeing those standing watch.

Arriving at his tent, Ta'ano pushed aside the blue striped cloth serving as a door and stepped into the small space. A single oil lantern sat on a camp stool beside the camp cot built big enough for two. The flickering orange flame dance on the cotton walls, his lover's shadow splashed against the white woven fibres.

Silently, Ta'ano came to sit beside his Silver God on the cot and took a pale hand in his own. The shock of the heat radiating from his beloved pulled him from the bed to kneel before the Blessed One. Still, the red eyes remained closed, his head lowered as to create a curtain of silver.

"*Kreidad.* What is it? What's wrong?" Ta'ano had never seen his beloved so...so ill. Dread tightened his chest. The celebratory sounds outside mocked his concern.

The Silver God shook his head. "I did not want to come on this campaign." His voice sounded rough and abused. "They said I needed to."

Ta'ano did not need to ask who "They" were. The Lady only spoke with Her son now. The paths to Their power had become too difficult for the Chosen to tread in this part of the world.

The Blessed One lifted his head and opened his eyes to stare into Ta'ano's. "Change is coming, and for the first time I am afraid of what it will create."

"Change is part of what we witness," said Ta'ano. "We stay the same so as to bear witness and be a living link through the ages to the Gods. You showed me this."

"In our time did we not witness changes affecting the Chosen?" The God canted his head to the side.

Ta'ano lowered his gaze to his beloved's lap. "The Chosen

have lost the ability to connect directly to the Gods."

"They have become Gods themselves."

The statement rocked Ta'ano and he gazed up. "Only in the eyes of the mortals."

"That is all that is required, my Ta'ano," said the Silver God. "In their hubris and in their inability to connect with those they once served, the Chosen have come to believe the lie."

"Not me!"

"No, my Ta'ano, never you." The corner of the Blessed One's mouth twitched into a smile. "But you have me and I you."

"Then what are you talking about?"

Ta'ano's beloved turned over and opened his fist. There, across his index finger, an angry cut remained unhealed, its edge darkened by cauterization. That in itself was shock enough, but it was the tendrils of black radiating from it that pierced Ta'ano's heart with fear. He took his lover's wounded hand. "The knife? The knife did this?"

The Silver God nodded.

Leaning forward, the Blessed One caught Ta'ano in an embrace.

"The world is change, my precious Ta'ano, and so too must the Chosen lest they become more than they were ever meant to be."

Ta'ano did not know what his beloved meant. His tremors matched that of his beloved's.

Ta'ano woke to the clamour of blades striking blades and men's shouts and cries. Sitting up in his cot, he watched his beloved dress in a tan hide cloak. Hastily, Ta'ano rose and tossed on a simple tunic. "What's happened? What's going on?"

The Blessed One turned, his pale face hidden in the depths of the hood. "Re's forces were attacked."

"How?" gasped Ta'ano, pausing to tie on a gilded belt.

"Deception," stated the Silver God. "The two *Shasu* lied."

Cries of the dying and those causing death crashed through the thin fabric of the tent. Horses screamed as the heavier four wheeled Hatti chariots crashed into the swifter two wheeled chariots under the Pharaoh's command.

"Re is trying to reach us," said Ta'ano's beloved.

"How is that we are standing safe?" asked Ta'ano. "Surely we would have been overrun by now."

"I have shifted us," replied the Blessed One.

Ta'ano moved to the entrance and pulled the door to the side. What should have been a scene of horrific proportions was inhibited by a dense swirling fog. He dropped the cloth back into place and turned to face his beloved. Never before had his God left them hanging between worlds. The effort required astounded Ta'ano. His Silver God used it to transport, never to hide.

A deafening crash trembled the earth beneath Ta'ano's bare feet, causing him to flinch. Despite the fact they were shifted, the violence seemed even worse than a moment ago.

"Why are we still here?" Ta'ano's voice rose in panic.

"I cannot leave," stated the Silver God.

"Why?" implored Ta'ano. He strode over and lifted hands that knew his body more intimately than his own. Ta'ano gasped, distressed by what he saw. Tendrils of black laced through argent pale skin. "Take off your hood," he demanded.

The Blessed One stood silently defiant.

"Take it off." Ta'ano's teeth grated together.

Another crash, followed by screams, sounded closer, but remained ignored as Ta'ano glared up at his beloved.

Removing his hands from Ta'ano's grip, the Silver God lifted black trailed arms to push back the cowl.

The blood drained from Ta'ano's face. Stumbling back, the edge of the cot caught him, forcing him to sit down on the crumpled covers. His beautiful beloved sported matching black lines webbing erratically over his face. Words fled despite all the questions surging in his mind.

Unable to remove his gaze, Ta'ano numbly watched his beloved lower himself to kneel before him, pain lacerating his ebon webbed face. Blood red eyes locked onto brown as an infected hand caressed Ta'ano's face, its head scalding to the touch.

"Know that I love you," said the Silver God, his voice raw with pain. "I have never loved another, but I need you to stay here."

Alarm gripped Ta'ano and he pulled the heated hand from his face, clutching it more firmly than intended. "What are you talking about? Where are you going?"

Lips laced in black lifted into a sad smile. "Rameses needs me."

"I need you!" Ta'ano refused to release his lover's hand.

The smile grew into one of love imbued happiness. "I know." He leaned forward and placed a gentle kiss on Ta'ano's lips. Leaning back, his smile disappeared into a mask. "Stay here. I need to know you are safe. Do not come out until nightfall."

Ta'ano released his beloved's hand as the Blessed One rose to his full height. "You're not coming back, are you?"

The Blessed One hid his face in the depths of the cowl. He took one last look at Ta'ano and left the tent.

Numb with shock, Ta'ano could only sit on the bed. The sounds of battle raged all about and still no act of violence penetrated the swirling protection. Above the clash and clamor Ta'ano heard Rameses' voice call out for his beloved.

A sudden silence and then the sound of Rameses' troops rallying to their Pharaoh's call came before the routing of Muwatalli's forces. Through it Ta'ano sat, a silent witness to the death of thousands, tears flowing rivers down his face.

Time inched on until darkness descended into the tent's confines. Still Ta'ano did not leave the false succor of the bed, his tears spent and his throat raw. With the last light of day vanishing Ta'ano rose on shaky legs and went to pull back the door. The scene before him assaulted his senses. The sight and smell of rotting thousands littered across the land pinched renewed tears into his eyes. He wondered if his beloved lay as offal for the scavenger's feast.

Ta'ano shook his head, denying the image, rejecting the loss and allowed the cloth door to swing back into place. It did nothing to halt the stench of horse and human remains. He could not stay in this place of death, of massacre. For what? Control of the centre of trade? To teach each other who on this earth held the greatest power? How many tens of thousands gave their lives for an idea? The only life he cared about he could not find.

Turning to his rucksack on the ground beside the campstool,

Karen Dales

Ta'ano lifted and discovered a strange pendant on a silver string laying atop a folded piece of papyrus. Curiosity lowered him to his knees and he lifted the argent phial by the string. There could be no doubt, the strand was his beloved's hair plaited. It then begged the question as to what was contained in the cylindrical pendant.

Careful of what the mysterious contents could be, Ta'ano popped open the cap. He did not need to breathe deeply to recognize the scent. Renewed tears flooded their banks and Ta'ano sealed the phial before hanging it around his neck.

Why? Why did you leave me? Mourned Ta'ano, gripping the silver cylinder in both hands as he rocked back and form on his knees.

No answer presented itself save for the folded yellow papyrus.

Wiping tears from his eyes, Ta'ano picked up the papyrus and stood. Unfolding it revealed a note in his beloved's hand. Too dark to read the hastily scribed hieroglyphs, Ta'ano absentmindedly stepped outside. The moon and errant fires still smoldering provided enough light to read.

> *Beloved,*
>
> *It pains me to no end that I must depart this realm, thus leaving your touch, your scent, your essence. Know that it is not my wish. If I could spend forever in your embrace, I would. Alas, what I wished for when I first came to live in your world has come to pass. The Lady has called me home, though home it no longer can be.*
>
> *The reasons for my departure are myriad. Predominantly, the People no longer need us, nor does it appear they want us. The Chosen have become their Gods. This hubris is their downfall. The People and the Chosen have lost their belief in us.*
>
> *I can well imagine the expression on your exquisite face, my heart, but you had me. Even though I could touch the hearts and minds of the Chosen, after a time it was not enough.*
>
> *I stayed as long as I could. The touch of the skymetal became the call.*
>
> *My sweet Ta'ano, please do not hold anger towards me because of this. It is time for you to walk your own purpose.*

THANATOS

What purpose, you may ask?

This is for you to discover.

The Old Ones are gone from the Land, from the People, from the Chosen. This need not be forever, but the People, as well as the Chosen, must learn what it means to live without our presence.

When the time comes the bridge between our worlds will come again.

The bridge will be with the People, but not of the People.

The bridge will be with the Chosen, but not of the Chosen.

In the same way the Lady had me come to live with and love the People, and you, so too will the bridge come to be.

If you make it your purpose, look to the heavenly lights. When the hunter bleeds red, then shall you know to whom the bridge will be Chosen to.

My beloved, know that you have always been my heart. Though I depart, know that I will always watch for you. Our lives are entwined though the distance is far.

I love you, my Ta'ano.

Thanatos clung to Bridget as she hugged him. Embarrassment rode the undercurrent of millennia old grief. He wanted to convince himself that fatigue was the culprit for his tears, but the truth would not be buried. After so long, speaking his loss for the first time released wounds he had forgotten.

Pulling back from the embrace, Thanatos pinched the bridge of his nose and wiped away the moisture from his face. "I'm sorry."

Bridget stood, towering over him despite her petite figure. "For what?"

Thanatos watched her return to her seat between Notus and Fernando. He desired to give an explanation, but the look on her face forestalled any further words.

"So you Chose me, knowing that I would find the boy?" Notus' question was more statement.

Thanatos nodded. "I knew it when I saw the Hunter bleed."

"The Hunter?" queried Fernando, clearly uncomfortable of

the emotionality that had gone on, and was happy to move on from it.

"The night Betelgeuse, the star at the left shoulder of Orion, turned red," explained Thanatos. "Before then, and for thousands of years, that star was yellow. That night, when it turned red, I knew. My beloved's note held truth. I had to be patient."

"That is why you had to leave me." Notus sat straight.

"Yes."

"I had to find him. Not you."

Thanatos inclined his head. "I wanted to stay with you. I couldn't. Had I done so you would not have found him and there would have been no reason for you to keep him."

Fernando lifted a finger, a querulous expression pinching his dark features. "But Notus is the Angel's Chooser. He's Chosen."

"He drank my blood," added Notus. "I witnessed his transformation into one of the Chosen."

"You're blood is my blood," explained Thanatos. "My blood is my beloved's. The Angel may have appeared to be Chosen, but the truth is that the Chosen are alike to the Blessed Ones. The ancient blood running through my vessels runs through yours and it awakened his."

"And each time he fed—"

"The more into his power he grew," finished Thanatos.

"But not this time," remarked Fernando. "After his accident, it left him human. How do you explain that?"

"The Angel is still very young," answered Thanatos.

"That's ridiculous! He's older than I am!" spat the Noble.

"Then let me ask you," Thanatos leaned forward, "have you ever seen him raise a fog in which—"

Fernando sat back as if slapped.

"We've seen the creatures in the mist," stated Bridget, her voice barely a whisper.

"That's not who he means, Bridget." Fernando did not relinquish his gaze on Thanatos.

"You've seen Them, haven't you?" asked Thanatos, pointedly.

The intensity of the Ancient Chosen's stare drained Fernando's face of all colour. "Yes," he hissed. "Three tall ladies similar in stature and appearance to the Angel."

"Their colouring," demanded Thanatos. "Tell me."

"One was all white, like the Angel, one red and the last, black as pitch." Fernando swallowed hard at the memory.

"And the Angel stood in a circle with them," prompted Thanatos.

Fernando shook his head. "We were at a church outside of Calais."

Thanatos' eyes widened and he glanced at the ceiling as if he could see the Angel recovering in his bed. A surge of hope blossomed and he returned to look at his guests. Whatever fatigue had gripped him released and he stood. "Please. We've been at this for quite a while. My home is your home. I will have Godfrey show you to your rooms."

He turned to leave, halting as Bridget cleared her throat.

"What of Jeanie?" she asked.

The unexpected underlay of meaning drew a frown on Thanatos' face. "That is a tale for another time. Now, if you please, it is late and Godfrey will be here soon."

Thanatos walked out of the study to find his manservant. Despite how exhausted he felt, he doubted he would be able to garner any rest.

The Angel had summoned the Lady without a circle. The implications numbed his mind. One thing he could not dismiss was the hope that the Gods of his People were finding their way back. If so, then he might see his beloved again…

He pushed that hope away as he brushed sudden tears from his eyes.

XXIV

is lungs expanded painfully, the gasp pulling at the burning ache centred around his stomach. The ceiling above swirled plaster into inconclusive shapes that played in the dark shadows the space gloaming created. One thing was for certain, he did not recognize this place.

With a grunt, he attempted to prop himself up on his elbows but something tugged the back of his hand, halting his attempt. Raising his left hand so as to see what pulled, he frowned at the sight of the intravenous tube taped securely onto the back of his hand. His scowl deepened at the sight of the red liquid filling the plastic catheter. Carefully, he pulled out the tube and noticed there was not a needle on the end. It helped to explain the lack of black tendrils and the pain they elicited.

Dropping the tube to dangle from the three clear pouches of nearly drained blood, he attempted to rise. The care he received did not quell concerns of the unknown.

His last conscious memory was of Jeanie running his sword through his abdomen, drew his ruby eyes wide.

Jeanie!

The image of her alive bolted him to sitting too fast for his healing body. A massive twinge threatened to fell him to the soft goose down pillows and comfort cradle of the bed, but he managed to keep upright.

The elaborate paisley inspired blue and gold comforter pooled in his lap, increasing his surprise. Still wearing the black trousers, he groaned as he lifted his hand away from the wound. Black stitches held closed the charred edges the impalement had created. No doubt remained that the pulling at his back was caused by similar stitchery. Whoever had rescued him wanted him alive. The question remained: for what reason?

Not wishing to discover the intention of his supposed benefactor, he placed his hands at his sides so as to push off the bed and halted. His right hand rested on something, or someone.

Twisting around, his eyes widened further and his breath caught. "Jeanie," he groaned.

Beside him, tucked under the covers, Jeanie lay in death. Her riotous blossom of crimson hair glistened on the pristine white pillow, framing a pale face slack in the mockery of sleep. Long eyelashes kissed over verdant eyes he had not beheld in a lifetime. No movement stirred beneath lids so pale as to be translucent. No breath lifted her bosom, her hands resting slightly curled over them.

Vertigo swept over him, his hand trembling as he reached out to caress her soft freckled cheek. The cold paleness brought tears to his eyes. This was not the future they had dreamed of together. To see her laid out as if for burial beside him pulled a sob from his tight chest. Here lay the evidence of his failure to protect the woman he loved.

Her death had been an insurmountable loss that dogged him through the decades. Seeing her here, a vampiric corpse, magnified his bereavement and ripped away decades of scarring to wrench open his wounded heart.

Tears spilled down his alabaster face. "I am so sorry I failed you."

Yet, she was no longer the woman he would die for. She was a Vampire, and she did not remember him. What did Corbie call her? Rose? He brushed his thumb across icy lips that had once held warmth. His Jeanie was gone and in her place resided a creature bent on the destruction of the Chosen, the Vampiress who had impaled him with his own weapon.

Ignoring the ache in his side, he placed a feather light kiss on her lips before pushing himself off the bed. On trembling legs he stared down at her, his heart pounding in his chest. He did not wish to relinquish the sight of her exquisite form, but he had to leave. Having Jeanie—or what Jeanie had become—beside him, proved that Corbie was not finished with him. A phantom ache throbbed through his wrists and down his back. No, he could not endure such torture again, especially if the instrument of his agony was the woman he loved.

He took a step back, his right arm cradling his middle as another twinge pulled. Only the pressure of his hand on the wound kept the pain at bay. Tearing his gaze away from Jeanie, he took in the opulent room. Wherever he was he did not believe he was at *Beyond the Veil.* The sunlight bleeding around the black-out blinds and the size of the space proved that the Vampires must have taken him elsewhere, but where?

Careful and slow steps took him past the king sized bed, past lavishly crafted dressers and wardrobe, to stand beside the cloaked window. One thing was certain, he had not been transformed into a Vampire. For that he was grateful, but if what he had experienced in his dreams were true, then he was neither human nor Chosen. Taking a tremulous breath, he widened the gap between window and blind enough to gaze out.

An extravagant yard of manicured trees, bushes and flower beds framed a concrete deck that surrounded an in-ground swimming pool, its water's clear and blue in dawn's light. Or was it dusk? He frowned, disoriented and displaced. If it were dawn, he would have time to escape his prison. If it were dusk…

He turned back to face Jeanie lying supine on the bed. He held his breath, waiting to see if any movement would indicated night's resuscitation.

Nothing.

His frown grew as he returned to face freedom. Still too weak the break the window, he also doubted his ability to survive uninjured from the jump.

Allowing the blind to fall back against the window, he turned and made his way to the door. He turned the crystal knob, his eyes widening in surprise as the door clicked open. Wherever he was, his captors did not believe he would be capable of escape.

Murmurs floated to his sensitive ears and he canted his head in an attempt to hear better. He could make out a couple of different voices, but not where they came from. Closing the door as quietly as possible, he leaned his back against its cool grain. He could not leave that way. Already tremors of fatigue wracked his body. There was no way he could fight off several mortal slaves.

Brushing his long, knotted hair from his face, he knew only one route remained. He hoped he had enough personal resources to do it. One last glance at Jeanie and the knowledge of what the Vampiress she had become would do to him hardened his resolve as well as brimmed his eyes.

He had to escape and that meant he had to try the impossible. Stepping away from the door, he stood by the bed, Jeanie's corpse beside him. The reanimation she could go through at any moment forced the ancient words to his lips. He had not attempted to call Them since his accident at the muscum. Belicf, or disbelief, in a thing could make something real, even if it were not. He could not allow such hampering. He had to believe.

The words flowed over his lips once, twice and a third time. Still nothing stirred. Gritting his teeth in frustration, he ignored the fatigue climbing up his lets.

"Come on," he chastised himself.

A glance at the fading glow around the blacked out window told him time grew short. He flickered his gaze at Jeanie, fearing to see movement. None appeared, but it was only a matter of time.

Returning his attention back to the open space in the bedroom, he took a deep breath and ignored the stab of pain in his side.

A faint sound of movement to his right told him it was now or never. He closed his eyes and allowed the words to flow over and over until he felt it.

He opened his eyes to see the area between the bed and the window fill with swirling mist, white diaphanous creatures swam about. He smiled in relief at the creatures that had once tormented him.

A familiar decaying white creature floated up to him and appeared to bow, its white skeletal features frozen in a ghastly snarl. "Ssssire," it hissed in the language Auntie had taught him. "It hasss been long. Too long. We are hungry."

"I know. I am sorry," he replied. "It was never my intention. I thought I had lost you."

The creature nodded and turned to the figure on the bed. "An offering?"

His eyes widened. "No."

Hollow sockets returned to face him. "We are hungry."

"Soon," he sighed. He could not continue this exchange too much longer. Nausea percolated in his gut as black spots formed in his vision. "I need your help."

The white faced demon swirled away and then back, intrigued. "We live to ssserve, Blessed One."

"Take me to the Lady." His voice sounded distant and the carpeted floor felt close. "Take me to Them and you will feast."

Darkness enclosed around him as he heard, "Asss you ssso will, ssso mussst it be done."

Jeanie stretched the life back into her body and opened her eyes. Two days in a row she woke in a strange place.

It all came back to her in a rush.

Sitting up quickly, she glanced to her left to find the Angel gone.

Panic struck, she spun around. Emerald eyes widened at the sight of the mist and its denizens fading from the room, the figure of the Angel with them.

Crying out her denial, Jeanie fled the bed and into the mist's strange embrace. Vertigo gripped Jeanie as the world she knew fell away to darkness.

XXV

rian closed the door to his quarters and stood alone in the hall. The door at the end loomed too near, the occupant within now someone he wished to ignore. He had barely made it to his bed before the sun stole his life for another day. Unfortunately, being dead did not allow for one to mull over what he had to do, and how.

Straightening the black silk shirt, pinstriped with silver, he gave the shirt tails a final tuck into the waistband of his tight dark blue jeans. If he was lucky, the confrontation would not occur tonight. It was a shame he did not consider himself blessed by the fates.

He took the several dozen well travelled steps towards the door that opened into his Dominus' apartments. For the first time since being placed bruised and bleeding on the audition block, Brian trembled in fear. Despite being a Dominus in his own right, one thing became noon-time clear, that nearly fifteen hundred years of being a Vampire paled in comparison to being Corbie's slave for even longer.

Brian's handsome face scowled at the thought and hated himself for having believed the lie for so long, his hand on the brass knob. He had allowed corbie to treat him as such, never believing he was free from the human contrivance of slave ownership. Brian knew he could blame Corbie for his continued enslavement, but Brian knew the truth and was shamed by it.

Turning the knob, Brian let himself into the grand parlor that imitated style from two centuries previous. From the luscious extravagance of the immense chandelier hanging in the centre, to the thick one hundred percent wool broadloom that mimicked the finest eastern rugs, and finally to the dark brown calf leather wing chairs set in positions around the room in a way so as not to promote socializing, everything screamed opulent power. Brian tried to ignore the originals of Goya's most gruesome paintings as he walked through the centre of the room to the dark wooden door opposite.

The next room would be the complete antithesis of this room and Brian entered to take in the expected white tiled floor, white painted walks and ceiling, and all the furniture appearing to disappear into the walls due to their absence of colour. The only contrast was the wall of monitors behind Corbie's white oak desk, now dark with lack of power, and Corbie himself, seated in state in the grand ivory leather office chair.

"Shut the door," ordered Corbie, his head lowered over his paperwork.

Brian did as ordered, the door closing with a click. His black leather loafers slipped against ceramic as he made his way over to stand before his Dominus. His hands clutched behind his back to halt any fidgeting, Brian stood silently waiting.

Time drew out, testing Brian's patience. It was a tactic Corbie often employed to ensure Brian's full attention. Brian recognized it for what it was. When they had both been mortal, Brian had tried to get his Master's attention by clearing his throat. The resulting punishment ensured proper obedience since then. Even once Brian was turned, the pattern to serve his Dominus remained deeply engrained.

"The shipment from the Liquor Control Board of Ontario is late. Have Cora contact them tomorrow morning and find out when it will arrive." Corbie continued to shuffle through a small pile of invoices, dark head still bent. "Go through our stock and see what we can water down. Whatever can't, pull it."

Brian's shoulders slumped at the directive. It meant that he would have to find a mortal to test the watered down drinks or do it himself. He suppressed a shudder at the thought of having to taste drinks fit for a mortal. Tonight would be one of customer complaints. "Anything else?"

Corbie placed the white gold Cross pen down beside the papers and raised his head. His blank expression, coupled with his pale hands coming to clasp over the papers, set Brian on alarm. "You tell me."

"Sir?" Brian tried to keep the worry from his voice. If he could have burst into a nervous sweat, he would have.

"You cut it quite late in getting in this morning." Black eyes bore down.

There was only one way to deal with his Dominus when he exhibited his paranoia. Crossing his arms over his chest, Brian canted his head to the side and raised a blond brow. "I didn't think you cared."

Cobie leaned back in his chair, his thin lips pursed in annoyance. "How many did you manage to bring back?"

"About a handful," replied Brian. Hopefully, he could dodge a potential landmine.

"That's it?" Corbie's widen in irritated surprise.

"What did you expect?" countered Brian. "By the time you ordered to go and by the time I got the Pearsons, most of them either had taken off so to get home in time for sunrise, or had already passed security. Without a boarding pass security wouldn't let me through."

"Always an excuse for your failure," spat Corbie.

"So what now?" Brian hoped to deflect Corbie's growing anger.

"Have them—"

The door opened, canceling the rest of Corbie's order.

Brian turned to find Marcus sauntering over, a pleased smirk accentuated the swagger until Corbie's dark glare halted him beside Brian.

"Report," commanded Corbie. He leaned forward, arms coming to rest on the desk, intent on what his coterie member had to say.

"Nothing." Marcus' clipped his tone with military precision.

Black brows drew down in a frown. "What do you mean?"

Marcus lifted a shoulder and dropped it. "Thanatos' place might as well be a fortress. When I left Cora, the place was locked up tight. No one in. No one out."

"And the Angel?"

"From what I could gather, he's still on death's door."

Brian groaned.

"What?" snapped Marcus, turning to face him.

No love lost between one who once served Corbie in the Roman legions and one who served as slave, Brian rolled his eyes and shook his head at Marcus' scowl.

"Enough!" Corbie's directive brought Brian and Marcus' attention back to the matter at hand. "Was there any sign of an attempt on Thanatos' part to follow through on his threat?"

"Not that I witnessed," replied Marus. "I'm on my way back, so if anything changes I'll call."

Corbie nodded, pleased with the news. "Good. It'll give Cora a couple of hours of rest before getting ready for opening."

"Do you really expect Thanatos to come?" asked Brian.

"Yes." Corbie gave a curt nod. "He's not one to threaten and not follow through."

A frown pulled Brian's lip downward. He hoped that Corbie would read it as concern and not the inkling of a plan taking root in his mind. The question remained: Would his coterie be patient enough to go along with it? If they were, then they—and him—would come off smelling like roses. He stilled the jump of the corner of his mouth and resumed an intractable mask.

The ringing emanating from Marcus broke the silence. Slipping the phone from his back pocket, he glanced to his Dominus. "It's Cora."

"Put her on speaker phone," ordered Corbie.

With a nod, Maruc slid his thick finger across the screen and touched the speaker button. "Speak." He laid the phone on the desk.

"Something's going on," Cora's musical voice wavered in fear.

"Report," demanded Corbie, rising from his seat to lord over the phone.

Brian heard a squeak, but was not sure it came from Cora or signal interference since they were below ground.

"There's—there's a strange mist—"

"Describe it," interjected their Dominus.

"It's weird, Mr. Vale," came Cora's nervous tones. "It's not rising from the ground, but seems to be appearing at the second floor, beside the room Marcus said the Angel was in."

"Is it doing anything?" asked Corbie.

"No, sir. At least from what I can tell. Do you want me to go closer?" Her trepidation belied her enthusiasm.

Corbie looked up at Marcus. "No. Stay there until Marcus arrives."

"Okay."

The phone went dead.

Corbie sat down, the calf hide creaking under his weight. "Go. Check it out."

"Yes, sir." Marcus picked up his phone, stuffed it back into his jeans and strode out of the office.

Brian watched Corbie's smouldering eyes follow the Vampire out. "What is it?" he asked once the door shut closed.

"Cora called Marcus."

Had Brian been mortal he would have sucked in his breath, instead he frowned at the door.

XXVI

 gasp tore through him as the sudden impact of soft earth felled him to all fours. Long white hair fell forward, allowing the false sun to warm his back. Despite the softness of the dewy grass, he sat back on his haunches and swept his locks out of view.

He could not help but to hang his jaw in stunned surprise. All of his previous visits to the grove paled in comparison to finally seeing it in the flesh. Verdant trees and bushes framed the grassy clearing and allowed the round stone bordered spring a place to nestle against. Its tinkling music filled the flower-perfumed air.

Breathing in deep gasps, he closed his eyes and tilted his face towards the bright canopy above. He sat there, his heart soaring at finally being here in truth. He knew what was beyond this hidden realm and that thought forced his eyes open in search of signs in the sky that had no sun. Nothing past the blue depths could be seen.

He rose to his feet and wondered why he could not feel the spongy grass between his toes. Black socks encased his feet. Frowning, he lifted one leg and then the other to remove the offensive clothing. He sighed as he wiggled his unbound feet, enjoying the cool delicateness of the grass. This was so much better than coming here in spirit.

Enjoying each step, he walked over to the spring and knelt down before it. Its gurgling song washed over him, raising gooseflesh across his scarred body. Even the sound of buzzing insects, bird calls and animal sounds from within the dense forest beyond added to the orchestration of the most beautiful music he had ever heard.

Across from him, on a flat stone, stood a chalice he had drunk from more times he could count, but that had been different. Anxiety swelled within him. A desire to drink from the bounteous well meant using the silver goblet, but what would the water taste like now? Would the flavor be foul or fruitful? Taking a shuddering breath, he reached across the spring, his hand coming to grip the cool, argent stem. Was it his imagination? Did the white aura around it grow brighter?

The wide squat base of the bowl settled onto both hands, its coolness traveling up his fingers, hands and arms. The strange lettering still accentuated the beauty of the goblet, and he knew the language it was written in. In reverence, he read the words, knowing the truth they revealed.

"I am She who gives the gift of joy unto the heart of mankind.
I am She that gives knowledge of the spirit eternal.
I give peace and freedom and reunion.
My name is Mystery."

As the last word rang through the grove, the fine silver chain melted away into nothing, freeing the chalice from the stone. With trembling hands he dipped the goblet into the water. The chilly liquid caressed against his flesh and he shivered. He desired the taste and sensation of the water, but chose not to rush.

The lip of the bowl singed his lower lip, frosting it with its cold. He tipped the chalice until the waters cascaded into his mouth and body. An explosion of flavour more intense and more powerful he had ever experienced pulled a groan of pleasure. A riot of blossoms with the undertone of blood caused him to close his eyes, the bliss threatening to sweep him away.

"Life tastes as you have lived it," came a familiar voice behind him.

Lowering the chalice, the contents half full, he turned around on his knees to start up at the Lady. "Then it should be fowl tasting." The response came unbidden to his lips.

"Life tastes as you wish to live it," replied the beautiful Lady in white, her ivory eyes smiled down on him.

"Life tastes as you deserve." The Red Lady, standing between the White and Ebon, offered her sun reddened hand.

He took it and stood, chalice in the other.

"You were lost," They chorused.

Shame filled him and he could not bear to be under their scrutiny. "I was," he whispered. "I'm sorry."

He felt a hand come to rest on his face, forcing him to gaze into sad, smiling eyes. "You are precious to us."

"I didn't know." Tears welled in his eyes.

"And do you now?" The melodious voice of a man turned him to see that there were others in the grove. They were of similar height and lithe appearance, but that was where the resemblance ended. Each bore a different combination of colourings. Of the indeterminable numbers, only two others seemed familiar.

The Silver man stepped forward, the crimson eyes so similar to his own. Long argent locks fell to his waist. Except for the difference of colouring, the Silver man could have been his twin.

"I see myself in you, too," smiled the Silver man.

His eyes widened and realization caused his hand to go slack. The chalice fell, spilling the spring's contents onto the green earth. Laughter erupted amongst those gathered.

"You did not answer the question," stated the Lady with the stars in her black hair. She stepped forward and knelt to pick up the chalice, a smile on her pale face.

Words choked him into silence. He could only nod.

"I once lived among the People," said the Silver man. His statement made sense to the ancient style of silver cloth that decked him in trousers and tunic. "I once loved one of the People. I still do, but I was called home. The People were forgetting us."

"Our power waned in the realm of the People," added a

woman with long waving crimson hair, her verdant eyes sparkled in sadness.

"And then the People worked a powerful magic," explained the Silver man. He lifted his hand and on his thumb a puckered scar showed red. "Death would take us."

"We could not allow one of our own to suffer oblivion," chimed the Lady.

He glanced down at the starbursts of silver scaring his wrists and similar striping on his forearm. "Yet you allowed it with me." Hurt tinged his words.

"It was never our intention," chorused the Lady.

"Time moved forward," said the White Lady.

"We were forgotten," said the Black Lady.

"History buried us," said the Red Lady. "The Chosen fell victim to mortal beliefs."

"The something strange happened," smiled the Ebon Lady.

"Something unexpected," grinned the Ivory Lady.

"Something wonderful," beamed the Crimson Lady.

"The People began to remember," They chorused.

"We heard their needs," said the White Lady.

"We listened to their laments," said the Black Lady.

"We felt the trembling of renewed magic," said the Red Lady.

"Our time was coming again," They intoned.

"And to fulfill the needs of the People—" said the White Lady.

"—and the Chosen," interjected the Black Lady.

"A bridge needed to be created," explained the Red Lady.

"Until such time the People can call Us, it will be through you that the magic will flow," said the Ivory Lady.

"Until such time we can walk once more among the People, it will be through you that the People will know we are here for them," said the Ebon Lady.

"Until we can Choose again, you will be the Chooser of all," said the Crimson Lady.

"You were born in the realm of the People," They chorused. "You have sewn the seeds of our return. You have journeyed with the Chosen. You know both life and death. You know both the realm the People and our realm."

The responsibilities They presented made him frown. "What if I don't want it?"

A collective gasp rang through the grove. He raised his gaze to take in all of them.

"What if...what if I want to quit this life, this existence." Pain tinged his words.

"Please. Please do not mean these words," pleaded the Lady with stars in her hair.

"Why shouldn't I mean them?" He turned to face the Lady. "All I've ever had has been suffering. Look at me. It's written over my body." He stood with arms outstretched.

"And scarred your heart," chimed the Lady.

He could not keep the tears from spilling.

"What can we give you?" asked the White Lady.

"What balm can be applied?" offered the Red Lady.

"What can we do to right our wrongs to you?" inquired the Black Lady.

He hung his head. "Nothing. There is nothing."

"What of the Chosen who care for you?" asked the Silver man.

"Notus?" He snapped his head up to glare at the one who had sired him. "He left me. He abandoned me when I needed him most." He could not believe the vitriol that spilled from his lips, but it felt good.

The Silver man lowered his head in defeat. "There are others," he whispered.

"Who see me as a weapon against the Vampires," he spat. "No, not them."

Silence filled the grove, stilling even the song of the spring.

A shout further back caused others to rush away from where he had arrived. Brushing past the Lady, he witnessed Jeanie stumble from a fog before collapsing to the ground.

"Stand back!" shouted someone.

"A Banished One!" screamed another.

Seeing her prone form on grass that shrivelled and curled black, he ran to her side. Gently, he turned her over. Every blade of grass that came in contact with her smouldered and died. His heart raced at the sight of her flaccid corpse face. Lifting her, he cradled Jeanie to his breast. "Jeanie," he whispered into her hair. "How is this possible?"

"That is what we would like to know," chorused the Lady. Anger flashed in Their eyes as They stepped in front of the others at the opposite end of the grove, far enough away to be safe from Jeanie's death-touch. "Send the Banished One back, now!"

"Banished One?" He wiped cinnamon strands from Jeanie's face. The last time he held her she had been dead. The memory tore a sob from him and an idea crystallized. "You asked me what you could do to make things right between us, to give me a reason to care to be who you want me to be. Choose Jeanie."

"That is impossible!"

"It cannot be done!"

"She is of the Banished!"

Laying Jeanie down on the scorched earth, he stood and strode over to the Lady, purpose in each step. "Make her Chosen," he said through clenched teeth. He would not give up on Jeanie again.

"We cannot do that," stated the Red Lady.

"It is beyond our power," explained the White Lady.

"The creature is a dead thing," continued the Black Lady.

There was something he missed. His wry grin did not match his hostile eyes. "If you can't, then who can?"

The Ladies glanced at each other before turning their attention to him. "You," They chorused.

He could not believe his ears. "How?"

"Be what you were born to be."

The cryptic answer from the Lady added to his frustration. "A bridge between here and there."

"And more," intoned the Lady. The three turned their faces upwards and the rest followed suit.

Curiosity lifted his gaze and he witnessed the diaphanous forms of the white faced demons as they descended. They spun and floated, but never touched the ground, never came close to the denizens of this place. They circled around him, touching and caressing him, the sensations oddly comforting.

"Do you now see?" asked the Ivory Lady.

"Do you now comprehend?" asked the Crimson Lady.

"Do you now know?" concluded the Ebon Lady.

"Out of us all," the Silver man stepped forward, "you know both sides. You have seen more, experienced more in your short time, than any here. Only you can traverse the realms."

"To transform a Banished One into a Chosen is something only you can do," said the Star Lady.

He frowned. "I don't understand."

"What are they?" The Silver man outstretched a hand to indicate the swirling mist.

The question stumped him. He knew what he called them but he did not know what they were. He shook his head in defeat, the white faced demons played with his swinging hair. He batted them away.

"They are the ones who failed to be Chosen," answered the Black Lady, sadness filling her visage.

"They are the ones who feared the Choice," replied the Red Lady in disgust.

"They are the ones who should never have been offered the Choice," sighed the White Lady.

Realization struck a grunt from his gut. "Those that died during the transformation did not go where all others go when they die. They became trapped. Here." His eyes widened even further. "They became hungry ghosts."

"In a way, yes," confirmed the Star Lady.

"But you call Jeanie a...a Banished One."

All gazes lowered to Jeanie's corpse. Disgust mingled with fear painted across their beautiful faces.

"One of the Chosen Chose poorly," said the Silver man, sadness filled him. "The one that was Chosen was soul split."

"Her body changed, but her soul remained prison with other failed Chosen. What returned was warped, twisted," continued the Lady with stars in her hair.

"We did what had to be done," chorused the Lady. "We banished her."

"The Light of Life would turn her to ash," explained the Ivory Lady.

"The strength of the Peoples' spirit would turn her," continued the Crimson Lady.

"The fear of the truth would banish her," finished the Ebon Lady.

"Bastia." The name slipped unbidden from his lips. It all made sense why the Vampires waged war against the Chosen. "Jealousy. She did not get what she wanted, so to remove the reminder of her failure she believed she had to destroy what she could not accomplish."

The Lady nodded, regret darkening their faces.

He glanced back at Jeanie's form, the truth running cold down his spine. Jeanie's soul flowed with the demons. During the night it returned, the trauma of dying every day forcing her mind to escape. Soul-split. It was worse than that.

Bringing his gaze back to the Lady and the others, he said, "I have to return her soul to her. Permanently."

"yes," chorused the Lady.

"You must mend what was broken," said the Black Lady.

"With blood you must bind what was wrongly displaced," said the Red Lady.

"To Choose her you must use your heart," instructed the White Lady.

He frowned. He needed exact details, but then he realized what held him back. Fear. Taking a shuddering breath, he turned to sit beside Jeanie and cradled her. The white faced demons swirled around him, brushing against them both and he closed his eyes. Could he do this? He did not know, but he had to try. He had to make up for his failure. He had to save Jeanie.

Centuries of mindful meditation made it easy to slip into a meditative state. This time he had to find Jeanie in the playful mist swirling around him. He thought back to what he had witnessed before his journey began, back to the outcrop where he had watched those who died move into the most beautiful lotus-light he had ever seen. Had Jeanie died in truth, she would have gone there. How? How could he call her?

Memories of her floated to mind and evoked emotions that

had scarred over. The scene of her holding his sword as he was made to watch her over painted lips twist in sadistic pleasure before—

Not!

Not that.

It would not do.

Taking a deep breath, he banished Rose from his mind and evoked memories from over a lifetime ago.

Jeanie stood in the kitchen of the flat he and Notus had shared before any of the Chosen knew of the Vampires. She laughed as Notus insisted that she try his newest concoction, unsuitable for both mortal and Chosen consumption. She turned to face him, grinning as she wiped errant curls from her face. His breath left him as green eyes caught his.

Fierce as a hawk, she matched him word for word as she fought for the right to save Notus. His heart broke witnessing the defeat in her eyes.

Stunned, he sat on his four poster bed, disbelieving the confession that fell from her lips. The cotton shirt she wore revealed more than he suspected she was even aware of. His feelings for her surged forward, refusing to be buried by self doubt and fear.

He moved within her, supple legs wrapped around his waist, guiding him deeper, riding him. Pleasure flushed her face. Cries of her need urged him. The taste and texture of her flesh as his tongue played with the skin over the leaping vessel in her neck was exquisite. The rush of her convulsing release as her blood cascaded into his mouth, ignited spasms of his own pleasure.

Memories flew fast. Her scent, her textures, her sound, her taste, her smile, filled him, each swelling his feelings for her in his chest. When the memory of finding her dead beneath the lamppost threatened to overwhelm him, he pulled back and opened his tear filled eyes.

Before him, spinning stationary, a light similar to those who flowed into the lotus, sparkled. He wanted to say her name, but could not. The beauty of her essence froze him.

Slowly, it descended until it hovered above Jeanie's brow. It appeared to hesitate for a moment before disappearing into her corpse. The swirling mist dissolved back into the aether.

Silence thundered through his ears as he searched her face for some sign of life. Sculpted eyebrows slightly darker than her disarrayed locks drew together at the same time her lower lip pouted. He held his breath, waiting, and was rewarded with the fluttering of her eyelids before they opened to reveal the deepest forest green of her eyes.

Relief exploded the breath from his chest, but the sense of victory vanished with the expression of horror twisting her face.

Jeanie pushed away with a cry and scrabbled to her bare feet, her blood dappled skirt and blouse wrinkled and twisted.

"The sun! It'll kill me!" Panicked, she turned around, desperate for a place to hide and was struck still at the sight of the Lady and the others near the spring.

Several of the realm's denizens stepped back, horror and terror marring their faces.

Still kneeling on the scorched grass, he watched in confusion until he saw the black patches that blossomed beneath Jeanie's feet. They were the same as which he sat upon. He had to do something before the situation worsened.

"Jeanie, stop!" he shouted, rising to his feet. The dead foliage crumbled into ash beneath him.

She turned to face him, eyes wild. Another patch of green succumbed to death. "Ye're...I—"

"Don't move!" he ordered, his hand outstretched in an attempt to soothe her. He took a step towards her.

A collective gasp from those by the spring accompanied Jeanie's retreating step. "Am I...am I dead?"

He shook his head.

"Then where am I?"

Her plaintive cry cut him to the bone and he winced. "That's difficult to explain."

She turned her hands over, examining them as if they belonged to someone else. "I dinna burn," she said. "Why dinna I burn?"

"The light here is different—forgiving," he replied. The answer spilled from him. *How do I know this?*

Jeanie looked up from her perfect hands, her eyes locking onto his. "But I'm still a—"

"Yes," he said. His heart lurched in his chest at the sight of blood tears welling in her eyes.

"Oh my God!" she cried, her hands covering her mouth as memories broke the damn of her tears. "All the lives I've kilt."

She sucked in a shuddering breath, her eyes wide. "I kilt ye! I took yer sword an' stabbed ye. I drank yer blood!"

He watched her descend closer to madness, his heart breaking. "That wasn't you."

Copper waves sparkled amber in the false sunlight as she shook her head. "Ye're wrong," she sobbed. "I took all those lives. I dinna want to, but I had to. I even took yers. I couldna stop myself. Corbie told me— Oh God. I'm a monster!"

He caught Jeanie as she collapsed to the ground, the sound and scent of burning filling his nostrils. Bundling her up on his lap, he held her, blood tears cooling on his chest. Through her weeping he held and rocked her, whispering placations to calm her.

In time, her crying came to a halt and she pushed away from his red dappled chest and gazed up at him. The hopelessness across her visage threatened to overwhelm him.

"I'm so sorry, Jeanie," he implored.

"But it's my fault. What I did to you—"

"I forgive you," he said. "Even while you— It doesn't matter because it was never your fault. If I hadn't agreed to have you wait under the lamppost while I freed Notus..." He could not finish. The memory twisted his gut and he relinquished his gaze into her eyes. "It's my fault. I should have been stronger. We should have spent this last century together."

Her hand on his cheek made him look into the face of the woman he loved—would only love. "I should have Chosen you."

"Is that what you wish, child?"

He had not noticed that the Lady now stood before them, but far enough away so that Jeanie could not come in contact with the three.

"Is it possible?" Awe widened green eyes. "I'll no longer be a Vampire?"

The three nodded in unison, a slight smile on their very similar faces.

THANATOS

"There is one question—" said the Ivory Lady.

"—that you must answer true—" continued the Crimson Lady.

"—or the Banishment will continue," finished the Ebon Lady.

"Do you love the Blessed One?" They intoned.

"I never stopped," replied Jeanie. She lowered her gaze. "Even when I couldna be anything but Rose, I knew part of me was missing." She looked up into his eyes. "When I saw ye in the newspaper, a part of me wanted—no, needed—to be with ye though I dinna know why. But it was when ye were there, on yer knees, I couldna stop myself. I had to have ye, and though I knew what I was doing, I dinna understand my feelings until...until…"

"You tasted my blood," he finished.

She nodded. "Though my mind had forgotten ye, my heart never did. I'm sorry."

He pulled her closer. The warmth in his centre rushed up into his chest. He wanted to jump and shout in glee at hearing her words, instead he sighed, worry and fear dissipated.

"Then Choose her," intoned the Lady.

He gazed up at the three. "How?"

The Star dappled Lady cane forward, dipping the silver chalice into the spring. Crystal droplets pearled at the base before falling to the ground as she strode over, her black and silver shimmering robe floating around her slim figure.

"Take this, child," she said, placing the goblet on the scorched earth in front of him and Jeanie. Where droplets touched new sprouts of green poked through.

"Ass I hae t'do is drink the water?" asked Jeanie. She slid from his lap to kneel before the chalice.

Gazing over Jeanie, he saw the Lady shake their heads before gazing down on him. "One other ingredient is required," The chorused.

He knew, at that moment, what he had to do. Standing, he walked around the woman he loved and knelt beside her to peer into the silver depths. *One ingredient*, he sighed. Lifting a scarred wrist to his mouth, he bit. At that taste of his blood, he pulled his hand away and held it over the chalice.

Ruby droplets splashed into the sacred water. His blood mingled with the water and rose the level within the chalice. Worry niggled at him. He still healed from the impalement. He needed the life sustaining blood, but Jeanie needed it more.

Light headed and hungry, his wound closed, stemming the flow. Within the silver goblet his blood shimmered, a living liquid ruby. Raising the chalice by its stem, he held it towards Jeanie. "Drink."

Wide eyed with awe and hunger, Jeanie took the cup, pausing long enough to gaze at the contents before placing the lip to hers to drink.

"You must imbibe it all, child," said the White Lady.

"You must take in all the good, all the happiness, all the love," said the Red Lady.

"You must drink the bitter dregs, accepting what you cannot change, forgiving of all trespasses done to you and you have done to others," said the Black Lady.

"In this way you will be Cleansed," chorused the three. "In this way you will be purged. In this way you will be Banished no longer."

He watched Jeanie as she drank in his essence mingled with the sacred waters until her head tilted back to devour the last drops. A worried smile met him as she lowered the chalice. He smiled back, taking the goblet from her.

A shock of pain stole her smile, forcing a wince as she doubled over.

Head spinning from the sudden change, he placed the chalice down and raced to Jeanie's side as she crumpled to the ground. Violent tremors seized her body.

"Jeanie!" he cried. He went to lift her.

"Do not touch her!" The command from the Lady trembled the leaves on the trees.

Stunned, he turned to face Them, torn to do Their bidding or do everything in his power to heal Jeanie. "Why?" he implored.

The Lady took a step closer, Their harsh tone replaced with compassion. "She must fight her demons if she is to return to you," said the Ebon Lady.

Impotent to help, he could only kneel beside her convulsing body. Each time a violent spasm shocked through her, he had to pull back from touching her, more to comfort himself than to alleviate her suffering.

"Please, Jeanie, stay with me," he prayed.

Time protracted, making each convulsion increasingly difficult to witness. Eyes only on Jeanie, he did not see the Lady, nor the others, come to stand in a large ring around them. On the edge of his consciousness he registered a hum of aetheric music reverberating through the grove.

Kneeling in vigil, his breath exploded at the sight of the swirling mist rising to flow around him and Jeanie. He had not called them. "Go back," he ordered, anxiety tightening his chest.

A denizen of the mist floated over Jeanie, its diaphanous tendrils fluttering against her convulsing form. Its black mouth opened, making its grotesque skull-like face even more fierce. "We came at the call," it hissed before floating away.

Swallowing the drying from his mouth, his head spun at the realization. They were here if she failed to make the right choice.

Panic gripped him. The thought of losing her because she made the wrong choice, thus damning her soul for eternity as one of the white faced demons, spurred him into action. Despite the Lady's warning, he lifted Jeanie onto his lap and held her tight through each passing seizure.

"Jeanie, don't go with them," he pleaded. "Stay with me." He rocked her, his head resting on her crown of cinnamon.

He tried to ignore the thickening of the fog, but at the sight of the spark he had freed rising from her forehead made cold dread still him. He could not lose her. Not after they had gone through so much. Not when they were so close. "No, Jeanie, you can't leave me." He tilted her head back to stare at her placid face. "I won't let you go."

Tears ran tracks down his face and he lifted his gaze to the white faced creatures floating dangerously close to Jeanie's brilliant spirit. "Go away!" he shouted, using his free arm to wave them back. "You can't have her. She's mine!"

Frenzied by his banishment, the creatures of the mist floated out of reach. The spark rose higher until he had to look up at it.

"Jeanie. No. Please don't go," he pleaded. "I forgive you."

"That is not enough," chorused the Lady.

"There must be a reason," said the Star dappled Lady.

"You must be the reason," said the Silver man.

A warm touch settled on his shoulder and he gazed up to see eyes similar to his looking down on him.

"There is only ever one reason to Choose another." The Silver man sadly smiled.

The blinking light of Jeanie's essence lifted upward.

Time was running out.

"Would you die for her?" asked the Silver man.

He gazed down at the woman he held and nodded. "Yes."

"Dying is easy," said the Silver man. "It is living that is hard. Would you live for her?"

A frown twisted his face, at the same time pain gripped his gut. "Haven't I done so?"

"Existing is not living." The Silver man knelt behind him. "Existing is all you have been doing. If she is to choose life, you must choose to live. The Chosen connect us to life as we connect the Chosen and the People to what is beyond life. It is only through our lives do the Chosen truly live. I ask again, would you live for her?"

His breath caught in a sob, the truth of the Silver man's words cutting deep. "I don't know how."

His words hit hard, bringing with it the knowledge that in all the centuries he walked the earth he remained hidden, apart, afraid. It was no life.

"I want to live," he whispered, gazing at Jeanie's face. "Jeanie. I want to live, but I don't know how. I never felt alive until you came into my life, and when you died, I did, too. I need you to show me how."

He pulled her into a fierce embrace. "I love you."

He buried his face into her soft curls. "Please, Jeanie. I need you."

He did not see the spark of Jeanie's essence descend and merge back into her trembling body, and nor did he see the white mist dissipate into nothing. At her sudden stillness he lifted his head, eyes wide at the thought that she was truly gone. Studying her face, he sought for any sign of life.

"Jeanie, please come back to me." He combed locks back

from where they had fallen over her face.

About to smooth her copper eyebrow, his fingers halted as her brows lowered. A gasp preceded the fluttering eyelashes before opening to reveal eyes the colour of the sacred grove. Stunned, he watched as she sat up, slipping off his lap to stare wide eyed at him.

"Gwyn?"

His breath rushed out. He had not realized he had held it. He could not believe his eyes.

Jeanie gazed down at herself, searching for evidence of change, before looking up at him. "Am I...am I Chosen?"

"Rejoice, child," chorused the Lady, coming to kneel before them. The burnt grass was fading as new shoots sprung up.

His gut wrenched and it took all his willpower not to crush Jeanie in an embrace. He smiled and nodded.

He caught her as she fell onto him, laughing and matching her kiss for kiss. Lips he once believed he would never feel again played against his own, his face, his neck. When she finally stopped, she was above him and he lay on new green.

"Is this real?" she asked. The bright glow of the sky highlighted her long waves, giving her a radiant halo.

He reached up to pull at a corkscrew strand and playfully let it go to bounce against her voluptuous breast. He could not take his eyes off her. "It's real."

"It is time," chorused the Lady, standing.

He gazed past Jeanie to find satisfied smiles on the three, the Silver man beside the White Lady and the Star Lady beside the Ebon.

Though he did not want to get up, enjoying the feeling of Jeanie's warmth against his body, he nodded to the woman he loved. *I hate to ask, but...*

Her eyes went round. "I heard ye, but ye dinna say anything!"

You're my Chosen, now, he sent. A smile curled his lips. *I can hear your thoughts and feel your feelings.*

Like this, aye? She closed her eyes.

Her need for him stiffened him. "Yes," he growled. "Like that."

Chuckles from around the grove sent a riotous blush to

Jeanie's face. Embarrassed, she climbed off of him and stood, eyes lowered.

He climbed to his feet and stood beside Jeanie, her fingers twining his.

The Lady came forward, loving smiles etched on exquisite faces. "It is time for you to go back," They intoned.

"Can I ask, who are ye and where am I?" asked Jeanie, confidence lifting her head.

"I can see why you picked this one," laughed the Silver man.

He gave Jeanie a side long glance. "I didn't pick her. She picked me." He gave her hand a gentle squeeze.

The Silver man nodded, his face serious.

"To answer your question—" said the White Lady.

"—is to ask who you are," continued the Red Lady.

"We have been with you from the beginning—" said the Ivory Lady.

"—and we will be with you until the end of time," finished the Black Lady.

"Know, child, that you are the first of the People who have traveled to our domain since our worlds were cut apart," said the Ivory Lady.

"Your presence here—and what has transpired—gives us all hope," said the Crimson Lady, taking Jeanie's small hands in hers.

"I dinna understand." Jeanie shook her head.

"Understanding is not for the mind, child," chorused the Lady. "It is of the soul. Now, go. Know that we will meet again."

The Red Lady released Jeanie's hands and stepped back in line with her sisters.

Placing his hand on Jeanie's shoulder, he met her confused gaze with a reassuring nod. *Let's go.*

But how?

"The same way we came," he said, taking her hand in his.

They walked the few steps to where they had entered the grove. The green trees and grasses dotted with wild flowers gave no indication of the portal that had been there. Not even a scorched patch of earth remained. With ancient words he summoned the spirits and was rewarded by the rising of swirling mist and the creatures it held.

"Wait!"

The call broke the natural silence, and he and Jeanie turned to find the Silver man trotting towards them.

"Please, wait a moment," asked the Silver man as he came to a halt.

Of a height to each other, white brows furrowed as he met eyes so unnervingly similar to his own.

"Before you go, I ask a boon." The Silver man pulled off what appeared to be a long argent chain from around his neck. "I beg you to give this to Ta'ano."

Taking the strand, he realized it was a thinly braided lock. He frowned, noticing that for the sake of a difference of shading they looked similar. He held out the strand to the Silver man. "I don't know a Ta'ano."

"No?" frowned the Silver man. "His scent is all over you, as is the scent of my blood."

The observation stunned him and he lowered his proffered hand, the braided argent hair dangling from his numb grasp.

"D'ye mean Thanatos?" interjected Jeanie.

"If that is the name he goes by now, then yes," nodded the Silver man.

"He's the one who saved yer life," explained Jeanie. "'Tis his bed we were in."

A smile filled with hope lit ruby eyes swimming in unshed tears. The Silver man ran his argent hand down an ivory arm, lifting the hand which held the braid. Winding the chain, he placed it in the an alabaster hand and closed long fingers around it .

"Give this to my Ta'ano," said the Silver Man. "Tell him I did not want to leave, but I would have died had I stayed."

A scarred silver thumb caressed the starburst. "I understand,|" he said.

"Tell him that I love him and one day we will be together again." Tears dripped down the beautiful silver face.

"I will." He nodded and grasped the clutched hands with his free one.

The Silver man released a shuddering sigh as he nodded. "Tell him I am proud of him." Red eyes peered intently into each other.

"He found you, and now Ta'ano and the rest of the Chosen will be restored."

"What d'ye mean?" asked Jeanie.

The two, so similar in appearance, turned their attention to her.

"Your beloved is the darkness in the day," explained the Silver man, a wry smile on his argent lips. "As he is also the light in the darkness. My Ta'ano will teach you."

The Silver man turned his attention to the swirling mist. "Now go. We will see each other again."

His hand released, he turned to face the mist. He clutched Jeanie's hand with his other.

He's yer sire, isna he? asked Jeanie as they stepped into the vapour.

Yes, he sent, a smile on his face. *They are my family, but you are my life.*

xxvii

 thought you were asleep, sir." Godfrey set down the full carafe into the coffee maker, his black mug bereft of caffeinated warmth. He turned to face Thanatos, concern etched his brow. "Was the room I set for you unsatisfactory in any way?"

Thanatos walked around the large kitchen island. The scent of his servant's dinner still lingered though all traces of the meal were swept away by Godfrey's meticulous cleanliness.

"I couldn't sleep," he said, coming to stand opposite to Godfrey. He leaned his weary body against the marbled granite of the island counter-top.

Surprise replaced worry in Godfrey's blue eyes. "IF I may be so bold to say, sir, I have never seen you so exhausted."

"I don't remember the last time I remained awake so long." Thanatos rubbed a hand over his face.

"Is there anything I can get you, sir?"

Thanatos shook his head. "Thank you, no. I heard you so I thought to join you. Please don't let me interrupt."

"I think it's a little late for that." Godfrey offered a teasing smile as he turned to fill his mug.

"It's times like these that make me glad I have you in my

life." Thanatos went and opened the freezer of the double sided stainless steel fridge.

"I can—"

Thanatos cut off the offer with a raised hand. "I can warm my own blood."

Godfrey stepped back against the stainless steel gas stove, his steaming mug in both hands.

In silence, Thanatos chose a bag of blood and closed the door, cutting off the flow of frigid air. Tossing the bag into the microwave, he set the timer and found a tea cup from the cupboard. It did not take long for the beeps to signify the blood was warmed. Retrieving the bag, Thanatos split the edge and poured into the cup. With a sigh, he sipped the contents and grimaced. It was then he caught Godfrey's knowing smile.

"This is horrible," remarked Thanatos, pouring the blood out into the sink.

Godfrey placed his mug down on the counter and went to get another blood bag. "You don't microwave blood, sir."

"Then how do you do it?" Thanatos crossed his arms with a wry grin. "I'm more of a traditionalist, as you know."

"Yes, sir," grinned Godfrey. "Straight for the jugular."

Thanatos laughed. "So?"

"One has to slowly warm it by using a double boiler." Godfrey pulled out the contraption from a lower cupboard. "If you over heat it, you cook it and, well...that doesn't do you any good at all."

Thanatos watched as his manservant demonstrated the process of making bagged blood taste and feel as if fresh.

"And that is how it is done, sir," smiled Godfrey, handing the filled cup to his employer.

Thanatos inhaled deeply before taking a sip. Perfection. "What would I do without you?" he sighed.

"I hope you never find out, sir."

Thanatos turned at the sudden seriousness of Godfrey's words. "You know why I can't Choose you, Godfrey. I can't take the risk after the last time I Chose someone."

"Yes, Bastia."

Thanatos followed Godfrey to the kitchen table and sat opposite to the young man who meant so much to him. "I can't risk having that happen to someone I care about again."

"I know." The words rushed out of Godfrey.

"What about the Angel?" asked Godfrey in an attempt to steer the conversation away from the painful topic. "It'll be dark soon and the Vampiress is with him."

Thanatos appreciated the change, but Godfrey presented the pressing matter. He stared into the cooling red liquid contained by white porcelain. "I should go up. Is there any blood left?"

Godfrey stood and walked over to the double boiler on the stove. "I'll take it up, sir."

"No," said Thanatos, eyes still on the ruby contents. "If given a choice, the Vampiress will feed from you, not the cup. I won't risk you."

"Thank you, sir." Godfrey placed the new tea cup and saucer down next to Thanatos.

Thanatos climbed the stairs to his room, the cup and saucer in both hands. He had felt the sun set and hoped Rose had not yet awakened, but it was not that which kept is pace slow. Worry clenched his gut at what he might discover of the Angel's status. The idea of the Angel lying dead in his bed chilled him. If that were to be discovered then all his hoping and searching would have been for naught.

Opening the door at the end of the hallway revealed a sight that gripped him. The Angel was not in bed. Neither was the Vampiress. With a panic driven push, the door slammed open, the knob embedding into the wall.

Eyes widening at the sight before him, the cup slipped from the saucer to land on the broadloom, splashing the expensive wool with red.

"What do you mean the Angel is gone!" roared the Master of Britain.

Thanatos wished in that moment that he had been able to achieve more than a handful of hours of sleep. The sound of the

Iberian's anger pulsed behind his eyes. Maybe it had been wrong to let his guests keep sleeping well after he witnessed the Vampiress follow the Angel into the mist.

The clock in the dining room chimed eleven.

"It's exactly as I told you," reiterated Thanatos. His elbows rested on the dark oak trestle, his head in his hands. He did not wish to meet the baleful glares of his guests, specifically that of Fernando who stood at the opposite end, bronze hands on the table.

"Why didn't you wake us as soon as you discovered them gone?" asked Bridget, her jaw tight with controlled anger. Sitting to his right, she crossed her arms and leaned back in the chair.

Thanatos lifted his pounding head to meet her icy blue gaze. "What would that have accomplished? The Angel and Rose—"

"Jeanie," corrected Notus, his voice quiet. Notus stared at his clasped hands laying on the polished wood, sitting to Thanatos' left.

"Jeanie," corrected Thanatos. "The Angel and Jeanie were already in the mist when I arrived in the room. What did you expect me to do?"

"Stop them," answered Fernando, born eyes burning with contempt.

Thanatos closed his eyes and released a tired sigh.

"It's clear that the Angel survived his injury," said Bridget.

"But where did he go?" demanded Fernando.

Anywhere he wanted. Thanatos refused to say.

"Bah!" Fernando threw his hands in the air and stomped towards the dining room's entrance.

"Where are you going?" demanded Bridget, standing. Her chair scraped against the wood floor.

"I need some fresh air," snapped the Noble without turning back.

They listened to Fernando's heavy footsteps until they were cut off by the slam of the front door. Bridget regained her seat with a trembling breath.

Silence thrummed in the tension of the remaining three.

"He's never gone with them before." Notus' meet words snapped the tension.

Thanatos stared at his Chosen. "Never?"

Notus lifted his tired gaze onto his Chooser and shook his head. "He would call them so as to defeat those what would harm him and the other Chosen."

Thanatos' eyes widened. He had never heard of the summoning being used in such a manner, and then he caught onto what he missed.

"Them?" Surely, Notus could not be referring to the Blessed Ones. His chest tightened at the horrible possibility that the Gods he grew up with had altered so dramatically.

"He calls them the white faced demons," explained Notus. "They exist in the fog the boy summons."

Did he see Bridget shiver?

Thanatos frowned. He did not know what to think. In the time before his Beloved left, the Summoning allowed for the People to connect with their Gods. When his Beloved used it, they were able to transport from place to place in an instant. Now it appeared that the Angel used it for something completely different. If that were the case, then... He could not continue with that thought.

Thanatos' jaw clenched. There had to be a logical explanation. One thing was certain, the Angel had survived, but where did he go?

The front door banged open, startling the three.

"Let me go!" shouted an unfamiliar voice. "You have no righ—"

A man stumbled into the dining room, shoved by a fuming Fernando. The man caught himself from falling by crashing into the table, which slid under the force. Thanatos, Bridget and Notus stood at the sudden movement of the trestle.

"Don't think about it," sneered the Master of Britain. He rolled up his shirtsleeves, his dark eyes flashing with the hope of violence.

The stranger stood and straightened his rumpled dark blue dress shirt before raking squared fingered hands through his dark hair. "Oh, but I always think about it," shot the man. He took a threatening step toward Fernando.

The promise of a brawl between the two spurred Thanatos.

"How dare you!" His imperious tone stunned everyone immobile. He walked around the table to stand between Chosen and Vampire.

"I found this Vampire on the roof, overhanging the Angel's room." Fernando crossed his arms, a smug smile twisting his lips.

Fury swept away fatigue. Thanatos spun to face the Vampire. "Did Corbie send you to spy on me—on us?"

Thanatos had all but forgotten Bastia's whelp and the promise he made if Corbie did anything to the Angel. It was apparent that he would have to follow through.

The smug expression stayed on the Vampire's face, matching gazes with Thanatos. He remained silent.

"He asked you a question," demanded Fernando, coming to stand beside the ancient immortal.

"Don't think of trying to escape." Bridget's hardened voice came from the other side of the table. Her blue eyes sparkled with bridled malevolence. "We're faster and stronger than you."

"I'd sure like to test that theory with you," said the Vampire. His lingering gaze took in her slim hourglass figure. He did not see the right cross that came out of nowhere, breaking his nose in a wash of blood.

The Vampire crumpled over the table, clutching his face as the run of blood trickled to a stop.

Thanatos' eyes widened at the unexpected assault.

"My, my, I didn't think you had it in you, priest," said Fernando, appreciatively.

Notus shook the pain from his hand. "I don't, but I've come to learn a lot from the boy."

"You'll pay for that," growled the Vampire. Still holding his healing nose, he glared at each of them. "All of you."

"Would that threat include me, Marcus?" Thanatos stepped closer and was rewarded with the Vampire's attempt to back away. The table halted his retreat and he lowered his gaze. "I thought not. Now, tell me why you were on my roof or you will have me to contend with."

Indecision flashed across Marcus' face before settling on a resolution. "Corbie sent me," he said, lifting his head.

"That's self evident, you ponce," stated Fernando. "Why?"

Marcus glared at the Noble. "Weren't you and your whore told to leave our lands?"

This time Fernando's fist connected with Marcus' square jaw, igniting the Vampire into violence. The two leapt at each other with blurring speed.

Thanatos backed away from the brawl. Stunned that anyone would deign to break his home's peace, rage erupted at the destruction of one of his handcrafted chairs as Chosen and Vampire crashed into it.

"Enough!" He yanked the two apart as easily as separating two young children. "I will not tolerate such behaviour in my home." He glared at each before releasing them. "Am I understood?"

Fernando scowled but lowered his gaze. His black shirt bore a pocket hanging half ripped off and his shoulder length hair was in disarray. Marcus glared at his unfortunate host. Neither replied. It was better than nothing.

"Marcus, tell me why Corvus would dare to place me under surveillance?" Thanatos crossed his arms over his chest, never lifting his hard gaze from the Vampire.

"It wasn't you, so much as the Angel," explained Marcus, constrained anger tinged his tone.

"Explain," commanded Thanatos.

"Corbie saw you take the Angel and Rose before dawn, on the security camera."

"He wanted to know the Angel's fate," stated Thanatos.

Marcus nodded.

"And what does he know?"

"That you saved the Angel and he's alive."

"What does Corvus not know?"

Marcus' impertinent gaze slid to the side, refusing to answer.

"Tell him," growled Fernando, taking a step forward.

Thanatos raised his hand, halting the Noble.

Marcus cast a glance at Fernando. "What assurances that—"

"This is not up for negotiation." Thanatos leaned forward until he was a hand's breadth apart from the Vampire. "If you wish me to be merciful, then you *will* tell me all I wish. May I remind you that the Chosen do not succumb to the day as Vampires do. If you continue to play this out, I guarantee that you will be a pile of ash to fertilize my roses. Now tell me."

Defeat deflated Marcus' stance and he leaned back against the table. "Cora saw—"

"Who's Cora," asked Bridget.

Marcus did not even bother to look at the Mistress of Britain. "She's Corbie's mortal assistant manager for the club."

"Go on," ordered Thanatos.

"She was sent to watch your house during the day," continued Marcus. "Shortly after sunset she called to say she saw a strange mist at the second floor windows. When I arrived I found the Angel and Rose gone. I was about to inform Corbie when the Master of Thugs found me."

"So Corvus does not know the Angel's fate?"

Marcus shook his head, a glimmer of worry etched his heavy brow.

"You're worried that the Angel has gone to take revenge," observed Notus.

"What do you think?" snarled the Vampire.

Thanatos reached out and gripped Marcus by his chin, turning the Vampire to face him. "I think that Corvus has misjudged where his greatest threat lies."

Music erupted into the silence, accompanied by a rhythmic buzzing.

"What's that?" asked Notus.

"Someone appears to be calling our unwanted guest," stated Thanatos, releasing the Vampire.

Marcus folded his arms over his chest, refusing to answer the call, a smug expression twisting his features.

"Aren't you going to answer it?" asked Bridget.

Marcus did not even shake his head. His smile grew once the phone fell silent.

Knowing he would get nothing more, Thanatos spoke, "Fernando, please bring the chair at the end. The one with the arm rests. Our new guest will be staying a while and I wish him to be comfortable."

Fernando did as requested, manhandling the Vampire until he sat. Standing behind Marcus' left, the Noble kept a firm grip on the Vampires' shoulder.

Once Marcus' immobility appeared secure, Thanatos addressed Bridget. "If you would be a dear, could you find Godfrey? He may be in his suite down the east wing. Please ask him for the spool of wire from the garage, as well as a pair of pliers."

The Mistress of Britain nodded with a smile and vanished from the dining room.

Thanatos returned to face the Vampire, his mouth pinched in irritation. Despite Marcus' sudden worried expression, Thanatos disliked what he was forced to do. Once, long ago, witnessing such fear in another's eyes would have provided a false balm to his broken heart, bleeding anger. Now, only disgust filled him at the actions required to gain the results he needed.

Bridget returned as though she materialized out of thin iar. A bobbin of fine wire and needle-nose pliers in her hands.

"Thank you, my dear," said Thanatos. "If you would be so kind as to tie Marcus in place. I believe a woman of your talents will find the most effective way."

An evil glint took root in sapphire eyes. "I'm sure I can manage something," she purred as she went to carry out Thanatos' request.

With Fernando's help, Marcus' wrists and ankles were tied firmly against arm rests and wooden legs, the wire biting into flesh. Thanatos' eyes widened at the brilliance of wrapping the wire across Marcus' neck in a way that if he tried to free his arms or legs the wire would decapitate him. It was clear that Marcus recognized this as he became very still, fear in his eyes.

Finishing touches done, Fernando and Bridget stood behind their prisoner, a length of wire held tight in the nose of the pliers held in her hand.

Thanatos inclined his head in appreciation of her ingenuity. "Very nicely done."

"I've had centuries of practice," smiled Bridget. "Though, I have to admit, I've never used wire before."

Flashing an appreciative smile to her, Thanatos returned his attention to Marcus. Seriousness replaced amusement. "Where is the phone?"

Marcus sat still, refusing to answer.

Karen Dales

"Bridget, if you please," asked Thanatos.

"Gladly." Bridget tugged on the wire, the garrotte cutting shallow before she released the pressure.

Marcus slumped as much as his restraints allowed. Had he been mortal, he would have panted with pain. Instead, Marcus closed his eyes and grit his teeth. "My back right pocket."

Passing the wire lead and pliers to Fernando, Bridget knelt behind the chair and slipped her hand between seat and back to gain purchase of the pocket.

"Uh-uh," tisked Fernando. "You don't want to squirm."

Thanatos watched Bridget extricate the device while Marcus did everything he could to stay perfectly still. By the time the pocket surrendered the phone, the wire had bitten deeper into ankles, wrists and neck.

Bridget tossed the phone to Thanatos. Sliding his index finger across the black screen woke it. The image of a naked girl bound to a St. Andrew's cross stunned Thanatos for a moment before he scowled. "What's the password?"

Fernando did not need to pull the wire for Marcus to relinquish the secret. Thanatos shook his head and the answer, typing "vampire" into the phone. Unlocked, it did not take Thanatos long to navigate to the call log. Tapping the call back icon beside the name and number, he raised the phone to his ear.

After a few rings, the sound of muted dance music interwoven with indiscernible voices heralded a singular voice. "Where the hell have you been, Marcus? I've been—"

"This is not Marcus," interrupted Thanatos.

Silence, except for the background noise. "Who is this?" replied the man on the other end.

"The one Marcus was sent to spy on," answered Thanatos, matter-of-factly.

"Thanatos?" came the response in a choked whisper.

"Yes, Brian. It's me."

Silence.

Thanatos had no doubt Corvus' slave was well rattled.

"Hold on a moment," stated Brian. A business tone set in to cover his anxiety.

Thanatos waited, listening as the sound of pounding music

and voices fell away to a humming buzz of night traffic.

"Where's Marcus?" asked Brian, his voice clearer away from the dance floor. "Is he dead?"

Thanatos smirked at the concern Brian showed towards his coterie brother. He knew there was no love lost between the two Vampires. The fear of Corvus' eventual reaction probably fuelled Brian's query. "Marcus is currently my guest. As to his continued longevity... well, that's completely dependent upon him. Neither I, nor my welcome guests, will have any hand in Marcus' demise, should he choose to act in a discourteous manner."

Silence.

Thanatos frowned. Something did not feel right. "I take it that you are reporting this to your Dominus?"

"No."

Thanatos' brows rose high. This was unexpected. "You are not going to inform Corvus?" He glanced at Marcus who appeared as shocked as he.

"I am not."

"What is going on, Brian?"

"Are you intending to follow through on your threat?"

"What game are you playing at, Brian?" frowned Thanatos.

Silence broken by a resolute sigh. "What if I told you that some of us are tired of the old regime and its incessant need for revenge?"

There was no doubt in Thanatos' mind as to the meaning of Brian's couched phrasing. "There was never a need for revenge. Bastia—"

"I know what she desired most," interrupted Brian. "I was there from the beginning."

"As was I."

"Yet you did nothing to curb her desires," stated Brian.

Thanatos lowered his head. The truth of Brian's words shamed him. "She was damaged, Brian. I tried to give her what she wanted, but the pain and the loss of realizing all that she believed in was a sham splintered her. She came back wrong, fuelled by hate. That was never my intention. You know this. Corvus knows this. Bastia knew it too, no matter what her broken spirit lied to her. She enacted the blood feud because she couldn't stand to see her utter failure whenever she saw me, or any Chosen. That infection continued down to her progeny."

"Corbie intends to become Imperator."

Thanatos sucked in a breath. He knew he should not be surprised, but he was. "Over what?"

"All of us."

Thanatos swallowed.

"Killing the Angel was to help solidify his power."

"And had he succeeded?"

"War."

"Oh dear Gods," gasped Thanatos.

"Her vision would be fulfilled."

"But the Angel lives." He hoped Brian and the others had no knowledge of the Angel's whereabouts. The sudden realization that Rose went with the Angel sent his stomach plummeting.

"Yes," said Brian. "An unforeseeable failure."

Anger surged and Brian's words. "What do you want, Brian?"

"Help."

Thanatos straightened at the unexpected statement. "What?"

"Corbie needs to be removed—"

"You traitor!" roared Marcus. "I'll gut you—" The wire dug deep, silencing the Vampire, but did nothing to cool his simmering rage.

Thanatos turned his back on Marcus and found Notus staring at him, a questioning expression furrowing his brow. "Why should I help you do that? What do you get out of it?"

"I get my freedom and we get what the Chosen want—Peace."

Thanatos' shocked expression matched that of Notus'. Could it be possible? "How do I know you're telling the truth?"

"Because this has gone on far too long, and if he gets what he desires, then not only will there be war, but he will expose both parties to those who could eradicate us all."

"Mortals," susserated Thanatos. The full comprehension of Corvus' schemes punched the breath from his lungs.

"Yes," replied Brian. "Now do you see?"

"Yes," nodded Thanatos. His head swirled at the enormity of their true situation. "I have no choice."

"None of us do." Regret filled Brian's voice.

Thanatos took a moment to gather his thoughts. Corvus defied him and despite everything he would rather do, he had to follow through on his threat. He glanced at his silver wristwatch. There was ample time to drive to the club and back before dawn. He did not like leaving without knowing the Angel's fate. "Is Corvus there now?"

"He is."

"Then I'll be—"

"No. Not tonight."

"Why not?" Suspicion flared.

"The club is open. Too many witnesses," explained Brian. "I also need to gather my coterie and you need to bring the Master and Mistress of Britain."

"Vampires and Chosen standing together," stated Thanatos. The mind boggled at the thought, but it also elicited a spark of hope.

"Yes," said Brian. A lightness in his voice indicated a smile.

"When?" asked Thanatos.

"Tomorrow, before the club opens. I'll leave the back door unlocked."

"What of the other Vampires, the ones loyal to Corvus?"

"I'll send them out."

"This had better not be a trap," commented Fernando.

"Tell the Master of Britain, it is not," said Brian. "On my oath to the old Gods."

Thanatos was struck speechless.

"Are you still there?"

Thanatos shook himself out of his shock. "Yes."

"Then you'll come?"

"Yes."

"Nine o'clock."

The phone beeped twice and fell silent, the call disconnected. Thanatos slipped the phone onto the dining table and stared at its black screen before turning to face his guests. "I'm sorry I've dragged you into this. It was never my intention."

"Drag us into facing and defeating Corbie?" asked Fernando, incredulously.

"You couldn't keep us away from taking out that slimy little tad-pole," smiled Bridget. Her eyes glittered with murderous intent.

Thanatos released a sigh. He would not be alone in this. It had been so long since one of his kind stood with him that the sense of relief threatened to overwhelm him. He turned to face his Chosen. "What about you?"

Notus pulled out a chair and sat down, staring at his hands that rested on his thighs. "I heard what Brian said—as we all heard—and despite his assertation of a possible peace between Chosen and Vampire, I have been a victim of Bastia's machinations, my boy even more so. I even stood at the boy's side as he did the Grand Council's dirty work." He looked up at his Chooser. "I don't think it would be wise for me to participate. In any case, someone needs to stay here to wait for the Angel's return."

"Notus is right." Fernando handed the pliers to Bridget. "Someone needs to babysit the Vamp, and I doubt you'd want to put your servant at such risk."

Conceding the salient points, Thanatos nodded. "In that case, please consider my home to be yours. I'll send Godfrey to your residences to pick up anything you may require during your stay."

"I'll go with him," said Fernando. He turned to address Bridget. "I'll pack up and check out."

"Thank you. I can't very well be seen in public wearing the same clothes I wore last night," teased Bridget.

Notus stood. "I'll go, too. All my items are in boxes."

"What about the Angel? He'll need clean clothes when he returns," said Bridget.

Notus' mouth pinched. "I no longer have any of his things."

The disapproving glare from the Master and Mistress told all that Thanatos needed. Turning on his heel, in search of Godfrey, he wondered if they would all be alive this time tomorrow.

XXVIII

espite his fatigue, Thanatos could not entertain the concept of sleep. Instead, he attempted to balm his rising anxiety by playing host. The distraction would work until someone mentioned the missing Angel, then renewed tension flowed. There was no need to say it, they were all concerned and none of them desired to leave to confront Corbie without knowing the Angel's fate.

Walking down the hall, Thanatos trod lightly in the attempt to not wake his guests. He snorted at the thought. If his nerves buzzed, it was likely neither Bridget, Fernando nor Notus could find any solace in the down filled pillows Godfrey provided in the guest rooms. The only ease of mind came that Marcus appeared to be co-operating, for now.

Thanatos halted by the entrance to the dining room. Still seated, the wires no longer cut into flesh as Marcus kept his eyes closed to his inevitable daytime death. Thanatos sighed and continued towards the large living room that Godfrey had turned into a media room.

Shouting, mixed with explosions and music that would make Wagner cringe, spilled out of the open door. Thanatos stepped into the theatre and found the remote control to the projector and sound system, plunging the room into silence and darkness. Light flowed in from the sliding glass doors that led to the backyard, the burgundy drapes pulled away. The prickling along his skin told him what his eyes insisted, the sun would soon rise.

The seated figure on the plush beige couch still had not moved. Thanatos patted Godfrey's leg. "Come on. Time for bed."

Lifting his groggy head off the back of the couch, Godfrey swiped a hand over his face and sat up. "Sorry, sir." He glanced around, a frown forming as he patted down disarrayed blond hair. "What time is it?"

"Almost sunrise," replied Thanatos. He placed the remotes into their cubbies where the consoles to the media sat on the back wall.

Godfrey stood and turned to face his master. "Shouldn't you be in bed, sir?"

Thanatos' shoulders sagged. "We've been through this, Godfrey. I don't think I could sleep even if I was knocked unconscious, but that doesn't mean you should neglect your needs."

"Alright, sir." Godfrey headed to the door. "Call me if you need anything."

"As always, Godfrey." Thanatos gave a fleeting smile.

Alone, the living room felt oppressively large. For a moment Thanatos entertained the thought of selling the mansion and purchasing something smaller, but he could not bear to strip Godfrey of the only home he knew. Until Godfrey chose to move on in his life or succumbed to old age, Thanatos would do what he could for the young man.

Waling to the sliding door, Thanatos took hold of the drape and froze. Eyes wide and heart pounding between his eyes, he could do nothing but stand stricken. On the far side of the pool, swirling white mist ascended from the manicured lawn.

The thick fog dissipated around him and Jeanie, leaving them standing on an emerald lawn next to the sparkling waters of a pool. It did not matter where the white faced demons left him so long as Jeanie was with him.

"We're back," he smiled.

"Aye," grinned Jeanie, turning to face him.

He ran an unencumbered palm down the side of her face and was rewarded by her contented sigh.

He finally had what he most wanted in his life: answers to his origins, and Jeanie. Nothing and nobody could take that away. He would not allow it.

Cupping her face in his hand, he bent and did what he longed to do. His lips found hers, and she welcomed his passion with desperate need. Through their connection he was unsure where she began and he ended. The idea of this sensation, coupled with wondering what sex would be like now between them, sent his heart thudding. For a moment he wondered who had had the thought and felt Jeanie's lips bow into a smile against his.

Pulling back from the kiss, he could hardly believe Jeanie was back in his arms as one of the Chosen—his Chosen. "I often dreamed of this," he said. "Please tell me it's real."

'Tis real, sent Jeanie. She closed the gap between them and rested against his blood dappled chest. "I'm real."

His arms wrapped around her, and he luxuriated in the warmth of her body pressed against his. Closing his eyes, he dared not pinch himself for fear that this was a dream.

"Does this mean we'll be together forever?" whispered Jeanie.

Her breath tickled his chest and he opened his eyes to find Jeanie staring up at him. Forever. With Jeanie. The dream made real still felt tenuous. "Yes." He held her tight.

"Should we find shelter?" Jeanie raised her gaze to the bluing sky.

A shock of fear caught his breath and he stepped away from the embrace. The sky was too blue, the sun had already crested the horizon. Panic set in as he turned to the east, just in time for the sun's golden rays to break over the neighbouring roof line. The burning impact of the full force of the sun stung his eyes to tears and his flesh to—

Through watering eyes he noticed that his skin did not erupt into flames. Instead, his pale skin began to redden. Stumbling, he made his way to the shade provided by the large house abutting the yard and pool. Tears flowed freely down his face. How could forever be so short?

He staggered onto the shaded concrete deck, the hard surface biting into his knees as he fell. Lifting to kneeling from all fours, he turned to face Jeanie's charred remains and found her untouched by the full brunt of the sun.

Through stinging eyes he watched her marvel in the golden rays.

Wiping his eyes with the tender back of his arm, he could not believe what he saw. In the daylight, Jeanie's hair glittered highlights he never witnessed by starlight as she examined herself.

"Ye never told me that the Chosen are daywalkers," she said. Her wide emerald eyes held the delectation of a child receiving a long awaited surprise.

"We aren't," said Bridget, stepping out onto the deck through the now opened patio doors.

Thanatos watched the fog dissipate, leaving the Angel and the Vampiress standing in his backyard. Every instinct screamed at him that the two would be dead in moments. He opened his mouth to yell a warning through the glass door, but closed it as bright sunlight poured into his backyard and over the Angel and Jeanie.

His mouth turned to the ashes Jeanie should have immolated into, his heart pounding painfully in his chest. The sense of contentment that had washed over him when the Angel arrived now hammered away with fear before mutating into awe. No doubt remained. The mixture of feelings flowing over his own came from the now kneeling Angel.

A hand a-lighted onto Thanatos' shoulder and he turned to find Bridget, Fernando and Notus standing behind him. He did not need to ask why they had come. Their stunned expressions said it all. They had felt the Angel's return, but it was witnessing Jeanie, no longer a Vampire, and the Angel not bursting into flames that widened their eyes.

"Ye never told me the Chosen were daywalkers." Jeanie's statement snapped Bridget's head back as if slapped. Shaking herself, Bridget stepped past Thanatos to open the sliding door and step out onto the shaded deck. "We aren't."

Fernando, eyes wide with fear, followed.

Thanatos turned to see Notus as he left the room for the dark passageway of his home. In awe and a large measure of hope, Thanatos stood in front of the opened door, the cool morning air caressing him as he watched.

He could not believe his eyes. "Bridget?" he asked, climbing to his feet. His stinging eyes widened further at the sight of Fernando stepping outside behind her.

"Who else would pull your ass out of the fire...again?" Bridget stormed towards him.

He stepped back, but not fast enough, nor far enough, before she punched him hard in the gut. "Don't you ever do that again!" she roared.

He clutched at the still healing wound and straightened. "I—"

His confusion was overridden as Bridget yelled at him. "Do you know how worried we were?" she railed, tears streaming down her face. "You went off without us and got yourself killed. Why didn't you come to us? Did you know what it was like to feel you die?"

Sobs rendered Bridget unable to speak, and he reached out, pulling her into an embrace. Feelings of loss, fear and joy flowed into him from Bridget as he held her close. He never considered that Bridget would have cared so much. Feeling her emotions humbled him and rose guilt to his chest. *I'm sorry*, he sent.

He looked over at the Noble, the black shirt, misbuttoned and left half undone. Anger mixed with annoyance twisted Fernando's lips. "IS that all you have to say for yourself?" snapped the Noble. "'I'm sorry?'" Fernando stepped up to the Angel. "This is one I will *never* let you live down."

Bridget pulled away from him and stood next to her Chosen, wiping away the moisture from her face with her fingers. "What are we to do with you?" She shook her head, sending blonde locks bouncing in the sunlight that crested closer to the house.

The brightness ached his eyes and he backed up even closer to the house. He thought he heard Fernando's shout of warning, but it came too late.

"No!" he shouted.

Through stinging eyes the Angel watched Jeanie pull the Master and Mistress of Britain into the sun bathed yard. Mouth dropping, he realized that the sun no longer burned the Chosen.

Laughing in pure joy once past the shock of not instantly immolating, Fernando lifted Bridget and kissed her, all the while spinning.

Jeanie's shout of warning came too late. Fernando's foot caught, tumbling the two into the pool with a splash. Both came to the surface, spluttering. Jeanie's laughter coupled with Fernando's demand that she help them out of the pool.

Trying hard to contain her mirth, Jeanie went to the pool edge and held out her hand to help them out. Too late to catch Bridget's mischievous grin, the Mistress grabbed Jeanie and yanked her into the pool.

Red curls flattened against Jeanie's head as she surfaced, spitting water. "That's no' very nice," she chided.

Fernando's guffaws were cut short as Jeanie splashed water in his face.

Stupefied by the sight of three Chosen rough housing in the pool with their clothes on while the sun beat down on them, the Angel could only stand against the brick wall. Unbridled joy flowed into him from the three as they realized their unexpected and unexplained reconnection to the day.

"Come in. I have feeling they'll be out there for a while."

The Angel turned to find a man with dark curling hair and large brown eyes beckoning him in. Uncertain who he was, or what his intentions were, the Angel decided to take a chance. It was clear that the Chosen were guests of this man. Ducking his head, he stepped under the metal lintel and into the dark confines of a large room that would make Fernando drool with envy. Sensations of hope mixed with trepidation flowed from the strange man, giving a partial clue to who this would-be benefactor was. "You're Chosen," stated the Angel.

And you are not.

The statement and how it was delivered straightened him.

"Please allow me to introduce myself." The man held out his

hand. "I am Thanatos."

The Angel recognized the name of his rescuer and went to take the man's hand but halted. The object in his grip would not allow it, and he frowned. The silver strand felt as though it wanted to leap from his grasp, and he remembered what was asked of him.

"I believe this is for you," he said solemnly. He opened his fist and pulled out the thin silver braid.

Thanatos' breath caught as trembling fingers took the strand in both hands. He held it as if it were some long lost holy relic. "Where?" His strangled voice caught and he cleared it. "Where did you get this from?"

"I…" He could not believe what he finally would say, the words choking him. "My father."

The statement snapped Thanatos' attention to him, his hand wrapping the braid around the other. "What did you say?"

The Angel glanced down at the silver chain of hair encircling Thanatos' hand and then back to desperate brown eyes. "My father," he said in a rush, the truth still difficult to believe. "He gave this to me to give to you—to Ta'ano." Thanatos' eyes widened and filled with tears. "He said that he did not want to leave you, but would have died had he stayed."

"The iron," mumbled Thanatos. He stumbled, as if mortally wounded, to sit heavily onto the suede couch, the wrapped strand held against his heart. "What else?"

The Angel sat next to the man his father loved. Both stared at the black screen on the wall before them. "He said to tell you that he still loves you and that one day the two of you will be together again." His eyes widened at the pain the flowed from Thanatos, and whispered, "He wants you to know how proud he is of you."

Thanatos' choked sob turned the Angel's attention to him. *He said that you would teach me. That the Chosen—*

Would be restored, finished Thanatos. He turned tear filled eyes onto the son of his beloved. "You know now what you are."

The Angel nodded and stared at his clasped hands on his lap. "But I don't know what that means."

Thanatos' hand found his and their eyes met. "You are the first Blessed One to walk the earth in over three thousand years. I have waited for this day for so long."

The sound of laughter from outside invaded the home, and the Angel and Thanatos looked up to see the three Chosen dripping water onto the carpet.

"This is incredible," exclaimed the Noble, wonder lit his face. "I stood in the sun for the first time in...in...in forever!" He grabbed Bridget, her soaked dress clinging tight, and pulled her into a kiss. She broke away, laughing. "I'm hungry!"

Fernando eyed the forgotten half-eaten bowl of popcorn on the table before the couch, grabbed a handful and popped the kernels into his mouth before anyone could stop him.

"Oh my God," moaned the Noble around a mouthful. "I've never tasted anything so *good*." He reached for another handful.

"How is this possible?" asked Bridget. "Are we mortal again?"

Thanatos released the Angel's hand. *I guess it's time for your first lesson,* he sent. An apologetic smile curled his lips as he stood. "No. You are not mortal," he answered. "You are Chosen."

"But we dinna burn in the sun." Jeanie came to stand behind the seated Angel. The sound of water dripping onto the couch caused her to back up a pace.

"And I can't stop eating this," said Fernando around another mouthful.

"How is this possible?" asked Bridget.

Thanatos glanced down at the Angel, a grin on his face. "The Angel has restored the Chosen to what they once were. By the nature of who and what he is, the Chosen are once again true immortals."

"But the Angel is—"

"A Blessed One." Thanatos cut off Fernando's protest. "He always has been."

"'Tis true," interjected Jeanie.

"Then why now?" asked Bridget. "Why not give us this before?"

The Angel inhaled deeply and stood, brushing back his long alabaster locks with a hand. *Because my blood wasn't pure,* he sent to all of them. *Until now.* He gave a wry grin. "It's what has allowed me survive this..." He held out his arms, showing off the silver scars.

Their eyes widened.

"You're saying that the Angel is the same as your Silver God?" asked Bridget.

Shock swung the Angel's attention to Thanatos who shrugged apologetically. *We had a lot of time on our hands,* he sent. *I'll be happy to share those stories with you later.*

Thanatos turned to Bridget. "Yes, and though still young for a Blessed One, his reconnection between this world and the realm of the Gods has restored the Chosen to what they once were."

"You never said that the Chosen could stay out in the sun," said Bridget.

"Or eat food," added Fernando, popping more corn into his mouth.

"I didn't want to raise hopes," answered Thanatos. "In case the Angel did not survive. When my beloved left, many Chosen died the next day, burning in the light of the sun. It was a tragic adjustment. The day was no longer ours and the only way to sustain our lives without the presence of a Blessed One on earth was to feed off the blood of the People and other living creatures. The Chosen descended into darkness because our light, and our connection to our original Choosers was shattered with the severing between this world and the Blessed One's."

Silence crashed down, allowing all a chance to absorb the truth.

"Will we still hae t'drink blood?" Jeanie's quiet voice cut the stillness.

"Sometimes," answered Thanatos. "It will depend on the Angel."

"What do you mean?" asked Fernando.

"The Chosen serve the Blessed One by protecting and doing what the Blessed One requires."

"No. I don't want or need—"

"How you connect with the Chosen is your choice," said Thanatos, cutting off the Angel's protest. "I mean, so long as you live your life force is linked to all Chosen."

"All?" asked Bridget.

"Yes. All," nodded Thanatos.

Fernando whistled. "That's a lot of Chosen, and not many like you."

The Angel scowled at his friend. He knew what Thanatos meant. SO long as he was hail and healthy, feeding off of life, then the Chosen would be true immortals. He frowned, wondering if he could do this and keep the white faced demons satiated.

He sat heavily on the couch and leaned forward to prop his elbows on his knees so as to cradle his head in his hands. A hand alighted onto his shoulder but he did not look up. He did not need to. The feelings of concern and protectiveness flowed into him. His father's lover had taken him under his wing.

"I think the Angel needs to get his rest," said Thanatos. "Why not get changed into dry clothing and go explore the day. I'd offer Godfrey to drive you, but the poor lad needs rest. I'll stay with the Angel. You can take my car."

"Are you sure about this?" asked Bridget.

He could sense her concern warring with the desire to do as Thanatos suggested. He leaned back against the couch and nodded. "Go. I'll be fine."

"I'll stay with ye, too," said Jeanie.

He turned to face his beloved. "Go with them. Have some fun. I'm not going anywhere."

She leaned over and kissed him. "If ye're sure. I wouldna mind clean clothin'."

"Shopping. Now you have my attention." Bridget grabbed Jeanie's hand and pulled her to the hallway.

Fernando groaned as he followed. "Do you know how much damage she can cause to a credit card?" he said on his way out. "Before she'd have an hour or two. Now she has the whole damned day. You've created a monster!" Fernando's voice called from the corridor.

The Angel smiled and shook his head at Fernando's plight, knowing that the Noble was actually happy at the prospect.

Alone once again with Thanatos, he looked up at the ancient Chosen.

"You didn't tell them," stated Thanatos.

"That the day is still denied to me, no. That would break their hearts."

"They'll find out eventually."

"I know," he sighed. "Everything's changed."

"Yes."

"I can feel the others."

"It won't be long until you will be able to communicate with them as you do with us."

"I know." The oppressive knowledge bowed his shoulders.

"You did notice that Bridget, Jeanie and Fernando took it as perfectly normal that you can send to them and they to you."

"I did."

"I'll help you with the others."

The Angel gazed up at Thanatos. "Thank you."

Thanatos sat down beside his new charge. "I have one request."

"Anything."

The Angel sat in silence as Thanatos laid out the situation with Corbie, and with Brian's turn around.

XXIX

He stepped out of the shower and wrapped the beige towel around his waist, still uncomfortable about Thanatos' generosity to allow him to stay in his master suite. The connecting bathroom, fogged from the water's heat, was built for a king. Walking to the porcelain sink that stood on a cream and caramel marble counter, he took a wash cloth from beside the basin and wiped away the condensation on the wall width mirror. Strategically placed halogen pot lights running along the ceiling next to the mirror illuminated his ivory skin and hair. He stared at himself, his crimson eyes unwavering, and for a moment thought he saw the Silver man—his father—in the reflection. The tracts of argent scars disavowed the vision.

A headache climbing from the back of his head to creep around and pinch the corners of his eyes told him his control slipped. He shut his eyes. More and more of the Chosen were becoming aware of their new state and with it flew questions and a kaleidoscope of feelings that threatened to crack his skull in two. There were so many of them and they all deserved answers he could not give at this time.

Taking a couple of deep breaths, he managed to reduce the pain to an annoying throb. He opened his eyes.

THANATOS

So much had changed and more would come, but to the man—no, not a man, but a Blessed One—in the mirror, he appeared very much the same.

He raised his hands and touched his face. He looked the same. He even felt the same. Every aspect of his physical being remained constant. Not even the healing abdominal wound changed that, but it was the blood, and the knowledge that came with it, that changed everything.

He lowered his hands and rested them on the counter, noting its coolness. Answers long sought after swirled in his mind too impossible to believe, but how could he not? He was never truly Chosen. He would have come to this state of being eventually. After all, Thanatos did call him young for a Blessed One. Now he knew what he was, and that evoked more questions.

An explosion of breath erupted from him.

A Blessed One, Thanatos had called him. A God.

He sure did not feel like one.

He shook his head. There was still much he did not know. One thing was certain, it was by his existence that the Chosen no longer need live in the dark and feed off the living. He would be that for them. He would continue to make the night his day and the blood of the living his sustenance. It was his sacrifice, but it still did not seem fair.

The sound of the bedroom door opening lifted his attention away from the mirror and he exited the bathroom to find Jeanie placing parcels on the bed. Her curling copper locks dangled from a thick ponytail. Dressed in one of Bridget's blue peasant skirts and white blouses, she appeared radiant.

She startled as his foot found a creak in the floor. She spun around to face him, her verdant eyes wide. Did she have more freckles on her face?

"Sorry," he muttered. He had not realized how tight of a reign he had on his senses.

"I dinna think ye were here," explained Jeanie. "I couldna feel ye."

He came to her side. "My fault."

She gazed up at him. "Are ye alright?"

He caught her hand before she could caress his face. "It's

going to take time."

"Aye," she smiled. "So much has changed."

Releasing his breath, he kissed her hand and let it go before turning his attention to the paper bags and boxes. "What's all this?"

Jeanie's smile grew. "Bridget and I went shopping." She opened a flat box and pulled out a man's dress shirt with silver pinstripes. "We couldna allow ye to walk about in bloody stained trousers."

He took the folded fabric and opened the shirt.

"I hope it fits ye." Her smile took on a worried tinge. "It's been so long…"

He crumpled the shirt to his chest. "It's perfect. Thank you."

"Let me help ye," she said, opening another box.

"You don't have to, Jeanie," he said, halting her action by placing his hand on her arm.

"But I hae to," she said, refusing to look away from the uncovered black jeans. "I did so many horrible things. I remember them all." She turned to face him. "The worst was killin' ye, and I almost succeeded. Despite that, ye still love me, still Chose me. I dinna deserve ye."

He ran his hand down her face, wiping away a tear with his thumb. "It's the other way around. I don't deserve you. I failed you, and because of that you will now carry memories of actions you should never have done. I can't undo those, and for that I will never be able to make that up to you. The only thing I can do is life every day of the rest of my life for you. Jeanie, you are my one true reason for living."

He found her lips with his, the shirt forgotten as she pressed herself against him and wrapped her arms about his neck. Greedily, he invaded her mouth and she moaned. The sound and sensation pulled a growl from his throat as a wash of heat tightened him, urging him on.

"Ah hem."

The voice from the hallway intruded, splashing freezing water on him and Jeanie. Reluctantly, he released their embrace to find Fernando standing beneath the lintel, a dark brow lifted high in amusement.

"Did I come at a bad time?" asked the Noble as he walked into the room.

Jeanie glared at Fernando.

"Stupid question," said Fernando, his smirk still plastered on his face.

"What do you want?" asked the Angel. Clearly, some things did not change. He kept an arm around Jeanie's waist.

"A word. In private."

Jeanie opened her mouth to protest only to be cut off by Fernando.

"It won't be long. Considering how much you piled up on my credit card, I believe a few minutes along with the Angel is more than fair payment."

Jeanie glanced up at the Angel and he nodded. *It's okay.*

I'll be back in ten minutes. She stepped out of his embrace, handed the shirt to him and headed toward the exit.

Once she had disappeared, Fernando turned and shut the door. It was then that the Angel noticed the long black box strapped to the Noble's back.

"Let's get something straight right off the bat," said Fernando, turning around to face him. "I do not want you Sending to me. I do not want that kind of connection with you. You keep out of my head and I'll keep out of yours."

Relieved, the Angel sat on the edge of the bed with a sigh.

"You're not upset at this?" Fernando stepped closer.

"No." He shook his head. His wet hair sticking to chest and back.

Fernando peered at him, a hint of concern on his face. "Too many voices?"

He glanced up, pinching the bridge of his nose. "Too many. Thanatos said it would happen later. I guess now is later."

"Shit."

He nodded, surprised by the Noble's seeming compassion.

"Well, at least you have one less to worry about," smirked Fernando. The smile evaporated. "Do you want me to ask—"

"No," interrupted the Angel. "It's okay. I have to learn how to deal with this."

"You are a stubborn bastard."

The statement shocked him, lifting his gaze to the Noble.

"You don't take help even when it's offered," explained Fernando. "It's what got you into this mess in the first place."

"I recall that you forced me into a partner—"

"And had I not, things would have worked out differently. Probably to all of our deaths, but we're here, now, and whether we like it or not we are all connected to *you*. Didn't Thanatos tell you what the Chosen are while Jeanie and Bridget were dragging me from one store to another?"

He opened his mouth to answer.

"Whether we Chosen like it or not," continued Fernando, ignoring the Angel, "and I sure don't like it, we are here to ensure you do not do anything as monumentally stupid as going off and getting yourself killed, again. If the voices of all the Chosen bouncing in your head isn't proof enough, you are not alone."

Silence fell in the room.

"Bridget sent you, didn't she?"

Fernando's bark of laughter was answer enough.

"She's still angry."

"Are you saying that or can you feel it?" challenged Fernando with a grin.

"If I lie and say—"

"You're a horrible liar."

He sighed. "I'm not good at—"

"Duh." Fernando crossed his arms over his chest.

"I thought you weren't going to be in—"

"Your head," finished the Nobel. "I'm not. I've known you too long. Listen," —he swung the box off his back and laid it on the bed with the others before sitting down beside the Angel— "regardless of everything, you and I both keep others at arm's length. It's part of who we are. It's what pisses me off about you, and I'm sure it's what annoys the fuck out of you about me. Despite that, or maybe because of it, you are the only Chosen I've considered a friend."

He looked at Fernando's proffered hand and all that it meant, and slipped his into the Noble's for a brief moment. "You know I'm not Chosen," he said, relinquishing the grip.

"Yep, but thinking that you're some kind of deity from

ancient times freaks me out."

"Me, too," he susserated.

He caught Fernando eyeing him strangely.

"This—you—everything is different," whispered Fernando.

He nodded.

"Did Jeanie tell you we went to a restaurant, sat at the sunniest table and ate the food on their menu?"

"No, she didn't."

"For the first time in about eight hundred years I *ate* real food and drank real wine, but it paled in comparison to sitting in the sunlight." Fernando turned to face him. "Just by being what you are has gifted me—us—with something we all thought was lost forever. Don't blow it, and don't think any of us will allow you to destroy that for us."

Humbled by Fernando's words, he dropped his gaze to the carpet. He felt the Noble's weight leave the bed and heard a click. When he looked up, he found the sword he had made for the Master of Britain lying across two tanned hands.

"I know none of us can stop you from confronting Corbie tonight," said Fernando. "But we'll be there to make sure you don't' do something stupid. Also, the Blessed One should have something to defend himself with." He held out the blade hilt first.

"I made it for you," said the Angel, refusing to take it.

"And as Master of Britain, I'm giving it back to you."

The Angel reached out and took the blade by the hilt, the heft of it settling comfortably in his grasp.

"When we get back home, Bridget and I will be calling a Grand Council," said Fernando. "I don't think I need to say why."

"No." The Angel gazed up at his friend. The weight of the world stiffened his shoulders. "No, you don't."

XXX

he cool spring night promised a glorious exhibition of starlight had the sky not been so light-polluted by the city. Navy blue in the east bleeding to sapphire in the west proved a sky devoid of the sun. The Angel stared at the hopefully unlocked back door to *Beyond the Veil*. From Thanatos' limousine he had watched Vampires leave their nest as Brian had promised. Now, standing on the small gravel parking lot he had died on, he stared at the black stain that still marked his demise. He shook his head at all that had occurred.

The grip on his right hand gave a reassuring squeeze and he turned to gaze down at Jeanie's apologetic features. He returned the grip with a tight smile. Despite his desire to rediscover their pleasures with one another, they had spent their time alone in the room talking about their time apart. It was a start to healing wounded hearts, a process that would take a long time, if everything went as well as they hoped.

"It's time," stated Thanatos. He lowered his arms, shaking the sleeve of his impeccable dark suit jacket to cover the expensive watch.

"Do you think he kept his word?" asked Fernando. Dressed in black trousers and sweater he appeared ready for a covert attack.

He held onto a white nylon rope that dangled as a cable-tow from Marcus' neck. Standing behind the Noble's right, the thin wire still circumambulated the Vampire's thick neck and remained attached around abused wrists at the centre of his back.

"There's only one way to find out." Bridget walked to the door, her flat shoes whispered over stone, to place a hand on the steel door knob. Without a click it swung outward an inch. She gazed over he shoulder. "It's open."

"Let's go," said the Angel. The weight of the sword on his right hip felt oddly comforting as he took a step forward. "Let's get this over with."

Their footfalls shushed over the rocks and stopped as Bridget pulled the door wide.

"You first." Fernando tugged on the rope, sending Marcus stumbling into the black opening. "Remember. You do as you're told and you keep your head. Do anything to compromise our safety and you'll lose your hands. Do anything to cause us harm and you will lose your head. If you can't keep your mouth shut, I'll cut out your tongue."

Defeat rounded Marcus' shoulders. He tried to nod, but halted the movement as the stained wire drew more blood.

"Good, boy," smirked Bridget.

"Take us to Corvus and go slow," ordered Thanatos.

Silence encapsulated them as they walked into the ground floor of the club. The sound of the door closing followed behind. Black walls, black flooring and the occasional red gloaming light added to the oppressive air. Heavy curtains of black and red velvet hid chambers better left to their secrets.

Fernando's amused gaze and Bridget's tight lips proclaimed they had a fair idea what went on behind drawn curtains.

What is this place? sent the Angel to Jeanie.

'Tis where patrons and vampires come t'play, frowned Jeanie. *Did you—?*

She shot a shocked expression at him before it dissolved into defeat. *I'd rather no talk about it.*

He gave her hand a gentle squeeze. *Sorry.*

They reached the end of the hall and found a set of stairs leading down. No lights flickered to guide wary steps. Absolute darkness met them, but did not deter their resolve. Each could see the steep descent and with a gentle shove by Fernando, Marcus led the way down.

Another black hall met them, as did a figure.

"Brian," hissed Marcus.

"Marcus," stated Brian, a smirk of pleasure twisting his lips. His gaze turned to the Chosen. "Thank you for coming."

"It's—" Thanatos' reply was cut short by Brian shaking his head and placing his index finger across his lips.

Thanatos nodded, understanding.

Corbie can hear all that goes on out here, if he has a mind to it, explained Jeanie.

The Angel sucked in a breath and relayed the message to Bridget who shared it with Fernando.

Please follow me." Brian turned on his heel and led the group down the hall.

Doors with numbers lined the hall. Some were cracked open enough to allow the occupant to stare at the newcomers. Clearly, Brian had not sent all the Vampires away. The sight of so many taking note of their passing tightened the Angel's jaw as he gripped the hilt with his free hand.

Fernando and I don't like this, sent Bridget.

The Angel did not need to reply. He could feel their unease, as well as Thanatos' growing anger and Jeanie's worry. Feelings from far off Chosen added pressure behind his eyes, and before he lost complete control to the inevitable bombardment he shut everyone out. The suddenness of the disconnection shocked the Chosen and heads turned to face him.

Sorry, he mouthed.

Bridget gave him a forgiving smile and continued on. Thanatos nodded his understanding before following the Master and mistress. Worried green eyes gazed up at him.

Unwilling to risk opening the floodgates again, he leaned over to whisper in her ear. "Give me time."

Jeanie nodded, her cheek rubbing against his. "I love ye," she said, her voice the barest of whispers.

Standing straight, he held her close and followed the others until they halted at the door. Without further explanation, Brian opened it.

Candlelight washed over them, momentarily blinding them. Eyes wide at the lavish room lined with gothic and horrific works of art, they followed Brian towards another door on the opposite side. This time his hand hesitated for a faction of a second before turning the knob and pressing inwards. On Brian's heels they followed into a room of stark white. The only colour was Corbie sitting at his desk.

Corbie lifted his gaze from his computer, his face hardening with anger at the sight of his unexpected guests. His eyes flickered from Marcus' prisoner status onto Brian who had the wherewithal to lower his. Leaning back into his white leather chair, Corbie lifted his chin, his hands on his lap under the desk. "Well, this is a bit of a surprise," he drawled, his black eyes hooded.

"I told you to leave the Angel alone." Thanatos took a step forward.

"You did, yes, but since you walked out of Bastia's life after your failed attempt to Choose her, I don't believe you have much say over her children." Corbie's thin lips twitched towards a smile at the surprised glances the Mistress and Master of the British Chosen gave the God of Death. "You didn't know? Such a pity."

"This has to stop Corvus," said Thanatos, ignoring the jab.

"What? What has to stop?" Corbie raised a placating hand to the sky. "The Chosen are obsolete, failed creatures, that should no longer exist."

"That's not what Bastia believed," stated Thanatos.

"You're right," smirked Corbie. "In her love for you she believed that the Chosen were superior. It was your failure of her that proved the truth to her. Now we know better, don't we. Evolution has an interesting way of dealing with obsolete creatures."

"And you believe you are the one to enact it?" said the Angel.

"Ahhh... I was wondering when you were going to chime in," said Corbie. His face turned ugly. "Of course. Who better? I took your lover and made her my plaything."

The Angel felt hands grip his arms, pulling him back. "Don't," growled Fernando, standing at his side. "If you do, you'll play right into his hands."

"You'd better listen to your little Chosen playmate, Angel," said Corbie. "Then again, are you so sure that you haven't already?"

The Angel and his cohorts turned around to find a little over half a dozen Vampires standing behind them.

Corbie stood, the chair's wheels squeaking as it rolled back, a gun in his hand pointed at the Angel, and walked around to the front of the desk. "You see, you were expected. It was a matter of when, not if."

"Corvus," growled Thanatos.

"What, old man?" snapped Corbie. "You think I didn't prepare for this once I knew the Angel was still alive and in your possession? What a fool."

Thanatos' jaw clutched tight.

"Jeanie's now Chosen," stated the Angel, his voice cold. He would have smiled at Corbie's surprise and the gasps behind him, but he kept the mask in place.

"Not possible," said Corbie. "Once turned into a Vampire there is no possibility of going back, let alone becoming Chosen." He glared at Thanatos. "If that were possible, you would have fixed Bastia and we would not be standing here."

"If I had had the power to do so, I would have," stated Thanatos, "but that is not within the abilities of the Chosen."

"Rose?" growled Corbie, believing the truth for a lie.

Jeanie stepped forward, a smug smile on her face wide to show off her teeth. "I'm no longer Rose, no longer yer plaything, no longer part of yer coterie," she seethed. "I'm no longer a Vampire. I've been Chosen by the Angel. I guess I should thank ye for reuniting us. If ye hadna done so, I'd still be a Vampire."

Confusion covered hatred for a brief moment as Corbie glanced back at the Angel, his eyes pinching in malevolent thought. "It doesn't matter," he sneered. "It just means one more Chosen to put into the ground. No longer will I leave such delicate matters to incompetent individuals. I wonder, if a sword won't do it, will a hollow tipped steel bullet to the heart?"

Chaos exploded at the concussive blast from Corbie's gun.

The Angel watched everything slow down, his heart pounding painfully in his chest as Thanatos crossed in front of him, at the same time Jeanie's scream slammed time back into place. Stumbling, the Angel caught Thanatos as he fell back against him. The scent of blood detonated throughout the room.

"Well, that's a new sensation," coughed Thanatos. Blood frothed on his mouth.

Fury painted the Angel's vision and he hardly recognized his voice ordering the others to take Thanatos from him. Before Corbie could pull back the trigger for another blast, he grabbed the burning barrel and twisted upwards.

Corbie cried out at the sudden pain in his wrist as at least one bone snapped. His knees gave way, but instead of falling to the floor, he found himself dangling by the throat. He scrabbled at the hands choking him, unable to utter a word.

"Don't even try," hissed the Angel as he stared up at the Vampire in his grasp. Hatred flowed through him. Here was the one who had orchestrated his misery and the deaths of countless Chosen in his attempted genocide. "I will rip your head off if you move an inch." He turned to face the other stunned Vampires in the room. "If you value this Vampire's life, or even your own, you will stay where you are."

Brian made no move except to wave the others back.

He glanced down at Bridget and Jeanie attempting to deal with Thanatos' bullet wound. Thanatos' eyes were wide in surprise and pain.

Fernando stood over them, Marcus' cable-tow still in hand, covering the Angel's back by keeping an eye on the Vampires in the room. "You're going to have to get the bullet out before it completely heals over."

"I know, Fernando," hissed Bridget. She ripped open Thanatos' shirt and found the bubbling wound. "It's in the lung." She caught Thanatos' eyes with her own. "This is going to hurt a lot."

Thanatos nodded, and then clutched his eyes closed as Bridget's long fingers descended into the bullet hole.

The Angel turned his attention back to the Vampire in hand. "This vendetta against the Chosen ends tonight," stated the Angel, malevolence slicked with ice. "I am done with this pettiness. You will not touch my Chosen. You will not do anything to harm my Chosen."

"Stop him!" Corbie managed to gasp.

"No," replied Brian, finding his courage, his coterie behind him. "I will not let you continue this madness. You have failed us, Corbie. We *will* be free from your tyranny, even if the Angel is the one to provide it for us. One way or another you are no longer the Dominus."

Corbie's eyes bulged at seeing his Vampires shoot hatred at him. Fury strengthened his resolve to break free of the Angel but the Angel squeezed tighter, halting any motion.

"No more," stated the Angel. The words of the summoning came to him and the tendrils of white slipped from the floor to twine around the Vampire. The Angel shook his head. He would not allow his demons to feast on one such as this. Fear rounded Corbie's eyes, immobilizing him. Something more would need to be done.

Once the mist flowed up high enough to wrap about Corbie's head, leaving his face uncovered, the Angel closed his eyes and searched. It did not take long. It was there, hovering close. Opening his eyes, he called it and it came.

A spark of light, diminished and barely flickering lifted up from the mist.

Corbie recognized the glimmer and panic renewed his ability to fight against the immovable grip around his throat. It did no good, but he tried nonetheless. Moans of pleading came from him and had he been mortal he would have soiled himself. As it was the Angel ignored the Vampire and sought into the creature's body for the other half.

Deep within Corbie, the Angel found it and summoned it out. The other half of the flickering light exited through Corbie's chest to circle around the dull light. Once. Twice. The third time fused the two together and Corbie gave a strangled cry. Tears of blood erupted down his face and his nose. The mist closed over Corbie's face, completing the cocoon, but not his muffled moans of panic.

A word in the ancient language slipped from the Angel's mouth, sending the flickering light up and out of the building. Once gone, Corbie hung slack with arms dangling. With another word, the mists dissolved back into the ground from whence they came. Uncovered, Corbie's terror fixed eyes bulged vacantly.

Scowling in disgust, the Angel tossed the flaccid corpse over to the side of the room and turned to face the others. "It's over."

"Is Corbie truly dead?" Brian stepped closer, eyes on the lifeless body.

"He will not be rising with any dawn from this time to the end of time," stated the Angel. He turned his attention to Bridget who held the ruby painted bullet between two fingers, eyes wide up at him. Thanatos sat cross legged, the wound closed over, smiling up at him.

Relieved to see Thanatos hale and healthy again, the Angel turned his attention to Brian and the other Vampires, recognizing them all from that fateful night not so long ago. He almost allowed a smile curl his lips as he watched each one of them lower their gazes as he glanced at each one of them until he settled on Brian. "This is over," he said.

Brian nodded, and startled as the Angel stepped up to him.

"The Chosen will stay in their parts of the world and the Vampires will stay in theirs," stated the Angel. "I will not suffer having Vampires in Chosen territory. Attempt another rising against the Chosen and *I* will eradicate you all."

"What if..." Brian's voice fell quiet under the imperious red glare, but he had to broach the topic and found his courage. "What if the Chosen come here?"

"Then I will deal with them, as is my right," stated the Angel. "If the Banished wish their continued existence, it will be by the rules I set forth."

"And what would those be?" asked a dark haired male Vampire from the back.

He turned to face them all. "It is as I've already stated, but I will add one thing: do not allow the mortals to become aware of you. You live in the dark. You will stay in the dark."

He offered a hand to Thanatos. "Let's go."

Thanatos rose to his feet, his smile growing. "I will stay here and help them."

The Angel nodded as he took Jeanie's hand and walked towards the door, the Vampires making way.

Fernando passed off Marcus' cable-tow to Brian as he led

Karen Dales

Bridget to follow. At the door, the Noble turned back, an evil grin on his face. "By the way, the Chosen no long burn in the sun. We've become true immortals. We are not limited to hunting you during the night. We can slaughter you all while you sleep."

Bridget's laughter mixed with Fernando's as they followed the Angel and his beloved to the surface.

epilogue

Sunlight spilled throughout the two bedroom condo, illuminating even the most awkward areas. Motes flickered where once electric lights glowed. Heavy drapes hung impotent beside large windows, no longer their outside cloths fading in bleaching light. Carpet, leather sofas and dark wood furniture speckled white with a fine dusting. Notus stood with his back to it all, his attention on the city below.

How different it all appeared in the light of day. More people than he could have imagined walked the sidewalks, each hurrying in the participation of their daytime lives. He had heard of the stories of congested traffic as people scurried in vehicles to jobs and meetings better conducted while the sun was up. Witnessing it reminded him of toy cars lined up for play.

Though the activity below entranced him, it was the sight of the pale blue sky populated by fluffy white clouds and the brilliant yellow orb of the sun that intoxicated Notus. The overwhelming miracle of finally being able to stand the day left dried tear tracts down his face. For two thousand years he had lived in the dark with the little hope of ever being restored.

Now, standing here, safely washed in sunlight, he felt his prayers come true. It also proved that the boy he had taken under his wing and cared for almost as much as his own children, had been the one he had waited for so long. The cruel irony twisted his lips and begged the unanswerable question: why now? Why, after he had so horribly failed and rejected the boy? Clearly, the fates had played him for a fool.

The sound of a throat clearing pulled is attention away from the sight beyond the apartment and Notus turned around to face one of the three young men in dirt smeared jeans and white t-shirt. "What is it?"

"We're almost finished packing the truck, Mr. Nathaniel," said the young man, a fair sized cardboard box in his hands.

"Thank you," replied Notus. "I'll be down shortly. You have the shipping orders?"

"Yes, sir. Mohammed's got it all organized. I'll be driving the truck to Pearson."

Notus turned back to face the outdoors, silently dismissing the young man. Eyes still focused on his new reality, he grew annoyed at the lack of sound of the young man's departure and turned around.

His breath caught.

Bridget stood in the doorway, clearly unhappy.

Without saying a word, she stepped in and closed the door, sealing the two of them in the room empty save for the furniture that the place had come with.

Notus wished he could be surprised by her arrival, but knowing her as he did, he sat down on the armrest of the couch, waiting for what he knew would come.

"Why did you leave?" Bridget glared at him from across the room.

Notus shook his head at the absurdity of the question. "Why should I have stayed?"

Bridget blinked at the unexpected response before masking her face in annoyance. "If *I* have to remind you, then you are a greater idiot than I could ever have imagined."

Notus expected such and stood to walk over to the Mistress of Britain. "I left because the Angel must learn to be who he is. I cannot help him. In fact, I've probably done more to limit his self discovery than anyone else."

"That doesn't make sense," snapped Bridget. "The two of you are renown for being Chosen and Chooser."

"Yes," interjected Notus. "Chosen and Chooser, but that's been a lie."

"Is your love for him a lie?" asked Bridget. She brushed past him to move further into the room. "Or is his love for you?"

Notus spun on his heel. "My love for him is not a lie. As for his love for me...well..."

"He loves you, Paul." She spun about. "Why can't you see that? Can you not feel him? Can you not hear him reaching out for you?"

"I've shut him out." Notus lowered his head. He had felt the boy's searchings, had sensed the boy's feelings, but it did not change what he had to do. "I failed him."

"And you made up for that."

Notus shook his head. He wished he could explain this more clearly. Instead he walked up to Bridget, took her hands in his and stared into sapphire eyes. "You've never been a parent."

"What does that have to do with it? We Choose others, it's the same thing."

"No, it's not."

Bridget pursed her lips, annoyance making her frown.

"Chosen do Choose, but those we Choose are not children," continued Notus. "They are adults making an adult decision. We do nothing to raise them, guide them, mold them into the individuals they become. They have already done most of the work themselves, with the help of their mortal parents."

"You're not making sense."

"I'm making perfect sense, Bridget. I, unlike so many Chosen, was a parent to three beautiful children that were never given the chance to grow up, never given the chance to become the adults they were meant to be. That truth still haunts me."

"What does that have to do with the Angel?"

"Don't you see? In my pain, and in his, I kept him from growing up."

"That's ridiculous, Paul!" Bridget pulled back her hands and paced a few feet away before coming to a halt. "He's who he is because of you."

"In spite of me."

Bridget released a huff.

"Bridget, please listen to me. I'm leaving not because I no longer love the boy, I do, with all my heart. I'm leaving because if I stay he will not have the opportunity to grow into the person he was always meant to be."

"A Blessed One."

Notus gave a one shouldered shrug. "The title doesn't matter. What does is now Jeanie is his Chosen and that is who he should be with." He gave an amused snort. "I guess it's taken all this time to become a grandfather."

"You're making no sense."

"I'm making perfect sense. The Angel must stand on his own, with friends who accept him for who and what he is. I would only hold him back and make him doubt himself."

"And what about Thanatos."

"Even grown adults need older adults as mentors."

"You have an answer for everything, don't you."

Notus smirk grew into a genuine smile. "I do, don't I?"

Bridget sighed, defeated. "What am I to tell the Angel?"

"Tell him that I still love him. Tell him that I will be there for him when he needs me. Tell him that I am proud of him."

"But you're not coming back?"

"No."

"Even after what he's given us?"

"Especially because of that." Notus walked up to Bridget and laid a hand on her shoulder. "My boy has surpassed everything I could have expected from him, but that's the problem, isn't it? He's still *my boy* and I will continue to treat him as such. This distance will give us the opportunity we both require so that when next we meet he will no longer be *my boy*, but the Angel, and I can be a friend to him."

"I still don't understand. You've left him for long periods of time before."

"Out of my own shame."

"And this is different?"

"Yes." Notus turned and walked back to the door and opened it."

Bridget walked to the door and stopped to face Notus one last time. "I still don't understand."

"You probably never will."

"Because I've never been a mother?"

"Because you've never been a parent."

Bridget lowered her eyes, her voice small. "Do you think it's possible now?"

The unexpected question pulled a laugh from his centre and he pulled the Mistress of Britain into an hug. "Wouldn't it be wonderful if it were so..."

Jeanie closed the door behind them, cutting the two of them off from the rest of Thanatos' house and leaving them alone in their host's master suite. The Angel walked past her, failing to ignore her concerned gaze, and sat down on the edge of the perfectly made bed. His head throbbed, the effort to keep the Chosen from his mind becoming more difficult the more tired he became.

He heard Jeanie walk up to him and he leaned forward, placing his head on her shoulder and sighed as he felt her comb his hair from his face. The voices and feelings from all the Chosen in the world subsided into a soft buzz in his mind, only Jeanie's love and concern for him filtering through.

Tired and hungry, and not a little angry, he had left the Vampires to their fate. Leaving *Beyond the Veil*, he was relieved to find Thanatos' limousine and driver still waiting for them. The blonde man-servant had immediately exited the driver's seat to walk around and open the back door for them. Worried blue eyes cast about for his master, but he did not ask. The Angel knew that look and he was about to offer the man words of comfort when Fernando and Bridget burst through the steel door to the building, their laughter cutting the night air.

"Thanatos is staying," blurted Fernando, coming to stand next to the Angel.

Bridget and Jeanie scowled in unison.

"Is he alright?" stammered Godfrey.

Bridget nodded and laid a comforting hand on the mortal's shoulder. "He's fine," answered Bridget.

Karen Dales

Godfrey frowned and he glanced down to the gravel, unhappy with his master's decision.

"It's okay," offered Bridget. "He's safe."

Still unsure, Godfrey lifted his gaze to meet the Mistress of Britain's. "What of Corbie?"

"Dead," blurted Fernando.

Godfrey's eyes went wide. "How?"

"The Angel," smiled Jeanie.

Watching new worry creep into the mortal's face, the Angel sighed. "It's as they say. The Vampires will threaten the Chosen no more."

"Why no' drive us back and ye can come back to pick up Thanatos after?" Jeanie smiled sympathetically.

Godfrey nodded, still holding the door open for his employer's guests to enter. Once the Angel and Jeanie were settled, they gazed out to the two Chosen still standing in the parking lot. "Are ye no' comin'?"

Fernando hooked an arm about Bridget's slim waist and drew her close. The Mistress of Britain laughed, turning her face to meet her Chosen.

"Nope," replied Fernando. "If there were ever a time to celebrate, tonight's it. We're going to paint the town red... well, not literally."

The Angel nodded, a slight smile on his face. How he wished to join them, but Godfrey gently shut the car door, leaving the two Chosen to their revels.

The Angel lifted his head off Jeanie's shoulder and gazed at the miracle standing before him.

"'Tis over. This horrible nightmare is over," stated Jeanie.

The Angel nodded.

"What happens now d'ye reckon?"

"I'm not sure." He reached up to pull at a corkscrew red lock of hair. He watched it bounce back up at its release before meeting her gaze again. "Everything is new, and for the first time I have what I most desired in the world."

"Me?" she squeaked as he pulled her into an embrace.

"Yes," he smiled.

He expected her to be happy, but seeing her frown as she reached to play with his long white locks, worried him. "What is it?"

"Notus," said Jeanie in a rush.

The unexpected name caused him to suck in his breath as if punched and he stood up. Jeanie backed a few steps away. Memories of his Chooser's abandonment when he most needed him tightened his chest and he turned away from Jeanie to walk to the windows.

"He was here," said Jeanie, following him. "He helped save ye."

The words struck hard. He could not deny that he still loved the man, maybe forgiven him, but the pain still hurt. "Then why did he not stay?"

Jeanie wrapped her arms about his midsection, snuggling against him as they stared out onto the moon dappled garden below. "I think he's afraid that ye'd still be mad at him."

The truth of the words caused him to close his eyes.

"If Paul had been here…"

"I don't know."

He felt her hand reach up to his face, turning it so he would have to look down on her. "He knows ye better than any," said Jeanie, softly. "His heart is sore for what he did. Maybe 'tis better this way. To give the two of ye time."

"That is what we have an abundance of, but I still miss him," he said.

"Aye, I do, too."

Together, the Angle and Jeanie turned back to watch the night, their arms encircled about each other.

about the author

Karen Dales is the Award Winning Author of the widely acclaimed and best selling series, *The Chosen Chronicles,* having won Siren Books' Award for Best Horror and Best Overall 2010. *The Chosen Chronicles* include *Changeling, Angel of Death, Shadow of Death* and *Thanatos.*

She is currently at work on the next book in *The Chosen Chronicles* as well as a historical romance novel, *The Sword and the Flower.*

When not writing, Karen teaches Creative Writing for the City of Toronto.

Born in Toronto, Ontario, Canada, she shares her life with three cats, one son and her husband.

Visit her website at www.karendales.com